PRAISE FOR

Alphabet Weekends

"[Noble's] best novel to date—a tale of three couples, of different generations, learning to grow up, grow apart and love each other all over again. It's mature chick-lit for people who've seen it all before but haven't quite lost hope."   —*The Mirror* (UK)

"Funny, touching and a reminder that true love rarely runs smoothly."   —*The Sun* (UK)

"Weaving an amorous alphabet from the romantic ups and downs of a clutch of characters, this warmhearted book by the author of bestselling *The Reading Group* is a reminder that no true love ever ran smoothly."
—*Mail on Sunday* (UK)

"Noble's ability to weave in secondary stories puts her near the top of the chick-lit class."
—*Herald Sun* (Australia)

David Galloway

About the Author

<small>ELIZABETH NOBLE</small> is the author of the internationally
bestselling *The Reading Group* and *The Friendship Test*.
She studied at St. Edmund Hall, Oxford University,
before working in British publishing for several years.
She lives with her husband and their two daughters in
New York City.

ALSO BY ELIZABETH NOBLE

The Reading Group

The Friendship Test

Alphabet Weekends

Love on the Road from A to Z

Elizabeth Noble

HARPER

NEW YORK • LONDON • TORONTO • SYDNEY

HARPER

First published in Great Britain in 2005 by Hodder & Stoughton, a division of Hodder Headline.

ALPHABET WEEKENDS. Copyright © 2005 by Elizabeth Noble. All rights reserved. Printed in the United States of America. No part of this book may be used or reproduced in any manner whatsoever without written permission except in the case of brief quotations embodied in critical articles and reviews. For information address HarperCollins Publishers, 10 East 53rd Street, New York, NY 10022.

HarperCollins books may be purchased for educational, business, or sales promotional use. For information please write: Special Markets Department, HarperCollins Publishers, 10 East 53rd Street, New York, NY 10022.

FIRST HARPER PAPERBACK PUBLISHED 2007.

Library of Congress Cataloging-in-Publication Data
Noble, Elizabeth (Elizabeth M.).
    Alphabet weekends : a novel / by Elizabeth Noble.—1st U.S. ed.
        p. cm.
    ISBN: 978-0-06-112218-7
    ISBN-10: 0-06-112218-1
    1. Friendship—Fiction. 2. Chick lit. I. Title.

PR6114.O25A78 2007
823'.92—dc22   2006046490

07 08 09 10 11 RRD 10 9 8 7 6 5

From the A of Abseiling to the V of Vegas
for who else but my friends
Nicola, Suzanne, Nicky, Fiona, Maura, Jenny and Kathryn

Acknowledgements

No author is an island, and I am more of a spit, so I need to thank: My friend Stephanie Cabot, for being the first believer.

The ever calm and kind Sue Fletcher, the meticulous and generous Hazel Orme, and all the heroes and heroines in production, design, sales, marketing, publicity and editorial, for being so patient and nice to an author who was far more trouble this time round than she meant to be. Kate Flemming, and Jenn and the wonderful staff at The Bellagio for a stupendous stay in Las Vegas. And to Caedmon, Pete and the staff at the Princetown Spirit of Adventure centre, for a life-changing one on Dartmoor.

Lovely Dr Pete Clarkson, who is the best kind of doctor, but who knows plenty about the worst. Any mistakes are mine, and not his, which is why it is best that he wields the scalpel, and me the pen.

Denise Hayden, for never making me feel as bad as I probably should have done, and for keeping us all going.

Jonathan Lloyd, for being brilliant.

Tim Barker and Kathryn Sweet for being copy readers par excellence.

My mum and dad, and the rest of my family, which now includes the miraculous Imogen and Louella, who fought so hard to get here as I wrote this book.

My friends Suzanne, Pam and Wendy, who deserve a special mention for their apparently endless willingness to help me out when I'm stuck.

And, as ever, to David, Tallulah and Ottilie, for being mine.

Prologue: New Year's Eve

Natalie and Tom

New Year's Eve. It was one of those things, wasn't it? You only looked good in a bikini for one summer (after breasts, before tummy), you only ever had one first kiss (per guy, obviously), and everyone, well at least everyone Natalie knew, had honestly truly only ever had one really, really brilliant New Year's Eve. Which, funnily enough, usually coincided roughly with the looking-good-in-a-bikini and the first-kiss year. All the years after that suffered by comparison. The summers-were-hotter-when-we-were-young principle – wasn't everything a bit brighter and louder and more vivid? Wasn't I a bit thinner and prettier and more fun? Wasn't New Year's Eve an altogether better experience? Like Valentine's Day – only really good when you were fifteen and waiting for a card from the guy who sat in the back row on the school coach and wore the really thin tie and listened to Led Zeppelin's 'Stairway To Heaven' *all* the time. A one-year deal, a once-in-a-lifetime thing.

Eleven fifteen p.m. on New Year's Eve was actually a great time to be driving. Everyone else was already 'there'. At the place where they were going to pretend to have the time of their lives, when actually they were thinking about that house party they went to in Cambridge in 1988, or that time in 1967 when they were so stoned

I

they didn't even hear midnight chime, or the New Year in 1992 when their boyfriend proposed to them in Times Square, or any year when the same ten people sitting round a suburban dinner table with them didn't seem quite so dull, or so snappy, or so needing to get home because their babysitter charged double time after midnight.

There was no one else on this bit of road. 'Dancing in the Moonlight' was blaring out of the stereo, and Natalie changed empty lanes a couple of times in a kind of Corsa salsa. She was cheering up a bit. Good idea. Good idea of Tom's.

She'd been going to stay at home, having a sulky night. Rose, possibly the only friend who could have jollied her out of it, had announced apologetically that her boyfriend Pete had got a deal on Eurostar – two nights, three-star in Lille (not Paris, that was two hundred pounds more and he hadn't yet finished his doctorate, after all). And would Natalie be okay? *Et tu*, Brute, Natalie had thought (saying a mean, silent prayer that Rose would not come back with a ring on her finger, and instantly feeling awful for wishing it), before she had hugged her friend, offered her lingerie drawer with an ironic shrug – negligées not thongs, obviously – and said that, yes, of course, she'd be fine, she'd go to some party. She'd then, obviously, turned down the two parties she'd had invitations to. Told both hosts she'd already accepted someone else, and managed to fall off the radar (which made her simultaneously relieved and alarmed – it had been pretty easy).

Both her sisters were a waste of time. Susannah was in Marrakesh, if you please, at some sort of New Year's Eve wrap party for the film Casper had just finished shooting. And Bridget was about ten months pregnant, which made her a very unlikely source of fun this evening. She and Karl were probably already in bed, with their angelic eighteen-month-old, Christina, nestled between them, reading the baby-name book, and toasting the New Year in sparkling apple juice.

Mum and Dad's? She'd rather be alone. A thirty-five-year-old at home with her parents on New Year's Eve in any year was bad enough, but after this last year, with the way things were at home . . . No, she couldn't have faced that. Not with everything that was going on.

She should have brought in a new flatmate when Susannah finally moved out. They'd liked it, just the two of them, after Bridget had left to get married three years ago, and the mortgage was pretty okay. Bridget had liked it, her room being unoccupied: she could still escape Karl and Christina, sometimes, for the odd night in town. But Susannah had gone so quickly, and apathy had set in. Well, not apathy. Anticipation. She shouldn't have been there much longer herself. It should have been happening to her, too.

None of it was how it should have been.

Right now, for example, she should not be bombing down the M4 listening to the radio, heading for the public house of her adolescent New Years' Eves. She should be in the Maldives, after an exhilarating day's diving, wafting fragrantly and goldenly around in something white and linen, drinking Bollinger imported at great expense. She should be in Simon's arms.

The bastard.

The complete bastard.

She was half-way through wishing him third-degree sunburn and jellyfish-stung gonads when the tears started. Damn. She thumped the wheel. I WILL NOT GIVE HIM THE SATISFACTION. I GAVE HIM SEVEN YEARS – I WILL WILL WILL NOT GIVE HIM ANY MORE.

Her New Year's Eve – The One – had been that one, the first the two of them had shared. Skiing in Switzerland. In a chalet belonging to someone's parents. A snowy, schnapps-fuelled rave in a pretty village square. A thousand people dancing to a hundred different tunes blasting through open windows, a million snowflakes on them all. That big, drunken, loving crowd vibe. Simon kissing her, his mouth so hot in the cold air. Making love in the drying room because it was too cold to do it lying on the snow (and they'd tried) quietly, so no one woke up.

That had been the one.

She'd forgotten about Tom. Well, not forgotten about him exactly. Tom was always there. He always had been. But she'd forgotten that he wouldn't have forgotten her.

Natalie and Tom had met in August 1977, the summer that Elvis Aaron Presley had died, when Natalie, her two sisters and their parents had moved in two doors down. Bridget had been the nesting one even then, unpacking boxes with their mother, arranging her enormous collection of Whimsies on the white melamine chest of drawers that separated her narrow single bed from Natalie's in the bedroom they were to share. Susannah had watched television for days on end – they'd showed all of Elvis's movies: *Viva Las Vegas, King Creole, Love Me Tender.* The new three-piece suite hadn't arrived so she practised the dance routines with abandonment in the living room, singing along. She would have enlisted Natalie, if she'd been given the chance, as extra chorus, but Natalie was sulking. She hadn't wanted to move. She'd liked their old house. Susannah always said she was change-resistant, and that you should embrace change. That was the sort of thing Susannah said a lot, using her long, graceful arms in expansive gestures, silver bracelets jangling.

Dad was going to be a branch manager, and that was why they had had to move. It was a promotion and a good thing and, anyway, no one had asked her.

She had been sitting on the low brick wall at the front of the house, poking at some earth with a twig, when she first saw him. Her mother had come out with some empty boxes just as his mother was walking by – she said they'd been into town to get him some new school shoes before the start of term, and that his feet grew like nothing else, and that he needed a new pair practically every term, and that was expensive enough before you even started to think about football boots and training shoes and wellingtons. Tom – whom Natalie judged to be about her own age but taller – looked mortified, and Natalie's mum looked sort of stunned, and nodded and smiled a lot, slightly sideways at her when Tom's mother said three daughters, how lovely and how lucky because their feet, girls' feet, probably didn't grow anything like so fast. Natalie had weirdly big feet, which seemed to grow only sporadically, incredibly quickly and usually just after her mum had bought her some new shoes. It was a bit of a family joke. He had stary eyes. Big stary eyes. And too much curly hair. Not down his neck, like a footballer, but all up on top of his head.

Natalie's mum told Tom's mum that Natalie was a tomboy, and Tom's mum said Tom would like that, that there weren't many other children his age on the street, and that they should be friends.

But, of course, it had taken weeks. Well into the new term at school. Weeks of self-consciously playing at the same thing (bikes, roller skates, toss-ups) in two gardens, two houses apart. It was Mrs Samways, the old lady in the middle, who finally got them together. She had this copper-pan thing she kept in her front room that she put sweets in and then got you to pretend that you had 'magicked' the sweets into it by rubbing it. Everyone, except perhaps her, knew there was no magic, but they kept going in anyway and rubbing the pan. Mrs Samways liked the company and the children liked the sweets, even if the front room did smell a bit funny, like she'd always eaten fish the night before. When she saw children in their front gardens, she would appear in her doorway, with a luridly coloured crocheted shawl round her shoulders and say, in her thin, tremulous voice, 'Anyone feeling magic today?' and the children would smile shyly and traipse over.

One particular Sunday, when the dads were polishing their cars and the mums were washing up after Sunday lunch, and the older siblings were listening to the top forty and writing the list down to memorise before school, they both answered the reedy call. Tom let her choose first, and afterwards, when they had let Mrs Samways ask them some questions about school, he had said to Natalie, 'Wanna go for a ride?'

'S'pose.' She had shrugged.

And that was how it had been between them, ever since. Tom was the instigator, Natalie the willing participant. He was older, in Bridget's class at school. And braver. And more foolhardy, Natalie's dad always said. It was Tom who had decided they should ride full pelt down the steep road and practise skidding to the left and right inches before the waist-high brick wall and, what was more he'd owned up to the idea, somewhat tearfully, in the back of Natalie's dad's car on the way to Casualty. It was Tom who had decided they should take the bottle of Martini from the drinks table at his parents' summer do, at which they were supposed to be taking coats and handing out peanuts, and drink it in the garage. No one had to own up to that. They were very sick very privately, and no one ever missed the Martini. He had done everything first. School trip to France. Cigarettes. Snogging with the lights off at a party when the parents had gone out. O levels, A levels, university . . .

They'd had one serious fight. The year Torvill and Dean won the world championships with 'Bolero' in those floaty purple outfits. He'd got off with Susannah – who did a lot of random snogging – at the school disco, and Natalie had told him she thought it was disgusting, like snogging your sister. He had

6

laughed, and said that Susannah was nothing like his sister, and that maybe snogging Natalie would be like snogging his sister, but that Susannah was a different kettle of fish. He had said it with an expression on his face that Natalie hadn't seen before, and didn't like at all, and she had slapped him – not across the face, but hard, in his stomach – and flounced off, and not talked to him for a whole week, until he bought her a Terry's Chocolate Orange and said, with a very serious face, that he was sorry and that he would never do it again.

And they had had one kiss, when she was nineteen and he was twenty, and she had been dumped and he was picking up the pieces. Again. She'd been in love with some guy at college, only he'd taken this old girlfriend of his to some big London house-party instead of her, and she'd come home to mope. Tom had been home, too, getting ready to go Interrailing for the summer, and she'd sat on the floor of his bedroom watching him put pants and T-shirts into his rucksack, moaning.

'You know what your trouble is?' he had asked. 'You have to fall in love. Every single time.'

'I'm a romantic – what's wrong with that?' She had pouted.

'Bollocks! It's just a bad habit. You can't possibly be in love that many times, Nat. Love isn't like that!'

'And when did you become such an expert? There's me thinking you're reading computer science.'

'I'm no expert. That's exactly my point. I've never been in love.'

'Diddums.'

'I don't need your sympathy, honey. I'm not the one sitting there with a gob on. I've been in plenty of other things, thanks very much.'

'Like knickers.'

'Well, yes, since you're asking. A few pairs. I've been in lust, I've had a laugh, I've cared, I've even really, really liked girls.

But love? Not yet. And I'm in no hurry either, especially if this,' he gestured at her, 'is what it does for you.'

'Boys mature less quickly than girls.'

'That's lame. You're missing my point, Nat. You're in love with love. You fall for the wrong guys, and you fall too bloody hard. And then we have to have this heartbreak fallout all over the place. It's stupid.'

Natalie had stood up, indignant. 'I'm so sorry to come round and burden you with my stupid "heartbreak fallout". How tiresome. I'll go.'

He caught her wrist. 'Shut up. I can take it. And the only place you're going is the pub, with me, now. If I can't reason you out of it, I'll have to drink you out of it.'

Several drinks later, they were lying on their backs in the garden, still talking about Natalie's heart.

'You know what your trouble is?'

Natalie's trouble at that moment was that she needed to pee, but she let her head loll to one side and looked at him. 'What, O wise one?'

'You've got the wrong criteria.'

'Huh?'

'You need to make more intellectual decisions, fewer emotional ones . . .' 'Decisions' came out a bit slurred.

'What the hell are you talking about?'

'You need to go for someone who won't let you down.'

'How are you supposed to know if someone's going to let you down or not?'

'I wouldn't let you down.'

She flopped her arm on to his chest. 'I know you wouldn't. You're my bestest friend.' Patted him. She really must get up and go to the loo.

Tom was suddenly up on his elbow. Close. Looking at her. And then he kissed her, just once, lightly, on the lips. At first she thought he must have missed. Maybe he was trying to kiss the cheek of the second Natalie. He had drunk three pints. But his face said otherwise. 'Shut up,' she said, although he hadn't spoken.

'I'll marry you.'

'Shut up!' A bit louder that time.

'Not now. We're too young.'

'Not ever. Never, you idiot.'

'Never is a long time.'

Natalie sat up. 'Shut up.'

'I think it's your wit and biting, incisive commentary I love most about you.' He was smiling again, and he looked more like Tom.

'Shut—'

He put his finger up to silence her. 'Okay, I will. Just remember this afternoon, Natalie. When you come back to me with another broken heart, and you're thirty and over the hill, and you've had enough of the hunt, I'll marry you.'

'Right. Jolly good. Nice to know. Thanks, Tom.'

Blimey – did we really think thirty was over the hill? Sixteen years ago it had probably seemed it. From the other side, of course, it was pretty young.

He'd been laughing at her then. Perhaps she ought to call his bluff tonight. Go down on one knee, take him up on his offer. He probably wouldn't remember – she was surprised *she* remembered herself. And it wasn't exactly the subject matter that most made her want to chuckle right now.

The pub must be heaving – there was nowhere to park. Natalie drove the Corsa up on to the grass bank that ran alongside the cricket pitch and got out. Blimey, it was cold. She pulled her coat tightly round her, tucked her hair behind her ears and trotted towards the pub door. You could hear the noise, as you got closer, and there was a sort of Ready Brek orange glow coming from inside.

Like a warm blanket, the voices and hands of her old friends covered her.

'Hiya, Nat!'

'Happy New Year!'

'How are you?'

'Get you a drink?'

She realised she felt a little elated. People were pleased to see her, and it was good to see them. The cast of her childhood and adolescence. Like the theme tune – sometimes you wanna be where everybody knows your name. Clever old Tom.

And there he was. He always drank like that. Arms folded, with his pint balanced on the inside of one elbow. Tipping forwards and backwards a little on his heels. He was nodding and smiling at someone, and he didn't see her for a few moments. Then someone backed away from the bar with a metal tray of drinks over their head, and he spotted her through the space. He winked and mouthed hello, and Natalie thought suddenly that she might cry.

Patrick and Lucy

Lucy heard Patrick coming back down the stairs, and came out into the hall. 'Thanks for that, love. Success?'

'Sort of. Ed is finally, three chapters later, asleep, but Bella is still insisting that at the great age of eight she's old enough to stay up until midnight.'

'What did you tell her?'

'I told her awake was fine, that it was up we had a problem with.'

Lucy smiled. 'Too right. This is you-and-me time. Come and have a glass of this.' She was holding an open bottle of champagne in one hand, and a half-drunk glass in the other.

She turned back into the kitchen. 'Grab another glass from the cabinet, will you?'

Patrick went into the front room. How long had he been upstairs with the kids? Their living room was transformed. She must have gone round like a dervish. The newspapers, which had previously been strewn across the floor, were neatly piled on the coffee-table. The kids' toys had been returned to the boxes behind the sofa, and the pine needles had disappeared from under the tree, which had been up for three weeks and was practically bald. That was how Patrick felt. Used up. Worn out by the festive season. His parents and her mother and a seemingly endless parade of friends, relatives and what he referred to silently as 'miscellaneous' had paraded through and been fed, watered and cleaned-up-after. Lucy was like Delia Smith on speed. Practically every other morning he and Ed had been despatched to Tesco with a scrawled list of obscure ingredients like saffron, vanilla sugar and goose fat, and every evening he had washed and dried the same saucepans and baffling food-processor attachments and put them away in readiness for the next day's onslaught. He had fallen into bed and into a coma every night. He'd be lucky to make it to midnight. New Year's Eve should be in March. Who the hell could be bothered now? Clearly, Lucy. She'd laid the table, two places, real napkins, candles, and put on a CD, which she almost never did.

Patrick stared at himself, pale and baggy-eyed, in the mirror above the mantelpiece and wondered if he should have tidied himself up.

'Patrick?' He grabbed a glass, one of the eight crystal flutes they had received as a wedding gift, and went back to the kitchen.

It smelt great. Lucy was stirring something on the hob, and her face was a little flushed from the heat. Two plates of gravadlax were waiting on the counter.

'This'll be ready in about twenty minutes. Give it here.' She filled the glass, then raised her own to clink against his. 'Happy New Year, darling,' she said.

'Happy New Year.' She kissed him. A kiss full of needs and promises. 'I can't believe you've still got the energy to cook, after the fortnight you've had.'

'I am pretty knackered,' she confessed, adding, 'but you're the most important. And tonight is just for us. And,' she smiled, 'it *is* from *10-minute Feasts*!'

'You're unbelievable.'

'And tomorrow Marianne's cooking for us, so I'll get a day off.'

'Is it just us?'

'Think so. Why?'

'I'd prefer it, that's all. If any more parents from Bella's class are there it'll turn into the same old thing. Teachers, curriculum, car park, cake sale . . .'

'Welcome to my world, honey!'

'I know . . . but it can get a bit tedious. It'll be more relaxed if it's just Alec and Marianne.'

Lucy didn't answer.

He drained his glass, poured more for himself and topped hers up. Then sat in a chair and watched her quietly. She didn't look different at all. Not older, or bigger, more tired or more staid. Just exactly like the girl he'd first met.

He'd followed her up and down three aisles of a supermarket. Fruit and veg. Tinned goods. Baking. She had a great wiggle. A happy walk. From a distance, filling his trolley with whatever he grabbed from left and right, he watched her talk to a couple of old ladies and a spotty youth stacking shelves, her auburn hair bouncing and shiny. He watched her take an inordinately long time to choose a handful of plums. Ludicrous though it sounded, even to him, he had pretty much fallen for her back view before he'd overtaken her on the corner of Toiletries and seen her lovely face, then Bella, strapped to her chest in one of those origami-like slings.

Lucy and Tom liked to joke that Patrick had invented supermarket cruising.

'Wish you were at the pub with Tom?' She was looking at him quizzically. His brother had called earlier in the week and invited them.

'No. Way too old for all that nonsense, aren't we?'

'Speak for yourself. I've still got a few epic evenings left in me. It might have been fun. We could have got your mum to have the kids, maybe.'

'So you're the one who wishes they were in the pub with my brother!'

'No way. Although he said Natalie was down, didn't he? I haven't seen her since the Simon thing blew up. Still, maybe she'll drop round before she goes back. And this is what we do, isn't it? It's tradition.'

'Have we got traditions?'

'Honey, we've got dozens. Hadn't you noticed?' Now she hugged him, and he smelt her perfume and her hair. He breathed deeply, and rested his chin on top of her head.

In a moment, though, she was back at the stove, stirring. 'Can you believe this is our seventh New Year together?' she said.

He smiled. 'We didn't get much peace that first night, either, did we?' Bella had been teething. He'd greeted midnight pacing the bedroom floor with another man's screaming child in his arms.

Lucy had said she would ask her mother to have her. She was embarrassed, Patrick thought, and it had made him sad. Will, her husband, had left her when Bella was three months old, and Patrick was the first man she had been with since. He'd wanted desperately to show her that Bella was okay with him, that her past could be part of his present and their future. He hadn't necessarily expected to prove it so utterly on New Year's Eve. It was the first time they'd made love. They were almost, but not quite, too tired by the time Bella had succumbed to a dose of Calpol, and it had been oh-so-quiet in order that they didn't wake her, and he remembered her saying that she never wanted to start another year without him there, then looking mortified, as though she had said something so clingy and so needy that he would leave immediately. He had hated how grateful she was, how reticent about her body, with its four angry red stretch-marks and its huge milky nipples. He just loved her. He didn't mind about all that. He had wanted to take care of her. He still did, all these years later. 'What are we having?'

'This,' she gestured towards the salmon, 'then king prawns in a tomato and champagne sauce – so I'll need a dribble of that, but don't worry, I stuck another bottle in the fridge – then strawberries.' She slid her arm under his shirt, and ran it lightly across his skin. 'Which you can eat out of a bowl or off me, whichever you prefer.' She kissed him hungrily. 'Mmm. It's been a while. In case you hadn't noticed.'

He had. It had been three weeks. Not since the day . . .

Anna and Nicholas

Nicholas took a handkerchief out of his pocket and rubbed it gently across the silver neck of the decanter. He had poured the red wine into it earlier this evening, through a muslin square, carefully and slowly, in the kitchen. He'd been in Anna's way, of course, although he had chosen his corner carefully, hoping not to be; she had shouted at him. But these things had to be done properly.

The table was beautifully laid. They weren't rich, but they

were of a generation that took care of its possessions, and over the forty years of their marriage they had amassed some beautiful things. Full sets of crystal wine glasses – none chipped; a Royal Doulton dinner service; the beautiful white linen tablecloth with matching napkins. All bought by themselves. For twelve Christmases, back in the seventies and early eighties, they had given them to each other. Anna had bought him one red and one white wine glass, and he had bought her one place setting. You could mark out his career by how easy it had been to pay for it. In the early years it had been a lot of money. By the end, it was just one of the gifts they exchanged – Christmas had become a much more elaborate affair. But they still did it. The girls thought it was dull – Susannah was always trying to talk him into jewellery, Bridget favoured perfumes. But it was what they wanted, a ritual that mattered. Anna wouldn't use any of them until they'd got six, and they hadn't been able to have eight 'smart' guests for dinner until Charles and Diana had got married. They'd bought the cutlery, in its small mahogany canteen, one year in the Harrods sale, with the only inheritance either of them had ever had: four hundred pounds from an old aunt of his. It was silver plate, of course, but it did justice to the china and glass. It hadn't ever been about showing off – Anna was no Hyacinth Bucket. It seemed to him that it had been about achievement, commitment and longevity.

The girls hadn't understood it then, and they never would. Everything was different now: Bridget had got her eight-place dinner service overnight – it was all itemised like an inventory on her wedding list. He'd spent fifteen thousand pounds on a wedding, she'd gone off on a three thousand pound honeymoon and come home to a hallway full of a ready-made life, carefully packaged by John Lewis. They laughed at him, gently, when he told them that the things you had to work for were worth more to you.

'War-baby,' Susannah called him, not unkindly.

Which, of course, was true. Born the year before war had broken out, to a mother struggling already with four other children, and a father who had gone away in 1939 and not come home for six years. Maybe they were right.

But Bridget had been married only three years, and she'd already had to replace a glass and two side plates.

Another New Year's Eve. Nicholas felt very old and tired. The three couples next door were the same six people he and Anna had spent New Year's Eve with for the last twenty-two years. Four of them they *only* saw on this one night in the year.

He ran one finger along his collar. Anna always required them to wear black tie. She said it made the evening more special. And more uncomfortable. He probably needed a six-teen and a half collar, these days, and his shirt was old and tight. In private Anna said she was damned if she was going to slave over a five-course dinner only to have people eat it dressed in jeans. They went to each other's houses in rotation. At Brian and Margaret's it was always curry, ordered by Margaret from the restaurant on the roundabout and collected by Brian early, so that he could drink, and served from the Formica breakfast bar, still in its cartons. They had holidayed with Brian and Margaret a few times when their boys had been friendly as teenagers with the girls, and Margaret had often gone braless, well into her forties, long past the age when it might have been a good idea. Nicholas supposed it was the same sort of thing with the food. Free and easy. At Shaun and Lindsay's there was always a theme. Thai, Scottish, cowboy. Lindsay dressed up, and Shaun matched the alcohol. Nicholas remembered the year Lindsay had appeared in a full kimono, bowing and scraping theatrically, and Shaun had served *sake* in egg-cups. They'd been made to sit on the floor, which had played havoc with his knees. Clive and Vicky were more conventional, but they ate in the kitchen and Clive always wore jeans.

He wondered what the others had talked about, getting dressed in their penguin suits to come here tonight. Maybe they liked it. They were all chatting away happily enough next door in the living room – Anna would be handing round the mini Yorkshire puddings with tiny strips of rare roast beef. He heard Clive and Shaun laugh their hearty male laughs.

Nicholas wanted to go upstairs, lay his head on the pillow, go to sleep and maybe never wake up. Or, at least, not until this endless night was long over. More than anything he didn't want to go back in there with them and start smiling his plastic company smile. He didn't want to eat his fiddly five-course meal, and watch his expensive red wine being poured down the throats of people who would have happily drunk Blue Nun. And, most of all, he had no wish and no energy to pretend that he was happy. To survey all that he owned smugly, and carry on this unbearable, pointless charade.

He almost jumped when the door opened behind him. Anna was backing out of the room, saying something sing-songy. The others laughed. When she turned to him, with her empty tray, her face changed; the smile faded instantly and her eyes narrowed. 'What the hell are you doing out here, Nick? I'd appreciate some help in there. You're the host, for God's sake, not one of the guests.'

Patrick and Lucy

They hadn't eaten the strawberries. Too many late nights and too much champagne. Patrick couldn't remember how they had arrived on the sofa, or whose idea it had been to switch on the ubiquitous New Year's Eve shindig, but they were both sprawled across it now, half listening to the enforced gaiety of some daemonic Scotswoman screeching to make herself heard above the roar of a crowd and some even more screechy bagpipes. He thought Lucy might be asleep, but when they started the crescendo of the countdown she shucked herself out from under his arm and nudged him. 'We should stand up or something.'

'Why?'

'You know. See the New Year in.'

'You're bonkers.' She did it for the National Anthem, too.

'Get up.' She was on her feet now, dragging at his arm.

'Three, two, one. HAPPY NEW YEAR!' Lucy threw up her arms and whisper-shouted. It would be a disaster to wake Ed now. He'd be up for the duration. With her arms still above her head, she added, 'Feeling a bit daft now.'

Patrick sighed. 'Luce?'

'What?'

The phone rang. It was, as she had known it would be, her best friend Marianne, calling from a party. 'Happy New Year, Luce,' she roared.

Lucy felt a stab of envy, as she listened to the revelry. Patrick hadn't wanted to go. 'And to you. Are you having fun?'

'*So* much fun!' She was drunk. 'Talk to Alec.' For a moment Lucy thought the line had gone dead or that Marianne had dropped the phone. Then she heard Alec's voice.

'Hello, you.'

'Happy New Year.'

'I wish you were here.'

Did she blush? She stepped back from the receiver as though it were on fire, and shouted into it. 'Yes, Patrick's right here. Here he is.'

Patrick wasn't right here at all, but she waited while he stood up and came over, the earpiece clasped to her chest. When he took the phone she went into the kitchen.

She was busy at the sink when he came in behind her. She didn't turn round. 'Sounds pretty wild, hey?'

'Lucy?' His tone was strained. 'I've lost my job.'

Anna

They'd only had four courses by the time the grandfather clock in the hallway struck midnight. Anna wouldn't have the television on. Immediately, they heard fireworks in the street outside, booming over their own soundtrack of Mozart. It seemed inappropriate to get up, sing and embrace, although Brian blew a kiss at Margaret, and Nicholas saw Clive take Vicky's hand across the table.

Anna excused herself to get dessert, and Nicholas busied himself pouring champagne into eight flutes.

'We can't make a toast until Anna gets back,' Lindsay protested, when he raised his glass. 'What's she up to out there? Shall I go?'

'No,' Nicholas said. 'I'll go. And drink up. It's sacrilege, you know, to let the bubbles disappear. We'll have another toast in a minute . . .' He opened the door to the kitchen and saw Anna, leaning against the back door, watching next door's fireworks. 'You all right, Anna?' Her shoulders gave one heave, and she made a strange little strangled noise.

He went to her, and she leant into him, crying openly now. 'What is it, Anna? What on earth is it?'

He was so very rarely allowed to touch her these days, and he so badly wanted to comfort her. For months and months she had been unapproachable, unrecognisable, unassailable. He knew she cried, but she never let him see. He tried to look at her face, pulling her chin up with his finger, but she pulled it away roughly and buried it in his sleeve. They stood still long enough for him to worry that one of the others would come in and find them like this. She'd hate that. And those people were supposed to be their friends . . . 'You have to talk to me, darling. We cannot go on like this.' He felt her nod, and cling to him.

'I'm sorry.'

'I know.' He did. 'I just want to help you.'

'You can't help me.'

'I want to try.'

For a moment she didn't say anything at all, and then what she said made his blood run cold: 'Why? I'm nothing.'

Natalie

At the pub, Natalie was finding it hard to cross her arms for 'Auld Lang Syne'. The person on her left kept proffering the wrong hand, damn him.

'Come here.' Tom grabbed her right arm and pushed it across her chest, then started pumping the left. '"Should old acquaintance . . ."'

Huh. Old acquaintance. Ancient-history acquaintance, more like. And, yes, he bloody well should be 'forgot'. Not tonight maybe. She had to be remembering him to say he should be forgotten, didn't she? But tomorrow he would definitely be so very 'forgot'. She had everything she needed here, after all. She had good friends, she had unlimited access to chilled white wine, she had Tom. Ah, yes, Tom.

It was very noisy. The first time she said it, his brow furrowed. 'What?' he roared.

'You're going to marry me, Tom.'

'What?' Except that this time he had heard.

'I said, *you* are going to marry *me*.' She had pulled her right hand away from the man on her left, and was using it to point, with emphasis.

'Course I am.'

She didn't remember much after that.

Until Tom's mum knocked on the door and, without waiting for an answer, came in and sat down on the end of the bed. She held out a mug of tea. 'Happy New Year, dear! I must say, this takes me back. It's been years since you slept here, hasn't it? It's lovely. I only wish Tom had told me he was bringing you. I'd have bought carnations, brightened the place up a bit.'

It was bright enough already. Natalie squinted between eyelids gummed together with last night's mascara. Lime green and violet. The result of a particularly lurid and unpleasant episode of *Changing Rooms* Cynthia had watched, and, more worryingly, been inspired by, in the mid-nineties. Natalie wasn't sure God had made a carnation to match.

Cynthia was still talking. That was the nice thing about her. No response necessary. Natalie didn't think she could speak, this morning. Had she been smoking? Her mouth felt like the proverbial parrot's cage, and her head was thumping.

'How's your mum, love? Terrible business, that. Still, glad it turned out to be nothing in the end. Must have given her a terrible scare. I've been meaning to go and see her for a while but, you know, with one thing and another . . .' Her voice almost trailed off. But she rescued the moment. 'Still, New Year, new start, all that.'

That was easy enough, then. Perhaps Natalie should explain that to her mother. They'd never been friends, not really. Cynthia was too noisy, too speak-now-think-later for her mum. Natalie had always felt a little embarrassed about her mother's attitude, to be honest. She could seem . . . aloof and superior. But Cynthia would never have noticed. Speaking of which, she'd have to go today, she realised, with a small shiver of dread. On a hangover. 'Where's Tom?' she croaked.

'In the shower, I think. He's in slightly better shape than you. Nice fry-up? Kill or cure!'

'Sounds lovely, Cynthia. Thanks.'

Natalie had retreated back under the duvet, and was almost asleep again when Tom knocked and came in.

'What is it with you lot?' she grumbled. 'Do you never wait to be invited in?'

'Don't be narky with me. If I hadn't practically carried you back here last night, God knows where you'd have ended up. You were in a right state.'

'Thanks a lot, Sir Lancelot. Whose fault is it that I was?'

'I can't see that it's mine. I don't remember making you drink ten glasses of wine.'

'Was it really that many?'

'Well, I wasn't counting, but I'd say it was a ten-glass stagger you had on you at the end.'

'Was I embarrassing?' She covered her face with her hands.

'Excruciating.'

She threw a lime-green pillow at him. He caught it in one hand.

'And why the hell are you looking so sprightly anyway?' she asked. He looked positively rude with health, hair still slightly damp from the shower.

'I've got things to do, people to see. There's a lot to arrange.' Natalie was mystified. 'It's not every day a guy gets proposed to.'

'What are you talking about?'

'I'm hurt that you don't remember.' He didn't seem hurt at all. 'Last night? You asked me to marry you. And I agreed.'

'You silly bugger.'

'Does that mean you've changed your mind?'

'That means last night I was out of my mind, and cannot be held accountable for anything I might have said or done . . .'

Cynthia called upstairs. 'You two! Breakfast is ready.'

Tom pulled the lime-green dressing-gown off the back of the bedroom door and threw it at Natalie, then winked at her and turned towards the stairs.

'Good news, Mum and Dad. Natalie and I are getting married. She asked me last night, and I agreed.'

Tom's dad John twitched the corner of his newspaper to look at them. 'Splendid. Welcome to the family, love.' His eyes sparkled with amusement.

He'd have been a real dish, years ago, Natalie thought, as she watched him. She hadn't noticed it before. 'We so are not.' She attempted to kick Tom under the table, but hit the mahogany leg instead, which really hurt. She rubbed her ankle ruefully, while Tom made a face of mock-sympathy that she longed to punch.

'And why not, I'd like to know? He'd be a great catch. He's handsome, clever, successful, kind . . .'

'All right, Mum. Remind me to take you on all my first dates from now on.'

'There won't be any, will there? Not now you're promised to Natalie . . .'

She couldn't cope with the banter. Her head was really hurting now and she felt terribly sick. She put her knife and fork down, mumbled her thanks to Cynthia and went back to bed.

It was several hours later when she emerged. Tom was in the garage with his father. Tinkering. That was what they called it. As long as Natalie had known him, John had had an Austin Healey, which he kept in something like a bubble that always made Natalie think about the end bit of *E.T.*, to protect it from the elements, and which he drove just once a year to and from a

Healey rally, providing it wasn't raining and there was no rain/hail/snow/plague of locusts forecast. The rest of the time he 'tinkered' with it, and when Tom was home, he 'tinkered' too. The fact that the garage was somewhere Cynthia never followed them to resume talking was, presumably, a bonus. They were listening to the horse racing on the radio.

'Nice overalls, chaps.'

'How are you feeling?'

'Better.' She smiled weakly. 'Ready, *je pense*, for *les parents*.'

'Wanna ride?'

'Drive me to the pub, and I can pick up my car there?'

'No problem. Hang on.' Tom peeled off the overalls and laid them over a workbench.

John put his arm round Natalie. 'Nice to see you, sweetheart, it really was. We haven't seen much of you, these last couple of years.'

'I know. Sorry.'

'Nothing to apologise for. You've all got your own lives now. We hardly see this one, either.' He gestured at his son. 'I remember a time when I couldn't move for kids. You two, Patrick, Genevieve. It sometimes felt more like a youth club in there than anything else. Miss it a bit, sometimes.'

'But, then, Patrick brings Bella and Ed over . . .'

'That's true. Then I remember!'

'See you in a bit, Dad.'

John kissed Natalie. ' 'Bye, love.'

'Do you want me to come with you?' They were leaning on Natalie's car in the bright sunshine.

'No, thanks. Bridge said she'd be over this afternoon. With a bit of luck we'll overlap.'

'Then what?'

'Then . . .' she sighed '. . . back to my new reality, I guess. I suppose I'm glad we never got a place together, me and Simon. At least I don't have to go through all that moving upheaval, sharing out CDs and all that.'

'True.' Tom didn't know what else to say, so he hugged her. 'You'll be all right.'

'Huh.' She felt heavy, lethargic and knackered. She didn't feel all right.

Tom kissed her forehead, unlocked his car and climbed in. As he switched on the ignition he wound the window down. 'And I'll see you in a couple of weeks. Friday night.'

'Have I forgotten something?' She didn't think she'd had plans on a Friday night with anyone but Simon for a long, long time.

'No. But you'll be free, won't you?'

She shrugged. 'S'pose. What are you on about?'

'I've made a plan . . .'

'What plan?'

'Well, you've got nothing better to do, let's face it, and I'm up for a bit of a challenge, so I've thought of one.'

Natalie couldn't help but smile. 'And . . . ?'

'And . . . since you're so sure I wouldn't make a decent boyfriend, and I reckon I might, I figure I'd better prove it to you.'

'And exactly how are you going to do that?'

'I'm going to spend twenty-six days with you. See what I did there? That's the number of letters in the alphabet.'

'And . . .'

'And, O cynical one, we're going to take turns to decide what to do on those days. Turn and turn about. I'll start, by the way, with A. You'll be B, I'll be C, you'll be D—'

'I do know the alphabet, Tom.'

'Exactly. Shouldn't have any trouble, then, should you, thinking up things to do?'

'And the point of this will be?'

'You're going to fall for me.'

'Yeah, right.'

'We're going to go out of our comfort zone. We're going to
see each other in new situations and new places . . . and you're
going to find out what you're missing.' He was grinning, and
Natalie didn't know whether he wanted to be taken seriously or
whether he was winding her up.

'You're mad. We've known each other for, like, twenty years.
I think we'd know by now if there was any chemistry between
us, don't you?'

'Maybe one of us thinks there is.' She rolled her eyes. 'And,
anyway, why are girls always going on about chemistry? You
never heard a bloke talk about that, did you?'

'Blokes don't need chemistry. They just need tits.'

Tom shook his head. 'You disappoint me with your general-
isations, Nat, not to mention your crude and base language.'

'Oh, shut up. Listen, I know, okay? You know, too, if you
stop being a clown for a minute.'

'One question, my little lovely. Have you got anything better
to do with your life in the next couple of months?'

'You know I haven't.'

'Well, then. Why not play Alphabet Weekends with your old
mate, Tom? Live a little.'

Natalie had no answer for that.

'See you next Friday, then.' And with that he sped off.

Lucy

It snowed overnight. Lucy couldn't remember the last time
snow had settled around there, but it had this morning – just a
couple of centimetres. The world looked pretty. Bella and Ed
were outside, coats and boots on over their pyjamas, building a

snowman, and she listened to their squeals while she waited for the kettle to boil.

'I'll cancel Marianne and Alec,' she said.

'Don't do that. No need.'

'If you're sure.'

'I'm sure.'

She was relieved. She didn't want to cancel. She hadn't seen him since the end-of-term carol concert. Alec had kissed her cheek just a little nearer her mouth than he should have done, and held her hand just a little longer than was, maybe, normal, when they'd said goodbye and wished each other a merry Christmas.

She knew she shouldn't want to see him as much as she did. 'And we'll talk about it tonight, shall we?' 'It'. Little word for a huge subject.

'Sure.'

Upstairs she dressed with care. She heard the children come in, giggling and chattering, and heard Patrick taking them out of their snowy gear, laughing along. When Bella came into her bedroom, there were two or three discarded outfits on the bed, and Lucy stood in her bra and pants examining herself in the long mirror. She smiled at her daughter, then twisted her mouth into a grimace. 'Think I've put on a couple of pounds over Christmas.'

'Mrs Smith says we shouldn't even know how much we weigh.'

'That's easy for Mrs Smith to say. She doesn't weigh an ounce over eight stone.'

'You look lovely, Mummy.'

She kissed Bella's forehead. 'Thank you, darling.' She took another skirt and sweater out of the wardrobe. 'This one?' Bella nodded approvingly. 'You're looking pretty good yourself, sweetheart. That's the cardigan Granny bought you, isn't it?'

Bella grinned and twisted happily. She was getting so grown-up. And she looked like her father.

Lucy hadn't thought much about Will in a long time. But Bella was increasingly similar. She had her own colouring, but the long, coltish legs and the long, curling eyelashes were all Will. Sometimes, when she was explaining something to her mother, Bella used her hands like he did, emphasising things with expansive gestures. She hadn't seen him for ages. There had been no need, while the divorce was being finalised and he hadn't asked to see his daughter. Lucy didn't even know where he was any more.

The last time they'd met had been the summer he'd left. He'd rung her mother and asked Lucy to meet him in the park near their home. He'd expressed surprise, as she approached the bench where he was, that she hadn't brought baby Bella with her. She remembered telling him that he didn't deserve to see her, and she remembered enjoying the pain and hurt that came across his face.

She'd felt strong. She'd had Patrick.

For a few years after the divorce, she'd lived in a kind of permanent fear that he would come back to try to claim Bella – fight for access or shared custody. She couldn't have allowed that. She didn't ask him for advice, money, or help. And he'd better not ask her for Bella.

People tried to tell her that Will had rights; legal entitlements. Bleeding hearts, and do-gooders, and even her mother. They said that Bella needed to know him. That Lucy was storing up trouble for herself and her daughter by not acknowledging him. They made her angry. She didn't want to be reasonable and civilised. She didn't ever want Will to have the chance to explain his actions to Bella. The mushroom cloud of rage inside her grew smaller and paler over the years, and it was displaced. But it never went away entirely. She didn't want it to.

But he hadn't fought for Bella, of course. He wasn't interested enough to stay around for her, and he wasn't interested enough to want to be a part of her life. If there was anything still unresolved in her head about Will, that was it. How could she have fallen in love with someone who could father a child, then walk away?

When Bella had been younger, Lucy had spent hours watching her asleep in her cot, or toddling drunkenly across the grass, or painstakingly feeding herself, and offered silent apologies to her baby: I'm sorry I chose someone like that to be your father. I'm sorry.

The divorce had been finalised long before Bella was sentient enough to remember the man who had deserted her when she was just a few months old. And there had been Patrick, who had wanted to care for them both. There had been no need to tell her, and she had always sensed that Patrick didn't want her to. So they hadn't. When Ed was born, it had felt like even less of a lie – they were a family, the four of them: father, mother, daughter, son. Why complicate it? Only very occasionally did she lie in bed and worry at it in her own mind.

One day Bella would have to know.

She shivered. Standing there now, gazing at this child who reminded her so much of Will, that time seemed suddenly closer.

'You're cold, Mum! Hurry up. I can't wait to show Nina my new skates.'

Lucy held out her arms and Bella bounded happily into them. She laid her head against Lucy's stomach and put her thumb into her mouth, and they stood there like that for just a minute until Lucy broke away and started to dress.

She should have been thinking about Patrick and his New Year bombshell. But she was thinking about Alec and about Will.

Natalie and Nicholas

'Hello, Dad!'

'Hello, darling! Happy New Year!'

'Off somewhere?'

'I was just going for a walk. Want to join me?'

'What about Mum?'

'She's asleep.'

'Is she okay?'

'Bit tired. You know what she's like . . . The last guests didn't clear off until about two and then she always insists on doing all the clearing up before she'll go to bed. By hand, since it's the best stuff. It was nearly four by the time she came up. I've left her there. Took her a cup of tea just now, but she was out for the count.'

'Then I'll come!'

Her dad looked pleased. Natalie slipped her arm through his, and they started up the road.

'How was your evening?'

'Boozy. Feel a bit crap today, truthfully. Fresh air'll do me good, no doubt!'

'Where were you?'

'I was with Tom at the pub. Went back and stayed the night at his mum and dad's.'

'I had no idea you were going to be so local. Where was Simon?'

Natalie took a deep breath. 'Forty foot under the sea, I expect.'

Nicholas looked perplexed. He'd stopped walking, but Natalie pulled him along, and carried on talking. 'I think he's in the Maldives, Dad. Diving.' She laughed. 'You thought I'd sent him swimming in concrete flippers, did you? Sadly, no. He dumped me, Dad.'

'Sweetheart!'

'Don't be nice to me, or I'll cry on the street. Very embarrassing.'

'I don't give a damn about being embarrassing.'

'That's because you're old,' she said. He smiled at her. 'Well, *I* do. Made a big enough fool of myself already, haven't I?'

'How? Unless you don't want to talk about it . . .'

'I probably should talk about it. No sense bottling it up, I suppose.'

'Never is.'

Natalie squeezed her dad's arm. He was so . . . so solid and reliable. She was suddenly glad that she'd come, glad to have it out in the open. She'd struggled, keeping it to herself last week at Christmas.

They'd come to the edge of the park near her parents' house.

'Fancy a sit-down? Not too cold.' He gestured towards the bench.

They walked over to it and sat. A boy was throwing sticks for a Labrador, and a few children were playing on the swings and see-saws in the fenced area, tired-looking parents watching them.

'So, what makes you think you've made a fool of yourself, my love?'

'All the time he was getting ready to leave me, I thought he was getting ready to ask me to marry him. I was so sure he was. He'd been acting a bit shifty and I thought he was up to something. And that time, in November, when we came down for Mum's birthday and he very specifically asked you to go to the pub with him for a drink – I thought he was asking you for permission. What an idiot!'

Nicholas couldn't remember what the two of them had talked about that day. He remembered being relieved to get out of the house for a while. But he would never have enjoyed a drink in the pub with Simon. He was one of those young men who patronised with almost every word. He didn't know what he would have said if Simon had asked for Natalie's hand. He wouldn't have wanted to say yes. Not that it really was about permission, these days, was it?

Nicholas really had had to ask Anna's father. He'd just finished his national service. Got a job as a clerk in the local bank. Anna's father had been a frightening, formidable man – huge, with a booming voice and a pipe. The women in his house were a little afraid of him, and, that day, Nicholas had been too.

'What happened?' he asked now.

'Well, I'd been kind of waiting, I suppose. For a few weeks. I kept thinking, you know, when we met up for dinner, that tonight might be the night. Let's face it, we'd been together long enough, and I'm not getting any younger. Maybe I started to smell of desperation or something . . . But no, actually, that's not right. It was the next step. The next obvious step. He knew it was what I wanted – what I expected, I suppose. But he didn't ask, and he didn't ask. I started to think Christmas – that would be a nice time to get engaged. God – I sound stupid.'

'You don't sound stupid, love.' Nicholas held her hand tightly.

'And then he started talking about going diving. Some mate of his at the hospital had been with his girlfriend and said it was brilliant, and he gave him the brochures of where they'd stayed. Simon seemed really keen – said it had been too long since he'd had a proper holiday, and what did I think of it and things.'

Nicholas nodded.

'I was so excited, Dad. I thought it was all going to happen. And I was so, so happy.'

'And?'

'And then he dumped me. Just like that. Came round to the

flat, quite late one night, the week before Christmas, and said he wasn't ready for commitment. Said it wasn't fair to keep stringing me along, when he knew that was what I wanted, and he wasn't in a position to offer it. He said he wouldn't be being fair to himself – something about just emerging from all these years of study and dedication and concentrating on getting himself qualified, and that getting engaged and married and stuff would just be another pressure on him, and that what he wanted was to be free, have fun, enjoy himself a bit, before he would truly be ready for all of that.' Natalie's voice broke.

'He said I could still go with him to the Maldives, if I liked.' Her brow furrowed. 'I suppose he thought of it as some sort of goodbye present. Or more of an *au revoir*. He wasn't quite brave enough to put a full stop to us. More of a question mark, or a colon.'

Nicholas snorted. He supposed Simon had thought of it as some sort of way to get laid on holiday without any hard work or responsibilities. 'I hope you added your own punctuation.'

'Of course I did. I told him if he didn't want me now, he could consider me off limits for ever. Except I didn't mean it. He knew that as well as I did.'

Natalie was crying quietly now, and she put her head on his shoulder. He reached up with his other hand and stroked her hair. His poor baby.

She'd always been the vulnerable one. Susannah – she was as tough as old boots. Beautiful, talented, confident. The only worries she'd ever given him and Anna were practical ones: where was she? How much bigger could her debts at drama college get? And Bridget was straightforwardly happy, even as a kid. You could put baby Bridget down on a two-foot-square mat in the living room and she'd never crawl off it. She would sit, playing contentedly with whatever was to hand, and never bother about what might be out of her reach. She didn't ever get dirty, and she had rarely cried. As a grown woman, she was the same. She'd found Karl, and they were gently, impressively happy together. No crawling off the mat.

Natalie was always the one who had worried him most. When she was about ten, he'd been working in London. She'd come up with Anna and the other girls one day in the summer holidays to meet him at his office and have lunch together, then go to Madame Tussaud's or somewhere. They'd passed a homeless guy, sitting in a thin sleeping-bag at the entrance to the tube, a scrawny dog lying in his lap. She'd talked of nothing else all day. How did he feed the dog? Why wasn't there somewhere they could go to sleep? How did they stay clean? Her big eyes had been wide with concern, and he remembered wanting to pick her up and hold her to him, protect her from all of the world. He had that feeling again now, as they sat on the park bench and she cried on his shoulder.

And it didn't get easier to protect her, it just got more difficult. And she hadn't told him, until now.

'Why didn't you tell us, when you were home for Christmas?' he asked.

'I don't know. Ashamed, I suppose.'

'Why would you be ashamed?' Nicholas had sounded angrier than he'd meant to.

'I feel like a failure, Dad. No one wants me.'

Nicholas's chest hurt. 'That's not true, my love.'

'I know what you're going to say, Dad, because you've said it before. It's his loss, he's the fool, I'm beautiful and lovely, and some lucky guy out there is waiting to make me happy. I've heard it before. I believed it before. I just don't believe it any more.'

'Because of Simon.'

'Yes. I really loved him, Dad. I really *love* him. Six years. For six years I did nothing but love him.'

'And do you really think it's over?'

'I don't know. Maybe. I don't know. But it's spoilt, isn't it? Even if he changes his mind.' She got a pack of tissues out of her pocket, and blew her nose noisily. 'And I didn't want to ruin everyone else's Christmas with my bad news. I knew Mum was already upset because Suze wasn't at home for long, and Bridge and Karl are so happy, and—'

'I wish you'd told us.'

'I do too. I'm sorry, Daddy.'

'Sssh.' Daddy? How long was it since anyone had called him that? 'That's all done with now. You've told me. I'm glad.'

'Will you tell Mum?'

'Of course I will, if that's what you want.'

Natalie nodded. It was exhausting, talking and thinking about it. And she couldn't second-guess how her mum would take it.

'Does Bridget know?'

She shook her head. 'Just Rose. And Tom.'

'And that's why you were at the pub with him.'

'Yep. My knight in shining armour – he rescued me. He stopped me staying in the flat on my own, drinking a bottle of vodka and drowning in a pool of my own vomit.' She laughed, a small sad laugh.

'Don't even joke about things like that,' Nicholas said. 'Thank God for Tom. I like that boy.'

'I like him too.' Natalie stood up, and shivered. 'It's bloody cold, isn't it?'

Nicholas hadn't realised his feet were numb. 'Bit nippy.'

'Let's go home.'

He held his daughter's hand all the way back.

Karl and Bridget were parking on the other side of the road as they approached the house. Christina leapt out and toddled headlong at her grandfather, squealing with delight. He picked her up and swung her above his head, then pulled her to him in a long hug. 'Happy New Year, Bean!' He didn't want to put her down. They were much easier to keep safe at this age. He held her tightly, until she squirmed for release.

Natalie had to stretch her arms wide to get them round her sister. 'You all right, Moby?'

'You wait!'

'Have a wild night round at *chez vous*, did you?'

'Crazy! Karl gave me a foot rub, and I packed a bag for the hospital.'

Natalie laughed. It sounded nice.

'You?'

'Far, far too much wine at the pub with Tom.' Bridget raised an eyebrow. 'Long story. Tell you later.'

'Okay.'

Karl kissed her cheek. 'Happy New Year, Nat. Where's Simon, then?'

Natalie looked from Bridget, who shot intuitive daggers back at Karl, to her father, who raised his eyebrows, then winked at her, grabbed Christina's hand, and started towards the house. At least, Nicholas recognised, it wouldn't feel so empty with them in it.

Patrick and Lucy

'You were quiet,' Lucy said. They were driving home. Bella and Ed, at the end of a fortnight of over-excited late nights, had dozed off practically as soon as Lucy had started the car.

'Mmm.'

'Are you okay?'

'I probably should have let you ring up and make our excuses. I wasn't in the mood.'

Lucy reached out and put her hand on his lap. 'I know. I'm sorry.'

'It's fine. You had a nice time, at least. And the kids had fun.' He looked over his shoulder at the back seat. 'They're spark out. That yomp finished them off.'

They had walked, after lunch, through the woods behind Alec and Marianne's house. The children had darted in all directions through the undergrowth, chasing the dog and making tiny snowballs from the scant traces of snow that remained after the night's fall.

Ed had tripped, and lain whining on the path. Lucy had crouched beside him, and Alec had hung back with her, so that Marianne and Patrick had got some way ahead of them on the narrow path. They were talking about something, Lucy couldn't hear what.

Ed staged a miraculous recovery from his life-threatening injury and scampered after the others. Alec held out his hand, and pulled Lucy up. He didn't let go straight away. 'It's good to see you.'

She tried to keep it light. 'Yes, it's been lovely, hasn't it?'

His grip on her fingers distracted her. They stared at each other for a moment. Then he dropped her hand and started to walk. But when he spoke again, it was in a low voice, only meant for her: 'Do you ever go to London?'

'What for?'

'To shop or . . . just come in?'

'Why?'

'I'd like to buy you lunch.'

She stared at him.

'Just lunch, Lucy. I'd like to see you, talk to you. That's all. There's nothing wrong with that, is there? Two friends having lunch?'

'Would you tell Marianne?'

He hesitated.

'Then there's something wrong with it, Alec.'

'I'm sorry.'

Patrick turned round. 'Coming?'

Lucy speeded up. 'All right, all right. Didn't realise it was a route march!'

Marianne had laughed.

They were home now, and the children didn't stir when she switched off the ignition.

'Let's see if we can lift them straight into bed, and then we can talk.'

'I'd like that.'

Bella had woken up enough to have a wee and put her pyjamas on, then fallen gratefully into her bed. As for Ed, Lucy made do with taking off his trousers and sweater, and tucking him up in his Power Rangers T-shirt.

Downstairs, Patrick was uncorking a bottle of wine. Lucy, who felt the beginnings of a headache, wasn't sure she wanted a glass, but she took one anyway, and tried to look reassuring, rather than pitying. She was pretending.

'So . . .'

'So.'

She wanted to hurl accusations at him. It hurt that he'd waited three weeks to tell her. It hurt that he'd let her go through Christmas, made himself go through Christmas, not talking about it. She didn't understand why he hadn't come to her straight away, the very day, and told her.

'I'm sorry I waited to tell you.'

'Why did you?'

'I wanted to protect you, I suppose.'

'I'm a grown woman, Patrick. I don't need protecting.' Her tone was harsher than she had meant it to be.

'I suppose I thought I'd sort it out.'

'Sort it out how? You've been made redundant. I had to be told.'

Patrick rubbed his eyes. It made him look tired. 'I know. I need you not to be angry with me, Luce.'

She put her glass down and went to him. 'I'm not angry, Patrick. How could you even think I would be? Of course I'm not angry. I love you.' She was very aware that she had made herself say that because he needed to hear it, not because it was the overwhelming thought in her brain. She put her arms round him, and felt him relax against her.

He was suddenly close to tears. 'I love you too.'

And then he was kissing her. It felt strange, after all these weeks. His hands pushed her sweater down over her shoulders and his fingers were fumbling with her bra. He was hard against her leg. He hadn't touched her like that for so long that Lucy was almost instantly aroused. She pulled him into the living room and down on to the sofa. He threw her bra on to the floor, and sucked hungrily at her nipples. For a moment she put her hands in his hair and held his mouth there, feeling the pull. Then his hand was up her skirt, yanking at her tights, and his fingers were inside her and he knew how much she wanted him. She lifted her hips towards him, willing him to hurry.

And then he couldn't. She felt him nudging himself against her, but he wasn't stiff any more.

His head was buried in the side of her neck, and he kept thrusting, but it was pointless. Lucy ran her hands down his back to his buttocks, holding him still. 'I'm sorry.' His voice was muffled.

'Hey. Don't be. Let me . . .' She rolled him on to his side, shuffled down the sofa and took him, soft and small, into her mouth.

'Don't Lucy. Nothing's going to happen, I don't think.'

Lucy pushed her hair back from her face, and smiled at him. 'Ah, well, too much wine at lunch, maybe.'

'Are you all right?' She wasn't: she felt high and dry. For weeks she'd wanted this, and now he'd got her going, then stopped.

And later, in bed, when he'd rolled away from her and gone to sleep, and she put her hand under the duvet and touched herself, gently, so as not to wake him, it was Alec's face she saw, and Alec's fingers she imagined were stroking her.

And she and Patrick still hadn't talked. And the New Year wasn't new any more.

Tom

Tom pushed open the door with his back, balancing the three coffees one atop the other. It still gave him a thrill to see the logo on the wall outside. They'd had the office for about nine months, taken the lease when they realised they could make their idea work. He'd given up his job six months earlier and been working out of the living room at his flat, but this felt great. A dedicated space. Eight hundred square feet of it. With one of those water-coolers, and a very cool espresso-maker that had cost more than the conference table and chairs, since they had come from Ikea and it had come from Harrods. Rob was better at all that stuff than he was. He'd thought he was quite happy working from home. It was Rob who'd convinced him that they needed to take out a lease on this place, and Rob's girlfriend Serena who'd kitted it out, and although it was a little spare for him, he could see, on the faces of the clients who came through the door, that it looked good.

They made a good team, the two of them. Three, if you counted Serena, who was omnipresent. Good job he loved her too or his nose might have been quite out of joint. A year ago he and Rob had been living a life of relative debauchery in the bachelor heaven that was their two-bedroom flat, running an increasingly successful website design agency from a corner of the living room that wasn't given over to X box, DVDs and CDs, and having a bloody good time doing it.

Now they were becoming increasingly grown-up. Rob had moved out and in with Serena, whom he had met at an industry conference. They had dinner parties and decent towels, and an inordinately · high number of cushions. Actually, while she might have put an end to some of the less salubrious elements of Tom's life with Rob, he had to admit that she'd been an undoubtedly good influence on them business-wise. She was brilliant. Her ideas were original – she could have sold snow to Eskimos – and everybody who met her fell a little in love with her. She was attractive, stylish and funny, but you just knew you wouldn't want to mess with her. Tom was always grateful he didn't fancy her. Although he realised she wouldn't have glanced twice at him since she'd met Rob – she called him Achilles in private, because he was her only real weakness. She'd missed a fascinating session on Internet copyright at that conference, chatting at lunch with him. And that was as weak as Serena got.

Tom quite enjoyed having the flat to himself. He was a bit of a slob, a flamboyant but messy cook and something of an insomniac: the freedom to leave his dirty socks on the living-room floor and cook green Thai curry at three a.m. was to be appreciated. They were making pretty decent money now, too, so it was fine. He was already earning more working for himself than his highest employed salary had been when he'd jumped ship last year, and he reckoned that wasn't bad going. Life was good.

Serena was there this morning. She raised an eyebrow when he handed her a coffee. 'Am I becoming too much of a fixture around here?' she asked.

'Good job you're decorative, love, that's all I'm saying.' Tom winked.

'Sod off. Decorative!' But Serena was laughing.

'Glad you're here, actually. Got a new project I need some advice on . . .'

'Shoot. Rob's at the bank, incidentally. Back in ten.'

'That's all I need. Now, the thing is, this has got nothing to do with websites . . .'

Rob came in five minutes later to hear Serena saying, 'I don't know if you're a genius, or a fool, Tom . . .'

' "The best geniuses are always a little foolish," ' Rob quoted expansively.

'What? Have you swallowed your dad's desk calendar of aphorisms?' Serena slapped his thigh.

He kissed her neck. 'What's he done?'

'He's making a move on his oldest friend.'

'And I've *told* him,' Rob quipped, 'that I'm spoken for.'

'Not you, mate.' Tom smiled. 'You're not my oldest acquaintance. Natalie. And it isn't so much a move as an experiment.'

'Which could blow up in your face, my friend,' Serena added, nodding sagely, and looking from Tom to Rob over the top of her achingly trendy black-rimmed spectacles.

Tom shrugged. 'Or make two people very happy.'

'Is someone going to tell me what the hell you're on about?'

Serena gestured towards Tom. 'Tom is making Natalie spend twenty-six days with him, doing alphabetical "activities", in an effort to prove to her that she should be with him, not Simon – or anyone else for that matter.'

'What's happened to Simon?'

'He dumped her. Just before Christmas and New Year, on pretty much the day she thought he was going to propose marriage or, at the very least, a tropical holiday.'

'The shit!' Serena was emphatic.

'So you think *now* is the time to make your move, do you?' Rob sounded like Claire Rayner.

'Stop calling it a "move". We're not extras in *Saturday Night Fever.*'

'Whatever. Doesn't Nat need some wound-licking time?'

'I'm going to lick them for her.'

'Gross.'

'Metaphorically.'

Serena laughed. 'Well, all right, Tom. We're in. We'll watch you make an idiot of yourself, and we'll pick up the pieces afterwards.'

Rob grinned. 'Should liven up those dull winter months.'

'But,' Serena went to him, and put her face unnaturally close to his, 'do not hurt her, okay? Don't.'

'I won't.' Tom kissed her cheek. 'Promise!'

Then he grinned, reached for the mouse, and clicked on to Encarta – he'd start with A.

Natalie

Christina, Bridget's eighteen-month-old baby, was asleep on the sofa. Arms and legs akimbo, her T-shirt raised to expose her soft, round belly, she snored gently, completely at peace. Natalie watched her for a minute, then picked up the remote control and switched off *The Fimbles*. 'She's gorgeous, Bridge.'

'You time your visits impeccably, sis. Not so gorgeous when there's a party in her cot at three a.m., believe me.'

'Surely Karl's doing most of those, these days?'

'He's not bad, bless him, but he's knackered. And he has to get up and go to work. At least I can hang out here with Christina and nap when she does.' She smirked. 'Once I've put a load of washing on, cleaned up from breakfast – by which I mean walls, floor and table, you understand – and providing I can get comfortable in any position, which is, frankly, less and less likely.'

Natalie clucked sympathetically. 'Shall I go away?'

'No, no – that's not what I meant.' Bridget patted the sofa beside her. 'Come and tell me more about this alphabet game. I can only think of obscenities – it must be the hormones. B for blow-job . . . C for—'

'Yuck! That's a whole other game you're thinking of. And what are you doing fantasizing about "it" in your state?'

'Because at least day dreaming about it doesn't give you leg cramps, or present major engineering problems, like actually doing it does.'

'Too much information. Shouldn't you be thinking pure thoughts?'

Bridget laughed. 'You've got a lot to learn, little sis.'

'Well, thanks, I'm in no hurry. In fact, I'm further away from being ready to sprog now than I have been for years, aren't I?'

'With Simon, maybe. Which, frankly, is a relief to the rest of us. Didn't fancy Christmas dinners and summer holidays with him for the rest of my life.'

'Bridget!'

'Well, I didn't! He was the most infuriating, arrogant, self-absorbed—'

'Okay, okay!' Natalie loved her for it, but enough was enough. 'You don't have to worry about it any more, do you? He's gone.'

'Now, Tom, on the other hand . . .'

'What's wrong with you? I got the same reaction from Susannah when I told her about it the other night on the phone. He's like our brother, for God's sake.'

'But he *isn't* our brother, is he, Nat? How is Suze, by the way?'

'Suze-like. Ten minutes on the souks and the sunshine, five minutes on Casper, thirty seconds on the rest of us.'

'Don't be rotten. She's just excited, that's all. Let's face it, her life is a bit more exciting than ours, these days, isn't it? And Casper waited a long time for this break.'

Bridget was always so reasonable – she was pathological about finding the good in people.

'I hardly think we're about to see him on Jonathan Ross. He's got about ten lines.'

'Which is a start.'

'Okay. Point taken.' Bridget made Natalie want to be nicer. When they were kids, she'd sometimes hated it, but now she had come to see visits to her sister as a bit of a confessional – she poured out her vitriol, spite and meanness, and Bridget sent her away topped up with warm fuzziness. Mostly. That was why her sister's view of Simon was so shocking – it was completely out of character for her to react to someone like that.

'Back to Tom. I trust you're going to do it?' Bridget asked.

'As Tom pointed out, it's not like I have anything better to do for the next few months, is it?'

'There'll be a fair amount of winding, feeding and nappy-changing around here . . .'

'Tempting as that sounds, Bridge, I take his point. We'll have a laugh – we always do. And if he wants to put himself out to cheer me up, then fair enough. But nothing's going to happen and nothing's going to come out of it. You just know, don't you? I mean, you knew with Karl straight away, didn't you?'

'Not straight away. It was after the first bed-bath, I think!'

Bridget had been nursing in a high-dependency ward at the hospital. Karl had come off his Ducati at 105 miles per hour, and arrived with his leg broken in four different places, five broken ribs, a shattered wrist and half of the grit from the M4 embedded in his flesh. By the time he came out of traction he was hooked, and although Bridget initially thought it was the painkillers and the boredom that made him so desperate about her, they were married as soon as he was off drugs and off crutches.

'You knew! I remember seeing you that week – and you were different. You had relaxed. Exhaled. You had found "the one". You know you had.'

'Okay – I'll admit he was different. But that was me – you're you. Not everyone falls in love the same way. You should give yourself a chance, Nat. Simon's really done a number on you. Remember how sure you were of him, and look what happened. Your instincts couldn't have been more wrong, could they? So that's where all this "the one" and "just knowing" nonsense got you. Broken-hearted and alone. Hardly a glowing recommendation.'

Natalie's face was unconvinced.

'And look if it isn't to be, fair enough. But I'm with Tom. Do it, play this game. For whatever reasons. Just have some fun. What possible harm can it do?'

They smiled at each other.

'And promise you'll come and see me when I'm stuck in the bunker up to my elbows in shit and milk and impossibly tiny clothing, and tell me all about it!'

Later, at home, Natalie took a deep breath and looked around. This place definitely needed to be de-Simoned. It wasn't so much that it was full of his stuff. It actually wasn't. Just that lots of things reminded her of him. Those pot plants – she'd dragged him out of bed at five thirty a.m. to go to the flower market and buy them. That checked blanket, on the arm of the sofa – she'd pulled that over him so many times over the years, when he'd fallen asleep in front of the television after a long shift. The candles in the fireplace – they used to light them on

Sunday evenings, drink a heavy red on the floor in front of them, listening to music and then, usually, make love and fall asleep there, to wake up a couple of hours later, cold and stiff. Everything had a picture of him imprinted on it.

She wandered into the kitchen. This wasn't a place that reminded her of him too much. He'd barely ever gone into it. She smiled a little. Lazy bastard. He always said that if you learnt how to make good tea, or eggs Benedict, you'd be stuck with making it for time immemorial. But on the back of the kitchen door there was one of those plastic photo-montage things, with about fifty pictures of the two of them. Faces together, smiling. In black tie. In swimsuits. Against snowy backdrops. Among Christmas decorations. Simon in drag, Natalie as sexy nurse . . . She took it down and put it behind the sofa, not letting herself look at it.

January
A for Abseiling

Natalie heard Tom's car horn at seven p.m. on the dot. He was never late. But Simon always had been. Not for patients, just for her. She was still on Simon time.

At seven ten he hooted again.

'All right, you bugger,' Natalie shouted, to the empty room behind her, as she slammed the flat door.

At least she had something to pack an overnight bag for, even if it was only Tom. Natalie liked packing overnight bags. She hoarded those little bottles you could buy at Superdrug, and sachets that came in magazines, and kept them in an Anya Hindmarch bag Susannah had been given once when she was upgraded on a British Airways flight. Ever ready. It made her feel glamorous − the thought that she could head off at a moment's notice to Babington House or Gleneagles. Now it was in her holdall (fake Mulberry, M & S), nestled alongside a travel hairdryer and two sets of matching underwear. Underwear always matched in an overnight bag.

If he'd booked one room he could think again. She wanted six feet of Frette linen all to herself, thank you very much. Thank goodness he had a bit of money. He might want to dress up the cheering-her-up process as this stupid alphabet game, but she knew they were both in it for a laugh. She was looking forward to a bit of pampering. Maybe there'd even be a spa . . .

Tom had opened the boot and was leaning against the passenger door. 'Come on.'

'Da-dah!' Natalie spread her arms and gave a little twirl. 'I'm ready for A. Or should I say, I'm Available for A, I'm Able to A, I'm Amenable—'

'You're L for late.'

She ignored him. 'Come on, then. Where are we going? Don't keep me in suspense!'

'We're going abseiling.'

'You have got to be kidding me.'

'Nope. Kit's in the car.'

'Kit?'

'Sleeping-bag, boots – you're a size five, if the shoes I read last week were telling the truth, Rescue Remedy, ingredients for packed lunch—'

'But you're kidding really, right?'

'I am totally serious. We're booked into a bunkhouse on Dartmoor tonight, and it's going to take hours to get there, so could you close your big guppy mouth and get into the car? We had a deal.'

'I don't remember any deal where I agreed to something life-threatening.'

Tom smiled. 'You'll be as safe as houses. Trust me.'

'Yes, well, that doesn't sound very likely, does it? Trusting you has ended me up here.'

Tom started the car, and pulled out into the traffic.

Natalie watched him. His brow was furrowed in concentration, one eyebrow – the one with the tiny scar from when he had fallen off a diving-board when he was fourteen – a little higher than the other. 'Abseiling? Really?' she said.

'Really.'

'In January? Really?'

'Really.'

An hour later, on the M5, she still didn't believe him. Maybe Exeter, somewhere like that. Topsham. There must be lots of hotels around there, the ones with linen sheets, posh shampoo and spas. He couldn't be serious.

And if he was, it would prove what she had said all along, ever since that stupid conversation in the pub on New Year's Eve. He so wasn't the right man for her.

She woke herself up with her own snore, head snapping forward, and realised the car had stopped. And that it was almost pitch dark. Driving rain smudged the view of what was clearly the only building for miles around, illuminated by pale lights through tiny windows.

'We're here.' Tom stretched beside her, his forearms flat against the top of the car. 'Thanks for the marvellous company.'

'I was tired.'

'Just as well, actually. I dare say you're going to get all princess-and-the-pea-ish about the bunkhouse.'

'Very probably.'

The smell of wet neoprene hit them as they opened the door. A drying room was immediately to their left, full of dripping wetsuits swinging like carcasses in an abattoir. To their right, the living room was occupied by a couple of mouldy-looking sofas, some Formica tables and chairs, and a family in perfectly co-ordinating fleeces, engrossed in a game of Scrabble. Everywhere signs advised them to 'switch lights out', 'behave with consideration' and 'deal responsibly with litter'.

Tom was watching Natalie.

'Brownie-camp flashback. What the hell have you done, Tom?'

'You'll be fine. Let's go and find our room.'

'Our room?' She trudged after him, up the stairs.

She was about to call him presumptuous, but then she saw the bunks. You'd need to be a contortionist, let alone presumptuous. The mattress was about two feet wide, with no sides, and, it appeared, no ladder to the top. Blimey.

Natalie stood in the corner while Tom busied himself un-rolling their sleeping-bags and laying them out. 'D'you want to go on top?' His eyebrows waggled suggestively at her. She was too horrified even to take the bait, and shrugged.

'So, do you fancy the pub, or a microwave meal with Mr and Mrs the Family Who Plays Together Stays Together down there?'

'Pub.'

'Are you planning to speak in whole sentences at all this weekend, or are these monosyllabic utterances the best I can hope for?'

'If you want a whole sentence you'd better feed me, then drive me home.'

He was pushing her down the stairs.

The pub helped a little. An open fire and a big bowl of chilli. Several whisky macs.

'So,' she asked, 'have you ever done this abseiling thing, then?'

'Nah. Bungee-jumped once when I was in Australia. Do you remember?'

Tom's year off. Her finals. He'd rung her at three a.m. once, off his face in some bar in Queensland, to wish her good luck in an exam. She nodded.

'I figure this can't be harder than that.'

'But you're about fifteen years older now,' she said.

'True. But I hardly consider myself to be over the hill. What about you?'

'You know I haven't!'

'But haven't you always wondered what it would be like?'

She stared at him as if he were mad. 'I can honestly say I've never thought about it at all before about seven o'clock this evening. And now that I am thinking about it, I'm bloody terrified.'

'That's the point, Nat. You've got to feel the fear and do it anyway.'

'Shut up. You sound like some stupid self-help book.'

'And you sound like a big girl's blouse.'

'Are you trying to goad me into doing it?'

'I promise I'm not. You don't wanna do it, you don't do it. You won't hear about it from me.' His face was suddenly serious.

And Natalie felt a little bit safer. That was okay, then. She didn't have to do it.

She awoke, feeling like a sixty-year-old, after an incredibly uncomfortable night. Every time Tom had moved above her, the slats of the rickety bunk had creaked alarmingly. She hated sleeping-bags – you couldn't spread yourself out in them. But she didn't moan. She ate the condemned man's breakfast in silence, while Tom chatted away animatedly to the fleece family. He was good at that: he could talk to anyone. She tried to imagine Simon in the bunkhouse. He wouldn't have stayed, of course, but if he had . . . He would have been terribly rude and funny about the other people there. About their clothes, their fresh-faced enthusiasm and their accents. Funny, but cruel.

They saw the viaduct about a quarter of a mile away, and it got taller and taller as they drove towards it in the instructor's grubby Land Rover. Clive, one of the young guys escorting them who, rather like policemen, these days, looked unfeasibly youthful, told them it was about a hundred feet high, but he was clearly lying – it was at least a thousand. The guys, completely blasé about the task ahead, started tying their knots and arranging their ropes. It still didn't feel real to Natalie. She wasn't that sort of girl – she didn't do things like this.

'Isn't there supposed to be a wall or something for your feet?' she asked Clive. 'Nah!' He smirked. 'This way's much more fun. Trust me. Just you and the rope and the air. Best feeling in the world.' She doubted that. A wall would have been better. 'This is typical of you,' she spat at Tom, who was climbing into his harness.

'How?'

'Remember that diving-board?'

Natalie had been eleven. It was one of those endless hot summers that didn't seem to happen any more, the kind where all the grass goes beige and parents sit around drinking in the evenings and forget to put you to bed. Susannah, Bridget and Natalie had gone swimming. Mum hadn't – she wanted to be in the garden, she said, not in some noisy, sweaty, cacophonous indoor pool that stank of chlorine and hormones. They'd been allowed to take their bikes, and Suze had packed a rucksack with some drinks and crisps in it. Bridget kept calling it an adventure, and Suze kept telling her to shut up. Her idea of an adventure was a little less tame.

On the way down the road they'd seen Tom and Genevieve, sitting listlessly on the long low wall at the front of their house – Patrick had been at Scout camp in Dorset – and they'd shouted at them to catch them up.

And Tom had made her go off the five-metre diving-board. He'd dared and goaded and practically bullied her into it.

'Bloody hell, Nat. You certainly know how to bear a grudge.'

'I remember it as if it were yesterday.'

'But it wasn't. It was 1977, or something ridiculous. I hadn't remembered it at all until just now. In fact, even now you've said it, I barely remember it.'

'That's because you weren't the one who did a belly-flop – which was agony, incidentally – *and* who lost their bikini top.'

Tom laughed. 'Did you? Really?' He scratched his head. 'You can't have had much worth looking at – I'd have remembered if you had!'

'I had . . . something worth looking at. But that's not the point. It isn't funny!'

'Look. This is different. You're fully dressed, aren't you? You'd have to go some to expose yourself doing this.' He pulled on the harness, which was tight round both thighs and his middle.

'It isn't different. It's about you making me do things I don't want to do – that I'm not capable of.'

'Now, there's a difference, Nat. Don't want to – that's fine. I didn't make you go off the diving-board, and I'm not going to make you go over this viaduct. But don't tell me you aren't capable of it. That's not true.'

'How do you know?'

'Because I know you. And I know you're capable of a lot of things that you don't think you are.'

Clive indicated that he was ready and Tom practically vaulted over the railing, then leant back confidently until he was almost sitting in his harness. He made it look irritatingly easy. He smiled cheekily at her. 'Piece of cake.'

Natalie stuck her tongue out at him. She didn't want to smile. She was so afraid that she rather thought she might cry.

'So, Nat, do it and I'll meet you at the bottom and you'll feel bloody fantastic, I guarantee it. Or don't do it and I'll meet you back up here, and I'll never, ever mention it again. Up to you. I'm off.' With that he released his tight grip on the rope, which fed itself at alarming speed through his hands, and shot him down.

Natalie rushed to the edge, and watched the top of his

helmet. Bloody hell. She didn't breathe again until she saw the guy at the bottom catch him. Tom circled, arms exultantly above his head, whooping.

Clive looked questioningly at Natalie.

'I'll show him . . .'

Twenty minutes later, Natalie was hanging by her arse, a hundred feet up in the air, swearing at Tom like a navvy. He was a dot on the grass below, but he could hear her. He knew her eyes would be closed. She never looked when she was frightened.

'Open your eyes!' he shouted up at her. 'It's beautiful.'

She opened them. It certainly wasn't. She snapped them shut again. She didn't seem to be any nearer the ground. She realised she was muttering to herself. 'Shit, shit, shit. Help. Please. Shit, shit shit.' A mantra of terror. She could feel the rope burning her hand. It was never going to end.

Natalie opened her eyes once more, hoping desperately she would see Tom's face, up close. She was nearer, but not much.

It was quite a good view, though. She made herself keep them wide, not looking at the rope, or at the ground, but straight ahead at the tops of the trees.

Tom was still talking: 'Well done, Natalie. Well done. Nearly here.'

By focusing on the horizon, and on Tom's voice, she managed the next ten, twenty, thirty feet, and then he had her, first by her boot, then her leg, and finally the instructor was unhooking her harness from the rope and Tom was hugging her. 'You did it!'

'I did, didn't I?' Nat looked up to where she had come from. Already it seemed unreal.

'I did, didn't I?' she repeated, a beam breaking across her face. 'How cool am I?' She was as high as a kite. What a feeling!

Tom's eyes sparkled. 'Told you you could.'

Nicholas

'Would you like another cup, love?'

Nicholas gazed blankly at the waitress.

'Another cup of tea?'

He glanced at his watch. Eleven forty-five. He'd been in here for an hour already. 'Yes, please. That would be lovely.'

She smiled at him, and took away the cup.

He wondered briefly what they thought of him. He came in often, these days, with a copy of *The Times*, which he would read from cover to cover, eking out two cups of tea over a couple of hours.

He knew he looked all right – there was no danger they would think he was a vagrant, seeking sanctuary from the foul weather. He always paid with a note, not a warm fistful of change. And he tipped better than most. But he knew they found him a curiosity. He saw them sometimes, glancing at him, commenting to each other.

Well, he liked it here. That was why he came back most days. He liked the music they played, compilations of soft, folksy songs. The tea was okay, and the tables were big enough to spread out the paper. The café was in the front of the shop, not the rear, which meant he could see out on to the high street and watch the comings and goings. And it was always crowded, mostly with women in pairs – friends or mothers and daughters. They chattered away, and he enjoyed the rhythm of it. Sometimes he listened, but more often than not he let it wash over him pleasantly. Anna was so quiet, these days, and now that the girls were staying away more and more, he missed that female sound at home. Some men joked about it – being a lone male in a house of women. Needing to seek refuge in the pub or a shed, being battered by hormones and biorhythms. He'd never felt that way. He'd liked it. They'd been his girls, the four of them.

The women in the café talked about their bodies, and their men, and they talked about holidays, and work, and they talked about cancer. They seemed, if not to ignore him completely, then not to mind that he was there. It's true, Nicholas thought, you do become invisible when you're old. It was a funny thing all round. It wasn't you who decided you were old. Okay, your body poked the finger at you once in a while – you felt the aches and strains of time rampaging, but they were nothing serious and, anyway, you fought them because you had the feeling that if you didn't it was the beginning of the end, and you weren't ready, not yet, for that. The rest of the world decided you were old. They retired you. Consigned you. Nicholas remembered the first time he'd offered his seat on the bus to a young woman and been rejected – on the ground that he needed it more. She'd been polite, and not unkind, but her smiling refusal, her you-old-boys-won-the-war-for-us-the-least-you-can-do-is-sit-down-on-the-bus-in-your-dotage face, had horrified him. He wasn't seventy yet. It was a bloody insult.

Although he knew, too, that last year had taken a greater toll on him than most. And the confusion he felt about what had happened – that was the nearest thing to old about him. He didn't understand it. He had thought he was going to lose Anna, and then he had found out he wasn't, and then he'd lost her anyway. Not her body, but his Anna. She felt lost to him and he didn't know how to reach her. And he didn't know why.

And it wasn't fair. This wasn't how it was supposed to be. He'd been a good man, he knew he had. A good husband, a good father. He'd been faithful – utterly faithful – since they had first met. He'd provided. He'd worked hard at the bank and at home. And then he'd stopped. And it wasn't supposed to be like this. They owned their home outright, he had a pretty good pension, they were fit, their children were launched successfully into the world and didn't need them any more – this was *their* time.

And they'd never been further apart.

B for Ballet

'Okay. Ready for your instructions?'
        'I can hardly wait! Bring it on.' She could hear the dimple in Tom's voice. In a minute he'd be laughing on the other side of his smug face. All she'd told him was to keep Friday night free. Now it was Friday afternoon, and he hadn't a clue what he was in for. 'Be outside the Hippodrome in Bristol at seven. I'm taking you to the ballet. Tchaikovsky, *Romeo and Juliet. There!*'

Tom kept his voice steady. 'The ballet. Very good. Nice to see you entering into the spirit. I might have gone for Barcelona, myself.'

'On my salary, mate? You jest. Besides, it isn't up to you. B is mine. And I've chosen ballet.'

'Absolutely. I'll see you there.'

'That's it?'

'That's it. 'Bye.'

Tom pushed the button with the receiver still in his hand. Speed dial button three, the one Rob used five times a day.

'Serena!'

'Hiya, Tom.'

'I need your help . . . What do you know about ballet?'

Three rows of people turned and stared at Natalie in irritation as the text-received noise pealed through the theatre. She fumbled in her bag, which was suddenly bottomless, then picked it up and tipped its contents into Tom's lap. The phone came out last, and she grabbed it, leaving him to put back the wallet, hairbrush, Filofax, makeup bag, mints and, yes, thank you, Lord, the obligatory Tampax that had landed on him without warning.

She pressed the READ button: 'Need you at the hospital. Karl.' Only he hadn't bothered with any capitals or punctuation. 'I need to go,' she hissed at Tom, who nodded and stood up.

The tutting and obstructive knees in their row took some negotiating, and Natalie felt irrationally angry with those who were tutting in disapproval and begrudgingly lifting their coats into their laps. Did they honestly think she was doing this on a whim? If a text message could have a tone, she was frightened by this one.

Out in the lobby, Tom asked, 'What is it?'

'Bridge. She must be at the hospital. Karl says he needs me.'

'Come on, then.' Tom took her hand and pulled her out of the door. He had found them a taxi before she had thought of raising her arm for one and piled her in. 'Hospital, mate, please. Quick as you can.' The driver nodded, and glanced at them in the rear-view mirror.

Natalie was gripped by fear, now that she was sitting still. She sank into Tom's shoulder. 'What if something's wrong?'

'Don't jump to any conclusions, Nat. We'll be there in a minute. Just wait.'

'Please don't let anything be wrong with my sister. Please,' Natalie murmured inwardly. 'Please don't let anything happen to her baby.'

It was Tom who directed the cab driver to Obstetrics and Gynaecology, paid him and held her hand as they walked to the desk.

Before she had had a chance to ask for Bridget, they saw Karl. He came towards them, white and wild-eyed. Natalie opened her arms to him. He came into them and rested his head on her shoulder. 'What's happened, Karl?'

'She was doing so well, Nat. It started this afternoon, and she didn't want me to tell anyone – she wanted it to be a surprise. My mum came to look after Christina, and we drove in, and she was doing so well. I thought we'd be free and clear by now.' He looked around suddenly, scanning the wall for a clock as though he had no idea of when 'now' was.

'And then?' Tom prompted him.

'Then the baby got . . . I don't know – stuck or something. She couldn't push it out. They tried all kinds of things to turn it round – you know, so that they could pull it out. Poor old Bridge. She's really been through it. That was when she asked me to try and get you. She wanted you there. But they couldn't do it. And then the baby got distressed – they had this monitor thing on her and the baby's in all sorts of trouble . . . And they've taken her down for an emergency Caesarean. Honestly, Nat, I've never seen people move so fast.'

Tom patted Karl's back. 'All right, mate. They're moving fast because they know what's got to be done.'

'Why aren't you with her, Karl?' Natalie asked.

'She said I was to stay outside. She said I'd hate it. There's this screen, apparently, but even so . . . That's your wife they're slicing up, isn't it? She said I should wait out here for you.'

Typical Bridget. She was right, of course. Natalie loved Karl, and no doubt he loved Bridget, but he would have been useless. He was shaking now, out here in the corridor. 'How long ago did they take her down?' she asked.

'About ten minutes.'

'Let's go and wait.'

Natalie took his hand, and they walked slowly through to the bank of seats outside the operating theatre. Tom followed them.

'She'll be okay, won't she?' Karl asked her.

Natalie didn't know how to answer. She was pretty sure Bridget would be okay: she was healthy and she was in the right place. But the baby? She didn't know about the baby.

Tom answered: 'Course she will, mate.'

Natalie just squeezed Karl's hand.

Hospital time passes slowly. It felt like hours, but it was probably only a few minutes, before a nurse in scrubs pushed through the double doors. 'Mr Murray?' She had an almost impenetrable Irish accent.

Karl sprang to his feet. 'Yes.'

She smiled. 'Your wife is fine, Mr Murray. She did brilliantly. You have a little boy. He's doing great, too. They've whizzed him up to Special Care, just to make sure – he's had a bit of a go of it, but he's going to be grand, just grand.'

Natalie felt all the breath and tension go out of Karl. He slumped beside her. 'Thank God.' Then he started to cry, his face in his hands. Noisy sobs emanated from him for a few seconds. She put her hand on his shoulder.

Behind her, Tom ruffled her hair. She turned and smiled at him, her own tears dangerously close. 'It's okay,' Tom mouthed at her, and she nodded fervently.

The nurse let them have their moment, then added, 'They're just finishing up, you know. Then they'll take her back to the ward – she'll have a room, bless her. She's had a rough old time of it. Do you want to wait for her there?'

'Yes, please,' Karl answered. The panic had drained from his face, but he was still knocked sideways: he kept running his hand through his hair, and nervously scratching his nose.

'Why don't you and me go to the canteen, Nat, get some coffee and stuff? Let Karl see Bridget for a minute.'

'Thanks, Tom.' And then, 'Thanks for coming, you two.'

'You're welcome. Do you want me to phone Mum and Dad for you?'

'I'd better ask Bridget. She didn't want me to call your mum before.'

'Okay. See you in a bit.'

In the canteen they sat nursing undrinkable coffee in styrofoam cups.

'Are you okay?' Tom asked.

'I'm fine. Bloody hell.' Natalie rubbed her eyes. 'It's all a bit bloody real, though, isn't it?'

Tom nodded.

'Thank you,' she said.

'For what?'

'For being here.'

Tom shrugged.

'You're pretty good in a crisis, you know.'

'I'm pretty good in general.'

'All right, Mr No Self-Esteem Issues Here. I was paying you a compliment. Accept it graciously.'

Tom doffed an imaginary cap. 'Yes, m'lady. Thanks, m'lady.'

Natalie stuck out her tongue at him. 'And I'm sorry about the ballet. Although I'm sure you're not too gutted.'

'Well, I'm particularly fond of the second act. There are some particularly moving sections of music, and one exquisite solo performance.'

Natalie guffawed. 'Get out of it.'

'But, basically, I already knew the ending. They pretty much all die, you know.'

'Really?' She raised her eyebrows.

'Yep. It's a real death-fest. Mercutio, Tybalt, Juliet, Romeo . . . In fact, as the *grand fromage* says, at the end of the play,

"All are punished." ' He said it punish–shed, as in garden, and Natalie laughed. 'I'm not the cultural desert you make me out to be, you know, Nat.'

'Clearly! You haven't seen it before, though, have you? Admit it. You've never been near a ballet in your life, have you?'

'That is between me and myself, honeybunch. Ask me no questions, I'll tell you no lies.'

'Well, technically, since we didn't see it all the way through, I should get some more tickets . . .'

'I wouldn't hear of it. On your salary? You're practically destitute as it is! I'll live with the disappointment. And who knows? There may be other opportunities as the game progresses . . .'

'Right!' Natalie conceded defeat: she wasn't going to get him to admit that he hated ballet.

And, besides, half an hour later, B sort of stopped being Ballet and became Babies, as the three of them, Karl, Tom and Natalie, stood around Bridget's bed admiring her son, who looked smooth, pink and remarkably untroubled by his difficult arrival into their world.

Patrick

He must have given a hundred exit interviews, as they were called. A chance for the soon-to-be ex-employee to say what he thought – gloves off – about the company he or she was leaving.

He supposed he didn't have to go. But he knew he would.

So he was sitting there, in his suit and tie, waiting for them to see him. Waiting for her.

He fiddled with his wedding ring, pulling it up to the very tip of his finger, flipping it, without losing contact, then pushing it down again. Lucy had never let him take it off; neither had she ever removed her own narrow gold band. She was superstitious about it. She'd never taken Will's ring off either – until he left her, and then her fingers were still so swollen from carrying Bella that she'd had to go to a jeweller in town and have it sawn off.

He wanted Lucy with him now.

But she wasn't: she was at home, worrying about him, and he was here, alone.

He tried to marshal his thoughts, but half-sentences kept forming in his brain. Truthfully, he didn't have much to say. He liked the company he was leaving. He didn't want to leave. He'd lost.

New boss. New boss hired new personnel person. New personnel person – sorry, human-resources person – was now, effectively, going to get his job. Although, of course, the corporate lawyers would have been all over it, making sure that wasn't how it looked or sounded. There would be a different title, subtle changes in the job specification. But everyone knew that was what was happening.

Patrick wasn't even sure it wasn't fair. She was good, Miranda Clarke, very good. People talked a lot of crap about redundancy, didn't they? They thought they were being comforting and philosophical and, let's face it, in that situation it's a hell of a lot easier to say the wrong thing than get it right, but what it all boiled down to in the end was that the people in charge don't get rid of the best people. They get rid of the expendable ones. The quite-good but not-as-good ones.

He'd taken a cardboard box down to his car on the way to her office. She was two floors higher, but he'd taken one down in the lift to the car park first. It had given him time. The box was a bit tragic. A photograph of Lucy and the kids. A miniature Zen garden with a tiny rake that Bella had given him for Christmas last year. She'd be glad to have it back – she was the only one who had ever tended it. Black tie from the back of his door, kept there in case. As though anyone you were giving bad news to would notice. A half-bottle of Famous Grouse and two shot glasses.

Miranda Clarke came out to get him. He was glad she hadn't sent someone else to usher him in. She fidgeted uncomfortably. He'd never seen her discomfited before.

She must be about ten years younger than him. When did that happen? When had he suddenly become so old that much younger people could be better at his job than he was? She was a pretty girl. Too neat and proper to be sexy, but still good-looking. She had big, wide-set eyes, and she always wore her long blonde hair in a pony-tail, tied at the nape of her neck.

This was the woman who had emasculated him. It wasn't melodramatic, to him, calling it that. He'd never say it a loud, of course, but that was how it felt. Like she'd taken away his manhood, much more than his job. He couldn't even make love to his wife – hadn't since it had happened. As that thought flew in and out of his brain, he hated her, just for that moment. He thought about bending Miranda Clarke over the desk, and fucking her roughly. He thought about the power. Just the idea made him feel like a rapist. He wondered if his cheeks had reddened.

She'd come with a reputation, and people like that almost always disappoint, but he had liked her, when they'd first met, and, even though he had known she and he were at war, a war that she had won, he still liked her now. He would not like to have been doing this.

He supposed that another man might make it difficult for her, but he wouldn't. What was the point? Even in his own head he sounded defeated. He sat down in the black leather chair.

'This is horrible, Patrick. I'm sorry. Would you rather not do it?'

'I'm fine.' Ed always said that, when you asked him how he was. Fine. A child's answer. Inaccurate and uncomprehending.

Miranda's hands were shaking slightly. She was fiddling with things on her desk. He'd thought she would be more professional than this. More guarded. But her youth was suddenly showing. For one last time, he took charge. 'I've been over the papers, had a lawyer take a look at them, of course. It all makes sense. And it's pretty fair.'

'Good. I would have hated it to be any other way.'

'I'll finish at the end of the week, as agreed.'

'Fine. Is there anything you'd like to share with me?'

He smiled directly at her. 'I don't think so.'

'Of course.' This was awkward. Strangely, he felt a little sorry for her.

'Have you made any plans?'

'No. I think I need a little time.'

'Of course.' She stared at her hands, clasped on the desk in front of her. She had one of those manicures – the kind where the tips of the nails are square and impossibly white. 'Patrick. I'm . . . I just wanted to say that I'm sorry about all of this . . . I . . .'

Patrick put up his hand to stop her, and smiled. All these smiles, suddenly. How very civilised. 'Never apologise, never explain. Isn't that what they say? I think it's particularly apposite in this case, don't you? You've nothing to be sorry for, and I certainly don't need it explained to me. I'm pretty clear on what happened.' That was the best he could give her. Should he have told her he knew she was better than him? Maybe. But he couldn't. He pushed the chair back and stood up. 'I think we're done here.'

They shook hands formally. Miranda opened and closed her mouth a couple of times, searching, he knew, for the right thing to say. Failing.

'They're having a party for me, apparently. In the pub across the road. Thursday night. You'd be welcome.'

She looked doubtful. 'Thank you.'

She wouldn't want to be there any more than he did.

C for Canoeing

R ob and Serena had argued about C.
'Surely it's time for you to go cerebral, Tom. I mean, ballet was a pretty highbrow choice, wasn't it? She's sending you signals.'

'No, she isn't. She was trying to send him mad, making him sit through that. I reckon she was trying to put you off the whole idea, mate.'

'But she did not succeed.' Rob was making a paper aeroplane. He launched it and Serena caught it nonchalantly in her left hand, crumpling it up. 'How old are you?' she admonished him gently.

'I only got away with it because Serena gave me some top tips on ballet.'

'Hardly!'

'You did. Not that I got to use most of my jargon, with Karl interrupting.'

'But he got you out of another two hours of men in tights,' Rob laughed.

'It wasn't as bad as I thought it would be. Not sure I'd want to go every Friday night, but it was all right – if it kept a girl happy, who was going to keep me happy!'

The men laughed, and Serena suppressed a smile.

'But don't you think it's time to pick something you know she'll love? You pick another thing she loathes, like the abseiling, and she'll definitely think you're not the guy for her.'

'No way, Serena. It's far too early for that. Besides, she only *thought* she'd hate abseiling. It was a bloody triumph, I tell you. And not just for me, for her too. Trust me, I'm right about this . . . I've got to get her out of her comfort zone first. There's no point in a bunch of girl dates – that won't take her mind off Simon, and have her thinking about me in the right way, will it?' Serena looked doubtful. 'Besides, I'm having too much fun with the other stuff.' He grinned. 'Is there a martial art that starts with C?'

'Don't think so.' Rob started typing at his computer. He was quiet for a few seconds, then he said, 'What about copulation? Or cunn—'

'Thanks, Rob,' Serena interrupted sternly.

'Girls *like* that, though. You certainly—'

'Yep. Thanks.' She was blushing. 'If you two are going to degenerate, I think I might find I have something pressing to do back in my own office—'

'Don't go, Serena. Shut up, Rob. I'll call on you if and when I ever, God forbid, reach the stage of needing advice on sex. Meanwhile, Serena is far more help to me than you are, even if she isn't seeing things quite my way just at the moment . . .'

'Is it just that you're desperate to see me in a wetsuit, or are you really just a sadist?'

'Bit of both. Although if I was really a sadist, we'd be doing this outside.'

'You'd be doing it alone!'

'Well, we're not doing it outside, are we, and I'm not alone, am I?'

'So why, exactly?'

'Because Rob says learning the Eskimo Roll in one of these things is one of life's little triumphs. Remember how great you felt at the bottom of that viaduct? And you do look pretty bloody good in a wetsuit, actually.'

It had been a while since he'd seen the contours of Natalie's body quite so closely. She had this really little waist that made him want to span it with his hands. Her chest was big for her frame, and her hips weren't as boyish as he remembered. She hadn't done the zip all the way up on the suit, and he could see a shadow of cleavage, which he found quite exciting.

'It's got a bloody tutu!' Natalie flapped the neoprene frill round her hips.

'A splash skirt.'

'I feel like one of those hippos in *Fantasia*.'

Why did women always see themselves like that? She was slight, for God's sake. But the girl just behind her . . .

He'd told the course organisers that they'd done this before – apparently if you hadn't had at least one session you couldn't progress to the Eskimo Roll. He'd also told them that the two of them were planning to go whitewater kayaking in the Rockies that summer, on honeymoon, but he hadn't shared that with Natalie.

She was talking to the hippo now. Typical Natalie – she'd make a friend wherever she was. She was one of those girls people wanted to be with – they wanted to tell her things. He remembered her at school, always in the thick of it in the playground. Not the leader, necessarily – they were often the ones who got into fights, and Natalie had never been bossy enough to be kingpin. Just popular. The kind who was always next to the birthday girl at the party.

Good at girlfriends. Lousy at boys.

Mark Johnstone popped, unwelcome, into his head. The first in a long line of lousy boyfriends. He and Natalie had 'gone around' the year of O-level options. This, from what Tom could gather, meant walking everywhere as though you were spot-welded together, hands clasped so that the simplest activity was almost impossible, and snogging anywhere and everywhere, with little regard for who might be eating a sandwich in the vicinity. She was so not fun that summer. She'd gone all grown-up. Funnily enough, it was one of the only times in his childhood that he could remember crying, other than with pain when he'd broken something, which he had with monotonous regularity. Leg, collarbone, wrist, other leg . . . Everything was changing and he hadn't liked it. It was frightening. Now he supposed it had been about not wanting to grow up, but at the time he had thought it was about Natalie, and why she wouldn't go bike-riding and den-building in the woods any more. His mum had caught him crying on his bed, when he'd thought no one else was around. Angry boy tears, snotty and aggressive. But he'd let her hold him. She told him that girls grew up faster than boys, and that girls changed in different ways from boys. She told him that the Natalie he loved would be back. Or, rather, that he would catch up with her, eventually.

He'd hated Mark Johnstone. Not because he was jealous – he knew now he hadn't been capable of those kinds of feelings then – but because he had sucked all the fun out of Natalie while he was sucking her face off in the common room, and Tom had lost his best friend.

They'd stopped going around eventually, of course. Mark Johnstone told everyone that Natalie was a lousy kisser and wore huge knickers, but Susannah had told Tom that really they had broken up because he had tried to make Natalie put her hand down his trousers at the cinema and she hadn't wanted to.

'What are you laughing at? Is it me? In this wetsuit?'

Tom wiped his eyes. 'No, of course not. I was just thinking about something, that's all.'

'Well, I'm thinking about D, and it's not looking good for you, mate.'

In the end getting into the kayak was the tricky bit, even in the shallow end. By comparison the Eskimo Roll was a piece of cake.

And the best bit was that she was much better at it than Tom was. She was cautious, and more aware of her balance. Tom kept trying to go faster than anyone else and reaching out too far with his arms and the paddle, which tipped him over. He would roll under and come up splashing and spluttering, looking like a seal in shock.

Natalie was weak from laughing at him. 'I can't believe we only got to C before I whipped your arse at something! How fantastic! I can hardly wait to tell Rose . . . and Serena . . . and Rob . . . and Lucy.'

'Tell anyone, and I'll definitely take you pot-holing.'

'P's my letter!'

'Worked it out, have you?' That pleased him. Enough to soften the blow of being humiliated in the pool. Even the fat girl could stay afloat.

Anna

Anna picked up the willowy lilac Lladro figure and ran the cloth under it. She sighed. She had been dusting some of these objects for nearly forty years. Now there were lots more things, of course. Furniture and books, photographs and ornaments. She remembered when it had taken about half an hour to do her housework. Their first home had been practically empty, but it had always been immaculate. A carpet-beater, beeswax and a cloth, washing-up liquid. That was all it had taken. Anna could remember being a newly wed, marvelling at the sight of double sheets on the washingline, pegging pillowcases side by side, and gazing sentimentally at them. It had all been about routine then. She had washed on Monday, ironed on Tuesday, baked on Wednesday, shopped on Thursday, cleaned on Friday. And she had loved it. The home she had come from, her mum's, had been chaotic – noisy and messy and filthy – and she could still recall the joy she had felt when she'd first walked into her own home, the bungalow she and Nicholas had bought, and realised that she would dictate what happened there.

They had been ridiculously happy. It was the early sixties, but they lived a pretty old-fashioned life. What she remembered most about it was how simple life had been. Nicholas had been paid in cash – she hadn't had a penny of her own. She had three old tea caddies on the windowsill in the kitchen for the house-keeping, the bills and her dream fund, which doubled as the emergency fund. She would put money in there, when there was spare, and daydream about a new three-piece suite or a holiday in Scotland. And that was it. Every morning now the postman poured a mountain of paper through their letterbox – insur-ance, pension, investments. Nicholas paid the bills and filed them in lever-arch files. She didn't need to look at them so long as he was around to do it. She had seen a greetings card in a shop recently: it had said that if you prayed for rain you should be prepared to deal with some mud. That had made her smile. They'd got the prosperity they'd dreamt about, and the security, so the complications were the mud. She had bought the card and put it on the windowsill in the kitchen, where she used to keep the three tea caddies – five houses and forty years ago. He'd been a good husband. A really good husband. And she loved him so. Still.

They'd had a lot of fun when they were poor. The girls refused to believe it now, when she told them there had been weeks when Nicholas hadn't had enough money to go to the pub – because you had to have enough for two pints, so you could buy one for someone else. The girls were of the cashpoint, credit-card world – how could they understand? If you didn't have it, you couldn't spend it. Alien concept. They'd had a car, which was more than most people, and sometimes enough to drive to the coast at the weekend. Spread a blanket on the sand and eat sandwiches.

When she talked about it Susannah called her Ma Larkin. And she was right, in a way: life was better then.

If she had to name one perfect year, it would be 1972. She'd been in her early thirties. The girls had all been born. Nicholas was doing well in his job – he'd passed most of the bank exams he'd spent years revising for late at night in the front room. He was going places in the bank, he told her, and his joy at that infected them all. She had her beautiful, beautiful girls. Three children under five, and no tumble-dryer. What would Bridget make of that? Bridget, whose buggy was practically a car, who did all her food shopping with a credit card on the Internet, and had it delivered by men who carried it right into the kitchen, and probably, soon, would be unpacking and cooking it too. A few years ago Nicholas had taken her to the Caribbean. She had never thought she would be so lucky. They had stayed on Antigua in a beachfront room. She had never been anywhere so staggeringly beautiful, and sat for hours each morning, not reading the book in her lap, just gazing out at the amazing colours of the sea and the water and the sky.

On the last day they'd taken a car tour of the island. Their driver was called Christmas, and on the way back they went to his home to meet his children. It wasn't so much a house as a shack, and Anna had watched in astonishment as nine immaculate children in white dresses, white ribbons in their cornrows, poured out of it. It was almost funny, all those kids coming out of that tiny place, like a visual gag on television. Christmas's wife came out last and stood proudly among her brood.

We're the same, you and I, Anna had thought. She had an old school photograph of the girls in her handbag, and she had shown Christmas's wife, and the two women had nodded and smiled at each other for a while.

She had made Nicholas give Christmas the last of their spending money as a tip.

An eight-by-four-inch copy of that school picture was on the bookshelf now. She dusted it carefully, and studied her daughters' faces. Susannah, Bridget and Natalie. She still had that welling up of pride and love. But there was something else, and although she reached for it in her mind, trying to understand it, she couldn't find it.

D for Do-it-yourself

Of course, Tom buzzed at ten a.m. on the dot. Ten a.m. on Saturday morning. In the old days – were they old already? – if Simon hadn't been working, she might have jumped up, thrown on some clothes and run down the road to buy the papers, two huge cappuccinos and Danish pastries from the deli on the corner. By ten o'clock she'd have been back in bed with him, warming her chilled hands on his chest, pushing herself against his back until he woke up and turned lazily towards her, reaching. Saturday mornings used to feel so full of promise, his suit on the back of a chair, a whole empty day ahead.

When they had spoken yesterday, Tom had asked her what he should wear.

'Just something comfortable.'

'I'm intrigued.'

'And it mustn't restrict movement too much.'

'Are those the only clues?'

'I wouldn't want to spoil the surprise, would I?'

'See? You're getting into this, aren't you? I knew you would!'

'You know me so well, Tom.'

'That's the whole point, Nat.'

Natalie giggled as she buzzed him in. 'Come on up.' This was going to be fun. She picked up her bag, and opened the front door.

'Morning, hon.' Tom kissed her cheek. 'Crikey. Ready already? Where are we off to?'

87

'Me, Tom. Where am *I* off to. Since you ask, I'm off to Inner Peace. Christmas pressie from Bridge. A whole day at Inner Peace. That women-only place in town. God knows what they get up to there, but Bridget assures me it's more yoga and *reiki* than colonic irrigation, so I figured I'd give it a go.'

'I don't understand.'

'Oh, sorry. Of course. Yoga is an ancient form of exercise, *reiki* is a healing art and colonic irrigation involves putting a—'

'Ha, ha. Thanks. That I understand. What I don't understand is where the letter D and I fit into this fabulous plan to get toned, healed and de-pooed.'

'Oh, that. Sorry. Again. Should have explained.' Natalie waved him in past her. 'These shelves. Bought them ages ago but never got round to putting them up. Not sure I know how, to be honest. Bit of a boy job, I reckon. That's where you and D come in. DIY. Do-it-yourself. Pretty high on every woman's list of requirements for a suitable life partner, wouldn't you reckon? Gotta check it out, Tom. Okay? Tool kit's over there. Not sure what's in it – Dad gave it to us when we moved in. Help yourself to tea and coffee. Might be out of milk. Sorry about that. I'll be back around five, I suppose, unless my *chakras* are a real nightmare to realign. You should be well finished by then.'

She blew him a theatrical kiss and left before he could say a word. She had walked four houses down the street before she was certain he wasn't coming after her to complain, smiled to herself and carried on.

From the window Tom watched her go. *Touché.* Now they were getting somewhere.

Lucy and Patrick

'You look nice, dear.' Cynthia smiled benevolently at her daughter-in-law. 'Have you done something different with your hair?'

Lucy patted it self-consciously. 'Just washed it.'

'It looks lovely.'

'Thanks for doing this.'

'It's nothing, sweetheart. I was watching television anyway – I may as well do it here as at home. And Patrick's dad says not to worry what time you get back. He'll come and get me whenever.'

'You could have slept over, you know.'

'I know, dear, but I do like my own bed these days.'

Lucy nodded distractedly. 'Ed's asleep, Bella's reading. There's tea and coffee, and some cake – we had a cake sale at school today, so you're quite safe, I didn't make it. Help yourself. And you've got our mobile numbers.'

'Don't worry about a thing.' Cynthia put her hand on Lucy's arm. 'You just have a good time, the two of you, you deserve it. And kiss Patrick a happy birthday from his old mum.'

'You can do that when we get back.' Lucy smiled weakly. How the hell did Cynthia think she wasn't going to worry? She had a husband with no job, who couldn't make love to her, let alone talk to her about how he was feeling. She had a man, this guy, on the sidelines of her life, creeping further into her brain and her thoughts, and the urge to go to him was stronger every day. And she was in the middle.

Patrick had said he would meet her at the restaurant. He had mumbled something about having things to do, but she knew he hadn't wanted to be at home when Cynthia arrived. He didn't want to talk to his parents about it. She supposed there ought to be some crumb of comfort in that, but there wasn't.

He was already there when she arrived, and stood up, formally, to kiss her. There was none of him in the embrace, though. He felt brittle and slight.

'Happy birthday, Patrick.'

He shrugged. 'Turning thirty-nine feels a bit like vinegar strokes – on top of everything else. I suppose I should be glad it isn't forty.'

He'd already ordered some wine. And drunk half the bottle. He poured a glass for her, and a splash spread across the tablecloth. The waiter hovered anxiously, dabbing at the stain with a cloth, but Patrick waved him away. His laugh was hollow. 'Don't seem to be getting anything right, these days, do I?'

Lucy reached for his hand. 'Don't say that, love. You've had a knockback, a bit of bad luck. There's no shame in it. It happens – it happens to all sorts of people all of the time.'

Her words seemed to make him wince. 'It doesn't happen to the best people.'

'What?'

'It doesn't happen to the best people,' he repeated, 'only to the expendable ones. As soon as she came into the office, as soon as she put one of her dainty high heels on the carpet on the fourth floor, I became second best. My days were numbered.'

'That isn't true. You're being far too emotional about it, Patrick. It's business, sweetheart.'

'The least I can do now is own up to it. It's about the only thing I have left – my honesty.'

'There's a difference between honesty and the truth.'

He shook his head a little. 'I don't know what you just said.'

'That's because you're tired, stressed and a bit drunk. We need to order some food and get you sobered up a bit so we can have a proper conversation.'

'Second best.'

He hadn't been listening. His eyes were down. His voice had become almost a mumble. Lucy wondered if they could stay there, with him like that.

'Probably always have been. I was never as clever as Tom. Never as popular as Genevieve.' He laughed. 'Hey! Maybe I was third best at home.'

Lucy felt irritation rise into her throat. This was his birthday, and she'd tried, really tried. He was ruining it with self-pity, self-loathing and self-doubt, and although she told herself it was her duty to sit and listen to it, she didn't want to. He was making himself look dreadful.

'And I know I was second best for you. So that's another.'

The irritation bordered on anger. 'What in God's name do you mean, Patrick?'

'Well, it's obvious, isn't it? You'd still be with Will if he hadn't buggered off. I was second best. Your safe harbour in stormy seas. Except I'm not so safe any more, am I? Bloody ironic, that, isn't it?'

'Did you have a drink before you came in here?'

'A couple of pints. It was my leaving do, after all.'

'Your what?'

'Oh, yes, the human-resources department was very generous. They put money behind the bar at the pub next to the office. Don't know how much. Enough, I suppose. The young came to drink as much free booze as they could get down them. The older ones came because they were grateful it wasn't them. I went because . . . Do you know? I haven't the faintest clue why I went. To drink to my second-rateness.' He laughed.

Lucy didn't mean to sound as angry as she did: 'I can take a certain amount of this, Patrick, although it's all bollocks, but don't you dare to say that you were second-best for me. Don't you dare!'

He stared at her, for long enough to make her squirm a little in her seat. When he said, 'Okay,' he sounded strange.

She wasn't hungry, but she didn't want to go home to Cynthia early and she didn't have anywhere else to go. So they ordered starters and main courses, coffee afterwards, and sent back plates that raised concern in the kitchen: a waiter was despatched to ask if everything had been okay for them. And they had an oh so polite conversation about Patrick's plans – where he would send his CV, which headhunters he thought it best to approach, and so on. It was the bones of the conversation that Lucy had known for some weeks that they had to have, but it had no blood, no muscle and no skin.

And all she kept thinking, as she chewed the food that tasted like sawdust, drank the wine, listened and nodded, was that he was right. He was second best. Not to Will, certainly. Maybe not to Alec. But to what she knew she wanted. He was second best.

Anna

The average GP's waiting room must be the best place in the world to go if you wanted to get sick. People were coughing up their guts here today. What on earth was she doing here? She'd promised Nicholas she'd come. He'd wanted to be with her, but she'd said no. She hadn't been able to stop him driving her, though. He was sitting outside now, in the car, reading the newspaper. She'd asked him not to come in, and even though he had made that sad face at her, she was glad. Anna flicked through a copy of *Hello!*, three years out of date. Almost every couple on its pages, photographed exchanging vows at absurdly over-the-top weddings, or frolicking, scantily clad, on sugary beaches or cradling designer babies in their arms, was now divorced. Living a different life.

An elderly man pushed his wife into the room in a wheel-chair, and parked her in the only available space, next to the Lego table. Maybe he'd rather be outside too, in his car, reading *The Times*. Except he couldn't be, could he? His wife needed him.

When Jim Callaghan, the former Labour prime minister had died, his obituary had made much of his marriage. He'd out-lived his wife by eleven days, having spent the last ten years caring for her as she grew more frail and ill. But he'd never complained, apparently. He once told someone that she'd spent sixty years taking care of him and now it was his turn to take care of her. And Anna didn't know whether that was the loveliest or the saddest thing she had ever heard. Both, maybe. She couldn't help wondering whether Audrey Callaghan would have wanted it to end like that. Carers find it hard to be taken care of, don't they? And he'd died so soon after her – one of those couples who become two halves of a whole, like con-joined twins, and can't live without each other.

Anna wondered what kind of carer Nicholas would have made, if she had needed it. It was about a year ago that they'd been here, waiting to be called in. He'd gone in with her, that time, had sat on the other side of the sprigged curtain as she had taken off her blouse and bra, laying them carefully over the chair. It had felt cold, and she had felt vulnerable, standing behind the curtain, topless, waiting for the GP to come behind it and tell her she was going to die.

It must be the baby clinic this morning. Four or five mothers were sitting on one side of the waiting room with their red books, waiting to painstakingly record each new ounce of their child on the graph. The babies were in their car seats, and their mums had loosened their fleecy suits, taken off woolly hats.

The GP came in for her next patient, saw Anna and smiled reassuringly. 'You're next, Anna, okay?'

Maybe she thought the lump was back. In a way, Anna wished it were. You could do something about that. You could stick a needle in and suck it away, cut it out with a scalpel, blast it with drugs and radio waves. You could fight it. You might lose – it might get you however hard you tried. But you could do something. At least you knew what the enemy was.

What was she going to say?

She tried not to stare at the young mothers. She didn't want to look like some mad old bag. But when she gazed into the middle distance all she could see was a long washingline of pure white terry nappies. She picked up *Homes and Antiques*, and tried to concentrate on Victorian sewing boxes.

Then it was her turn.

'Anna? You can come in now.'

The GP had four children. Blonde, willowy, blue-eyed. Two boys and two girls. There were new pictures this year. The youngest must have started school – there she was, all pigtails and oversized blazer, sitting proudly with her siblings. Anna thought she liked Dr Jackson – not in a doctor-patient way, but if they were seated together at a dinner party, or if they'd had their children at the same time and had met in the playground, she would have liked her. In a person-to-person way. She was blonde, like her children, but less willowy. She always wore black trousers – wool in winter, linen and cotton in summer – that were a little too tight for her and gave her a small roll of flesh above the waistband that Anna found endearing. She was from the West Country, and her slight burr made her sound a little ponderous, but her eyes told you she was as sharp as you like.

'How are you, Anna?'

To her shock and horror, Anna burst into tears. Real, noisy tears. She didn't know where they had come from. They sprang into her eyes and ran down her cheeks. She couldn't stop. She tried to speak, excuse them somehow, but she couldn't say a word.

Dr Jackson waited for a few minutes. All she did was hand Anna a tissue. Then she looked away from her, at her computer screen, and made herself busy for a moment. 'Okay?'

Anna blew her nose. 'Sorry.'

'Don't be. Occupational hazard. Don't give it a second thought.'

Anna nodded.

'Want to tell me what it is?'

'I wish I could.'

'Have you found another lump?'

Anna shook her head. 'No. No. Nothing like that. I'm not ill.'

Dr Jackson wheeled her chair out from behind her desk so that she was next to Anna, and waited.

Anna was terrified that she would start crying again. 'I'm sorry about that. I've never done that before. I'm . . . I'm in a bit of a state, I'm afraid.' She felt as humiliated as if she had wet herself there in the doctor's room.

'Has something happened?'

Dr Jackson was kind and concerned, but she had only seven minutes. Anna was so angry with herself. 'No. Not really. I – I can't sleep.' That was a place to start. And it was true. She fell asleep, all right, but she always woke up at around two or three in the morning and never really went back to sleep.

'Are you anxious about something? I presume you've tried the usual things – warm milk before bed, not watching TV or reading, making sure the room is aired properly, lavender in a bath . . .'

She hadn't, but she knew it wouldn't have made any difference. It was her mind that was waking her up. 'Yes.'

'Well, then, my best guess is that there is some underlying

stress. Do you think it relates back to what happened last year? It really wouldn't be uncommon.'

'I don't think it's about the cancer scare.'

'That suggests to me that you know what it's about, Anna. You don't have to tell me, but . . . I'm not keen to prescribe something long-term to help you sleep . . .'

'I do know. I hate my life, Doctor. I feel like I'm finished . . . Like I outgrew any usefulness years ago when the girls left.'

The doctor nodded sagely. That's not right, Anna thought, panic rising. She thinks I've got empty-nest syndrome. That's not it! That's not it! She wrung her hands in her lap, pulling strands off the tissue the doctor had given her.

'I'm jealous of my children. I'm jealous of them having what I worked so hard to give them, and I almost hate them sometimes for having what I didn't. I could have had a different life. I could have been something, done something, and I didn't. And they are. And I hate it. I hate it because it's eating me up, and I hate it because it means I'm not even a good mother. Because a good mother wouldn't think that.'

She had finally found words for it. They had been spoken and heard.

Anna started to cry again.

Anna and Bridget

Anna had been sitting with the baby on her shoulder, his head in her neck, for almost an hour.

'I should probably put him down, Mum. Don't want to spoil him.'

'Why not?'

Bridget felt irritable. That was easy for her mum to say – she had nothing else to do but sit there nursing. It would be a different matter when Toby expected to be cuddled while she was trying to feed Christina, or get some washing done, or cook supper for her and Karl. 'Because he has to learn to go to sleep on his own.'

'That's what Gina Ford says, is it?'

'That's what I say, Mum. Give him here.' Bridget lifted her son's tiny body off her mother, and, in one seamless movement, put him into the Moses basket next to the sofa. 'There you are, darling. Good boy.'

She had sounded perfunctory. Anna felt bereft. There was a row of tiny cardigans drying on the rack. She started folding them carefully, laying them on her lap.

'You don't have to do that, Mum.'

'I want to help.'

'And you have. You put Christina down for her sleep while I fed Toby, and you've looked after him while I cleared up from lunch.'

'That doesn't seem much.'

'I don't want you to come here to work, Mum.' Bridget tried to keep the impatience out of her voice but knew she was failing. She was just so tired. She could cope with the kids, but Mum as well . . . She felt close to tears. She checked the clock on the mantelpiece. Still another three hours before Karl came home.

'I'm not ill, you know. It was a cancer *scare*, not actual cancer.'

Now Bridget really had to bite it back. She knew it was a scare, for Christ's sake. And scare was the right word. It had scared the shit out of all of them. But she wasn't the one behaving like the end of the world was nigh. Neither were her sisters, and nor was her poor father. It was Mum. She'd been like this for months now.

'I know that Mum.' She took a deep breath. She really didn't want to do it now, but maybe it would be better than this atmosphere. 'I do. But you've been so . . .' she struggled for an adequate word '. . . weird ever since. We never know what we're going to get.'

'What do you mean?'

'You're so up and down. One minute you're fine, the next you're snapping everyone's heads off. Or, worse, all Uriah Heep, like you're a burden or something. It's exhausting, a bit, Mum, to be honest . . .'

Bridget's voice trailed off. Her mother was profoundly sad, and she wished fervently that she hadn't started this. What was she doing? She wasn't equipped to wash her face and brush her teeth, let alone have this conversation.

'Is that why you didn't want me at the hospital?'

Bridget had been about to deny it, but then she said, softly, 'Yes.'

'And why you didn't call me to look after Christina?'

'No, Mum. I explained that to you. Karl's mother had specifically asked if she could. You can see her point of view, can't you? Karl's an only child, she hasn't got a daughter of her own, she knew I had you . . .'

'Only you didn't, did you? You didn't need me there.'

'I needed my mum there. But, these days, you don't seem much like her.'

'So you'd rather call Natalie?'

'Mum!' Bridget was exasperated. 'It's not a question of "rather". You're so unpredictable!'

'You're talking about me as if I'm mentally ill. Is that what you're saying?'

'No, of course not. I don't know *what*'s wrong with you. Nor do Nat and Suze – or Dad. None of us knows what to do! Dad's at the end of his tether – surely you can see that?'

Of course she could. You aren't married to a man for forty years without knowing when he's at the end of his tether. Anna just didn't know what to do about it. 'Are you all talking about me?'

'Of course we are.' Bridget was almost shouting now, and Toby snuffled and shifted in the Moses basket beside them. 'We all love you, Mum.' The tears that are never far away from a new mum sprang into Bridget's eyes. She was remembering last summer.

Breast cancer. God – that word. The disease that had killed their grandmother at fifty-four.

It hadn't been a long wait, from lump to biopsy to result. But it was long enough, because they had all believed it was inevitable that the oncologist would say, yes, he was very sorry but the lump was malignant. Certain. Anna's mother had had it, hadn't she? All any of them had thought about, as they waited that day – Nicholas at the hospital, the girls in their respective homes – was the inexorable progression of the disease and Anna's death. Their father's loneliness. A funeral. Grandchildren growing up without knowing her. They had been so sure.

And they had been wrong. It wasn't cancer, just a cyst that could be simply removed, with no side-effects, no radiation, no chemotherapy, no baldness, nausea – no death.

And life could go on.

'I'm sorry, darling. Don't cry, please. Come on.' Anna was Mum again, and Bridget laid her aching head on Anna's chest, and let herself be patted and soothed.

Natalie

These places – spas, health farms and beauty shops – always smelt so good. Natalie loved them. Not that she got to go very often. And the effect was not quite the same at the local sports centre, which smelt more of soggy nappy and adolescent boy, and had none of the calming balm that pervaded everything. Sometimes Susannah took her, when she was home and flush. Susannah always said, with an absolutely straight face, that maintaining a beautiful self was essential to her work, and that, therefore, spending the rent money on a day at the Sanctuary was more of an investment than a treat. It was a theory that worked well for Natalie, too, although looking good made little difference at the radio station, where she was pretty much invisible to all. She felt a little pang, now, for her extravagant, exuberant, theatrical elder sister. She hadn't seen nearly as much of her since Casper had been on the scene. And not at all, now, for weeks. Apparently she'd promised Mum she'd be at home for Easter, but that felt like a long way off.

Natalie took a deep cleansing breath of the aromatherapy-ish air and shrugged her shoulders further into the soft, thick towel. Beside her lay the schedule of daily activities available to her, but lying around was lovely enough. She'd swum a lazy ten lengths of the pool, sat until she was pruny in the Jacuzzi, and singed her nostril hairs in the sauna. Now she was wallowing contentedly in what they called the Silent Space. The walls were painted aubergine, and it was lit dimly with uplighters around the floor. The steamer chairs had thick cream cushions, and pointed away from the door to ensure privacy and tranquillity. Bridget had said she should persuade Rose or someone to come along, but Natalie was glad she was alone. She didn't really feel like speaking. She lay still, with her eyes closed, and let herself wander through her own mind. It didn't take long for it to settle on Simon. She'd never gone so long without seeing him. She realised she'd stopped thinking that he was on every ringing phone or had mailed every mysterious envelope in the post but she hadn't entirely accepted it. It felt, to her, unfinished – they would see each other again. She just didn't know what would happen when they did.

These last few months she'd filed him away. In Silent Space – where no one could hear you scream, as Tom would probably say – she felt strong enough to unlock her memory of him.

She and Simon had met when she was twenty-one. So he'd been around, or at least the idea of him, for the whole of her adult life. He was the brother of a friend of a friend at university. He'd appeared as the friend's 'date' at the ball to celebrate finals, and the first time she'd set eyes on him he'd looked like a young Sean Connery, all dark eyes and dinner suit. The eyes followed her around the crowd – she could remember feeling them on her, like a touch – and performing for him: she was only doing the things she would have done if he hadn't been there but she was concentrating on how she did them because he was watching her. It was sexy, that – the certainty that whenever she turned back to where he was sitting, his eyes would be on her.

At the end of the evening she'd been hovering accidentally-on-purpose near the exit, when he left, and his eyes had laughed at her. He'd kissed several girls goodnight, but he'd put his thumb under her chin, lifted her face and the kiss had landed almost over her lips. When he'd pulled away, his eyes were regretful.

She hadn't forgotten him. She wouldn't have called it pining, and she made no brave attempts to see him again, but she daydreamed about him sometimes, for years afterwards. She was sure that in her head he was darker, more handsome, and that his eyes were more attentive, more sorry at the end. But that was okay. He was just a daydream, wasn't he? He could be Prince bloody Charming in a daydream if she wanted him to be.

She had almost forgotten about him when she met him again. And she had loved the fateful randomness of it. Nothing to do with their respective friends and siblings at university – all of those chances – if they ever existed, had evaporated. A friend from work, Stella, had asked her to be godmother to her baby. Stella's husband, Ross, had asked Simon to be godfather. How fabulous was that? As meeting stories went, Natalie thought it was a damn good one. It certainly sounded fantastic when she rehearsed telling it to their grandchildren. When she was alone, of course.

He had been late. The rest of the party had assembled at Stella and Ross's house, then walked the short distance to the village church together. Simon arrived as they were singing hymn number 321. Stella hadn't said much about the other godparents, except that one was to be her brother, and the other an old schoolfriend of Ross's, whom she had described as 'a bit up himself, actually'. The late arrival came slowly up the aisle behind Natalie, and took a place at the end of the pew directly in front. Ross handed an open hymn book to him, and rolled his eyes, as the broad shoulders shrugged an apology. It was the hairline, straight and definite, like a cartoon hero's, and the colour of the hair, the black that was almost blue – L'Oréal called it Raven, but there was no doubt that this was natural. Natalie felt excited. Then, like those moments in pop videos and films, she had waited for him to turn and reveal a different face, the wrong face.

She walked behind him to the font, and as they arranged themselves round it, he saw her face. His eyes were pleased and surprised, and he raised an eyebrow at her. She was almost shocked that he remembered her. Like an Exocet missile, her gaze sought out his wedding finger. Bare. Did he see her looking? He was smiling now, and Natalie felt herself blush. As befitted a romantic heroine.

The baby, Hector, was vast, and bore an uncanny resemblance to Alexei Sayle. He wailed and wriggled in Simon's arms, and on several occasions almost succeeded in freeing himself from his godfather's untrained grasp. He seemed desperate to get into the font. His hands grasped angrily for the edge. Natalie giggled, and the dark eyes twinkled at her. The years evaporated.

Afterwards, when the regular worshippers were energetically singing 'He's Got the Whole World in His Hands', he whispered, 'Christ, I thought he was going for the full immersion, then, little brute.'

'That's our godson you're talking about.'

'Oh, yes, our first child together.'

She didn't know what to say.

'In a manner of speaking, of course.'

Still stumped. She was usually better at it than this, but this was a full-on assault, and they weren't even out of the church.

His mouth was even closer to her ear when he said, 'One of ours would, of course, be far, far better looking.'

Now she curled her lip. 'Could you be any cornier?'

He laughed. 'Probably. Wait until I've had a glass or two of champagne.'

Stella was glaring at them, puzzled and slightly annoyed. Natalie held up the hymn book between them, and sang in her best schoolgirl voice.

Outside the church, Stella grabbed her arm and hissed, 'How the hell do you know him?'

'I don't, really. We met once, years ago. Guess we remembered each other.'

'I guess so. Never expected to have the air on the altar so heavy with sexual tension at the baptism of my firstborn child.'

'What can I say? I'm unforgettable and irresistible.' At that moment, it was how she felt.

Stella was called over for photographs, and Simon sauntered in her direction. 'So, what is your connection with the happy parents and the elephantine child?'

'Stella is a friend – we work together.'

'As what?'

'Radio producers, at the BBC.' She thought he looked a bit impressed. He wasn't to know she meant assistant producer, and regional at that. 'And you?'

'I was at school with Ross.'

'And now?' If he could be economical with language, so could she.

'And now I need a drink. When the hell did christenings get like weddings? How many hours are we expected to stand out here while they snap away at young Algernon like he was David bloody Beckham?'

'Hector. And it's only been about ten minutes. Are you always so impatient?'

'Yes.'

He was a surgeon. Well, almost. Turned out he was younger than she was. He hadn't looked it, in 1989, and he sure as hell hadn't acted like it. He'd been almost nineteen, and just about to start his pre-clinical studies when they'd first met – at St Thomas's in London. Now he was an SHO, he said, and about to start training as a surgeon. 'Another long haul. That's why I took some time off,' he said. After he'd qualified, he'd been round Australia and New Zealand working stints in A&E departments to fund dive courses and extended holidays in the Whitsundays and on the Barrier Reef. He'd only come back three months ago – that explained the tan: he had the kind of skin that held colour. 'Theory, practical, specialisation . . . It'll be another few years before they start letting me cut people up on my own.'

'So, you're going to be the kind of doctor who doesn't have to be bothered by his patients because they'll all be unconscious – is that right?'

His eyes narrowed, and then he smiled. 'How incredibly perceptive of you.'

'And is it a calling?'

'It's a living.'

'A pretty good one, I suppose.'

'Not yet. I'm pretty much destitute right now. But it will be.'

That was the first time she'd paid for dinner. Mind you, that was two all-day breakfasts at a Little Chef on the motorway so it hadn't even cost her a tenner.

He'd hitched a lift back to Bristol with her, after Hector had declared the end of his party by yelling so loudly that he threw up over his three-generations-old Belgian-lace christening gown. Simon didn't have a car of his own. Which didn't stop him implying that her battered red Fiat Uno wasn't a proper one. His superiority and self-assurance were attractive, which surprised her: she hadn't known arrogance did it for her. 'You're going to have a proper God complex, aren't you, when you're qualified?'

'Absolutely.' He grinned at her. They both felt it, the new thing between them, and they both liked the feeling.

In town, Natalie had dropped him by a bus stop. 'I'm not going your way.'

'I could be going yours, if you liked.'

She didn't know how, but she managed to resist. 'You'll have to try harder than that.'

'I'd like to be going your way. Please.' He made a face like a spaniel.

Natalie laughed. 'Not tonight, Josephine.'

He acknowledged defeat with a nod. 'I suppose it's up to me, then, isn't it? All those years ago I let you walk out of my life, and now you're going to do it again.'

'Oh, please. Where are you getting this stuff? Have you got a Mills and Boon stuffed up your jumper? Or is Barbara Cartland feeding you dialogue into a hidden earpiece?'

He laughed. It was a good sound. When he spoke again he seemed younger and more vulnerable. 'I really like you. You can see through the bullshit, can't you?'

'Helen Keller could have seen through those lines.'

He shook his head. 'So, cynical one, can I see you again? I'd really like to.'

Of course he could. And in reality, the only thing she could actually see through was his brown eyes, and what she could see was the rest of her life, with him. And he knew that better than she did, even then.

February
E for Equine

Tom had called Natalie and offered her a ride home. Said he was passing vaguely by the radio station.

It had been a draggy afternoon – it was ages since he had called. Natalie was hormonal and bored and scratchy. She ate a whole bar of Cadbury's Fruit and Nut while she waited for him.

Tom's afternoon had been rather more successful. He'd landed a new client at his meeting. He was feeling a bit smug, and rather playful. Which meant that he didn't recognise that the girl with the slightly chocolatey lips who got into his car wasn't the sashaying, smiley-eyed girl who had left him in her flat hanging shelves last week. This girl had dark circles under her eyes, which weren't all that smiley, and her shoulders were hunched and tense under her overcoat.

'I was going to go for Eating. It's almost Valentine's Day, after all. I thought perhaps a nice, romantic, candlelit dinner . . .'

'Sounds good to me.' Natalie rubbed her mouth, inspected her fingers, and rubbed again, until the chocolate was gone. 'I'm starving.'

'. . . but then I remembered how you lured me to your place under false pretences and forced me to spend most of the day grappling with some shelves and their obscure instructions written in pidgin English, and I'm not so sure that you deserve a nice meal. So I rethought my letter.'

'Sounds ominous.'

'Enema. I almost booked you a colonic irrigation at some clinic in town.'

'Yuck.'

'Yeah. And I'm not that mean.'

'I'm glad.'

'Not *quite* that mean.'

'Are you sure I don't deserve a nice dinner?'

'Don't even think about using that little-girl-lost voice on me, Nat. I am so much more than sure that you don't.'

'Come on, then.' Natalie sighed, but Tom didn't hear it. 'Put me out of my misery. What hideous E have you got planned for me?'

'Don't you want to guess a little longer? I mean, there were plenty of possibilities. I toyed with Eco-warrior—'

'What? Make me sit up a tree all day with people whose personal hygiene leaves a lot to be desired?'

'It would have pissed you off.'

'But you'd have had to do it too, and you're not up for that.'

'Exactly right. That ruled out several options. Until I came up with the perfect thing.'

'Tom!' Natalie was exasperated, but also a little scared. He looked like he was enjoying this.

He did an imaginary drumroll with his hands, biting his bottom lip. 'E for . . . Equine.'

Natalie raised her eyebrows

'All things equine. Equestrian activities.' Her expression was unconvinced. '*Horses.*'

'What about horses?'

'Nothing extraordinary. We're going to ride some.'

'No, we are not.' Natalie shook her head petulantly like a toddler.

'Says the girl who jumped off a viaduct less than a month ago.'

'That was different. I've never had a bad experience with a viaduct.'

Tom chortled. 'Oh, come on. That was years ago.'

'It was enough for me.'

She'd broken her pelvis, which would have been enough for most people, during the summer after her O levels, when everyone else had been celebrating, partying. She'd thought she was going to die. The mare she'd been riding wasn't big – although she'd felt it when she landed on Natalie, after they'd fallen. There weren't many things from her childhood that she remembered so exactly. Crystallised moments held in perfect lucidity in her mind. Hardly anything, actually. She remembered their mum sitting on the stairs and crying when the three of them had chickenpox. She must have been four or five. She remembered driving away from their old house, when they moved, and watching it get further away until Dad had turned left and it disappeared. First filling, first kiss, first period, last time Mum had smacked her. But she remembered nothing as well as the terror and pain of that accident. And the girl who had loved riding, who had claimed it as her own thing, while Susannah tap-danced and Bridget sat still, had not been near a horse since.

She realised that Tom was curiously absent from her memories of the time right after the accident. It had happened at the start of the summer holidays – he must have been in Cornwall with his family. They had always gone, to the same place for two weeks as soon as term finished.

She remembered him visiting, now that she concentrated – sitting on the edge of her bed, telling her about the pubs in Newquay and taking the rise out of her.

'Come on, Nat,' he wheedled now, and something in Natalie snapped.

'No. Tom. No. What part of "no" is confusing you? I don't

want to do it. This is just some stupid game to you – I get that, okay – but I can't get on a horse. And I won't. Not for the game and not for you, and, most of all, not because I'll be conquering some inner demon. I'm quite happy with my inner demon, thanks very much.'

She opened the car door before he had had the chance to say anything.

'Tom, you're my friend, not my therapist. At least, that's what I thought.' And got out. She didn't exactly slam the door, but then again, she didn't look back at him as she went in through her front door.

Tom sat there for a few minutes, feeling strangely embarrassed and a little too ashamed to get out and knock on her door. He'd been mean, he thought. He shouldn't have suggested it. He hadn't remembered, or maybe had never acknowledged, how much the accident had upset her, and he'd used what he knew about her as a cheap stunt.

Natalie had seemed tired today, strained, and he had made himself part of the problem rather than part of the solution, and that was so far away from what he had set out to do that he wanted to bang his head against the steering-wheel. What a prat! Serena would kill him.

Natalie didn't get much further than the hall. She dropped, cross-legged, to the floor, and put her face in her hands. She would have liked to cry, but couldn't. It was a bit like when you've had food-poisoning, and you keep retching long after your stomach is empty. she'd cried too much since Simon had left her. No more tears – that was what was written on the shampoo Bridget used on Christina. No more tears. That was what she had now. Bad day. That was all. You knew there would be bad days. At the beginning they were all bad. Then one or two okay ones surprised you, then a good one. And eventually, probably, hopefully, there would be more and more good ones, fewer and fewer bad, no more truly-dreadfuls. And then a bad day would surprise you and there would be no more. This one had been a bad day, that was all. Shitty, actually.

After about five minutes of sitting in the hallway, long enough for her knees to protest about being in the lotus position, Natalie raised her head and smoothed back her hair. Sometimes she missed being half of a couple. And sometimes she just missed him. The smell of him, the feel of him, the sound of him. So much.

Tom wasn't supposed to make it worse. The whole point of Tom was to make it better. To make her better. And today that not being the case was the last straw on the camel's back. It wasn't about the sodding horse, not really. Although, actually, it had been mean of him. And she hoped he was sorry. It was about what he was supposed to be doing for her.

Even as she thought it she had a quick glimpse of how selfish it made her sound.

Then, Natalie remembered something. She had had a huge row with Simon once, a couple of years ago. He'd been working crazy hours, as he did, and Natalie had felt as though she hadn't seen him for weeks. Not properly. She'd tried hard to get it right for him. To help. She'd even done his laundry. Cooked him stuff. Pinched herself properly awake when he came in at all hours of the night so that she could have a proper conversation with him, if that was what he wanted, or let him make love to her, if he preferred (although, if memory served, he mostly liked her to make love to him). And then he'd announced, the first free night he'd had in ages, that he'd been invited for dinner with some medical-school friends – people she didn't know, he said, although she'd met them. Hadn't liked them much. Cliquey. The kind of people who pepper almost every conversation with references to the past – a past you had had nothing to do with, but which was obviously so much more fantastic than the present that you felt superfluous and spare. She'd been incensed that he would rather be with them than her, that apparently she hadn't been invited, that he would actually consider going and leaving her.

It had been a vicious row – Natalie self-righteous and hurt, and Simon undoubtedly tired, but also indignant and defensive. 'What's the big fucking deal, Nat?' he had ranted. 'You don't even like them, for Christ's sake. You made that pretty clear when you met them before. Don't ask me to choose between you and my friends.' His tone was dangerous. It felt like a threat. 'We're not joined at the bloody hip or anything, are we? It's not like we're married or anything!'

And that was it. They weren't. Married. Or even anything. She had her mortgage, her sister-flatmates. He had his rent, albeit on a flat so squalid and so devoid of someone who would do laundry, dinner and fellatio at all hours of the day and night that he spent all his time at her place. And being married, or anything, obviously equated, for him, to being conjoined. Which was so obviously not a good thing as far as he was concerned. And he was telling her that, despite the laundry, the dinner and the fellatio, if she made him choose, he would choose them – people he didn't even see that often. Choose freedom.

She didn't often cry. But she had then. She'd crumpled into the sofa and cried. Which had made Simon incredibly angry. He had spat something nasty at her about clingy women and he had gone.

Just for a moment, she couldn't believe that he had walked out on their row. On its vast, iceberg-like agenda. She remembered half crawling to the window to scan the street for his car. Surely he would be sitting in it, head in hands, wondering what had gone wrong, how he could have been so unkind, and contemplating what to say when he came back in. But of course he had gone.

And he had come back, of course. Late. A little drunk. (He'd left the car, and Natalie remembered that she'd driven him to pick it up the next morning, and they'd been invited in for a coffee, and the friends had spent half an hour reminiscing about the night before, as they would.) And very sorry. He'd breathed garlic and red wine and apology and love and excuses into the back of her head as she lay curled tensely on the edge of her bed.

And she had rolled over and breathed forgiveness and longing, of course.

Now she stood up, and rubbed the small of her back ruefully. She walked over to the window, just as she had that night.

And Tom's car was still there.

When she opened the front door again, Tom saw that she'd brushed her hair and put on some lipstick. He wound down the passenger window, and she stuck her head in. He started to apologise, but Natalie raised her hand. 'Complete overreaction. Bad day. Not bad friend. Bad idea, maybe, but not bad friend.'

'Lunch? You choose.'

'Sushi. Much better. E for Eating.'

'Get in.'

Nicholas and Anna

'Happy birthday, sweetheart.'

Anna rolled over and saw Nicholas at the door, with a lap-tray. She'd bought it when Susannah got her A-level results. Each of the girls had had a Bucks fizz breakfast in bed, with a flower in a bud vase, and a scary brown envelope to open. She'd forgotten they still had it – he must have climbed into the loft to get it. She sat up and smiled at him. 'What's this?'

'Breakfast in bed for my beautiful wife.' He put the tray down.

A pile of cards was tucked into the side. He was trying so hard. The doctor had given her pills, not Prozac, but something like it, and gone on about how depression was nothing to be ashamed of, it was chemical, and just as much in need of treatment as ingrown toenails or even breast cancer. She'd given her a three-month prescription and asked her to come back in April. But she'd urged her to talk to Nicholas about the root causes of her unhappiness as well. Of course.

And, of course, she hadn't. Not yet. She didn't know how. She'd told him about the pills and they'd picked up the pre-scription, and she'd seen his shoulders unhunch a little with relief. She'd been taking them for a couple of weeks. Silly to think they'd magic everything away overnight, although she did feel a little lighter and freer. She was sleeping better too.

There'd been a woman, Sally something, three doors down, when Natalie was a newborn, who'd had what was clearly post-natal depression. That had been more than thirty years ago, of course, and they didn't call it that. At least, not as far as she knew. And not out loud. 'Baby blues' came on the fourth day with your milk.

Anna remembered helping her. She'd had to, really. Sally had looked so awful all the time. She didn't wash her hair, and she had grey skin beneath her eyes, which were red from crying. She had put Sally's baby, Amanda, beside Natalie in the big Silver Cross pram and taken her for walks, or let them lie side by side on a blanket in the summer sunshine while Susannah watched them. Bridget was no trouble – she always sat still.

Anna had helped in practical ways, but she hadn't under-stood. She remembered thinking that Sally should pull herself together and be grateful she had a healthy baby to care for. She wondered now whether Sally had known. She'd got better eventually. She and her husband had moved away, and for a few years the two families had exchanged Christmas cards. Sally never had another baby: she had said in one card that she was afraid of what would happen. Now, Anna understood. If you could ever manage to pull yourself out of this terrifying dark place, you'd do anything – anything – to stop yourself falling in there again.

Did Nicholas think she should pull herself together? Did the girls?

She smiled broadly at him. 'Come and help me eat this toast.'

She opened her cards. One from Nicholas, from Susannah and Casper, Bridget and Karl, a homemade one from Christina, on computer paper stiff with too much paint, and one from Natalie. To my wife, to my mum, to my lovely granny. A woman's whole life encapsulated in three relationships.

Anna hadn't needed friends particularly. Friends had always been ephemeral. Before she'd married Nicholas, there'd been girls in the bakery where she worked. To giggle and talk about boys with. To dress up and go out with, then forget about. After the babies, there had been other mothers. She supposed she'd always felt a little superior to them. Her children were cleaner, cleverer and prettier. She'd never wanted those co-dependent relationships other women craved. She hadn't wanted to spend whole mornings drinking tea in someone else's kitchen, revealing details about her sex life. That was private, and she was self-sufficient. Anyway, the intensity of those friendships didn't last. The kids grew up, too.

They had friends, of course. The people who came for New Year. The women whose husbands had worked at the bank with Nicholas, who played golf with him at the club. He had a friend he'd done National Service with, for God's sake. But not people who knew secrets about her, because pride had never let her tell one.

It didn't make sense, really, any of it. So Anna stood the cards up – the one from her husband, the three from her children, the one from her granddaughter, and smiled benevolently at them on the mantelpiece, and she didn't talk to Nicholas about it, because, after all, what would she be saying?

'I've got a surprise,' he was saying. 'Instead of the same old birthday treat, I'm taking you away for the night. Here.' He handed her, with a flourish, the brochure of a country-house hotel. 'I thought it would make a nice change. Just the two of us.'

His lovely familiar face, so desperate to please. She put her hand to his cheek and caressed it. 'Thank you, darling.'

Nicholas pulled her into an embrace, and held her tight.

F for Family Get-together

'I know about your cousin's wedding because your mum told me at New Year, and I know it's coming up soon, and I'm sure you can wangle me an invite. Anyway, I know for a fact that your invitation is for you plus one. I want to be your plus one.'

'It's as simple as that, is it?'

'Not quite. I want you to pretend to your cousins, your aunts, Uncle Tom Cobbleigh and all that we're an item . . . Think of it as trying me for size.'

'When I already know you're a perfect fit?'

'Shut up, corn man. You know I like weddings. I like your family. Lucy and Patrick will be there, won't they? I haven't seen them for ages.'

'Sounds like an easy way of wriggling out of thinking up a proper F to me.'

'I resent that. It certainly isn't. Family get-togethers. Number three on the list of things couples argue about. After money and sex. Crucial!'

'Where are you getting these statistics, Nat?'

'*Trisha.*'

'Must be true, then. Can't we deal with one and two first?'

'You wish. I've got no money, and we're having no sex. So I can come?'

'I wasn't even going to go myself.'

'Well, you are now. Think of the Brownie points you'll get with your mum.'

'You win. We'll go. God knows why, but we'll go.'

* * *

121

'Oh, this is going to be even better than I thought!' Natalie squealed with delight.

'They aren't the most stylish branch of the family, it has to be said. You were warned . . .'

'Warned? We should be filming this. You'd sell it to Endemol for a fortune.'

The bridal party were having a fag on the pavement outside the town hall. The bride (sticking to tradition by appearing to be six feet wide) was concerned about getting ash down her polyester taffeta so the bridesmaid, a vision in strapless maroon, was holding the cigarette for them and they puffed away, oblivious of the page-boy, with his waistcoat and shaved head, who stood between them, pulling at their skirts and demanding, 'Toilet.'

Shoppers wove their way through the small crowd, largely ignoring them. There was a wedding on the half-hour at the register office on a Saturday, and, frankly, all this well-wishing and confetti-tossing got in the way.

Tom and Natalie were on the other side of the road. 'Let's leave it until the last moment,' Tom had pleaded.

It was a while since she'd seen him in a suit, Natalie thought. He looked pretty good. She'd bought her suit and hat last year, for the radio station's annual outing – to the evening races at Windsor – and been almost as horribly overdressed there as she was here, but she loved it. Besides, she was in character, wasn't she, so it was her costume? The dress was terribly low cut – Susannah had talked her into it – and chiffon, the lightest mint green, with white devoré flowers, and the coat, very Countess of Wessex, she'd thought – was a shade darker. The hat was what Susannah called a 'fascinator', an unfeasibly expensive concoction of feathers, net and seed pearls that was pinned to her head at a jaunty angle. In the mirror at Dickins and Jones, she had looked, to herself, like someone else. (A surgeon's wife, perhaps?) At this wedding she was the smartest guest by a very wide margin.

'Bloody hell,' Tom had said, when he'd arrived to pick her up. 'What have you come as?'

'Don't be rude. I've come as your girlfriend, of course.'

'You look more like a Tory wife.'

'Piss off.'

She had the grace to feel a little self-conscious now. Although the groom and his best man had on maroon cravats with their ill-fitting hired suits, most of the men had open collars and gold chains. And tattoos, which was only fitting, since the bride appeared to have Robbie Williams's face – palm-sized – inked on to her left shoulder.

Tom's cousin, christened David but known by all as Pinhead, for obvious reasons, crossed the road to greet them: 'Tom. How are you, mate? Cheers for coming.'

'I'm fine, Pin – Dave. Thanks. This is Natalie, my girlfriend.'

She experienced a little frisson to be referred to in that way after so long. Even if he did say it a bit funny.

Dave pumped her hand enthusiastically. He had sweat patches under each arm. 'Nice to meet you, love.' Then he gestured over his shoulder. 'Looks all right, doesn't she, the old girl?'

'She looks beautiful.' Natalie fixed her face into an expression of sincerity. Tom, she noticed, seemed fixated by something on the ground. She put a four-inch mint green heel on top of his black shoe and pressed, ever so gently.

'Your mum and dad here yet?' Tom asked.

'No, not yet. They're coming with Patrick and Lucy and the kids. Must be running a few minutes late.'

Pinhead nodded. 'Right. Right. Better get on. See you in there.' He darted back across the road.

'Is Genevieve not coming?'

'You must be joking. She'd rather poke sticks in her eyes. Although I think she's legitimately away somewhere this weekend – working or something. Lucky cow.'

'Shut up, Tom. This is going to be great. I *love* weddings!'

Tom's parents appeared round the corner, Cynthia clutching her hat to her head, and John holding a large silver-wrapped parcel. Behind them, Patrick and Lucy dragged one child each.

Lucy's face lit up when she saw Natalie. 'Nat! Fantastic. Tom told me you were coming. I'm so glad . . . Mystified, but glad! I haven't seen you for ages.'

Cynthia was straightening the tie of any male member of her family whom she could lay her hands on. Ed fidgeted with his shirt collar, and Cynthia smoothed his wayward hair with a wet finger. 'He's cross,' she said, to no one in particular, 'because we've told him he can't have his Power Rangers in the service.'

'Don't worry, mate.' Tom bent down to talk to his nephew. 'It only takes about ten minutes, and then you can have them back.' Ed smiled worship at his uncle.

'Natalie, sweetheart! You look wonderful.' Now Cynthia was kissing her. 'Well done for getting Tom here. So nice to have my family around me – it's a shame Genevieve can't be here too.'

Pinhead's mother was Cynthia's sister. They weren't close. Pinhead's mother had married someone the family hadn't entirely approved of. Cynthia's father had gone to his grave referring to him only as Billy Bigelow.

'Let's go in.' And with that Cynthia led the charge across the pelican crossing like Monty himself.

Natalie wasn't sure it had taken even ten minutes. It had been pretty soulless. Unless you counted the extraordinarily powerful emotional effect of Atomic Kitten being played on the tape-recorder as Pinhead and his lovely bride Mandy walked the five metres back down the aisle (or gap between the chairs) after the ceremony, grinning happily.

Cynthia leant across her husband, and hissed at Tom, 'Don't even think about a civil ceremony. I want a church, with flowers, a vicar and hymns.'

Natalie did her best demure-Lady-Di at him. 'Me too, Tom.' He slapped her leg.

Cynthia was hissing the other way now: 'I haven't told them, by the way, about you, Patrick. No need, is there?'

Lucy's heart sank. Sometimes Cynthia should think a little longer before she spoke. Beside her, she felt Patrick shrink a little. She squeezed his hand, but he didn't squeeze back.

The reception was being held in a hotel a little along the street. Round tables, with maroon tablecloths, surrounded a dance-floor with a disco set up at one end. The food was laid out on a buffet to the side. Tom went to the bar with his father and brother, while Cynthia spoke to some elderly – not to say cryogenically frozen – relatives who'd come down from north Wales for the day.

'So, what are you doing here really, Natalie? Can't you think of anything better to do with your Saturday?'

'F for Family-get-together.' Lucy was puzzled. 'Long story. Tell you later. I suppose I dared Tom to bring me.'

'Is something going on between you two that I should know about?'

'Is there heck! Come on, Luce. You of all people! But it's nice to see you. How are you? I'm sorry about Patrick. Tom told me. I hope it's all right, me knowing? I haven't said anything to him about it. Heard Cynthia in the church, though. She doesn't change, does she?!'

'We're not brilliant. I think Patrick's far more upset than he's letting on, even to me. And I don't think I'm being as patient about it as I should be. I want to get on, you know, deal with the practicalities. May be I haven't given him enough time to get used to the idea.'

'But Tom says he reckons Patrick knew about it before Christmas.'

'He did. Didn't tell me until New Year, though, and I suppose I'm a bit cheesed off about that. I don't know why he wouldn't want to tell me.'

'I guess he didn't want to worry you at Christmas.'

'But we're meant to be married, Natalie. His worries, my worries, our worries. They're supposed to be the same thing, aren't they?'

Now Natalie shrugged. 'You're right. It does sound like he's having a hard time getting his head round it. You've just got to give it some time, Lucy. It'll be all right.'

'I know it will. We're fine. Honestly.' She smiled. 'Marriage. That's all. What about you? Simon definitely off the scene?'

'I don't know. I can't imagine that he is, but I think that's just because he's been around for so long.'

Lucy smiled. 'Habit!'

'Suppose. But, that said, I haven't heard from him since before Christmas. Which seems pretty final.'

'You look fantastic.'

'Heartbreak. I've lost half a stone since he left me.'

'Not all bad, then?'

Natalie laughed. 'I'm okay, you know. Okay.'

Lucy put an arm round her. 'You'll be fine.' From her, it didn't sound patronising but true and comforting. Natalie laid her head on her friend's shoulder.

'Now, quickly, before the boys get back . . . what gives with you and Tom?'

*   *   *

From the bar, Tom watched Natalie surreptitiously. She was talking to Lucy, their heads conspiratorially close together. Ed arrived, and Natalie lifted him on to her lap unselfconsciously. He started pulling at that daft concoction she'd pinned to her head, and she stopped talking to Lucy to blow raspberries into his neck so that he giggled. Cynthia came back and stood between the two women, and they all laughed about something.

She fit. Bit of an own goal for her, the letter F, he pondered.

Two hours later the food had all gone but the drink still flowed. Pinhead had removed his jacket and cravat, the bride had relaxed enough to smoke her own fags, and the toe-curling speeches had been made. Packs of children careered round the room, skidding dramatically on the dance-floor and being shouted at by their parents. The DJ, in his lurid Hawaiian shirt, was warming to his theme, and the volume was increasing, so that everyone over sixty was being driven to the back of the room, where decibel levels were almost tolerable.

When Jennifer Rush's 'The Power of Love' started beating through the room, Natalie had to put the corner of her napkin into her mouth and bite down on it as the happy couple's first married dance together was announced, and Pinhead and Mandy shuffled uncomfortably round the floor for a couple of minutes. When he stepped on her train, she slapped him. Mandy's father stood nursing a pint, tears of pride and beer glistening in his eyes.

As the first dance segued into the second – no less mortifying – the DJ exhorted all 'couples, in love, young and old, male, female, whatever' to join the newlyweds. Cynthia dragged John to the middle of the floor, and Patrick and Lucy took up a less obvious station at the edge to watch Ed and Bella trying to dance with each other.

Mandy's mother was doing the rounds of the tables, shooing

people towards the centre of the room. 'Come on, you two beautiful young people. Get up there!'

Natalie raised an eyebrow at Tom, who was trying to eat a chicken wing. He put it down reluctantly and wiped his fingers on a maroon napkin. 'Come on, bird.' He reached for her hand.

'Since you ask so nicely.'

They'd known what they were doing in the old days, Natalie reckoned. Modern dancing – even that pelvic thrusting, grinding stuff they did in clubs – wasn't half so sexy. A man's hands round your waist, your thigh slipping between his, and the slide of chiffon up your leg . . . now, that felt nice. Even if it was Tom.

'We haven't done a lot of dancing, have we?'

Natalie thought about it. 'No. School disco, college bop stuff. Did we dance at Bridget's wedding?'

'You were with Simon.'

That was a no, then. 'Sorry.' She grimaced up at him. 'Who did you bring?'

'Genevieve. Who proceeded to get off with one of Karl's mates, as I remember. Another great wedding for me.'

'This one's been okay, hasn't it?'

He supposed it had.

'I thought you were going to be a lot more embarrassing. Not that your idea of being embarrassing would even register on the Richter scale here . . .'

'The night is but young, my love. And that sounds like a challenge. Is that a karaoke machine I see behind me?'

'You wouldn't dare.'

'Two more Bacardi Breezers, and there's almost nothing I wouldn't do.'

'Nothing?'

'I said almost.'

'Can't blame a bloke for trying.'

You couldn't. Natalie pulled him to her, and they danced.

Anna and Nicholas

'There's one more thing.' Nicholas looked like a kid.

They had had a lovely day. When she'd checked that her anti-depressants were in her toilet bag she had been reminded of her contraceptive pills in the late seventies. Not that they'd gone away much, of course. There had been a very occasional weekend when Nicholas's parents had taken the children.

This hotel was beautiful, all roaring fires and stuffed animals on the walls. They'd arrived in the afternoon, had a leisurely swim in the pool, and then she'd fallen asleep beside it on a lounger, trying to read some impenetrable novel Susannah had sent her. Then they'd had the kind of dinner where you don't recognise most of what's on the menu and you talk mostly about how nice the food is.

Despite her afternoon nap, Anna was tired again. But Nicholas clearly had other plans. She wondered if they would make love. But he went to his suitcase, and pulled out a beautifully wrapped gift. It looked like a CD, and Anna was surprised that he should give it such a build-up. She smiled her gratitude at him, and peeled off the silver ribbon.

It was an unmarked DVD.

'Da-dah,' he said, pushing back the doors of the heavy mahogany cabinet opposite their bed. 'I have just the thing to play it on.'

'What is it?'

'You're going to love it. Just wait and see.' He took the disc, pushed it into the machine, and fumbled with the controls.

The television came on, and the volume was ferociously loud.

'Sssh!' Anna giggled.

Finally he had mastered it, muttering all the while about how complicated machines were 'these days'. My God, Anna thought. We're old.

As the juddering images started, he came and sat beside her. 'I've had all the old cine film put on to DVD. Been meaning to do it for years. Had to get it all out of the loft without you seeing. That was where I found the lap-tray.' He nodded, like Watson on a case. 'I haven't watched it. Wanted to do it together.'

There was only about fifteen minutes and there were huge gaps – where they'd been too poor, or too tired, or too busy to film. But there it was. The best years of her life, flickering away on the screen.

Nicholas gave a running commentary, as though she didn't know what she was watching. 'Bridget's christening . . . Look how slim you are . . . and that hat . . . Oh, look at her. I'd forgotten she had so much hair . . . I remember that day. Pepperpot Hill. Bless her – she was chubby then, wasn't she? And look how much taller Susannah was . . . That's the day you brought Natalie home from the hospital. God, the girls missed you, didn't they? And I remember those things they made you . . .'

When they had watched it all, Nicholas realised that Anna was holding his hand tightly, as though she were falling and she needed him to save her. She was crying and when she turned to him, he saw desperation in her face. 'Oh, my lovely girl. What's wrong?'

She told him.

G for Gone with the Wind

'What are you wearing?'
                'Rob's cycling shorts.'
'Why?'
'Padded.'
'Is that supposed to make sense to me?'
'Padded crotch.'
'Still not getting it, although they look very fetching.' They
did. Tom had great legs. Except they were pale blue. It was a
grim February Sunday, and the wind was howling past them
round the grey concrete of the buildings in this part of town.
'Built-in comfort, for sitting through long periods.'
'Have you got haemorrhoids?'
'No! But I'm going to be sitting down for a long period.'
'Because?'
'We're going here.' He gave a dramatic flourish with his right
arm and opened the door. Natalie bundled gratefully inside.

Gone With the Wind
UNINTERRUPTED SHOWING. TODAY 12P.M.

Natalie's favourite film. She turned to him, open-mouthed.
Tom shrugged. 'I've never seen it – thought it was time I
found out what all the fuss was about.'
'I haven't seen it for years either.'
'Thank God for that. I'd have been a bit stumped if you'd
said you watched it last week.'

133

'I can't actually remember when I last saw it – with Susannah, I expect – but I can't remember when. Thanks, Tom. I love this!' She smiled at him with genuine pleasure and excitement, and Tom was glad. Grateful too: Serena had spotted the advert in the *Guardian* Weekend section and drawn it to his attention.

The cinema was, bizarrely, almost full. Natalie nudged him as they groped around in the dark for their seats. 'See? I'm not the only weirdo out there.'

'No, but I think I'm the only straight guy in here.'

'And you're wearing padded shorts!'

'Shut up and sit down.'

Now Tom took off his rucksack and opened the zip.

'What's this?'

'You can't honestly expect me to sit here for five hours, or however long it is, without sustenance, can you? And I've brought a couple of bits for you.'

He started handing her things. It was dark, and she had to lift up each item to the light to see what it was. A bottle of Tizer. A Cellophane packet of liquorice catherine wheels. A bag of Quavers. And a Terry's Chocolate Orange. Her favourite things.

Tom wished he could see her face. 'That do?'

'It'll do,' was all she said. But in the dark, as the white typography started rolling up the screen, telling the story of the American Civil War, her hand crept briefly into his lap and found his hand.

Tom couldn't believe how riveted she was. Natalie barely took her eyes off the screen. She sat still and quiet, utterly engrossed. He fidgeted. He finished his snacks, and gazed around at the slightly freaky crowd of daytime cinema-goers. And at Natalie's lovely profile, with the ever-so-slightly tilted nose, the full lips and the chin that always looked a little stubborn, even when it wasn't moving in speech.

It was dark outside when they emerged, mole-like, from the cinema, but the wind had dropped.

'Now tell me that wasn't the greatest film you've ever seen.'

'*Please! The Good, the Bad and the Ugly*, the first Star Wars trilogy, anything the Coen brothers ever made. No competition.'

Natalie pulled open the pub door. They went to the bar where she ordered a pint and a glass of white wine.

'But it wasn't as bad as I was expecting.'

'Praise indeed.'

'All that Atlanta burning stuff was cool.'

'You're so deep.'

'Rubbish ending, though.'

'How else could it have ended? Were you looking for a happy-ever-after, Pollyanna?'

'I don't know, but that was just crap. Were we honestly supposed to believe the spell was broken for him, and that he was suddenly over her?'

'God, no. He just couldn't take any more. But he was never going to be over her. She was the love of his life. In fact, they're one of the great cinematic examples of a couple with chemistry.'

'Didn't he have halitosis?'

'I'm not talking about Vivien Leigh and Clark Gable. I'm talking about Scarlett O'Hara and Rhett Butler. Chemistry, big-time.'

'But don't you think that Scarlett O'Hara and Ashley Wilkes is the ultimate being-in-love-with-love story? And that Scarlett's big mistake was ignoring what was right under her nose all that time, dreaming of some illusory romance that could never live up to her idealisation of it?'

'Christ, Tom, you sound like Germaine Greer.'

'You can't handle me – a mere male – understanding your silly film perfectly well, can you?'

'Oh, yes, I can. But what are we talking about here? *Gone with the Wind* or us, huh?'

'Definitely *Gone with the Wind*. Don't know what you're alluding to.'

Natalie laughed, and punched him gently in the stomach. 'Well, I loved it. It's been a long time since I saw it.' It had been a long time since she'd seen any film she might have chosen. Simon liked violent, noisy, fast-paced stuff. *Die Hard*, *Matrix*. And those bloody Tolkien films. She'd had to wait, if there was something she wanted to watch – for Bridget to have a free night, or to persuade Rose to abandon Peter for once, or for the DVD to make it to Blockbuster, then for Simon to be out so that she could watch it without his acerbic commentary. How pathetic was she? She almost laughed at herself.

'What?'

Natalie shook herself out of the memory and back to Tara. 'Nothing. Just thanks, Tom.'

Nicholas and Natalie

Natalie's phone rang at twelve-thirty p.m. It was Donna from Reception. 'Your dad's here.'

'Thank God,' Natalie muttered, to no one in particular. Her boss Mike was in a particularly bad mood today – the kind where everything she did was wrong. He'd named and shamed her on air, too, for apparently getting some information muddled, and it hadn't even been her fault. God, she hated him. She grabbed her coat and made her escape.

'Hiya, Dad. How are you?' They hugged. 'I'm glad to see you. I'm having a really grim day.'

'Don't let them grind you down, darling.'

She smiled at him. 'Shan't. Besides, you're here, and you're taking me out for lunch, so the day is definitely looking up. And I've snaffled some freebies that were sent to Mike, so I've had my little bit of revenge.'

'Well, normally I might have an ethical issue with that, but I'll make an exception.'

'Quite right. The man is amoral anyway. No point wasting my scruples on him.'

'Well, okay. What do you fancy, daughter of mine? Italian? Chinese?'

'Don't mind, so long as it's warm. Let's go here.'

Tucked into a corner booth, they studied the menu.

'We haven't done this for a while, have we, you and me?'

'Not for ages. It's nice. Do you remember when I was at university?'

Nicholas remembered. He had dropped by sometimes – work took him up that way – and bought her lunch from the deli on campus. He'd loved being there. University hadn't been an option for him, but the vicarious experience, seeing how it all worked, he'd loved it – and watching his too-thin daughter eat heartily – he'd liked that too. 'Long time ago.'

He was glad about Simon. They hadn't been so close when he was on the scene. He knew it was silly, but Nicholas hadn't liked the idea that what he had told her she might tell Simon later. It had made him uncomfortable. Maybe that was hopelessly insecure for a grown man, but it was how he had felt.

'I want to talk to you about your mum.'

Natalie had thought that might be it when he rang.

'But I don't think she'd want me to so I need to talk to you in confidence.'

'And not tell Mum?'

'And not tell Mum.'

'Okay. It's not the cancer, is it?' Natalie felt a drizzle of terror run cold down her spine.

'No, no. Physically she's fine.'

'Thank goodness. What is it, then?'

'She's depressed, Natalie, clinically depressed. She's been to the doctor, who gave her anti-depressants.'

'Mum?'

'Yes, your mum. And she would probably hate you knowing that, so you must promise me—'

Natalie waved aside his concern. 'I promise, Dad. You know you can trust me. Although it's nothing to be ashamed of . . .'

'But she is ashamed.'

'That's daft.'

'She feels like a failure, I think, and that she's letting me down, and that she's being ungrateful . . . lots of things. She's utterly wretched about it.'

'Poor Mum. I suppose it explains . . . you know . . . why she's been so weird lately. Do they think the scare last year triggered it?'

'It's possible, I suppose, but I think it's more complicated than that.'

Natalie listened.

'Your mum feels like nothing.' Nicholas was suddenly almost tearful. 'I'm sorry. I find this so difficult.' Natalie reached across the table and took his hand. The waitress arrived with their meals, and Nicholas looked at his lap while she offered them mustard and arranged their cutlery. Then he carried on talking.

'It's really hard to explain. You think there's some big drama, or some big secret or something, but it's all much more subtle than that. Your mum spent her whole adult life raising you three, and part of what she feels is that there's nothing else for her now that she's done that – apart from waiting around for Bridget to ask her to babysit or whatever. She loves you all so much, but she's found herself at the other side of it, and she knows that she could have been so much more. She's frustrated, and resentful, and thwarted, and angry. And she feels guilty and stupid about it, and as if she's taking it out on me and you girls, without you understanding why. Part of her thinks you three have no appreciation of the person she is, or even the person she might have been. She said she feels one-dimensional, and that she never realised it wouldn't be enough. And I think that the cancer scare made her believe she was going to die, which made her think about the life she'd lived, and now she's having a hard time coping with the feeling that she didn't live it as she wanted to.'

It was a lot to take in, and Natalie didn't understand it all. But she understood her father's distraught face. 'When did she tell you all this?'

'On her birthday. She broke down and it all came pouring out.'

'Poor you.'

'Poor her. She knows she's being bloody hard work. She thinks you're all fed up with her.'

'That's not true. It's just that it isn't easy – you never know what mood you're going to find her in. And I don't like the way she treats you. Even now you've explained all this, it isn't your fault, is it, Dad? And she's horrid to you.'

'You mustn't worry about that.'

'But I do. She jumps down your throat all the time. It's like she can't be bothered with you. Like you just irritate her all the time. I could feel myself wincing at Christmas, nearly every time she opened her mouth. You were starting to look like a rabbit caught in the headlights. God, Dad, three days of it was hard enough – but you have to put up with it all the time. It isn't fair on you.'

'I'll be fine. And it isn't all the time. She has bad days, that's all. Some days we're perfectly normal. Like we were before. You and your sisters only see her at her worst. Which is one of the hardest things about it. I love her, Natalie. I just want to help her.'

'How are you going to do that?'

Nicholas put his face into his hands, and rubbed his eyes wearily. 'I don't know.'

'How can I help?'

'Don't abandon her. Don't stop coming round, just because she's difficult. She needs you, Natalie, all three of you.'

'Okay, Dad. Okay.' Natalie was holding his hand again, across the food they were unlikely to eat. 'I promise.'

H for Hotel

'I thought you were broke.'

'I am. Freebie someone sent to the station. These guys sponsored some festival or something . . .'

'And they gave it to you?'

'Well, they sort of didn't happen to notice that it came in the post . . .'

'You're a dark horse.'

'Well, perhaps if the lazy shit ever opened his own mail, he might have found it.'

'Fair enough. Don't get me wrong. I have no problem with stealing from the rich to give to the poor – very Robin of Sherwood. I just wondered what we're going to do at this hotel. Where's it near?' Tom was holding the map and peering at it and the road signs were passing alarmingly fast. He'd forgotten quite how fast Natalie drove. Always as if she was late for the most important event in her life, hunched forward earnestly over the steering-wheel like an old lady.

'Oh, that doesn't matter. We're going to be having sex. Frankly, I hope the scenery takes second place.'

Tom had just taken a gulp of Coke, and spluttered it across the dashboard. 'What?'

'Well, I know it's been a while since you were in a serious relationship, but you surely can't have forgotten that it's a pretty important part of things. Sex, that is. I know they say it's like riding a bicycle, but I have a lot more gears than a three-speed, frankly. And how am I going to know about you if you don't show me you can cut the mustard in the bedroom department, if you know what I mean?'

'You're kidding. Cut the mustard? Where the hell did that come from?'

'I'm deathly serious.' She looked at him over the top of her glasses.

Although, of course, she didn't think she was. Sex with someone who wasn't Simon was a terrifying thought. She'd had lovers before, of course. Although describing them that way was probably overstating. 'Fumblers' might be better. They hadn't known what they were doing or how to get her to do what they wanted. Not the kind of lovers who see you naked in broad daylight. And not many of them, to be honest. She'd done all her real learning with Simon. She hadn't even liked sex much until him. Romance had always done it for her before. She might never have admitted it but sex was always the squelchy bit that came at the end of the romance and before the cuddling. Of course, Simon had shown her that she felt like that about it because the others hadn't been doing it properly. He said doctors made great lovers because they understood the human body better than other people. Natalie thought it might be more to do with all the practice he'd had: Simon had lost his virginity to his teenage babysitter when he was fifteen. His parents, who were naïve, kept paying her to come around long after Simon needed to be cared for because she'd got an A in English O level, and Simon struggled a little with that subject. His mother never really understood why he ended up with a C, but if she'd ever returned early from an evening out she would have discovered that what the babysitter was teaching him was not on the syllabus. After she'd gone off to university he'd moved on – and on, and on – and each girl had taught him a little something, so that by the time he had started with Natalie he was an expert. With him she had seldom required a huge amount of romance beforehand, and quite often, afterwards was more interested in doing it again than in being cuddled.

But someone else? After all those years with Simon? Maybe the best thing to do was get drunk and just do it. With anyone. So why not Tom? She knew where he'd been, pretty much. She knew he'd be kind. Why not with Tom? Alcohol was the key, maybe.

He laughed, delighted. 'You're bluffing, Nat.'

'Just you wait and see. I've an attaché case full of my best M&S lacies and a twelve-pack of Durex. I'm not afraid to use them. How about you?'

Tom hadn't had sex with anyone except himself since the previous summer. He'd never been much of a shagger, as Rob called them. He was one of those men who couldn't see the point of sex for the sake of it. He'd never been much interested in the porn videos that various friends and housemates had held in such high regard. The girls looked much the same after a while, with their implausible, unmoving boobs and their perfect round bums, and the act itself became dull and mechanical to watch. One particularly unsavoury friend of a friend at university had ridiculed him for this lack of 'normal' interest. Called him a poof. Which couldn't have been further from the truth. Tom loved women, and he loved sex, when it was the right kind. The sexiest part of a girl, for Tom, was her face when he was making love to her, or the secret bits that pushed her buttons, which only he knew about – like being kissed on the top curl of an ear, or stroked behind the knees.

He'd had a lot of girlfriends, and he'd slept with a fair few, but he hadn't lied, years ago, when he'd told Natalie that he hadn't been in love: there were many complex layers of caring. He hadn't fallen in love until he was twenty-five, and only once more since.

He hadn't been in love with the woman last summer, but he'd

thought she was pretty amazing. He'd been scuba-diving in the Red Sea, working towards his open-water PADI certificate, and she'd been on his course. She was Dutch, but her English was fluent, with a rolling accent he found instantly appealing. What had done it for him was her zest and enthusiasm. She was older than he, in her early forties; she had come to diving relatively late in life and loved it. She rattled off the bookwork, in a language that was not her native tongue, and was itching, every day, to get into the water. Back on the boat after a dive, she was always still for a while, as though readjusting to the air, then effusive about what she had seen and how it had felt. It was infectious, and rare among the hardened show-offs, dive log bores, and macho single men on the course. She made him think of mermaids.

One evening she'd asked him out, and after dinner they had walked along the beach, and she had said that she liked him very much and invited him to go back to her room with her. So he had, and she had made love the same way she dived – excitedly and heartily. And was quiet and reflective in his arms after-wards. They had done this every night until the end of the holiday. On the last night, as she lay beside him, she told him that she would always remember him, and how wonderful he had made her holiday. Her husband had left her, she said, the year before, and Tom had shown her that there was something else for her in the rest of her life. It was the first time she had mentioned anything about a life away from the Red Sea, and Tom had been so glad for her.

They hadn't exchanged numbers, or even surnames, and on the morning she left, she had kissed him lightly on the lips and said goodbye. There had been nobody since. And – presumably – Natalie had only slept with Simon in the last few years.

She had to be kidding. But it didn't stop Tom feeling nervous. He wasn't sure if it was Natalie's driving or the thought of having his – admittedly slightly rusty – technique evaluated so academically.

Perhaps he needn't have worried: twenty minutes later, Natalie turned triumphantly into the long country-house drive-way of a famous health farm. The kind where has-been footballers went to dry out, and pop stars went to do photo-shoots when they'd divorced their cheating husbands or lost the half-pound they had put on in pregnancy.

'You said it was a hotel!'

'And so it is.'

'It's a health farm.'

'Which is pretty much a hotel with . . . extra stuff.'

'Yeah, extra stuff for girls!'

'Rubbish. There'll be tons of blokes there.'

'There might be men, Natalie, but they won't be blokes.'

'Don't be so narrow-minded. You might like it.'

'I might not. I might rather stay home and push sticks under my fingernails.'

'They probably have a treatment like that here.'

'Treatment? It sounds like a madhouse. Frontal lobotomy, Miss Jones?'

'Treatment. And I got three each thrown in, so get ready.'

'And what about the sex? I've been promised sex. You can't just lead a boy on, Natalie.'

'Play your cards right. You never know. It's still a hotel.'

'Health farm,' Tom muttered, under his breath, while Natalie reversed the car into a parking space between an Audi TT and a soft-top Beetle. 'Health farm full of wankers.'

It was delicious to see him so uncomfortable. The dressing-gowns they were handed at the front desk were clearly one-size-fits-all, which meant that for Tom, and half the women there, it was a shortie.

'The English rugby team have stayed here, you know.'

'They're not here now, though, are they?'

'But there *are* men.'

There were three men, to be precise. Two halves of a couple, so clearly and delightedly gay that they practically sashayed down the corridors between 'treatments', and one middle-aged, paunched man in flip-flops who followed his vast wife around like a temple eunuch.

Natalie was studying their schedule like Indiana Jones on a mission. 'You've got a facial in half an hour, then an Indian head massage, and while you're doing that I've got a full-body blitz. Then we're meeting up in the thalassotherapy pool.'

'A few problems there, Nat. First, a facial? Then, what the hell is a thalasso-whatever?'

She consulted the brochure. 'It's a relaxing and stimulating vigorous massage by water jets in a pool rich with salt and minerals.'

'Thanks for clearing that up.'

'You're welcome. You've to wait here until someone comes to get you, and I'll see you down there in an hour.' Natalie winked at him and disappeared.

How could she do this to him after *Gone with the Wind*? Tom shifted uncomfortably in his seat.

An hour and a half later, he was waiting for her outside what looked like a giant Jacuzzi.

Natalie came in, and beamed at him happily. 'Nice hair!'

Tom smoothed his curls, self-consciously. They felt greasy. How could women love this shit?

'That was *wonderful*.' Natalie was practically purring. 'I feel fabulous. How was it for you?'

'Ridiculous!'

Natalie closely examined his face. 'Looking good.'

'Apparently I need to exfoliate more.'

'We'll pick something up in the boutique, shall we?'

'Right. What torture next?'

'The therapeutic water jets.'

'Oh, goodie.'

'Then dinner.'

'And what delights await there? Carrot juice and celery sticks?'

'Don't be daft. Health farms aren't what they used to be, you know. I bet you can even have a glass of wine.'

'I'll count the minutes.'

Their therapist came in, followed by a group of chattering housewives. She gave them an explanation of the beneficial effects of the imminent treatment, which Tom was not sure would stand up to serious scientific examination, then ushered them into the room and told them to take off their gowns. Tom was momentarily horrified. These women weren't going to be naked, were they?! Fortunately, they were all wearing costumes.

Tom was aware of seven pairs of middle-aged eyes appraising him frankly, and was quite glad he'd started going to the gym again in earnest, in the New Year. This must be how the Chippendales felt. He couldn't take his eyes off Natalie. She was fantastic. When had that happened? Her chest was fuller than he remembered, round and firm. Her skin was creamy, perfect and smooth. He wanted to touch it. And her bum, when she turned round to hang up her dressing-gown . . .

Tom was glad when they were told to get into the water. He was only human.

That wasn't any safer. Natalie climbed on to a sort of grilled lounger under the water, and lay there as the bubbles rose around her. Her head was thrown back and her eyes were closed. The bubbles made her chest bob. Bloody hell. No wonder blokes didn't spend time in places like this. He closed his eyes, stuck his head under a powerful jet and tried to think of something else.

They were allowed a glass of wine at dinner, but the menu 'recommended' no more than two a day, and the waitress removed their empty glasses with alacrity, which cramped their style a little. Tom felt strangely tired.

'That'll be all the detoxing, and the lavender oil and stuff.'

'Of course.'

'Do you fancy a last swim?'

He didn't, but she did, and ten minutes later she reappeared in that swimsuit and headed for the pool.

'Have you left a full hour since eating?' He spoke in his health-farm voice.

'Forty minutes. But we didn't eat much. Why don't you have your coffee facing the pool so you can see if I need rescuing?'

So he watched her. The pool was empty, and Natalie stood on the edge for a moment, then executed a perfect dive into the water. The ripples caught the moonlight flooding in through the skylights, and she seemed almost ethereal, gliding evenly up and down. Beautiful.

Tom was in trouble. He'd thought he knew what he felt. He hadn't expected waves of lust to break over him. He tried to tell himself that it was biological, that it wasn't because of Natalie. But, of course, it was. She had taken his breath away this afternoon, and it was gone again now.

The other times – on Dartmoor, and at the pool in a wetsuit – had been different. She had been making him laugh, making him care, maybe. More than he had thought he did, even. But she hadn't been making him want her.

Back in their room, Natalie changed into mumsy flannel pyjamas, which ought to have done the trick, but they didn't. He could see her breasts moving under the material, and when she put her arms above her head, the top rose and he could see her navel, the curve of her hip, which tantalised him.

'Why are you still looking so grumpy?' she asked.

'It's only ten o'clock. There's nothing good on TV, and there's no bloody bar in this place.'

'They have DVDs in Reception. We could go and check them out. And there may not be a bar but I've come prepared.' She opened the top drawer and produced a bottle of Jack Daniel's with some miniature cans of Coke. 'Contraband!'

Tom leapt up. 'You beauty!'

Back-to-back episodes of *The Simpsons* on TV became miraculously more entertaining after a couple of stiff Jack Daniel's, and an hour later, Tom was feeling more relaxed than he had done all day. 'How's your mum?' he asked.

'They've just been away, actually. Dad took her to this dead posh country-house place for her birthday. Part of his plan to cheer her up. She'll snap out of it, I'm sure. Sometimes a change of scene is what you need to make you see things differently, isn't it?' Was she talking about her mum or about him?

'Do you understand what's been going on with her?' He tried to concentrate on talking to her, although the whisky was going to his head. She was lying on her single bed, eyes closed. Five minutes ago he'd thought she was asleep, but then she'd sat up and poured herself another Jack Daniel's. If she was aware of him in some new way, she wasn't letting it show. He made himself not look at her. There was about fifteen inches between them.

'I don't know. Maybe. Can't explain it now. Wrong side of the whisky.'

'Do you think it's empty-nest syndrome?'

'Get you, with your fancy analysis!'

'Do you?'

It felt like Natalie didn't want to talk about it, and like he was pushing.

'Maybe. I know she lived for us.'

'What else could it be?'

'Lots of stuff. Dad retired, didn't he? That's pretty new. And maybe the cancer thing last year.'

'But that was okay.'

'I know . . . but I suppose it makes you think about your life . . . maybe.'

Tom nodded. 'I guess. I feel a bit sorry for your dad.'

'At least his marriage has only gone sour now. Your poor dad's had to put up with your mum for decades.' She didn't want to think about this now – she was too mellow. She'd go and see her mum when she got back.

'But he loves her.'

'He must do, to put up with that incessant chatting for so long. He's such a quiet man.'

'She's not so bad, you know They're yin and yang.'

Natalie laughed. 'Oh, I know. She's got a good heart, your mum. A big bloody gob, but a good heart. How else could she have raised you three? You're all right, aren't you?'

'Am I?'

She rolled on to her side, and smiled at him. 'You're very all right.'

'And you're very tipsy.'

'It's the aromatherapy oils.'

'Okay. Powerful things, mixed with Coke.' His smile twinkled.

'Exactly!' She closed her eyes again, and flopped on to her back. Suddenly she pulled her legs up and kicked them in the air, like a kid.

'What are you doing?'

'I'm happy.'

'Are you?'

'I am. And it's been a while.'

'I'm glad.'

Natalie looked at him, hard. 'Come here and give me a cuddle, Tom.' She didn't know exactly what she wanted or what he might want. She sat up, and moved her legs round so that she was on the edge of the bed.

Against his better judgement, Tom went to kneel on the floor in front of her. She put her arms round his neck, and pulled him to her. She smelt unlike herself, of all the potions and lotions she had been smothered in, but it was nice. And she felt nice, heavy on his shoulders. He put up his hand and let it rest on her soft hair.

She started it. She definitely started it.

She turned her head in the embrace and kissed his neck. Then his ear. Brought her hand to the back of his neck, and kissed his ear again. Tom pulled back, and gave an awkward laugh. 'Who am I?' he asked.

She opened her eyes briefly, then closed them again. Her voice, when she answered, was soft. 'You're definitely Tom. Tom.'

When saying his name didn't change what she was doing, Tom kissed her. She kissed him back, and pulled him closer, tighter.

It felt fantastic to be kissing her.

Tom stroked her back, over the flannel, then slipped his hands underneath and on to the skin he had wanted so badly to touch that afternoon. It felt as soft as he had imagined it would. His hands came round to the front, and across her stomach, and then up, under, to cup her breasts. He ran a speculative thumb across a nipple and groaned as he found them hard.

Natalie slipped off the bed on to his lap, and he pushed his hips into her, wanting more. For a while she met his thrusts, and they sat yearning into each other. But when Tom pulled at her pyjama bottoms, aching to get to her, something seemed to snap in her and she pulled back.

He was almost afraid to look at her face, and when he did, she was wide-eyed. Then she started to giggle. 'I'm sorry, Tom, I can't. I just can't take you seriously, not like that.'

'Did you ever think you would be able to?'

Natalie looked shamefaced. 'I don't know.'

Tom shucked her off his lap.

'I'm so sorry.' She put her hand on his arm. 'Really I am. I so didn't want to offend you, or hurt you.'

He didn't say anything. She patted his forearm. 'Or get you all wound up, for that matter. I haven't, have I? You know what I mean, don't you? It just doesn't feel right, does it? Us doing . . . that.'

It had felt pretty bloody right to him. But if only one of them was into it, it was pointless.

Her face was imploring him, as only Natalie's could, to let the moment pass, make things okay.

'Don't be cross with me, Tom. Please.'

'I'm not cross with you, Natalie.' He stood up. 'Forget it. Not my first drunken grope. Or the last, I shouldn't reckon.'

But he was cross. With both of them. With Natalie for saying she was going to sleep with him, and with himself for believing it. She'd so obviously been winding him up. She'd never really meant it. She was playing the game with him, that was all. And hadn't he asked for it? He'd been an idiot for trying it on. And after she'd had a few drinks.

'And we're okay, are we, really?'

He smiled, and said, yes, of course, they were okay, except that he hadn't quite forgiven her for the H, and she'd better watch out for the I.

Natalie climbed back on to her bed, and was asleep within

five minutes. She must have had more Jack Daniel's than he'd thought. Tom felt momentarily guilty. He wished he hadn't kissed her.

But then he lay down on the other bed and watched her. Her face was smooth and expressionless in sleep. Her mouth was slightly open. She had no idea what she was doing to him, did she? Because she didn't think of him that way, and she still hadn't really got the message that he did. That he fancied her rotten. That he was lying here now, with a stonking hard-on, wanting her. Someone who didn't know her as well as he did would call her a prick-tease. Maybe he would, too, if he didn't adore her so much. Perhaps he was making excuses for her behaviour, telling himself she didn't know what she was dealing with.

God, he was turned on. Frustrated. It had been a while, and he felt a dull ache. He thought about going to the bathroom, but that felt bad, so he turned over irritably, and tried to think about something other than ripping her pyjamas off. He had no choice now but to spend the night next to her. Then get up in the morning and pretend he hadn't been any more serious than she was. Let them both make a joke out of it to get over the embarrassment.

It took Tom ages to get to sleep.

March

Natalie and Anna

She'd come for her dad. She'd promised. It felt strange.

She hadn't lived here, with Mum and Dad, for years, but it looked the same.

She hadn't been since New Year. Normally she'd have been for her mum's birthday, but not this year. She'd been ready to make excuses, but there'd been no need. Mum hadn't seemed bothered either way when they spoke on the phone.

And Christmas had been so awful.

Long silences and high tension were so wrong in this house. It wasn't like that here. Even though she'd long since moved out, Natalie knew she still wanted to see her home and her parents as a sanctuary, a refuge. She felt hugely resentful of her mum for stopping it feeling like that.

Bridget was a bit too knackered to think about it, and Susannah was too selfish, but Natalie had thought about it a lot after Christmas. Realised that she was angry with her mum. Tried to reason with herself about it, and make it go away. Natalie wasn't good at confrontation, and the idea of fighting with her mother was abhorrent.

The conversation with Dad had made sense of some of it, and she was relieved not to be angry any more. But it still felt awkward.

She'd rung up and made an appointment to visit. At least that was what it had felt like.

It obviously felt just as weird to Anna. She made tea. 'Your dad's told you, I suppose.'

Natalie was wary. She didn't want to get her father into trouble.

'It's okay. I think he probably needed to tell somebody. And he's closest to you,' her mother went on.

'He's worried about you, that's why he told me.'

'And he asked you to come and see me, right?'

Natalie lied: 'No. Of course not. I don't need to be told to come. You're my mum.'

Anna smiled broadly for the first time since she'd arrived. 'You never were any good at lying, Natalie, even as a child. Susannah lied like other people breathe, and Bridget always went along with the majority, but you . . . I always knew with you.'

She was right.

'Besides, not one of you has been to see me voluntarily since New Year.'

'Susannah's been away . . .'

'Oh, I know, and Bridget's had another baby, and you've got your own things going on. I know all that.'

There was an awkward pause.

'And I also know that no one has wanted to come. I know how I've been. I can't blame any of you.'

'Christmas was a bit difficult.'

'It was for me too.'

'Was it?' It had felt like she hadn't wanted them all there. Natalie hadn't understood why.

Anna was staring into the middle distance. 'I stood in the kitchen with the turkey, all arranged on the platter, as usual. The same platter. Bird cooked the same way – butter-basted and golden. All those stupid little sausages wrapped in bacon. More bacon across the breast. Same stuffing, the one everyone

likes. The one everyone expects. And I wanted – more than I've
ever wanted to do anything in my whole life, I think – to pick it
up and throw it across the room. I wanted to hear the smash of
that platter, and watch the turkey explode on the floor.'

'Mum!'

'I felt like I was going mad.'

'Why didn't you tell us – tell Dad at least?'

'Because I was afraid to say it out loud.'

Natalie stared at her mum. Who could sew, and make papier-
mâché, and play the best party games in the world, and knew
the names of flowers. Who had kissed her grazed knees, and
stroked her fevered forehead, and held her hand on the walk to
school every day, and waited every day to bring her home and
listen, as though it was really interesting, to everything she had
to say about her day.

And realised that now it was her turn.

Lucy

The swimming-pool was always quiet at this time in the
morning. The office workers and commuters were long gone,
and the rush of mums hadn't started. They were all nattering at
the school gates, or picking up a few things in the supermarket,
or gathering for coffee. Lucy and Marianne liked to get there
early. Then they could have a lane each and plough up and
down for twenty minutes, uninterrupted by the flailing limbs of
others. By the time the pool got busy, they were having their
ten-minute reward Jacuzzi, and by the time there was a queue
for the showers, they would be on their way home.

Lucy closed her eyes and enjoyed the feeling of her muscles
pulling her through the water, weightless and silent. She
thought about Alec. She always seemed to, lately. It passed
the time. She didn't count lengths any more. She swam for

twenty blissful minutes, imagining things she should not. Alec undressing her. Alec kissing her. Alec's full length along hers. The two of them making love on a beach at night. Or slow-dancing under trees filled with fairy-lights.

Then she opened her eyes and saw Marianne's head emerging from the water, and wondered if she should feel like a bitch. Was it normal to think about someone else's husband like that? Or was it harmless?

In the changing rooms she looked surreptitiously at Marianne. She had a beautiful body. Smooth and taut and the colour of honey all year round. What could Alec possibly see in her, when his wife looked like that?

Yet she knew he did see something in her. That there was a connection. An invisible cord that they could never explore, or discuss, or acknowledge to anyone, even to each other, but which joined them whenever they were in the same place.

And still she wondered why she didn't feel worse about it. Lucy knew she wasn't a bad person. She was a loyal friend, wasn't she? She always had been. She had friends she'd known since nursery.

She told herself she didn't need to feel bad because nothing would ever happen. They wouldn't let it. She never would. And she guessed that Alec couldn't be as wonderful as she thought he was and be the kind of man who would do something like that to his wife. So it was safe, this schoolgirl fantasising. It was harmless. An ego boost, a diversion from the everyday.

They weren't doing anything wrong. That was what she told herself.

Natalie

Rose was cross with her, and Natalie hated that. They were having brunch with Bridget a few days after the health-farm débâcle, as Rose had insisted on calling it since Natalie had rung her that Sunday afternoon and told her what had happened. Almost all of it. She hadn't confessed to telling him, en route, that there would be sex. Good job. They were cross enough.

'It's no good looking at me with those puppy-dog eyes, Nat. I'm not going to let you off the hook. You had no bloody business kissing him. I don't care how much Jack Daniel's you'd had. Am I right, Bridge?'

'Absolutely. Poor bloke. Take him to some health farm – when you could have taken us, by the way – get him all wound up and not go through with it. Really rotten.'

'So you're saying I should have done it?'

'We're saying you should never have put yourself in that position in the first place, Nat, not that you should have done something you didn't want to. But I mean, come on, you were asking for trouble, weren't you? Two of you in the same hotel room. That's some dangerous game you're playing, girlie. What the hell did you think would happen?'

'You two are ganging up on me now.'

'We're not seven-year-olds! We're not ganging up. We just agree that you've behaved less than well.'

Natalie knew they were right.

Rose was still talking: 'We know Simon hurt you, Nat, but that doesn't give you *carte blanche* to lumber about doing whatever damage you like to other people.'

'He said it was okay.'

'And maybe it is. I don't know how Tom's feeling. My point is that you don't either.'

'I think she does. A bit,' Bridget was saying. 'And I think she quite likes having him lavish attention on her.'

'Don't talk about me in the third person, like I wasn't here. And incidentally, who wouldn't like having a great bloke lavish attention on them?'

'Which is all fair enough, so long as no one is getting hurt. And that includes Tom.'

'I honestly think you're worrying about nothing.'

Bridget raised her palms in surrender. 'All right then, if you won't be told. I wash my hands. I've got to go anyway. Karl'll be wondering where I am. Two children under two for two hours makes him a disagreeable boy. And I've got to get nappies on the way home.'

She kissed them both and stood up. 'How's Mum?'

Natalie got to her feet too. 'Better. I've been to see her a few times.'

'She told me. I've been over quite a bit, too with the kids. She loves it.'

Natalie was glad Bridget was making the same effort. They hadn't talked about it, not properly. She remembered something that Bridget had said to her, though, after Christina had been born, that being a mother made you think a lot about being a daughter.

'Suze is going to come at Easter, isn't she?' Bridget said.

'Far as I know. Mum's looking forward to it, isn't she? I think, after Christmas, she really wants us all to be together.'

'Someone should talk to Suze before she gets there. You know what she can be like.'

Natalie nodded. 'Mum says she's the one who's most like her.'

'That's why they spark so much, I suppose.'

'I'll talk to her.'

'Great.' Bridget kissed her again and urged Rose, over her shoulder, to 'Talk some sense into her about Tom, will you?'

'I've got a plan, actually,' Rose smiled.

'Oh, no.'

'Oh, yes. I think this alphabet game is fine up to a point, but it seems to me that you need to meet some new people. Peter and I are having a dinner party, and you're coming, and I'm inviting new people for you to meet alone.'

'That sounds gruesome.'

'Thanks a lot.'

'No, Rosie, you know what I mean. Being set up sounds gruesome. I shan't come.'

'We'll see about that . . .' Rose sat back in the banquette and folded her arms like Les Dawson across the washing-line.

I for IKEA

'This is definitely Dante's seventh circle of hell. No, it's the eighth. I just cannot believe that people come here seriously – I mean other than for bets, punishment or alphabet games.'

'Well, they do. In their thousands.'

'I know. They're all bloody here today.'

It had taken them fifty minutes to park on the top storey of the blue and yellow car park, and now they had joined a stream of lemmings on the escalator, all clutching stubby pencils, rulers and huge blue plastic loot bags.

'Don't crack on like it was my idea to come, Tom. I was your letter, if you remember . . .'

'Yes, well, blame Serena. She's the one who wants me and Rob to have this stuff.'

Serena had requested more chairs and a matching console for the meeting space. She had waited until she knew the letter I was coming up, then suggested that the yellow and blue jungle might be a good place for Tom to take Natalie. 'I know. Genius.' She and Rob had laughed.

'Besides,' Rob had gone on, 'you're the one into DIY and this is the kingdom of the flat-pack, so I'd have thought you'd be thrilled.'

Natalie had laughed. She'd asked for it, she supposed. '*Touché*! But what exactly is this supposed to be showing us about each other? At least with D there was a point. Can he, or can he not, put shelves up straight and strong?'

Between kitchens and sofa-beds, a red-headed toddler lay spreadeagled in their path, screaming angrily. His mother, heavily pregnant, was sprawled across a sofa-bed about twenty feet away and shouted, 'Shut up, Callum,' but Callum was beyond verbal reasoning, teetering very near the edge of a fit. Politely, Tom and Natalie steered their trolley off the walkway and round the little boy, as the twenty trolley-wielding shoppers before them had.

'I know they were straight. How about strong?'

'Haven't put anything very heavy on them yet. But, believe me, you'll hear about it if I put my collected works of Walt Whitman and Shakespeare up there and they can't take the weight.'

'Don't see that as an imminent risk. The latest Penny Vincenzi, maybe.'

'Oy! I read the classics.'

Tom raised an eyebrow.

'Okay. I did read the classics. I own them, anyway, which is all anyone really does with those books. They're in Mum and Dad's loft, I think.'

'Don't judge everyone by your own shoddy standards of integrity and intellect.'

'All right, smartass. What was the last classic you read, apart from *Classic Car Monthly*?'

He didn't miss a beat. 'It would have been the new Ian McEwan.'

'That doesn't count!'

'Why not? A classic of the future.'

'Tenuous. And maybe you did, but did you really, really enjoy it? I mean, if you went on *Desert Island Discs*, for example, right now . . .'

'Love to. I've had a bit of a thing about Sue Lawley ever since *Nationwide*.'

'Be serious. If you did, you'd say something pretentious and clever, wouldn't you, for your book, but you wouldn't mean it?'

'I might.'

'Come off it. Nick Hornby. At best.'

'What would you say, then?'

In Bathrooms, a couple were arguing about towel colours. Apparently he was a stupid colour-blind git while his wife, allegedly, 'wouldn't know good taste if it smacked [her] in the arse'.

'Well . . . you get the Bible and Shakespeare, don't you? So I'd have to say . . . the fattest sex-and-shopping novel I could find in the bookshop. Lots of characters. Lots of filthy sex scenes.'

'You so would not say that on Radio Four!' Tom laughed at her. 'What about music?'

'That's much tougher. It's a different ten every time, isn't it?'

'Not for me. Rolling Stones, Cream, plus Clapton's live "Layla", bit of Queen . . .'

A small, balding man was fighting with two trolleys that were stuck firmly together. Despite the abundance of single trolleys available to him, he seemed determined to have one of the conjoined ones. He was swearing under his breath, and a thin sheen of sweat had appeared on his forehead. Tom manoeuvred their trolley around him, and they left the man behind.

'And you'd have the nerve to admit to all that on Radio Four? No Schubert? No duet from *The Pearl Fishers*?'

'Nope. I've nothing to prove to anyone. Like I said. We're not all so worried about what everyone else thinks of us, Nat.'

She grimaced at him and wondered briefly about smacking his smug face with a three-pound IKEA frying-pan.

'Bet I know what your best song would be, if you weren't doing the whole Schubert thing, that is . . .'

'And . . .'

'Katrina and the Waves. "Walking on Sunshine".'

Damn him. 'Maybe,' she admitted grudgingly.

Tom nudged her. 'Come on. It's your favourite, I know. You used to call it your happy song.'

'You know too much.' She still did. Occasionally, alone at home, she put it on, turned it up loud and danced like a crazed thing.

'And I'm still here. Flattering, don't you think?'

It probably was. Natalie changed the subject. 'Back to IKEA. Although a desert island sounds infinitely more appealing. What are you here to show me about you?'

'What great taste I have?' They'd entered the warehouse bit, and were searching for the aisle and shelf where Serena's booty ought to be stored. Natalie pushed the trolley and Tom walked a few paces ahead.

'If you had great taste, we'd be at Heal's. Next?'

He stopped, triumphant, and began to lift flat-packed office chairs on to the trolley. 'How manly am I?' The trolley had no brakes and the wheels moved it forward so that he couldn't set the pack straight on the metal base. He tried kicking it into place, but the box was longer than his leg, and he couldn't reach. He dropped it awkwardly and tried to wedge the trolley against the shelves.

Natalie stood back, grinning broadly. 'Yeah. Dead hunky.'

'Piss off and give me a hand, will you?'

Like most men, Tom's usually effervescent sense of humour and ability to laugh loudest at himself was most under threat in places like IKEA. 'Stop laughing.'

'Sorry.' Natalie made a mock-serious face, and braced herself against the trolley while Tom put two more chairs on it.

'Where's the console?'

Tom consulted his scrap of paper. 'Should be . . . just . . . Oh, fuck.'

'What?'

'Out of bloody stock.' He kicked the trolley. 'I bloody hate this shithole.'

'I get it!' Natalie proclaimed. 'You've brought me here to show me how you can keep your head when all around are losing theirs. Like in that Rudyard Kipling poem. Then you'll be a man, my son, or something, isn't it? Good job, jobbed.'

For the second that Tom raised his face to look at her, there was no laughter in his eyes. But as he advanced towards her, hands raised as if to strangle her, the corners of his mouth turned upwards, and by the time his fingers were round her neck, pushing her back against the shelves, the smile had reached his eyes. 'And what do you want to show me about you? How much fun you can make everything every day? Hey?' His smile was very close to her mouth.

Natalie pulled away his hands, and darted out quickly from under his arms. 'Not my game, mate. Not my game.' But she was smiling in the same way.

'Let's get out of here.'

The couple who had had a disagreement about towels were now having an amazingly similar chat about bathroom cabinets.

'You know what happens to seals and penguins and stuff if they put them in pools too small for them in zoos? Disturbed, repetitive behaviour? Clearly happens to humans too . . .'

Natalie laughed, and they pushed their hard-won chairs towards the pay desk and the natural light they could see on the other side, beyond the plastic hot dogs and the bottomless Pepsis.

Natalie

A dinner party. Party? Not so much. God, this was dull! Even Rose was acting all peculiar tonight. As though she had aged about ten years, and developed a sudden interest in reading the *Guardian*. Which Natalie happened to know she hadn't. The *Daily Mail* would be a step up for Rose, who was infinitely more interested in who was sleeping with whom than in who was at war. She didn't think she'd had, or heard, a proper laugh all evening. She glanced at her watch, and tried to disguise her dismay. Eleven o'clock. She couldn't possibly think about leaving until midnight or Rose would sulk for weeks. She stifled a yawn. Rose was no Nigella Lawson. The food was okay, but the ambience left a lot to be desired. Pete's bosses were here, his accountant bosses, with their wives and girlfriends. Enough said. Rose hadn't told her it was going to be quite so grown-up or she might have made an excuse. Five past eleven. She still might.

The man on her left was clearly intended to be 'hers' – Pete's suggestion, Rose had whispered to her in the hallway, thus absolving herself of all responsibility. Which was fortunate. Because he was a bad choice.

Funnily enough, both Simon and Tom would have been hilarious about this. One kinder, perhaps, but both fairly scathing and probably quite badly behaved.

Tom had gone out with Patrick and Rob tonight for a curry. She could have been with Lucy or Serena. Or at home with a face mask on – or poking cocktail sticks into her eyes. Most other possibilities seemed appealing right now.

She couldn't figure out whether this guy meant to be offensive or was just thick enough to assume that everyone else shared his views on homosexuals, asylum-seekers and Oasis.

When Rose got up to collect the dessert dishes, she winked at Natalie and twitched her head to the side. Natalie jumped up and followed her into the kitchen, balancing a few plates in one hand.

'Christ, Rosie. How did I offend Pete?'

'I know, I know. I'm sorry. He's a complete tit, isn't he?'

'What on earth made Pete think he and I might get on?'

'I don't think it was a deep and meaningful connection he foresaw. He just said he'd only joined the firm recently, and that he was good-looking. And he is, in a way, isn't he?'

'He's all right until he opens his bloody mouth.'

'I'm sorry, babe. Really. God, it's dull in there.' The real Rose was back. She put her old persona back on when she'd stepped through the kitchen door and tied the Cath Kidston apron round her waist. Now she was taking cellophane off the kind of cheeseboard that hadn't come from the supermarket and didn't have any Cheddar on it.

'What the hell is that? It can't possibly be cheese.'

'Don't panic. It's an organic fig cake. Goes really well with cheese, apparently.'

'So does Branston pickle. Chuffing hell, Rose, cheeseboards are for thirty-somethings.'

'We *are* thirty-somethings, Nat.'

'Speak for yourself. I'm not that kind, at least. Have you got anything to drink out here?'

'Cooking brandy. I flambéd the kidneys in it earlier. There's loads left.'

'Thank you, Dr Lecter. That'll do. Pass it here.'

Rose reached for two glasses from the cupboard. 'Me too.'

They drank the first shot in one, then poured some more.

'Do you think this'll make Enoch Powell any more attractive?' Rose giggled.

'Not a chance.'

'So . . . my noble experiment didn't go so well.'

'Are we talking about the food?'

'No! The food was sublime.'

'Course it was, honey. I like my pork escalopes rare.'

Rose smacked her arm lightly. 'It was cooked to perfection.'

'Ask me tomorrow.'

'I mean my experiment to help you realise that there are men out there who aren't either Simon or Tom . . .'

'If that in there represents the cream of that particular crop, I'm in big, big trouble.'

The brandy tasted a little like meths but got more palatable with each mouthful.

'Besides,' Natalie added, 'I thought you were a yes vote for Tom.'

'I am, I think. I love Tom. I just don't want you to fall into something because it's easy and comfortable. And because you're afraid that's all there is. I want it to be a conscious decision. That's the only way it can work.'

Natalie looked fondly at her friend. 'You really love me, don't you?'

'Of course I do, you soppy eejit.'

'And you really love Pete, don't you?'

'God, yes.'

'That's really lovely. I love you too.'

'I know.'

'And I love Pete. Despite . . .' she gesticulated with the brandy bottle in the direction of the door '. . . this, I really love him. You two are so great together.'

'And you really love cooking brandy as well, apparently.' Rose prised the bottle out of Natalie's hand, and put it back beside the stove.

Pete came in. 'Everything all right out here?'

Rose smiled. 'Better than in there.'

'Christ, I know. Mogadon in human form. What the hell were we thinking?'

'I was thinking I'd lost the will to live.'

'Can I die in here with you?' Pete jumped up on to the worksurface. 'I don't think they'll notice I'm missing.'

'Stay with us, then. Come over to the dark side . . . cooking brandy?'

Pete shook his head, then nodded. 'You two are incorrigible.'

'Absolutely. Then perhaps you'd like to explain to Natalie exactly what you thought she and your friend might have in common.'

Lucy

'Chicks' night out?' The waiter was grinning at her. He was absurdly young.

'Definitely hens, I'm afraid.' Lucy smiled back.

'I'll bring these over for you.'

'Thanks – I can manage.' She picked up five wine glasses in one hand and tucked the two bottles of wine under the other arm.

The other mums were being pretty loud for an early-evening Monday in town. It was only seven, and they'd had two bottles already. She normally avoided these things like the plague. School dinners and Mark Warner holidays weren't her favourite subjects to discuss over a glass of average Chilean red, but just now they beat a night in front of the telly with Patrick. He didn't want to talk to her – or do anything else with her for that matter – so he feigned interest in every wildlife, home-improvement and reality show going. It was driving her mad, and she had shut the door behind her this evening with relief.

'Come on, Lucy.'

'We want to know how you and Patrick got together.'

'Yeah! Did you know Lorna and Steve were at the same infant school?'

Lorna was anxious not to sound too dull. 'But we didn't see each other for about ten years after O levels.'

'Sweet!'

'We were just a bog-standard dull office romance. Eyes met across a crowded boardroom sort of thing.' This was Sasha. 'Actually, it took me about three months to get him to stop concentrating on his figures and start focusing on mine, but I got there in the end!' Her laugh always ended in a little snort. It was the kind of line Lucy knew she had used for years but it still made her snort.

'So what about you?'

'Let me catch up a minute, will you? I haven't even had a glass of wine yet. Someone else go.' Lucy wasn't sure she could talk about it tonight.

'Marianne? What about you and Alec?'

Lucy felt a little shiver. Of anticipation or dread? She didn't want to hear this, but Marianne had leant in conspiratorially, and was warming to her subject. 'Qantas. Economy section, of course. Christmas 1985. I was visiting, Alec was going home.'

'I'd forgotten he was Australian.'

'His accent has almost gone, hasn't it?'

'And.'

'Well, you know how on those long-haul flights you walk up the aisle of the plane in complete dread of who you're going to end up sitting next to – like, please don't let me get anyone vast, or smelly, or mind-numbingly dull? – for twenty-four hours? I got him. Actually, there was someone pretty vast, smelly and mind-numbingly dull in the window-seat, but he swapped with me and went into the middle so he had her, not me.'

'What a gent!'

'Exactly!'

'And?'

'We just started nattering. And it was the quickest flight. We

landed in Bombay and Bangkok, got off and stretched our legs –
I remember him buying Chanel No. 5 in Duty Free for his mum
– but the time in the air passed really fast. I didn't even watch
the films.'

'Ah!'

Sasha was waggling her eyebrows lasciviously. 'Did you . . .
you know . . . mile-high club and all that?'

'No one ever actually does that. It's an urban myth.' Lorna
shook her head.

'Certainly not,' Marianne added. Then paused. 'Not on the
way out, at least.'

Sasha snorted again. 'Tell us more.'

Lucy took a long drink. She wasn't enjoying this.

'We swapped numbers and stuff, but he was incredibly busy
with family and I was doing my own thing – I met up with some
people out there, these friends of my parents, who had kids my
own age. I'd gone to spend Christmas with them and Alec and I
didn't see each other. We spoke a couple of times – he rang on
Christmas Day – and there was a sort of plan to meet up at
Sydney Harbour on New Year's Eve, but that never happened.
You know what it's like. I suppose I didn't think I'd see him
again, and that was sort of okay – I mean, we'd got on really
well on the plane, but you're young, aren't you, and things are a
bit more easy come, easy go? I really liked him, but I wasn't in
love or anything stupid like that.'

The others were engrossed.

'But he rang me at the beginning of January, and we did
spend a day together – on Bondi Beach, actually. A great day.
It was hot as hell, and really crowded, and we just had – I
don't know – one of those golden days, you know? Perfect
days. The kind you'd like to bottle . . .' Marianne's voice
trailed off.

Sasha prodded her elbow, and she started talking again: 'And that night – although I didn't know this at the time – he changed his flight home, so that he would be on the same plane as me. He hadn't been due to fly out for another couple of days.'

'He must have been smitten.'

She smiled shyly. 'I guess so.'

'And?'

Marianne giggled. She sounded about fifteen. 'Well, let's just say it isn't entirely urban myth.' Uproar. 'You have to be the right heights . . . and quite quick – and a hell of a lot more brazen than I am now!'

'I cannot believe you!'

'I cannot believe I've just told you that. Alec would kill me. He's coming in, in a minute. I got a sitter – he's going to take me to the cinema. Don't you dare let on!'

'I shall look at him in an entirely new light.' The others were still laughing excitedly.

'Oh, come on – it isn't that *risqué*, is it?' Marianne looked them in turn. 'Don't tell me none of you has ever done stuff like that? Sasha? Didn't you guys ever do it on the boardroom table when you thought everyone else had gone home?'

'Certainly not!'

'Really?'

'We tried it on the beach once, but Steve got sand in a very sore place, which knocked it on the head, if you'll pardon the phrase.' Lorna giggled.

More laughter.

Sasha was trying desperately to think of something to add. 'We did it in the car once.'

'Well done, Sash. Ten points. You'd have got more if the car had been on a cross-Channel ferry at the time or parked outside a supermarket.'

'You're disgusting, the lot of you.'

'*Were* disgusting, you mean. It's been a while since Steve and

I did it anywhere other than bed. And I mean beds on holiday, by the way.'

Marianne laughed. 'You're exaggerating, surely?'

'Only a bit.'

Lucy tried to read Marianne's expression. They never normally talked about this sort of thing. She hadn't even known how they'd met. She tried to interpret Marianne's raised eyebrow.

'What about you, Lucy?'

'Yes. You're being very quiet.'

'Do you mean have I done it in an aeroplane loo? No.'

'Not that. You and Patrick. How did you two get together?'

'No way – I can't follow Marianne's story.'

'Rubbish. I've heard this – it's lovely.'

'How had you heard it?' Lucy didn't mean to sound so sharp.

'Patrick told me,' Marianne answered, 'a long time ago.'

'Well, his story might not quite stack up with mine.'

Marianne's face was quizzical. Lucy knew she sounded fed up, and saw Marianne make up her mind to rescue her, even if she didn't know why.

But she didn't have to. The wide oak door to the bar swung open and Alec came in, his eyes scanning the room for them.

Lucy had a sudden mental image of him, trousers round his ankles, hammering into Marianne in an aeroplane loo. It made her feel turned on, jealous and angry. What the fuck was wrong with her?

Sasha couldn't resist a snort when she said hello.

'Having a nice time, ladies?'

'Illuminating,' Lorna said.

Marianne stood up and kissed him. 'And a little bit drunken, if the truth be known, love.'

'On a Monday night, too!' His eyes were sparkling with amusement. He bent to kiss Lucy on both cheeks, his hand on the back of her neck with just a little too much pressure. He smelt wonderful – wood and smoke. Familiar and forbidden.

'What are you guys going to see?'

'That new Keanu Reeves film, the one that opened on Friday,' Marianne told them.

'Chick-flick, I'm afraid.' Alec shook his head ruefully.

Marianne winked at Lucy. 'And you're coming too, aren't you, Luce?'

Was she? Marianne was still on a mission to rescue her. Why did everyone always do that? But Marianne had taken Lucy's coat from the stand with her own and was proffering it now.

The others topped up their glasses. Husbands were at home looking after children, and they were just getting started. Now that Marianne and Lucy were off they could return to school dinners and Mark Warner holidays.

Outside, Marianne put her arm through Lucy's. 'You can, you know, come with us, if you want. Can't she Alec?'

He didn't answer.

'Hang on a second, let me get some money.' Marianne turned to the cashpoint and fumbled in her bag.

Lucy stood awkwardly, shuffling from foot to foot. When she glanced at Alec, he was staring straight into her eyes, his face unreadable. 'Course she can come,' he said.

'I'd better get back.'

'That's okay too.' Marianne was tucking notes into her purse. 'Long as you're all right.'

'I'm fine.'

Marianne stared hard at her. 'You're not.'

'I am.'

'Okay. Go. Go home to Patrick.' She kissed her friend, then turned back to Alec and linked her arm through his.

'Night,' he said, and Lucy mumbled in reply, then turned to cross the road to where her car was parked.

'Lucy?' Marianne was calling her.
'What?'
'Yours is a nice story too. It really is.'

The supermarket cruising had been only the beginning, really. She was still married to Will when Patrick first spotted her, pottering up and down the aisles, filling her trolley, stroking the top of Bella's downy head and stopping to let old ladies admire her.

Still with Will. Still a family. Still believing she had the perfect, happy life.

No one ever really believed those stories, did they? The girl who comes into Casualty with food-poisoning and ends up having a baby. The baby born at the bottom of the garden because the mother was hanging out the washing and didn't have time to get back to the house when the contractions started. The mile-high club. The husband who disappears with absolutely no warning. Cynics tell you that there must have been signs, clues.

And they're right, of course: Will had left signs and clues. And she had had months to find them. After he'd gone. Because, of course, she hadn't been looking for them beforehand. She had been catatonic. She had been euphoric. She had been obsessed with Bella – with every infinitesimal detail of Bella's routine – how much milk she took down and brought up, how long, and in exactly which position she slept, which perfect white, pink, aqua or yellow outfit she would wear today, whether she was just warm enough or too warm. Whether she herself was ever going to be able to wear clothes without elastic waists, or stop leaking, or watch the news without crying.

She had thought that Will felt the same about Bella. Like all the other mums from the antenatal classes, who had all read the same chapters in the same books, she had worried about juggling her role as a mother with that of being Will's wife. One of her new friends had sat at a coffee morning, when the babies were about seven weeks old, taken a deep breath and told them that she was going to drink a large brandy and shag her husband that evening if it killed her, which she thought that it might, on account of the Bayeux tapestry of stitches she'd had after her episiotomy. She said her mother had told her to forget lying back and thinking of England, but to think of the exercise, do a few pelvic-floor exercises at the same time and remember that a serviced husband was a happy husband. Fifteen minutes, that's all it takes, she had told her, and think of the benefits. They had all laughed, some more nervously than others. Lucy had let Will back into her bed, and into her body, weeks earlier than that. The health visitor had said it was okay, if you wanted to, and they both had. Or, at least, she had, and she'd thought he had.

Afterwards she had wondered whether he was repelled by her. Or whether he was confused, like the books talked about – the hackneyed madonna-whore theme.

It was a long time before she stopped trying to figure out what she had done.

You'd have thought damage like that would have made her so suspicious, so untrusting – surely it took some getting over.

But not with Patrick. He wasn't like that.

He'd talked to her, that first day in the supermarket, even though she'd had Bella strapped to her chest. He'd joined the queue behind her, and made grocery small-talk. He'd put her shopping bags into the trolley for her so that she could push them to her car. He had a nice face. And she remembered it, the encounter as well as the face, because she had been so chuffed to learn that a man – a random, free-thinking man – could still find her attractive. She could tell, of course – even through her sleepless fug – that he did. The middle-aged woman on the checkout, so bored with her job that she barely made eye-contact with most customers who passed her till, even she had noticed. Not threatening, not invasive, not dangerous in any way, but definitely interested. Smitten, she'd have said.

Lucy remembered it well enough to recognise him the next time they met at the supermarket. She was having a watery coffee in the grim canteen annexe, Bella asleep in her arms, when he passed with a tray and sat down at the next table. They smiled nervously at each other and Lucy ventured a hello.

He was interesting. Nice-looking, in a watered-down sort of way. His brother, Tom, was brighter, somehow, the same looks, but more vivid, and stronger. Tom's hair was darker and curlier, and his eyes were darker, too, the lashes thicker. But she met Patrick, not Tom, and nice-looking was a good way to describe Patrick. With one long dimple, on the left cheek, that appeared only when he really smiled, as he had in the canteen when she'd said hello.

He always shopped on his way home from work, he told her. He wore a blue suit. She always shopped at this time because Bella was calm, she replied. He had to shop several times a week, he said, because he was a lousy cook, and couldn't plan ahead. She shopped several times a week because she liked being out and about with the baby. Now that the weather was nicer she was walking, putting the shopping into the bottom of the pram.

The third time he said, 'We have to stop meeting like this,' as they passed in the aisle, but Lucy was being pursued by a grumpy woman with three rampaging children imprisoned, standing, in her trolley, grabbing to right and left for random goods, so they couldn't talk.

Then he had sat beside her on the bench outside, and they had both eaten a Cornetto in the late-afternoon sunshine. He was in personnel management, he told her. That fitted. You would want to tell him things – he had that open sort of face, patient. He had loosened his tie and taken off his jacket. He leant back, after he'd finished his ice-cream, and sighed contentedly. They weren't flirting, and he didn't make her pulse race, but she had started to look out for him when she shopped, half expecting to see him round every corner.

By the sixth time, Will had left her. He had got home late one night, after she had fallen asleep, and she had stirred when he came to bed, acknowledging his arrival with a murmured hello and a perfunctory pat on his shoulder. But she was tired. The next morning, Bella slept uncharacteristically late, and Lucy woke, at first relaxed and refreshed, then almost instantly panicking. She ran to Bella's nursery in time to see her daughter raise tiny arms to punch the air in triumphant wakefulness, and put her hand on her pounding heart, telling herself how silly she was to have worried, and feeling the calm descend once more. Will must have gone to work so she took Bella into their bed for a precious half-hour of raspberry-blowing and gurgling. When they got downstairs, she tied the baby into her bouncing chair and collected a clean bottle from the steriliser. The letter was propped against the tin of SMA, which was logical, at least. Bella was a hungry baby, he knew that, and needed two good shots of formula milk every day to supplement Lucy's supply.

Lucy, I can't do this. I'm sorry, but I have to go. Will

That was it. Nothing to pore over, analyse. How long had he sat and wondered what to write? Had he started with 'Dear Lucy', then scrubbed it out, anxious not to convey her dearness to him. Had he contemplated asking for a divorce, or explaining to her that the home-and-contents insurance policy was in the top right-hand drawer of the desk in the living room, or giving her one single clue as to why he couldn't do this? He hadn't given her much to go on.

Lucy made up the seven-ounce feed, warmed the bottle in a saucepan of boiling water on the stove, sat down in the wicker chair in the corner of the kitchen that faced the television and fed Bella. She didn't cry and she didn't tell a soul. Not her mother. Not the well-intentioned health visitor, the bank manager or the girls at the coffee mornings. No one. A combination of shock, pride and fear made a liar of her. Eventually, she knew, it would have to come out. There were things to sort out, of course. But for two weeks Will was just away on a business trip, for anyone who asked.

Until she bumped into Patrick at the supermarket. She still didn't know, never would know, why she had done it. Where was her pride when she had seen him, basket in hand, choosing a steak in the beef, pork and lamb aisle and just started to cry?

J for Job Swap –

Rose poured herself another glass of wine, while Natalie served up two steaming bowls of pasta.

'You've got to help me,' Natalie was saying. 'My H was frankly disastrous, and his I wasn't much better. I need a good one for J.'

'Since when did you care so much?'

'I don't *care* care. I just like it. You kind of get into it after a while. I'm having fun.'

'I'm glad. Simon?'

'Simon who?'

'Simon-who-broke-you-into-a-million-pieces and left-you-lying-around-for-the-rest-of-us-to-pick-up Simon.'

'Oh, him!' Natalie wound a strand of spaghetti round her fork. 'Was I really that bad?'

'You were worse.'

'I'm sorry.'

'Don't be. It's in my job description. Under "Tell You When Your Bum Looks Big".' Rose hummed her approval of the first mouthful of pasta; the sauce dribbled down her chin. Natalie handed her a napkin. 'Actually, it could have been worse. A lot worse. Thank God for Tom.'

'Because?'

'Because he did most of the work for me. Picked you up, dusted you off, started you all over again . . .'

'Is that how you see this?'

'Well, I don't know about the starting all over again . . .'

'You think that would be a bad idea, then, do you?'

'Don't put words into my mouth.'

'But you do think it's too soon.'

'I never said that.'

'It is, though, isn't it? I mean, if I started something with Tom now, it would be a rebound relationship. A get-over-Simon shag thing. And I can't do that to Tom, can I? It wouldn't be fair. On me or him. Unless . . . Oh, I don't know.'

Rose was listening, with amusement on her face, next to the sauce.

'One of the things I absolutely love about you is your ability to have a whole argument with yourself without anyone else needing to be involved. You're like your very own Punch and Judy show.'

'Shut up. Pass the Parmesan, and help me think of a J. What about Japanese? I could take him to Wagamama's.'

'Nothing very original about a bowl of Odun noodles and a hard bench. You could take him to Japan.'

'Yeah, right. With all the air miles I accumulate in my glamorous career.'

'What about Ju-jitsu?'

'Is that a martial art?'

Rose nodded. 'Think I did it once at uni. Fancied some guy who dragged me along.'

'Glamorous?'

'It's a martial art, Nat. You do it in pyjamas.'

'That's out, then. What about vodka Jellies?'

'Do you ever worry about your need to tackle emotional scenarios with alcohol as a crutch?'

'All the time. No vodka Jellies.'

'How about another go at the horizontal mambo? You need a letter, though.' Rose thought so hard, she practically stroked her chin. 'I've got it. Jiggery-pokery. That's what my uncle and aunt who live in Fuerteventura always call it. They do it on their sun terrace a lot, in the afternoons, apparently.'

'Yuck. Thanks, Rose. But no Jiggery-pokery. Could you be serious for a moment?'

Rose thought it unlikely, but she put down her spoon, and made a Paxman face. 'It seems to me, Natalie, that what you need is something that gives Tom some insight he doesn't already have into what makes you tick. What makes you who you are? What shapes you?'

'We're back to alcohol, then.'

'Hang on, hang on. I'm on to something. What do you spend probably half your life doing?'

'Sleeping?'

'Not that.'

'Removing unwanted body and facial hair?'

'No! Working. You need to find a way to do a job swap. J for Job Swap. Let him walk a mile in your shoes down at the station.'

'Brilliant!' Natalie stood up. 'Brilliant, Rose. You're a star!' Rose bowed in her chair.

'Boss would never go for it. Come to think of it, I don't know if Tom would. I could do a lot of damage to his hard and his floppies in one day.'

'Oooh, Matron.' Rose giggled. 'Okay. Well, then, call it Job Swap, but figure out some other way to get him in . . .'

'Work experience? I last did that in 1984, when the careers teacher at school sent me to a biscuit factory for a week. The one with the hair-net.'

Natalie remembered the hair-net. 'Don't worry – the radio station doesn't need you to wear one.'

'What does the radio station need me to do?'

'I've squared it with Mike. He thinks he's doing the local community good – probably reckons he'll get to open the school fair or something like that, sad bastard. You're supposed to be coming in for the week – to add credibility. Don't worry. After your first day I'll tell them you've got glandular fever or something.'

'Great story.'

'Believe me, this guy doesn't listen to two per cent of what comes out of my mouth, so it doesn't matter. I could tell him you've got Lassa fever and he wouldn't even blink.'

'Okay. And I'll be doing?'

'Making tea and coffee, greeting guests, bit of research, probably. That sort of thing. Nothing too difficult, I promise.'

'I'm still missing the point of this, Natalie. I thought this game was supposed to be fun.'

'Yeah, like the abseiling was fun.'

'The abseiling *was* fun. Admit it.'

'The point of this,' Natalie went on, admitting nothing, 'is to give you an insight into what my professional life is like. To help you further understand *me*.'

Tom was hiding a smile behind his hand.

'And if it works out well, I thought I could do the same thing at your work.'

'Right. Know a lot about web design and computer graphics and program-writing, do you?'

'About as much as you know about radio producing, I imagine.'

'*Touché*, Nat. I'll be there. Shall I bring an apple for the presenter?'

'It's not him you've got to impress.'

Mike Sweet had worked at Radio One for about three weeks in about 1982. Which didn't stop him wanting to sell tickets to himself, as Rose put it. The man had a mullet, for God's sake, and a taste in shirts that veered towards the Polynesian pimp. Versace by TK Maxx. He had wandering hands, and a voice so unctuous it could soften dry skin at ten paces. Natalie hated him. Everyone else hated him, too, but they worked on other programmes so their contact with him was limited. Lucky buggers.

Mike Sweet thought he had done great things for Natalie's career. In the five years she had been working with him, he had – under relentless pressure – condescended to let her read first the traffic, then the weather on the half-hour during his three-hour show. He was 'considering' letting her have her own slot – a twenty-minute radio book club every fourth Thursday afternoon. Every second Tuesday since last October, when she had put together the proposal and shown it to him, she asked him how the consideration was going, and he always replied that good things came to those who waited. And once, when he'd eaten a dodgy curry and had terrible trots, he had let her read the news headlines and introduce Culture Club's "Do You Really Want To Hurt Me?" before he sent her out to get him some Imodium. How she had resisted the temptation to substitute Dulcolax for the white pills she would never know. She might have had her own late-night culture-vulture programme by now if she had.

Mike Sweet was the vainest man she had ever met. When all the jocks had had their pictures taken for some magazine a couple of months ago, he had insisted on being in the middle, and on leaping out of the elaborately arranged shot to look at the photographer's Polaroids every five minutes, making sure his chin wasn't too fleshy or his eyes half closed. He had the kind of highlights that make your head look like a leopard's, and she knew, because he had upended his sports bag once by accident, that he wore thong briefs, which was, frankly, appalling.

He claimed to know the lyrics of every pop song ever written, and his favourite game was to get you to tell him one line and let him tell you the next. He was actually very bad at this, unless the song was by Huey Lewis and the News or Kajagoogoo. He knew those because he'd been at primary school with Limahl, and called him a close personal friend. History did not relate what Limahl called him. Rose used to say that Mike Sweet was the kind of man who should be banned from entering the Friends Reunited website. 'Can you imagine him popping up on your PC?' she said.

Of course, he popped up on Natalie's PC all the time, having installed himself starring in a newspaper article as her screensaver. '*Mike Sweet Brightens Up the Children's Ward*' was the headline. He was sitting on a hospital bed, with a few un-willing-looking children smiling weakly beside him. 'As if chemotherapy wasn't tough enough,' Rose had said, when she'd first seen it.

'Is he for real?' Tom's mouth was wide with incredulity. They were in the kitchen. One of the researchers had just been in and walked out again, choking on a Bourbon biscuit from laughing so hard. 'The man is a walking cliché.'

'Welcome to my world.'

'And patronising! I don't think I've ever been spoken to like that. Even when I was working at the biscuit factory.'

'I know.'

'Do you think he was suspicious? I mean, I know I'm wearing well, but a thirty-five-year-old work-experience boy?'

'I told him you were a city analyst looking for a change in direction. And then I told him you were a massive fan. That kind of distracted him from everything else.'

'You told him I was a fan?'

'A massive fan.'

'Thanks. Great.'

'It is great, actually. He's going to let you do his on-line research for the councillor who's coming in this afternoon. Local-issues stuff. It was six months before he let me do that. And I had to let him "accidentally" feel my arse in the lift.'

'Remind me to Dettol that arse before I go near it again.'

'Again? You wish. Now, get on with the tea!'

'All right, but later you can tell me what the hell you're still doing in this job.'

Natalie thought about it for the next couple of hours. She thought about it so hard, she forgot to put through the irate caller wanting to complain about bins to the councillor during the interview. Mike Sweet came out during a record and told her to 'Look lively, sweetheart.'

And she was still thinking about it at five thirty as she watched Tom through the big glass window. He was trying to say goodbye to Mike, who was waving him away, trying to shrug on his leather blouson jacket and talk into his mobile phone at the same time. She smothered a giggle when Tom stuck two fingers up at him and backed out of the door genuflecting.

'I need a drink, badly. It's no wonder you're practically an alcoholic,' he said.

As they strode towards the wine bar by the river, he said, 'You're quiet – although I imagine a day with him takes some unwinding from. The guy's a tosser.'

'I'm thinking about what you said to me.'

'Which particularly insightful remark was that?'

'You asked me what the hell I was still doing there.'

'Ah, yes.'

It was only just dawning on her what she was still doing there. She was remembering a conversation she had had with her old colleague Stella, at Stella's leaving do a couple of years ago. Stella was pregnant again: 'See how desperate I am to leave. Desperate enough to get myself pregnant!'

'You don't mean that.'

'Course I don't. I need a sibling for Hector. Someone else for him to torture.'

By this time, the spherical baby they had christened the day she'd met Simon again was a spherical toddler, who wouldn't have been out of place in the front row at Twickenham, and bit everything that came within ten feet of him. Last week he'd bitten the family dog. Natalie had serious fears for the new baby.

'And thanks to you, I move a step closer to him.' Natalie was being 'promoted' into Stella's job as producer.

'You should move too. You don't even need to do anything as drastic as getting yourself pregnant.'

Natalie was remembering the certainty she had felt that this job was temporary. That she was treading water, bringing home an okay wage that could just about stretch to keeping her and a fledgling doctor with ambitions, and waiting. Waiting for Simon to marry her. Waiting to have babies, who would be beautiful and wouldn't bite people or animals, with him. That she could put up with Mike being a shit, and with doing the same thing day in and day out, because it wasn't for long. Because soon her real life would be starting, and this would all be just an unpleasant memory that she could make sound much funnier when she talked about it at coffee mornings than it actually was.

Jesus.

They were sitting down now, and Tom had just put a large drink in front of her. 'Talk me through it, then. Tell me how you ended up settling for this, Natalie.'

He sounded like someone's dad, and for a second she was annoyed.

He was right, though. She had settled. And it was unsettling to admit.

At school she had wanted to be a television presenter. She used to 'do' programmes all the time. Tom vaguely remembered being an extra in some of them. She used to talk to herself, whenever she was working at something – give a running commentary. Natalie bakes cakes. Natalie washes her dad's car. Natalie tidies the Wendy house.

Susannah had spoilt that. She was going to be the actress and Natalie could see that Susannah had something she didn't even as a teenager. Susannah was luminous and engaging, and people wanted to watch her. If you looked at family photographs – always taken by Dad – Mum, Bridget and Natalie were at the back, and Susannah, in some stage-show pose, was draped along the front of them. Natalie couldn't compete.

She wasn't bitter about it. She never had been. It was simply something she'd known. How could you not love Susannah, and delight with her in all her small triumphs? And keep your fingers crossed that, one day, she would get her big break.

And Bridget had always wanted to be a nurse. She'd had a little uniform when they were kids and called herself Nurse Bridget. From when she was about eleven, she'd used her pocket money to buy the *Nursing Times*.

Natalie used to wait for a sense of vocation to fall on her. But it never did. So, once she'd given up on wanting to be a television presenter, she spent ten years wanting to be, and she wasn't sure of the exact order, a hairdresser (to the stars), a landscape gardener, a corporate lawyer, a tea-shop owner and a marine biologist. These ambitions were usually informed by what she was watching on television, or reading about in books and magazines. None of them got off the drawing-board, except for hairdresser, but that fringe trim she'd done on Bridget had not been universally acclaimed.

At university, like many of her contemporaries, she had read what she was best at, which was French and German – even though German was always a bit of a struggle. She didn't like the way it sounded, or the way her mouth moved when she spoke it. She loved French. She was always the one who got sent into the *boulangerie* on family gîte holidays in the Dordogne. The others could muster a question, but were flustered by the stream of French response and gave up.

She hadn't done a great deal of work at university reading French and German, of course, but she'd had a lot of fun. Except for the falling-in-love-and-getting-her-heart-broken stuff, which had happened about twice a year. She'd fall for someone in the autumn and agonise over him until Christmas. Have one term of bliss in the spring and spend the summer term breaking up. She could usually manage to squeeze in a potted version of that during the long summer vacation, too – except during the year she'd worked in the food hall of Marks & Spencer where there were only middle-aged women, who taught her a lot about varicose-vein stripping and hysterectomies but offered limited potential for love.

Her companion on the roller-coaster of her life was Rose, whose own life was more of a steam train, which, thankfully, left her limitless energy to deal with Natalie. They'd met in French tutorials in the first term of the first year, shared a fridge shelf in the second, and an incredibly ropy apartment in Carcassonne in the third, during the obligatory six months' living abroad. Rose worked in Reception at a beautiful old hotel. Natalie had an unhappy love affair with the bell-boy. She thought he looked like a young Richard Burton, which Rose let slide, and when she wasn't lying happily in bed with him, or unhappily on the sofa without him, she worked on the travel and weather desk of a local radio station.

So, university had brought her half a dozen broken hearts and a best friend in the form of Rose. If she could tolerate all that wailing and gnashing of teeth squeezed into four years, the rest of life should have been a breeze. But she was no nearer a career.

She'd done different things for a while. She'd taught English as a foreign language to sullen European teenagers for a couple of years, and she, Bridget and Rose had gone travelling after Bridget had qualified as a nurse. Then Natalie had fallen back into radio. Which was okay. She didn't love it, but Mike hadn't joined the station back then; so she didn't hate it either. She'd worked on the drivetime show, which meant she didn't have to get up early, and the hosts were young and energetic. One, Georgie, did the breakfast show on a major London network now – she was the main presenter's much funnier sidekick – and the other had moved into kids' television. They'd had a lot of fun, and it didn't really matter that Natalie wasn't 'getting anywhere' fast.

And then she had met Simon again.

'God, Tom. I was just waiting to give it all up and be Simon's wife.'

'Come on, you can't be serious. This is the twenty-first century.'

'I know. But I think I was. I think that's what I thought would happen. That there was no real point in flogging myself silly trying to get on, or even trying to find something I was really good at, because I was waiting to stop.'

'Natalie!'

Tears welled in her eyes. 'My God. What a stupid, stupid woman. So now I'm sitting here, and I'm thirty-five bloody years old, and I hate my job, in which I am subservient to a complete prat, and the guy I waited years for has buggered off and left me. Great. All this time I was worrying about my love life and not noticing that my career was in the toilet too. My life has no meaning.'

'But plenty of melodrama! Don't be daft! Your life isn't short of meaning – a lack of focus and momentum, maybe, but thirty-five isn't old, you know.'

'Depends what time frame you're working to.'

'And you've always been working to the wrong one, by the sound of it.' He smiled at her.

'Is that a patronising smile?'

'No.'

'You'd be entitled. I mean, look at you. You're the same age as me, and you weren't even as clever as me at school,' Tom raised an eyebrow, 'and yet here you are, with your own company and your own flat . . .'

'You've got your own place.'

'Yeah. The deposit was paid by my poor father, while Bridget – who works in the NHS, for God's sake – and Susannah, with those bloody coffee ads she did after drama school, contribute to the mortgage.'

'So do you!'

Natalie sat sulkily.

'What did Simon think about all this?'

'I don't know. It wasn't really about my career, was it?'

She had that right. Tom associated Simon with a lot of things, not many of them good, but pretty much all of them connected to his flourishing career as a surgeon.

He remembered the first time they had met. He had been with Frankie then, the first girl Tom had fallen in love with. She had walked into his office one day, and it seemed to him afterwards that she had brought his heart to life. Not straight away, of course. He wasn't Natalie. But gradually and inexorably. All that stuff he had listened to Natalie spout for years made sense to him for the first time.

Frankie seemed exotic. She was half Argentinian – her father owned a lot of land there – but she had been educated in England. She sounded posh, and she had the self-assured polish of the rich, beautiful and well-educated. He didn't remember being intimidated by a woman before – that wasn't his style – but she made him feel like a kid. Until she took him to bed, where she made him feel more of a man than anyone else ever had.

Natalie had hated Frankie on sight. Although what she had actually hated, on reflection, was the way Frankie made both of them feel. Tom was quite un-Tom-like around her. Not so much fun. Serious, and absorbed in her. Like there was no one else around. It was so weird seeing him like that. She'd told him, once, that it freaked her out. He said it was unfair of her: he'd been watching her behave like that around men for years, and put up with it, and that she, too, would have to learn to.

Secretly, he thought Frankie made Natalie feel insecure. She made most women feel that way: always immaculate, and always being watched by every man in the room, regardless of who that man was with.

It hadn't lasted long. Tom always thought of it afterwards as a short, sharp shock. As though loving Frankie – which there was no doubt he had done – was akin to the electrical therapy they give to mental patients: mind-altering and violent. He was not the kind of guy she was going to end up with. That much was obvious. It was clear enough, too, that Frankie was not the sort of girl he would have been happy with long-term.

He remembered being surprised by the way his heart had betrayed him. Why would his physiology work that way? Let him fall in love with someone who didn't suit him? A few months later he was actually glad that she had left him. It felt a little like being saved.

The four of them had had dinner once. It had been Natalie's idea. He'd appreciated that she tried with Frankie – it was hard to imagine two more different women – and he understood her pursuit of a neat friendship between them. But Tom couldn't stand Simon. He was of a type he had known throughout his life and never liked. Self-absorbed, self-important, self-righteous. A total slicing and dicing bore, who was only animated when he was talking about himself or his work. His patients clearly didn't matter to him, except as nameless, faceless bodies that might be helpful in the fulfilment of his ambitions.

The evening had been a bit of a disaster, and they had ended it early.

It made him smile now to think that a woman like Frankie and a man like Simon might indeed have been very happy together.

Lucy

Lucy swept up the last of the crumbs and dust bunnies and stood up straight at last. She was knackered. Bella's Pop-stars birthday party was finally, blissfully, over. Seventeen eight-year-old girls had learnt the Macarena, been made up to look like Jodie Foster in *Taxi Driver*, dressed in neon brights, and generally run riot in the village hall to an inordinately loud soundtrack, which still hadn't drowned their glass-shatteringly high voices, all shouting and giggling at once.

'Thanks so much for your help, you two. You were lifesavers.' Marianne had stayed. Alec had collected Ed, who was looking horrified at the prospect of an afternoon of pink pop mania, to drop him and Stephen off at a school football session. But he had come back, and the four of them had finally cleared the debris. Bella and Nina were sitting on the stage, watching their parents benevolently as they worked.

Alec took the dustpan from her. 'You look done in.'

Patrick came in from taking out the rubbish sack and added, 'Yeah, you do.'

'Thanks, guys. I feel great now! Don't the boys need picking up? I'll go.'

'No, you won't. I will.' Marianne stuck her head round the kitchen door.

'I'll come with you,' said Patrick.

'Us too,' the girls chimed in, anxious to escape any jobs that might still be lurking.

Alec gave Lucy the briefest glance, but she couldn't read his face. She couldn't believe their families were forcing them to be alone together. 'Let me go,' she offered again.

'Don't be daft – you've been on your feet all day. You stay here and Alec can make you a cup of tea. Patrick will take me, won't you? We'll feed them at Burger King on the way back. Then, maybe, if you feel like it, we could get a curry in, have a couple of bottles of wine. The kids'll please themselves. If you've got nothing else on tonight?'

Patrick spoke first. 'Sounds great, Marianne. Thanks.' He doesn't want to be at home with me, Lucy thought.

And then they were gone.

It felt shocking to be alone together. All those months they had avoided it. For a moment they stood awkwardly in the hall. Alec spoke first. 'Cup of tea, then?' They both laughed, at nothing.

'Sounds great.' She followed him into the kitchen, watched him fill the kettle and switch it on, collect mugs from the hooks under the cupboard, take teabags out of the caddy. 'This is weird.'

It felt a little like a trap and a little like a chance.

In the end, Alec was braver: 'So, what are we up to, Lucy, you and me?'

'What do you mean?'

'I know it isn't just me. Is it?'

She couldn't look at him. 'No.' Her voice was very quiet.

'You know me, don't you?'

'I think so.'

'I think so too.'

Tiny staccato sentences. Vast distances.

'I can't stand it, never being able to talk to you – really talk.'

'I know. I feel that too.'

'So, let's talk now.' And now it was the last thing she wanted to do. It felt like you felt on Christmas morning, when you come roaring into the living room and see all your presents lying there, and you don't know which to open first because you're desperate to rip the wrapping off all of them. She wanted to talk to him, she wanted to listen, she wanted to touch and be touched. And it seemed like this was the only chance, the only moment, that they were ever going to get. She was aware of a flutter of hysteria. 'What do you want to talk about?'

'Tell me, Lucy-who-knows-me, I-don't-know-how. Tell me how I feel about you. I want to hear you say it all.'

'Okay.' And then the words were there, spilling out: 'You care about me. We're in a room together, with a hundred other people, and you know where I am, who I'm talking to. We enjoy each other. We're a bit alike, but different enough. You see things in me that you don't see in your wife and you know, deep down, that if we had met in another time, when it wasn't impossible for anything to happen between us, that we could have had something. And you think it might have been spectacular. And you know you might be a different person if you were with me, and that scares the hell out of you. And when you've had a few drinks, you fancy the arse off me.' She looked him squarely in the eyes. Her heart was hammering with the effort and the excitement of saying the things that had been in her head for such a long time.

He gave her a little sideways smile. 'Nearly right.'

She raised an eyebrow. God, this felt good.

'Wrong on just two points.' He was suddenly nearer. She could feel his breath. 'I don't have to be drunk to fancy you.' His lips were near her ear. 'And it isn't impossible for anything to happen between us.'

'Isn't it?'

They both knew the answer.

'Just to be sure we're both clear on this, I'm about to kiss you, Lucy.'

Just once, she thought. Just once. Perhaps she was telling herself that it would burst the unbearable bubble of suspense. Perhaps she was telling herself that it couldn't hurt. Perhaps she wasn't telling herself anything, just feeling, not thinking.

At first only his lips touched her. Rested against her mouth so gently that they almost tickled. It felt to Lucy that they stayed that way for a full minute, adjusting to the change between them. Her nerve endings screamed. She leant into him, and at that signal he pressed himself against her and they opened their mouths and kissed hard. Lucy felt as if she was falling into him. She felt their thighs, their hips, their ribs meeting. And everything disappeared. It was like being drunk, when you could only think about one thing at a time. There wasn't room, there wasn't time, for Patrick or Bella or Ed, or for Marianne. Just for the two of them, and for how fantastic it was, after all the months of thinking about it, fantasising about him.

When the kiss ended, he pulled her to him and held her tightly, his face buried in her hair. Muffled, he said, 'I . . . hate . . . you.'

Lucy leant back, and took his face in her hands. 'I hate you too. I was happy.'

'I was happy too.'

'So what are we doing?' Creeping fear. What had they done? It wasn't just one kiss, was it?

'I've seen something I haven't seen before, and now I've felt something I haven't felt in the longest time. If I ever did.'

'This isn't something you do, then?' She knew it wasn't, didn't she? A young tanned couple on a beach skipped through her mind, but they seemed so detached, so alien. They didn't belong in this moment, did they?

He looked almost stern. 'Never once. Never.' He was holding her again. 'I don't know what this is, Lucy. I don't have a neat name for it. But you have to believe that it is about you. It's all about you.'

She knew it was. That made it worse. That was what she wanted it to be.

K for Kids

'How's the old man?'

Lucy put two steaming mugs on the table and sat beside Tom. She felt utterly discomfited. Weirdly, it was harder to be sitting with Tom, Patrick's brother, now, than it had been to greet Patrick, Marianne and the kids when they'd got back that afternoon. The lie felt bigger. Why would that be?

'Not great.'

'Where is he now?'

'He's at an interview, with a recruitment specialist.'

'That's good, isn't it?'

'I don't know. He's already had a couple and nothing's come of them.'

'You're all right for now, though, aren't you?'

'We're fine. It was a good pay-off. They gave him the car. We've got redundancy insurance on the mortgage. It's not the money, not really, not for a goodish while, anyway . . .'

'What is it, then?'

'It's Patrick. He can't seem to pick himself up.'

'I'm sure I'd be the same.'

Lucy looked at him quizzically. 'Are you? You don't seem the type for self-pity.'

'That's a tough word for it, Luce.'

'Is it? That's what it feels like. He can't get past what happened – it's starting to feel like he's wallowing in it.'

'Really?' Tom wasn't used to feeling this rush of defensiveness. It had never seemed necessary before.

Lucy shook her head. 'I'm sorry, I don't mean to sound like a bitch. I don't really know how he is, that's the truth. He won't talk to me, Tom, not really, really talk to me.'

'That's just pride, isn't it? He wants to sort it out himself. You know what he's like.'

'But I'm his wife.'

'Still. He's him.'

'The other night I told him I was thinking of going back to work. There'd be a little retraining to do, but it shouldn't be too hard to find something. Something local, a bit flexible with hours around school holidays and stuff.'

'That sounds good.'

'Exactly. And it's something I've been thinking about for a while – since before all this came up with his job. Ed's not a baby any more, and I can't imagine not going back to work.'

'And how did he react?'

'He went berserk. Gave me this long speech about how he was capable of taking care of us all, how he was the provider.'

'Sounds a bit Victorian.'

'Too right. He told me I was undermining him, that it was the last thing he needed right now.'

'And that doesn't sound like Patrick.'

'Come on! You know he's always had this thing about protecting me. It's a joke, isn't it? That he was my knight on a white charger.'

'But that's what it was, Lucy, a joke.'

'I'm not so sure.'

'I don't follow.'

'Maybe he views our entire relationship in terms of him being the provider and the protector, and now that he isn't those things, he feels like a failure. I really can't talk to him, Tom.' She was close to tears.

Tom had had no idea things were so bad. He stood up and

went to her, put his arm round her shoulders. 'It'll be all right, Lucy.'

Why did people say things like that – issue platitudes when they had no idea if there was any truth in them?

'How, Tom?' She batted it right back to him.

'He needs time. You two need a bit of space, maybe.'

And what about me? Lucy thought. He doesn't even know the half of it. He sure as hell wouldn't have his arm round me if he did. 'Oh, yeah. Spoken like a childless bloke. How are we going to get that? And don't even think of suggesting Cynthia. You saw what she was like at the wedding. She's the last person he wants help from right now.'

'Let me have the kids for a couple of days.'

'I couldn't do that.' But already there was hope in Lucy's voice. She desperately wanted to remember why she had chosen to spend her life with Patrick. She wanted him to push Alec away for her.

'Of course you could. How about next weekend? Book something. I'll move in here with Bella and Ed. Do the crazy-uncle thing for a couple of days. The two of you can grab a bit of sanity back. Have the chance to talk properly. That's all it'll take.'

'Do you think?'

'I'm sure.' He patted her shoulder.

She laid her head on his hand, then kissed it. 'You're a poppet, Tom. Thanks. They'll run you bloody ragged.'

'You haven't heard my plan yet!'

Tom's mobile number flashed on her phone. She pushed the green button, tucked it under her ear and took another bite of her sandwich.

'What the hell are you eating?'

'Sandwich.'

'With gravel in it?'

'Pickled onions, if you must know.'

'That's disgusting.'

'Did you ring me to discuss my choice of sandwich fillings, or was there something else?'

Tom loved the laugh in her voice. She just sounded happy. The radio station should give her that plonker's job – she'd be a reason to switch on. 'There was, as it happens. This week's letter. My choice, I believe. The good news is, you don't need any special equipment for this one.'

'That *is* good news.'

'Hang on – you might actually need a hard hat.'

'I'm not, not, not going pot-holing, Tom. I really do draw the line at that.'

'Since when did pot-holing start with a K?'

'You're such a smartarse.'

'And you have disgusting taste in sandwiches.'

'I may hang up before you get the chance to tell me.'

'Don't do that. I know you can't wait, really.'

Natalie yawned theatrically into the phone.

'K,' he announced, 'is for Kids.'

'Aren't we back at H for Hotel, now? And you remember what happened there!'

'Don't flatter yourself, darling. I don't mean *our* kids.'

'Please tell me it's not goat kids.'

'It's not goat kids. It's Patrick and Lucy's kids. Bella and Ed. I'm borrowing them for the weekend.'

'Why?'

'Apart from the whole K thing? I want to evaluate your skills as a parent.'

'Fuck off.'

'There'll be no swearing, for a start. Not very maternal at all.'

'Why, Tom?'

'Seriously? They need a break. Lucy's pretty frazzled, and she and Patrick aren't getting along brilliantly. I figured they needed a bit of space and I can give them that.'

'And I get to help, I suppose?'

'Well, yes. Strikes me we can kill two birds with one stone. Help Luce, and tackle the letter K. Unless you really fancied Karate or Kayaking, which I don't imagine you do after the canoeing episode, or the previous front-runner, which was Karaoke . . .'

'Kids will be fine. As long as you're not going to be all Victorian about it. I'm not just chief cook and bottle-washer, you know.'

'It'll be an excellent opportunity for you to observe my positively Pied Piperesque way with little people. Part of my irresistible charm, you probably aren't aware.'

Natalie laughed. 'Okay, big-head. Although you should know that the real Pied Piper was a very dodgy bloke indeed, who kidnapped real children and did horrible things to them. So let's go with Mary Poppins, shall we? Sad though I am to be missing the chance to hear you massacre Sinatra, I'll go with K for Kids. What time d'you want me?'

Kids were probably not this much fun if you had them all the time, Natalie reflected, as she washed up the tea plates, and listened to Tom upstairs, supposedly putting Ed through the bath, although it sounded a lot more like what her dad would call rough-housing. Ed's infectious giggle was getting louder by the minute.

They'd had the best day. Tom had been brilliant. He'd driven them all to Longleat, despite the drizzly, grey March weather and they'd spent their time exploring happily. Bella was so grown-up, suddenly. Not that Natalie saw her often, but she was a changed kid from the one she had been, say, last year. She was in that phase where she badly wanted to be sensible and listened to, and ten years older. She had told them she wanted to be a vet, and stood for ages reading the information posted around the park about the various animals. But, really, she still wanted to be mucking about with Ed and Tom, pulling faces at them, and talking endlessly about the size, texture, colour and smell of their respective waste products. She had spent the whole day battling with herself and her age-related schizophrenia.

Natalie knew she was fascinated by her, because she remembered feeling like that when she was young. Anna and Nicholas had had some friends with a grown-up daughter, who had taken Bridget and Natalie into town once, years ago, when Natalie was about eleven, she supposed. She remembered this girl – Chloë had been her name – buying perfume, for herself, with a cheque and a cheque card, and thinking how impossibly glamorous that was, and aspiring madly to get to that point herself, when she could buy perfume for herself, which wasn't Charlie. Bella kept saying things to her – she liked Natalie's scarf and hat, she liked her hair, she liked her bag. Natalie was tickled. 'Are you Uncle Tom's girlfriend?' Bella asked.

'Well,' Natalie had been unsure how to answer, 'I'm Uncle Tom's friend and I'm a girl . . .'

Bella had smiled coyly. 'You know what I mean.'

Natalie had bent down conspiratorially. 'I do know, Bella, yes. I'm not really. Sorry.'

'I think you should be.'

God, Natalie thought. Out of the mouths of babes.

'Because then you could marry him, and you'd be my auntie.'

Tom had appeared at her elbow. 'I agree, Bella. Auntie Natalie. It has a lovely ring, hasn't it? How about it?'

'How about you buy us an ice-cream?' Natalie retorted.

'But it's freezing.'

'All right, then, a hot chocolate would do, wouldn't it, Bella?'

Bella wasn't to be dissuaded. On their way to the cafeteria, she tugged at Natalie's sleeve, and said, 'And if you did marry my Uncle Tom, could I be your bridesmaid? I've never been one, and I'm afraid time's running out for me.'

Jesus. Natalie stifled a giggle. If time was running out for Bella, that certainly explained why she sometimes felt a rising tide of panic.

Ed was not so complicated, and pretty adorable. At four, he was still enough part baby to make you want to pick him up and blow raspberries on his stomach, and enough part boy to find that distinctly embarrassing. He looked a lot like Tom had as a kid, and as she and Bella sat, finishing their hot chocolate, watching them rugby-tackle each other on the lawn, she realised that they could almost have been father and son. It struck her, in that moment, that Tom might have children, one day, with someone else, and that felt a little strange. Tom was hers, wasn't he?

Tom picked up Ed under one arm, and walked towards her holding him like a rugby ball. When he got near, he hoicked him up on to his shoulder, and said, 'You and me, Nat. This could be the future! Say the word!!'

That was when Ed threw up his hot chocolate down the back of Tom's jacket.

She went out for a takeaway curry, and when she returned, Bella had gone to bed with her book, and Ed had fallen instantly, utterly asleep. They ate the curry on their laps, with a bottle of beer and vacuous Saturday night television.

'I'm absolutely knackered,' Tom complained. 'Bloody hell, Nat, I'm never going to volunteer for that again.'

'You loved it. You were the biggest kid of the day.'

'I loved it – I love them – but, blimey, it's hard work!'

'Another beer?'

'I can't be arsed to get up and get one.'

'I'll go, old man.' She stood up and collected their plates.

'You do want kids, though, don't you?' she asked, when she'd come back with the beer, and settled on the sofa.

Tom put his feet, uninvited, on to her lap. 'Haven't got the energy, just this minute. Wait until after *Match of the Day*, will you?'

She pinched his little toe.

'Ouch!'

'I mean, eventually – they're part of your plan, yes?'

'Yes and no.'

'That's cryptic. Explain.'

'Well, with me it's not a biological thing. I don't yearn for them for their own sake. I don't think about sitting around in sixty years and figure that I have to, have to, must have had them.'

Natalie wondered whether she did. She supposed so.

'For me, they'd be part of the right relationship. Do you know what I mean? I'd have to meet the mother of my children before I knew for sure that I wanted them. Does that make sense?'

'Yeah.' It did. 'It must be different if you haven't got a uterus.'

'I suppose. Although I don't think having one necessarily means you have to feel that way – it's a bit prescriptive, isn't it?'

'Yeah, of course. I don't know. I guess I've always assumed I'd have them. That probably isn't the right way to go about it, though.'

'You'd be a great mother. You should have kids.'

'What makes you say so?'

'Your wide hips?'

'And?' She did *not* have wide hips, so he could just about get away with that.

'Everything about you. You're kind and warm, generous, smart and creative. You'd be a natural.'

'I don't know.'

'I do.' He was smiling at her.

Then the phone rang.

'That'll be Patrick or Lucy. I told them not to check up on us.'

Natalie stood up, tipping Tom's feet off her lap. 'I'll give 'em hell.'

But Tom had already reached behind him and picked the telephone out of its cradle on the table next to the sofa. 'Don't you trust us?' was his opening gambit.

Then he sat up and didn't speak for a long time. When he did, his voice didn't sound amused any more. He said, 'Okay. I'm sure she'll want to come right away. Okay. Hold on. Goodbye.'

Natalie felt frightened. Tom took her hand, and pulled her down beside him. He didn't know how else to say it so he just said it: 'It's your dad, Natalie. He's in hospital. They think hc's had a stroke.'

L for Luvvies

'Luvvies.'
  'Luvvies. Yes, Luvvies. You know, theatrical types. Susannah and Casper have invited us to a wrap party. It'll be heaving with thesps and luvvies.'

'Sounds horrendous.'

'Sounds great. Apparently Hugh and Jemima are going to be there. He had a cameo in Casper's film.'

'You mean the one he shot in Morocco?'

'No – they finished this one last summer so I suppose it isn't technically a wrap party, only the director had to go to America straight away after they finished it to do this other film, and this is the first chance they've had back in London, since most of the cast and crew are British, they're having it here and we're invited!'

'Tenuous, Nat, very tenuous.'

'So, Saturday night. We need to leave in the afternoon, I guess. And we can crash at Susannah's, she says. Oh, and dress glam. Very glam.'

'Do you mean as in the Sweet glam?'

'No.' Natalie spoke very slowly, as if Tom was a half-wit. 'I mean smart and trendy. Take Serena shopping at lunchtime – let her choose you something.'

'I can do smart and trendy without Serena's help, thanks very much.'

'Well, see that you do. People are going to assume we're together – I don't want you showing me up.'

* * *

Susannah and Casper had a basement flat in Arundel Gardens. It was tiny, a little damp and quite dark. But it was Notting Hill, and it was rent-free. Casper's grandmother, a wonderfully eccentric Jew, had lived in it since the war, collecting lovers, and Chinese pottery for the stall she had in Portobello Market, and had left it to her grandson when she died in 1995. They'd stripped it out, painted the whole thing white and fitted a thousand-pound IKEA kitchen that looked like twenty thousand pounds' worth of Poggenpohl. Against this neutral background they dressed the apartment like a film set, changing it with their mood. Just now it was Morocco. Ornate leather stools in pastel colours, cushions with mirrors and diaphanous fabrics. One vast tagine filled with perfect green apples.

Susannah opened the door to them. 'Darlings!' She pulled Natalie to her and hugged her tightly. 'I am so, so pleased to see you, sweetie.'

'Ab-fabulous to see you too, Suze!'

'And Tom! I haven't seen you in ages. Welcome.'

She ushered them in. The flat smelt of joss sticks. Natalie rolled her eyes at Tom. 'Very souk in here.'

'I know. Isn't it beautiful? And you cannot imagine how cheap.' Susannah pushed her hair back from her face, a thousand silver bangles jingling on each wrist. 'Mint tea?'

'I don't suppose you have PG Tips?'

'Absolutely not. You should try the mint. It's delish.'

'Mint tea it is, then.'

'Make yourselves comfortable.'

Tom doubted that was possible.

'Where's Casper?'

'In the pub.' Casper might have been educated at Stowe, but his inner Stan craved the odd pint of Boddington's.

'Bloody good idea,' Tom whispered.

Natalie grimaced at him, then said, 'The one at the end of the road?'

'Yep. Think so.'

'I might join him for a quick one.' And Tom was off.

'Good. Now we can have a chat.' Susannah brought the mugs over to the cushions, and sat down beside her sister. 'It's so good to see you. I've missed you.'

'Have you seen Bridge?' Natalie asked.

'I'm going up next week – I've got a couple of days. How is she?'

'Knackered. Happy. You know!'

'I bought the baby the most beautiful white linen things in the souk.'

'White linen? I'm no earth mother, but even I know white linen and newborns don't mix.'

'Rubbish! At that price, they're practically disposable anyway. And they're adorable. Made me and Cas quite broody.'

'Really?'

'Well, not really, no, of course not. I haven't done nearly enough nude scenes yet to think about ruining my body.'

There was a certain Susannah-like logic to that. 'What about Casper?'

'He's fine with it. I think he still wants me all to himself. Not ready to share me yet with some mewling, needy little ankle-biter.'

'You two really are the most selfish people on the planet, aren't you?' Natalie was laughing.

'I'm hurt, sweetie.'

'I don't know how we came out of the same womb. Me and Bridget, I can see. You? You must have been adopted.'

'I wish. So much more glamorous than being born in suburbia to married parents. A foundling. I'd have loved that . . .'

Natalie slapped her leg lightly. 'Sssh.'

'Speaking of the married parents, how's Dad?'

'They're both okay. Mum's brighter. I think it's having Dad to look after again. And he's doing well. It wasn't bad, as strokes go. A warning, I think. They only kept him in for a day or two, and he's taking bucketloads of pills and stuff. He always seemed so well, didn't he? They'll be looking forward to seeing you, I should think. You still coming home for Easter?'

'I said I would, and I will.'

'That'll be good. They've had a funny old year. First the cancer scare, then Mum's turn, now this.'

'Did you ever get to the bottom of what that was about? It's about fifteen years too late for the menopause.'

Susannah was so removed from it, Natalie thought. It wasn't that she didn't care – or she hoped it wasn't. 'It isn't that.'

'This all started when she had the scare, last year, didn't it? Do you think there's something she's not telling us?'

'What? Like she really has got cancer?'

'It's possible.'

'It's not. She isn't ill. She hasn't been going to the hospital or even the doctor. She hasn't lost weight. It isn't that, I'm sure. Dad would know, and I don't think he'd be able to keep it to himself.'

Susannah shrugged. 'What, then?'

'She's depressed, Suze.'

'Really?'

'Yeah, chemically. You know, properly depressed.'

'Have you told her that?'

'Stop it! It's not funny. The doctor told her, put her on something.'

'Mum? On Prozac? She'd hate that.'

'She is, although it's called something else. And she does hate it, but she recognises that she won't get better unless she does something about it.'

'I know it isn't funny. I'm sorry. I do tend to leave it all to you and Bridge, don't I?'

'You're away a lot.'

'It isn't just that. I can't cope, really. Too selfish, like you say. Now I don't know which one of them to worry about more – Mum and her happy pills or Dad and his stroke.'

The sisters sat there for a moment. 'I don't think you need to worry about either just now. Mum's having help, which I have great faith in, and Dad's going to be fine,' Natalie said.

Susannah looked uncertain.

'And you're coming home at Easter, which they'll love. We can make a point of all being there together and it will be lovely.'

'Has Mum stopped being so mean to him? It did seem to me that she was taking something out on him when we were home at Christmas.'

'She's much softer, since, yes.'

'I'm glad to hear it. It was all I could do to get away on Boxing Day without rowing with her about it.'

'I know!'

'I'm the only one who ever stands up to her.'

She was right. She was probably the only one of them who wasn't a little afraid of their mother. Susannah and her mother had always had a sparky relationship. Anna used to say, when Susannah was a teenager, that it was because they were alike. Which was a red rag to a bull, as far as fifteen-year-old Suze was concerned. What a heinous thought! Natalie remembered her saying, once, in a booming, disgusted voice, 'I am nothing like you!' and storming out for two days. Suddenly Natalie was very glad that her sister was coming home for a while.

The mint tea was surprisingly good. Over a second mug, Susannah asked about Tom. 'How's it going?'

Natalie smiled. 'Why does everyone keep asking me that?'

'Because everyone wants you two to get it together?'

'Et tu, Brute? I thought you, of all people, would be on my side.'

'What side is that?'

'The side of romance. Mr Right. Thunderbolt City.'

'And, to a point, I am. I don't think you should dismiss someone like Tom because there was a time when you knew him and those things weren't there.'

'*Is* a time, don't you mean? Do you see sparks flying?'

'Only in your denial, sweetie. Methinks the lady doth protest too much.'

'Piss off.'

Susannah laughed her deep, fruity laugh. 'Okay, then, tell me this. Have you ever just got a bit drunk and gone for it with him, just to find out if he can make you see stars?'

'I can't believe you'd even suggest it. That would be horrible.' She wasn't about to admit to the health farm. She'd been severely chastised by Rose and Bridget – she didn't need Susannah's disapproval as well.

'Why?'

'I couldn't use him as an experiment!'

'Isn't that pretty much what he's asked you to do, with this alphabet game?'

Natalie thought about it. 'Yes. But I don't want to hurt him.'

'And you think you would?'

'I do.'

'So that means you think he's serious about you?'

'I suppose I do, sort of, maybe, yes. Oh, I don't know, do I?'

Susannah picked up the two empty mugs. 'Have you noticed how cute he is?'

They both laughed.

As if on cue, the door to the flat opened and Casper and Tom poured in, also laughing. Casper was so not Natalie's type. He was tall and unbelievably thin, all elbows and cheekbones, which, apparently, the camera loved. Behind him, Tom was broad and strong. Susannah had a point. He *was* pretty cute. Trouble was, she remembered his face in all its incarnations. The Churchillian baby of his mother's mantelpiece, the cheeky boy she had first met, the gawky teenager, slightly spotty and making a bit of a mess of shaving. Now she could morph his man face back through time to the 1970s. Perhaps she should stop it.

The party was in an achingly trendy nightclub in which every surface appeared to be made from glossy white melamine. Natalie thought it looked like the kitchen their mother had ripped out of the house they'd moved into in 1977 and replaced with only slightly less awful pine, but when she said so Susannah and Casper got a bit sniffy, so she kept further observations to herself and Tom. The food seemed to be made for Lilliputians, tiny lumps of indeterminate stuff on cocktail sticks and single prawns glazed with three sesame seeds. Natalie watched Tom take two at once. Perhaps a kebab on the way home?

Arriving had been surreal. The entrance to the club looked for all the world like the door to a sewer or some Victorian horror location, under the arches in an unsalubrious part of town, south of the river. Opposite, the paparazzi were camped out, drinking tea and talking in loud Mockney. They'd ignored the four of them when they arrived, despite Susannah and Casper's best efforts to move in a famous sort of way.

Natalie had heard the murmur go round, 'It's nobody much.' Crikey! Hanging around with famous people was really good for your self-esteem. Her boss would be seriously, seriously hacked off that he wasn't there. On account of him being a J-lister. Natalie smiled to herself. J for Jerk. She must remember a few names to drop into conversation on Monday morning. It was all like some incredibly complicated caste system, wasn't it? Here, she was nobody. Having been here, however, would put her at the top of the pile at work for a while. The games we play . . .

She felt like the only girl in the room who had dressed herself. Everyone else was so 'groomed'. Puffy perfect hair, flawless faces, frocks she recognised from the pages of her magazines, the kind of frocks that cost a month's rent. She and Susannah had got ready two hours before, in the same bathroom, with Natalie dipping her fingers into the same pots as her sister, so how was it that Susannah looked completely at home and she felt like a poor relation?

'You look fine!' Tom had been a little exasperated.

' "Fine". The word a girl longs to hear. Thanks,' she had hissed at him in the taxi, but he had only chuckled.

She recognised practically every other face. Admittedly, some from *Hollyoaks* and *Coronation Street* – Susannah called them Rent-a-C-listers – but definitely some from the catwalk, and more than one from the silver screen. All behaving perfectly normally, as though they spent their whole lives being photographed and stared at by strangers. Which, of course, they did. At least models looked completely strange in real life – like newborn genetically modified giraffes. They were freakishly thin, like lollipops with giant, fluffy heads. She wished Rose was here: she'd have a field day.

There were podiums strategically placed around the room, with pole-dancers gyrating on them. Allegedly, this had what Casper called 'resonance with the themes explored in the script'. He and Tom were taking the time to note the artistic integrity. Or were they, option B, staring at the spread-legged, barely clothed girl with the huge tits and the smashing sense of rhythm? Tom was feeding himself a miniature something enthusiastically. He reminded Natalie of Ed, eating his tea in front of *The Fimbles*. She pulled his arm, so that he put his head down, and shouted in his ear, 'My mum can do that.'

It was an in-joke. They'd gone to see the cricket at the Oval a few years ago: England being crucified by Australia – hard to narrow it down to a particular year – and some brash Australians sitting behind them had waved a banner proclaiming that 'their mum [could] do that' whenever the Poms dropped a catch. Tom laughed a lot. But didn't immediately stop watching.

'I need another drink!' She nudged him. She didn't know why she disliked it so much, but she did . . . Feminist principle, probably.

Tom sauntered off reluctantly in the direction of the bar. Natalie hugged a dark corner of the room and just watched the people around her. She could see Susannah draped over Casper, talking to some similarly lithe luvvies over near the door. Then she watched a young actor from a medical drama she watched avidly, dancing with some beautiful girl wearing a dress apparently made out of macramé.

Tom had been gone for ages. She came round the corner a little, and scanned the bar for him. There he was, at the far end. Looked like he already had the drinks – but he was still talking to the girl who'd served him. Or, rather, she was talking to him. Flirting with him, if Natalie wasn't very much mistaken. She knew that body language – every girl within a hundred metres would have been able to tell you what she was interested in, if every girl was watching, instead of doing the same thing herself. It was all there, classic Desmond Morris stuff, the kind of thing they wrote articles in *Cosmopolitan* about. Hair-tossing, mouth-touching, direct eye-contact, fingers tracing down her own neck. She might as well have had a neon sign round it.

Natalie was affronted, which brought her up short. She didn't like it one bit, and that surprised her.

231

But as she stood in her corner, watching, she liked Tom's response even less. He was doing a bit of it back. Quite a lot, actually. She waited for him to turn round and make sure she was watching – it was bound to be part of the game, wasn't it? But he didn't and he didn't, and he carried on, leaning into the bar and talking to the girl with all the hair and the perfect cleavage.

She was shocked to recognise a flash of jealousy. The kind she used to have when she saw Simon talking to pretty nurses, or girls at parties. That had come from left field. Natalie realised Casper was by her side.

'You okay, Nat?'

She smiled at him, the kind of smile that was more of a rictus. Casper had watched her watch Tom. The same Tom who, three hours earlier in the pub, had confessed to him that he was mad about her, and terrified of blowing it again, and afraid that nothing was ever going to happen between them. Not that Casper knew whether this flirting with the waitress stuff was part of Tom's masterplan (which seemed a little flawed) or genuine attraction. She was a bit of a knockout. Casper, who was actually a bit simple, in the way that terribly well-educated public-school boys can be, didn't know what to say for the best.

'Fine. Great party. Wish I had a picture phone.'

'They'd haul you out if you used it. Celebs value their privacy, you know.'

'I can see that!' Natalie gesticulated towards the medical actor and his macramé girlfriend, who were by now engaging in their very own form of dirty dancing. 'Very private people!'

'Oh, him – I know him of old. He was at drama school with me. He'll hump anyone who stands still long enough. Want to meet him?!'

'I do not.' Natalie smiled. 'Besides, I'm a little overdressed for him. I'm wearing knickers.'

'Sure he'd find a way round that.'

'I'm sure he would. Still not interested, thanks, Cas.'

'Spoken for, are we?'

Natalie nudged him in the ribs. 'Stop fishing, brother-in-law. It's not so much that I'm spoken for as that I enjoy being spoken *to*, rather than just rogered . . .'

'Ah, hard work, then. Not sure he'd go for that.'

But Natalie wasn't really listening any more. She was watching Tom and the waitress, who were still talking.

He did come back, eventually. Susannah had caught up with them by then, and the three of them had found a free banquette. Tom handed Natalie her drink. She had an almost irresistible urge to throw it at him but she took it, ungraciously, and stuck the straw into her mouth like a petulant child, without saying thank you.

Susannah threw her a questioning glance. 'What's the matter with you?' she hissed, when Tom was talking to Casper.

'Tom was all over that waitress for about ten minutes!' She sounded indignant.

'Which one?'

'That one with all the bloody hair, at the bar.'

Susannah looked. 'She's pretty!'

'Thanks, Suze.'

'You mean he was kissing her?'

'No. He just looked like he wished he was.'

'Really?' Natalie couldn't read her sister's tone.

'What, really?'

'Do you think he's trying to make you jealous?'

'No, I think he's trying to make the waitress.'

Susannah laughed at her sulky tone. 'Well, honey, sounds to me like a bad case of "I don't want him but I'm darned if anybody else is going to have him."'

Natalie hated it when Susannah was right.

'And I'm afraid that unless you're expecting him to enter a seminary or join the French Foreign Legion, which I'm not even sure you can do any more, you might have to get over it.'

Natalie wasn't sure about that.

Later, on the way home, where Casper had promised bacon sarnies for all, Susannah sat between them in the back of the cab. 'Good night?' she asked Tom.

'Great. Thanks for taking us. Made a bit of a change. Very glamorous. Bit more Nat's kind of thing than mine, I'd have thought.'

'You looked quite at home,' Natalie threw back at him. She couldn't see his face. Or she would have seen the smile.

April

Lucy

This was the first time that Lucy had been alone with Marianne since she had kissed her husband. She'd avoided her at school, for a while, pretending to be busy – rushing here and there instead of chatting in the car park after the bell had rung. Avoided her well enough for Marianne to seek her out determinedly one morning and tell her that she had to come out with her. They'd agreed to do a bit of shopping, then have lunch. The bit of shopping had been fine, although Lucy had felt curiously shy about undressing in the changing room. There was a queue. Marianne had said they would share – 'Got no secrets, have we, Luce?' She was trying on a dress for a wedding she and Alec were going to some time in June. Lucy had half-heartedly picked up a skirt she didn't much like. It wasn't as if she and Patrick had money to splash around just now anyway. Marianne stripped down unselfconsciously to a grubby-looking bra and knickers, while Lucy had shrugged on the skirt under the one she was already wearing.

The satin dress had looked terrible, even on a woman as svelte and toned as Marianne, and she frowned at herself in the full-length mirror. 'Christ! Look at the state of me.' She had turned this way and that, pulling in her stomach, and flexing the muscles in her bottom so that the material jumped. 'I think not. What did someone once say – it looks like two pigs fighting under a blanket?' Lucy didn't say anything. Marianne had looked her up and down appraisingly. 'Skirt's gorgeous, though. You should get it.'

'Oh, I'm just along for the ride. Not really in a spending place right now.'

'I'm sorry – am I being incredibly insensitive?'

Lucy had shaken her head.

'Bugger it! Let's go for lunch. I'm buying. Come on.' Marianne had peeled off the unfortunate garment and stuck it back on the hanger. 'And I'm having chips!'

Now they were at lunch, and they'd drunk two big glasses of wine each. Lucy wondered vaguely about driving to get the kids and looked at her watch. They were okay for a while yet. As long as they ordered a coffee, and she finished that fizzy water. Drinking in the daytime made her feel sleepy, but she was terrified of letting down her guard with Marianne.

'Are you okay, Luce? Is this Patrick stuff really getting you down?'

It was, but that wasn't it.

'I mean, he's bound to get another job soon, isn't he? And you're not on the very edge, are you? You told me things would be okay for a while?' Her voice was kind and concerned.

'Oh, they are. We had a big enough cushion, so long as we don't go mad. It's just that . . . the longer it goes on, the more it affects Patrick's mood – he's very down and grouchy.'

'And that's no fun to live with, is it? Even though you understand and want to help and blah blah blah – they can still be buggers, can't they? They don't realise how their mood pervades the rest of the house – like a stink bomb.'

'Alec never seems that way to me.'

'He wouldn't, though, would he? You only ever see him at his best. Like I only see Patrick that way. They save the truly gruesome behaviour for their lucky, lucky wives.' She took a gulp of wine. 'Mind you, I daresay Patrick doesn't know I get wicked PMT and only shave my legs in the summer.' She laughed.

This felt almost as much like cheating as the kiss itself. 'Let's not talk about it. It's depressing. You're right – it will all be fine. Patrick will find a job, he'll perk up, problem solved. I thought you brought me out to cheer me up. Tell me some gossip.'

Marianne leant in conspiratorially, with a glint in her eye. 'Funny you should ask . . .'

One of the mothers on the PTA was having an affair, apparently. Someone or other had seen them somewhere or other and told someone or other in complete confidence. It had been the talk of the playground for days. Lucy was sure her cheeks were red. 'That's terrible,' she said, because it seemed like the right thing to say.

'Oh, I don't know.' Marianne pondered slowly. 'You never really know, do you, what's going on in someone else's marriage? You only know what they tell you or what they show you. We've all got something to hide.'

'What do you mean?' Lucy was instantly terrified.

Marianne gazed at her, long and hard, as if she was considering something. Took another drink. 'I had an affair.'

An explosion of relief took place in Lucy's chest. Followed immediately by horror. 'You did?'

Marianne nodded. 'Yep. Yonks ago. Bit of a show-stopper, isn't it?'

'It is a bit. You don't seem like the type. You two seem happy.'

'We are. I'm not. I don't really believe in people being "that type". That's a pretty adolescent view of the world, in my opinon. Adulthoood isn't black and white – it's a thousand shades of grey. Or taupe. It's not who you are, it's where you are. It was a long time ago. We were having a crap time. Bit of a cliché, really. We'd stopped making each other feel good, and I found someone who did. He wasn't anyone Alec knew – for God's sake, however desperate you are, you don't shit where you eat, do you? He was a bit random, actually, someone I used to work with years ago. We met up again, got talking – I fancied him, he fancied me. We had what was without doubt, and still is, I regret to say, the very best sex of my life. For about six months. That was mostly what it was. I didn't love him, and I'm damn sure he didn't love me. But we couldn't keep our hands off each other. Chemical. Any time, any place, anywhere. I can't believe the risks we took. I always . . . you know . . . had to have him.' Lucy remembered the aeroplane loo.

This was excruciating to listen to. It would have been at the best of times, but now, it was torture. She couldn't bring herself to ask Marianne anything, but it wasn't necessary – her friend seemed lost in the rhythm of her memory.

'And then . . . we stopped. I stopped it, as it goes, although it was only a matter of time before he did.'

An unspoken why.

Marianne shrugged. 'It couldn't go anywhere, could it? I wasn't going to leave Alec for him. I know it sounds ridiculous, but it was like . . .' she sounded as if she'd rehearsed this explanation in her head '. . . this flame, sort of thing. Magnesium, or something. It burned incredibly brightly, but only for a while.' She smiled. 'And then I came back to my well-bedded coal fire, I suppose.'

'Did Alec know?'

'God, no. Christ. We took risks, but not like that. He didn't need to know. It wasn't about him. It was about me. I did it and, all right, I'm not proud of it. For a long time after it stopped, a part of me wanted to tell him – I felt tainted by it. I seriously thought that maybe we couldn't go on with it between us. We could, we did and we have. But I know our marriage is better because of it, if that makes any sense.'

It did and it didn't.

'And it was the two of us – we hadn't got any kids. I couldn't have risked hurting children.'

'But hurting him?'

'I didn't.'

'You sound a bit calculating about it.'

'Do I?' Marianne seemed surprised, but not offended. 'I don't mean to. I wasn't. At the time, I mean. I was a mess inside.'

'Do you think he could have forgiven you, if he'd found out?'

'I don't know. I thought about that a lot. And I still don't know.'

'Well, could you forgive him, if the tables were turned?' What was she doing, for God's sake? Asking for bloody permission?

'That's a good question.' She thought about it. 'No. Not now. I don't think I could.' She swirled her wine glass, watching the liquid come closer and closer to the rim. Then she looked at Lucy. 'You think less of me, now, hey?'

Lucy smiled. 'No I don't.'

But she supposed that, really, she did.

M for Meeting New People

'It's a bold move,' Serena had said.

'Faint heart never won fair maid,' Rob had chipped in.

'Exactly. I think. I've got to shake this thing up a bit, haven't I? I'm pretty sure she was seriously pissed off with me for talking to that waitress at the party.'

'I agree completely. Does she know what she's showing up for?'

'No. I like the element of surprise.'

'But will she?'

'Who the hell knows, mate?' Tom said, ruefully. 'Women! Who knows?'

'Speed-dating!' Natalie heard her voice, so high it might have shattered glass, if they hadn't been drinking out of her thick IKEA wine glasses.

'Yeah, under the banner heading of Meeting New People – hence the M.'

'With the purpose of . . .'

'Well, you made it pretty clear at the health farm that you didn't think you could get serious with me in a million years, so the next best thing for a mate to do is make sure you find someone good. What better way than introducing you myself? Or, at least, being in the room when it happens.'

'And what will you be doing while I'm doing the speed-dating?'

'Well, I'll have to do it too, of course. You don't get allowed in if you're not playing, and if I'm not in there, I can't very well look after you, can I? And you never know . . . I might end up with someone too. How perfect would that be?'

'Perfect.' The sarcasm in her voice made his tummy flip. 'So, how does it work?' she added.

'Well, I'm no expert, but I know this guy through work and he's done it a few times.'

'A few times? That's not a great advert, is it? Shouldn't you only have to do it once, if it's so effective? What's his problem?'

'No problem, as he sees it – apparently so many babes show up at these things, he's happy playing the field.' Careful, Tom, he thought. Don't be too obvious. 'And I'm sure the same applies to girls. There's no stigma attached to finding romance through these organised methods any more. We live busy lives . . . You're just having help sorting the wheat from the chaff. It makes sense, if you think about it.'

'But what if I'm everyone's chaff?'

'Well, you won't be, will you? I think we do nine or ten of these things. We get three minutes with each guy or girl. At the end, if there are any we're interested in, we tell the organisers, and if those people have also given our names, then Bob's your uncle and Fanny's your aunt. You get their details and you're on your own. Sounds simple enough, don't you reckon?'

'Sounds humiliating.'

'Tough, girlie. You agreed to the game. I've exfoliated with a bunch of fat women with hairy legs for you. You're doing this for me. Drink up. It starts at eight.'

Oh. My. God. By man five, she wasn't humiliated any more. She had had no idea how incredibly interesting and stimulating she was. In comparison to them, she was a bloody shoe-in for *Parkinson*. The first guy was a sheep farmer and a young Conservative, with an Adam's apple nearly as big as his head.

She couldn't stop staring at it, marvelling as it bobbed up and down, and he had to keep sinking lower in his seat to make eye-contact with her, so that by the end of the three minutes he was practically on his knees (not that begging would have done him the slightest bit of good).

The second one taught physics – physics! – at the local comprehensive, and had three cats named after Ancient Greeks.

The third was all-right-looking from the neck up, but completely musclebound beneath – of the kind who can barely raise their arms above their heads because of all the hard knobbly bits – and only seemed interested in telling her how many 'reps' he could do, and that Mariah Carey was his idea of feminine perfection.

The fourth lived with his mother. Natalie stopped listening after that.

And the fifth, the first who had seemed vaguely normal, was sweet and smiley, but just plain boring.

Natalie's fixed smile was beginning to hurt her cheeks. She would kill Tom. This was the very worst letter so far.

The bell sounded and number five got up. As he moved away, and before number six took his place, Natalie glanced up and down her row. What sort of girl came to something like this? They all looked normal and nice – pretty, even. There had to be better ways. She felt the beginning of a crushing depression. Was this what she had to look forward to?

She saw Tom moving along the line. He must be her last. She tried to catch his eye, so that they could gurn at each other in silent agreement about its awfulness. But Tom, it seemed, had eyes only for his next date. Natalie followed his gaze and saw . . . The waitress from the party. How? How? Why?

Number six was talking to her in a thick Brummie accent and she had to turn to him, but afterwards she couldn't have told you a single word of their stilted three-minute conversation.

* * *

'Is she looking?' The girl's voice was full of giggles.

Tom bet she'd be a lot of fun to go out with. 'Think so. She definitely saw me come and sit down here. Listen, Eve, thanks a million for doing this – I appreciate it more than you know.'

'It's no problem. How could I resist after the story you told me at the party? So cute! I'm a sucker for a love story and I've been meaning to come back and visit my folks for months now. Good excuse.'

'Well, it's brilliant of you.'

'Actually, I've been trying out some different characters – I've been Welsh, very Catherine Zeta Jones, and Irish, and I'm going to try my South African on the next guy. I've got an audition coming up in a few weeks for something shooting in Cape Town, which I'd love to get.'

Eve, like every third waitress in London, was an aspiring actress. And now, it appeared, Tom was an aspiring con-artist. They had talked, a lot, at the bar at the party. And he'd loved Natalie watching them, and he'd loved even more how apparently pissed off she was with him afterwards. And when Eve had said she had family around here and that she must get home and visit . . . He'd been dazzled by how quickly his fiendish plan had fallen into place.

And it was working perfectly. Natalie had looked like a guppy when she'd seen her, blowing bubbles of indignation into the room. Fantastic!

'So, Tom, let's check. I'm supposed to say that I'm interested in hooking up with you?' He nodded. 'And you'll say the same. So they'll pass on our details to each of us?'

'That'll be great.'

'No problem. It's been a laugh. Will you let me know if it works?'

'Of course. If you're not filming in South Africa.'

Only about a minute left. Tom felt sorry for Natalie's

bloke. Out of the corner of his eye he could see her craning her neck to watch him and Eve, almost completely ignoring the poor sod.

'Big finish, then!' Eve was saying. And she leant across the table, her T-shirt cut so low that the top of her pretty pink bra was clearly visible, and kissed his cheek, lingeringly, her fingers on the other side of his face. As she drew back, she smiled suggestively and whispered, 'Are you allowed to put down two names? I saw a guy about three blokes back who works out. It's a look I really go for, no offence. And I think he liked me too – he said I reminded him of Mariah Carey.'

'Four! And one of them is you.'

'See? I told you it'd be good.'

'Four isn't good. Every one of those blokes would have been lucky to get the time of day from me.'

'Nice to see your self-esteem back to full strength.'

'I don't mean it like that.'

'You didn't mean to sound quite so conceited, I take it?'

Tom was laughing at her. He knew exactly what she meant. Surely. 'They were dweebs, Tom. Dweebs who aren't interested in me!' Her indignation made her voice squeaky.

'Maybe you just weren't dweeby enough for them.'

'Maybe this was a bad idea. What about you?'

Tom didn't want to tell her that he had five. It didn't seem like a smart move. He hastily balled up two of the small cards in one hand. 'Just three. Two, really, since you don't count. But thanks anyway.'

'Huh. And I suppose I know who one of them came from. What on earth was she doing here anyway?'

'Do you mean Eve?'

'Oh, sorry. Eve. Yes, I mean Eve. I didn't know her name, since we've never been introduced.'

'That's a whole other evening of speed-dating you're thinking of . . .'

'You haven't answered my question.'

'Her family live around here.'

'And?'

'And what?'

'And she just happened to be here tonight because it's so hard for a girl who looks like her to get a date in London? Did I blink and miss the part when the West Country becomes a mecca for desirable single blokes? 'Cos I haven't exactly been falling over them lately.'

'I don't know why she was here, Nat. Honest.'

'You had three minutes with her.'

'And we weren't talking about what happened to have brought her here.'

'Excuse me. Of course. How dull. What were you talking about?'

'Work. Cars. Travelling. That sort of stuff.'

'It doesn't make any sense.'

'Maybe she likes provincial guys.'

Natalie narrowed her eyes. 'Like you?'

He pretended to be reading the card for the first time, squinting at it. 'Yup. Like me. I've definitely made it on to her shortlist.'

'Well, you would, wouldn't you? It's, like, fate or something.'

'Sarcasm does not become you.'

'And what about you? Did you put her down?'

'I did.'

Natalie scowled. Tom laughed. 'What is your problem, Natalie?'

She didn't answer. 'You going to get her details, then?'

'You going to give me a reason not to?'

She wanted to shave off his incredible performing eyebrow, and stove in his dimple. 'Don't flatter yourself.'

'Okay, then. Yes.' Tom walked towards the desk where Cupid – in the guise of a middle-aged woman wearing too much foundation – was the keeper of all numbers.

He turned back briefly. 'You getting any numbers?'

Natalie balled up her cards and threw them at him.

She waited for him, though. She had to – they'd come in his car.

Tom ostentatiously put the card into his wallet, next to his driving licence, and patted it gently as they walked towards the car park. 'I must say, Nat, you do seem very stroppy all of a sudden. It isn't my fault she showed up.'

'Isn't it?'

Tom shrugged his shoulders. 'What are you talking about? You're being completely paranoid. If I'd wanted to do something about Eve, I could have done it when we were in London for the party, couldn't I?'

She remembered. Yes, he could.

'So why would I go to all the trouble of staging something like this?'

He was getting quite near the knuckle. But she was too sulky to think it through properly. She climbed into the car, and fastened her seatbelt. They'd gone two miles before she said, 'Are you going to call her?'

'Maybe. I might. I'm not a monk, you know.'

She turned on the radio, and looked out of the window as though the streets they were driving down were new and exciting to her.

The next morning he told Serena about it. She sucked in her cheeks and exhaled slowly. 'I don't know, Tom. It sounds like she's either on to you – and she'd be pretty thick not to be, wouldn't she? – or she's really, really pissed off with you.'

'You can't make an omelette without breaking eggs, Serena.'

'She's not an egg.'

Tom smirked.

'Admit it – you liked her being jealous.'

'Oh, I'll admit it, all right. I bloody loved it.'

'And are you going to confess?'

'No way.'

Serena stood up. 'On your head be it, Tom. Hell hath no fury like a woman scorned, you know.'

'I haven't scorned her.'

'It's an expression.'

'It's a load of rubbish. She blinking well scorned me, didn't she? Can't take me seriously in that way, can't she? I beg to differ. She was pretty flipping serious last night. If she thinks I'm sitting around pining for her like some loser, she's never going to work anything out, is she? If she thinks someone else might be interested . . . well, that might just galvanise her . . .'

Serena wasn't sure.

Lucy

Patrick had a job interview. In Leeds. Lucy didn't want to move to Leeds, but she didn't want to tell Patrick that. She hadn't a clue whether or not he wanted to do the job. They weren't talking on that level. She laundered the shirts and gave advice about the ties, and cooked the breakfast that would sustain a man on a motorway and didn't ask. She kissed his cheek, waved and beamed at him from the door, watched until his car had disappeared from view. Recognised that she was relieved he had gone, and instantly felt bad about that.

And then she made a mug of tea and two phone calls. One to a friend with a son Ed's age, to ask her to pick up the children the following day: she claimed she had a dental appointment, an emergency crown thing they could only slot her in for late in the day. She was staggered by how easily the lie came out, and she felt bad when the friend said yes, of course she would, and why didn't they stay for tea? She would bring them back at bedtime, because crown things were horrible, and Lucy wouldn't feel up to it.

Perhaps she was a complete bitch after all. For a second she saw herself as the mothers in the playground would see her.

And then she phoned Alec.

'Let's go somewhere,' he had said at once, when she told him. He didn't seem to consider work. It was flattering and frightening.

'I don't want to go to bed.'

'Okay. That's not what I meant.' Had it been? 'I just want to be with you.' She believed him, because it was what she wanted too.

Alec took her to the beach. It was a couple of hours' journey, and they talked all the way. Really talked. She and Patrick might have talked about where to stop for petrol, or what had happened to Bella at school that week, or whether they could get away with not having the front of the house painted this summer, but they already knew everything else about each other. It seemed to Lucy suddenly that nothing was new any more. It was different with Alec. Awkwardly at first, but then, like detectives, they asked questions that filled in for them the broad brushstrokes and the tiny details of each other. It was much more than a first-date conversation. They knew each other, didn't they? They'd known each other for years. In that long but not wide way of most relationships.

And he kept her hand under his on the gearstick. No one had done that to her for a long time, and it felt good.

Afterwards she remembered laughing a lot.

It was a blustery day, and the seaside town was practically deserted. They arrived at lunchtime and ate fat chips from paper cones with wooden forks, leaning on groynes. It reminded Lucy of being a little girl. And then they walked, hand in hand, almost as far as the eye could see.

Alec talked about Australia, where he had grown up. He'd lived near a beach, he said, and had marked out the years of his childhood by the passing of seasons on it. Summer, when it filled with escapees from Sydney to the south, and winter, when he had it to himself most days. All his neighbours had been wonderful, noisy Greeks, he said, and he laughed, telling her stories about blazing Christmas days on the sand, and raucous New Year's Eves. He'd smoked his first cigarette there, drunk his first beer, had his first kiss.

'Why would you choose to make your life somewhere so landlocked and relentlessly grey?'

'Marianne, I suppose.'

Lucy felt she should take her hand out of his, but he held it more tightly.

'I'm sorry. I shouldn't have said.'

'Of course you should. We're talking about our lives, aren't we? They're part of them. Hell, they're the biggest part of them. Of course you should.'

She stopped walking. Alec came round to face her. Suddenly she felt wild. 'We must be bloody mad. What in the name of Christ do we think we're doing, day-tripping like a couple of teenagers? Like it makes any difference at all, putting a few miles between us and our lives . . .' She closed her eyes, and let the wind blow straight into her face. The waves were crashing behind her.

She felt him put his arms round her. 'Sssh. Stop it, Lucy.' His mouth was on her hair.

'We're wrong, Alec. We're wrong.'

'I know.'

They stood like that for a moment. Then Alec stepped back from her, and stared into her face. 'And I don't care.'

All they did was kiss. For hours. Not because it was too cold to do anything else. Not because Lucy didn't want to go any further. She wanted to. She'd had sex a hundred times feeling less desire than she did now, today, to make love with Alec. They kissed themselves insensible on the sand. Until their mouths hurt, and her skin was raw.

She asked him if he thought she was pathetic. 'I'm not even a proper adulteress.'

Alec lifted her chin with his finger. 'I'm glad. It's more Lucy. And I think you're lovely.'

She went into a loo, and when she came out, Alec was checking his Blackberry. 'We should go,' she said. His face made her add, 'I don't want to.'

'I don't either.'

But they went. Home.

'What's going to happen, do you think?' Alec asked her, a few miles from where he would drop her.

'Can we stop at this?'

'Or have we started something we can't stop?'

Neither of them had answers.

N for Nemesis

'Nemesis. It means just punishment, Tom.'

'I love it when you're all dominatingy.'

'You won't. Just punishment for previous sins.'

'It's also a rock band, a computer game, and, if I'm not very much mistaken, the title of a *Star Trek* film.'

'That's very impressive, Tom, but irrelevant.' Her face was totally straight. 'What you did to me at the speed-dating certainly qualifies as a sin. It showed you to be devious, manipulative and, actually, cruel.'

'Oh, come on! You missed out mean, dastardly and utterly brilliant.'

'I'm talking!' She banged the kitchen table hard, with her open palm.

'Is there going to be whipping and chains? Because – I've gotta tell you – I've always thought I'd look quite good in a gimp suit.'

'You've met your nemesis. That's all I'll tell you. But here's a couple of things to give you food for thought. N was going to be Nature. I was going to take you to an RHS garden. To walk and appreciate the beauty around us.'

'Well, that's a relief. Sounds pretty dull.'

A smile played around Natalie's lips, then she recomposed her face. 'And you might dwell on this. Having your nemesis chosen by someone who has known you incredibly well for more than two decades, who knows your deepest fears and your darkest secrets . . . Well, frankly, it should scare the hell out of you. Remember, if you will, equine . . .'

For a moment, it almost did.

Natalie wasn't going to tell Tom that Serena had taken her out for a drink and told her about Eve. She'd promised her that she wouldn't. Tom underestimated the loyalty of women. And that was to her advantage. She'd known it hadn't smelt right, Eve turning up like that, but she hadn't put two and two together until Serena had shown her the way. And even if she had, he'd proven himself more devious than she had ever imagined him to be. Pretty audacious. All Serena had asked for, as reward for her double-agenting, was to be there when Natalie exacted her revenge.

Which was why Rob and Serena were in the car, heading up the M6 obscenely early on the next Saturday morning.

It had taken her a whole hour in the bath to figure it out. She'd missed *EastEnders* thinking about it. Then there had been a eureka moment. Thorpe Park. School trip. Summer before his O levels. She'd jumped out of the bath and dripped down the passage to phone Bridget, who was trying to watch *EastEnders*, and answered her questions distractedly for a couple of minutes. 'Yes,' she said, 'he was absolutely terrified.' And very very sick. 'I don't think it was the adrenaline thing that frightened him most,' she said, 'it was the being sick.'

The rest had fallen into place beautifully, and even provided her with the N. Natalie hoped he hadn't grown out of it.

'Alton Towers?'

'Yep. Alton Towers.'

'So what? This is the office outing?'

Rob snorted. 'Wouldn't want to miss this, mate.'

'Miss what, exactly?' Tom asked.

Natalie pulled the sheet of A4 paper out of her bag. Serena, who was driving, looked at Tom in the rear-view mirror. 'Rita, Queen of Speed, which goes from nought to a hundred kilometres per hour in two point five seconds. Or Oblivion, which plummets two hundred feet with a four point five G-force. Or Submission – that's a double inverter. Or Air, or Ripsaw, or the Blade, or Spinball Whizzer, or Enterprise. Or Nemesis, which has a greater G-force than a space shuttle takeoff. We wouldn't want to miss seeing you on any of those, Tom. Tom?'

Tom was green. And the M6 was straight. 'You know, don't you?' His tone was incredulous.

'Know what, Tom? Know that you set up that stuff with Eve? Of course. It was obvious. Or know that you're terrified of roller-coasters? I know that too. Or, rather, Bridge does. And was happy enough to tell me, once I told her what you did . . . Oh, yes, Tom,' and she gave a slightly maniacal laugh, 'I know.'

'You're not really going to make me go on all those rides, are you?'

'Oh, yes, one after the other. All of them. And I have a shortcut pass, too. Amazing what you can book on-line now. No queuing. You can just go from ride to ride to ride, without so much as a sit-down. Isn't that clever?'

None of them remembered the last time Tom hadn't had an answer.

Even without queuing it took almost three hours for Tom to ride them all. Natalie saved Nemesis until last. Rob and Serena rode all the same rides, but with gusto and enthusiasm – although Serena staggered off Oblivion wondering whether her fertility was at risk from the G-force – rather than the gut-wrenching, tummy-flipping, nausea-induced reluctance with which Tom joined each line. Each time, he gazed at her imploringly.

'For God's sake, Tom, you look like a seal that's about to get clubbed. Take your medicine like a good boy. No reprieves, however pathetic you are.'

'I've never noticed this streak of malice in you before, Natalie. It's not altogether attractive.'

'Tough.'

Actually it was quite attractive. Only he felt too sick to think about it. 'And you're not going to go on any? You're making me do it alone?'

'I might go on one, later. But first, I need to watch you suffer. It wouldn't be half as much fun if I couldn't. Besides, I hate the things. They make me sick.'

Rob was eating a hot dog. Fluorescent yellow mustard and ketchup squelched out of the edges. Serena was picking pieces of pink candy floss off a stick and eating them daintily. Tom winced. 'Urgh. How can you?'

Rob chuckled, and Serena pinched his cheek maternally. 'There, there. Over soon.'

Natalie went on one. Nemesis, obviously. Poetic, she thought. The front two seats were free. She pulled Tom towards it. 'The front? Really?'

'Really. It's the best seat in the house.'

When they were strapped in and waiting to start, she turned to him. 'Got your wallet?' Tom felt in the top pocket of his jacket.

'Yeah. Why?'

'Give it to me.'

He pulled it out and passed it to her. She opened it and fished out the card from the speed-dating night from behind his driving licence, then handed it back to him. 'I should have known you'd still have it in there.'

'I still have my university library card too. I don't clear it out very often.'

'Mmm.' She passed him the card. 'This is what we're going to do. Arms above your head, please . . .'

Which was how, when Nemesis reached the zenith of its torturous sixty kilometres an hour journey to hell and back, a small white card – barely visible – fluttered in the air and floated serenely to earth behind the hot-dog stand.

O for Opera

'Bugger it. Let's not go.'
      'But you've bought the tickets.'
   'So? Let's flog 'em.'
   'Where?'
   'Outside the place. Like proper ticket touts.'
   'Isn't that illegal?'
   'Natalie! So righteous. So law-abiding.'
   'I can't help it – I've always been like this.'
   'I remember. Except in the car. You've always been pretty lawless in the car.'
   'Lawless but safe, I like to think.'
   'So, look, if it worries you, I'll do the touting. You can keep lookout. Pretend you don't know me if the busies show up.' Natalie giggled.
   'That might work.'
   They wandered towards the theatre. 'So, what was it again?'
   'Wagner's *Ring Cycle*. Hours and hours and bloody hours of fat women wailing. No costumes, no sets, just wailing.'
   'You sound like a real fan.'
   'Not bloody likely. Most I've ever done is sat through *Carmen* and *La Bohème*, and they're, like, the easiest ones. The most "accessible", which I took to mean the ones least likely to make you want to slash your wrists.'
   'I saw *La Belle Hélène*, with my godmother, on about my tenth birthday, I think. It was pretty.'
   'Never heard of it.'

'If you're such an opera loather, why buy the tickets in the first place? Not stumped, were we?' She cocked her head at him.

'No. A bit. Okay – completely. Plus I was looking for a bit of revenge myself, after the whole vomitorium that was Alton Towers.'

'So, what changed your mind?'

'Well, two things, really. First I realised that if you had to sit through a Wagnerian performance that lasted half your natural lifespan I would have to sit there with you. The phrase cutting off one's nose to spite one's face springs to mind.'

'And second?'

'I remembered that despite your escalation of what I admit was a bit of a dastardly M into a downright unpleasant N, this is not an episode of that Japanese game show Endurance, but a rather sweet game being played between great friends. I thought it was up to me to bring honour and morality back to it.'

'And you couldn't face it.'

'And I couldn't face it.'

'Thank Christ. I'd better ring Rose. I told her to text me with some plumbing crisis at ten o'clock.'

'You bugger.'

'Me genius. You'd have escaped too – we came in one car, remember?'

'What a pair of Philistines we are.'

'Hurrah for us. What shall we do instead?'

'Well, let's see how much we can get for the tickets and then decide. Maybe McDonald's, maybe Le Gavroche . . .'

Tom was rubbish at touting. He looked shiftier than a pimp on a street corner, standing on the steps, whispering to passers-by, most of whom looked considerably less likely even than he was to want to sit through the *Ring Cycle*. Natalie's attack of giggles didn't help. In about five minutes, when the doorman of the theatre had started giving him regular hard stares, Tom lost his nerve and bundled Natalie round the corner.

'McDonald's it is, then.' She was still laughing.

'Hardly Bonnie and Clyde, are we?'

'Makes for a longer life . . .'

'Rose and Pete are at the pub.'

'Let's go.'

'What shall we tell them? This looks a bit pathetic – showing up ten minutes after the thing has started.'

'Tell them we got thrown out for singing along.' Natalie put her arm through Tom's and they marched off, still laughing.

P for Paris

'Don't go mad – it's just for the day, Tom. Thought we'd avoid any hotel-room horrors.'

'But April in Paris, Nat, your best letter yet, without a doubt.'

'Worth getting up this early for?'

'Absolutely.'

It was horribly early, and still quite chilly at Waterloo. Natalie was dressed for Paris In Spring Sunshine (inspired by a section in last month's *In Style* magazine entitled exactly that, and which Google Weathersearch had promised); she shivered as they waited for the ubiquitous security queue to subside. The night before they'd stayed with Casper: Susannah was away overnight at an audition. Casper had been smoking dope with friends before they arrived, and fell asleep on the sofa in front of *Coronation Street*. He hadn't been awake when they left this morning, surprise, surprise.

Natalie had persuaded her dad to buy her a day return on Eurostar as a birthday present. Actually, he hadn't taken much persuading. He'd gone a bit misty. Apparently he'd taken her mum to Paris for their tenth wedding anniversary. Natalie didn't remember that. She and her sisters had been left at home with their grandmother and chickenpox. 'Your mum didn't want to leave you.' He smiled. 'You were the worst – Susannah only had a few spots, and Bridget, well, she was always a Stoic, but you were absolutely wretched. You had spots where we didn't know you had places. And you made a hell of a fuss. I had to practically drag her to the airport, and she cried half-way there. It was probably the first time she'd left all three of you for more than day or so, bless her. But, oh, we had such a good time, her and me.'

He'd been doing a bit more of that lately, Natalie had thought, as she'd left with his cheque. Talking about the past. It made her inexplicably sad. Maybe her parents would never go back to Paris. Getting old was horrible. Having to think about all the things you wouldn't do again, or were doing for the last time. She remembered her granddad, who'd had the scruffiest old suit to wear to funerals, weddings and christenings, because from about the age of sixty-five, he'd refused to buy a new one, claiming that he'd never get enough wear out of it to justify the cost. How bloody sad.

Natalie had found the cash for the second seat, but if Tom wanted much more than a baguette and a carafe of the house red for lunch he might have to finance it. Last night Rose had dropped by. 'I've bought you something for your birthday.' She told her what it was before Natalie opened it. Rose always did that. She was usually far more excited about her present than the recipient was. 'It's four of those diddy bottles of champagne, like they have at posh parties in *Hello!* and *OK!*. And they have the cutest little things, look, that you slot in the top when you take the cork out and then you can sip them – see? Through there – and you don't need a straw or anything. And it's Veuve Clicquot, darling, not just any old plonk. I thought you could have one each on the way there and save one for the journey home. Do it in style, you know.'

Natalie had hugged her. 'Thank you – it's perfect!'

'Well – you know, the capital of romance!'

'Why does everyone keep calling it that? Even my dad did!'

'Him, me and the rest of the world, honey. Including Tom.'

'What do you mean?'

'I don't mean anything. Just that you're taking him to a city that the entire world considers the most romantic place in the world outside the Taj Mahal, which you couldn't afford.'

'Mistake?'

'You tell me.'

'I hate it when you're cryptic, Rose. Be obvious.'

'Only a mistake if you're not up for romance.'

'We're only going to be there for about ten hours.'

'Only takes most blokes ten minutes.'

'Rose!'

'Sorry.' Rose tried to look serious. 'Look, Natalie, as I see it, you're in denial of something that is undeniable. Tom has the patience of Job. He can see it, we can see it. Everyone gets it, except you. It's obvious.'

'It's a day trip.'

Rose put up her hands in a gesture of surrender. 'Fair enough. I presume friends can enjoy a glass of Veuve Clicquot on a train, same as lovers can?'

Natalie smiled. 'Course they can. Thanks, Rosie. I love you.'

'I love you too.'

She picked up her car keys, and stood up to leave. 'So does Tom,' she muttered, under her breath.

'Rose!'

The sun was out by the time they arrived at the Gare du Nord. Natalie had pored over her *Time Out* guide the night before and had planned an itinerary that wouldn't have disappointed a coachload of Japanese tourists. They were to have lunch within sight of the Arc de Triomphe, ram-raid the Louvre to see the *Mona Lisa*, meander down the Champs-Elysées, climb the Eiffel Tower, take a short ride on a Bateau Mouche and end up, at sunset, beside Notre-Dame. An early supper on the Île St Louis, then back to the station.

'Blimey. When do I get a Gauloise and a coffee in a pavement café?'

'First?'

'First sounds good.'

They wandered towards the nearest authentic-looking café, and sat down on the varnished wicker chairs outside.

'You don't really want a Gauloise, do you?' she asked, as the black and white waiter approached.

'No. Just joking. Although if any capital city was going to make me want to smoke, this is the one. A coffee would be great.'

Natalie smiled at the waiter. '*Deux cafés, s'il vous plaît.*' That was the only part of the conversation that Tom understood. The waiter asked her something, she answered, gesticulating and rolling her shoulders like a native. After a couple of minutes of this, the waiter glanced at him, laughed, shrugged and wandered off indolently.

'What were you saying to him?'

'Just passing the time of day.'

'Just taking the piss, more like. I'd forgotten you were fluent.'

'Not fluent, I shouldn't think. Not now anyway. I'm a bit rusty.'

'You sounded like a Frenchwoman to me.'

'*Merci, monsieur!*'

It was funny, that, wasn't it? Tom thought. You knew someone for so long and all this stuff about them, but you forgot it. Like the roller-coasters, which was definitely best forgotten. And the French, which was a lovely surprise to rediscover. She had sounded confident, relaxed and accomplished. He smiled at her. '*De rien!*'

'Not so bad yourself.'

'Don't get excited. That's about the only phrase I remember.'

'Good job I'm here to do your talking for you, then, isn't it?'

'Very good job.'

Their coffee came, and tasted fantastic.

'So, Natalie. I don't want to hold us back. I know how busy we are today. Just tell me, do you want your birthday present now or later? Don't know why I'm asking, really. You're a now-girl, I know, not hugely into the concept of delayed gratification.'

'Oh, yes, now. Now, now, now.'

Tom laughed at her.

'Where is it? Where?' She was tapping at his pockets. 'Can't be big, whatever it is – no lumps.'

'It's not here. It's at Cartier.'

'What do you mean?'

'We haven't bought it yet. We're going to get you a new watch. You've been wearing that Swatch for years. In fact, I remember the Christmas you got it. I was at university, so that makes it at least fifteen years old. I can't believe it still works. Or that no one else ever bought you another.'

'Mum and Dad did. They gave me this old-lady-type gold one – remember? – when I was twenty-one. Had it engraved, and everything. Can't stand it!'

'Why didn't you tell them? I'm sure you could have swapped it!'

'I'd never have done that. It would have hurt their feelings. They'd gone out and chosen it for me, hadn't they? And I'm sure it wasn't cheap.'

'So you've had it shoved into a drawer all this time?'

'Sort of. I wear it for family stuff. Come to think of it, I haven't seen it for a while. I might have lost it.'

'So you wouldn't swap it, but you'd lose it happily enough.'

'Not on purpose.'

'It never is . . .'

'Anyway, we're not talking about my bad habits. Or my old

watch. We were talking about the purchase of serious consumer durables. By you for me. A Cartier watch? Are you serious? I've seen them on eBay. They're gorgeous. With that D on the strap. But they cost a fortune! Are you sure? Tom?'

'Stop spluttering on. Course I'm sure. Bound to save a couple of euros, buying it over here. And it's about time you had a decent watch. So, can we shave a bit of time off the critical path and go and get it?' He looked at the list. 'Louvre. We can certainly do without that. I've seen her. Nothing enigmatic about that I've-got-a-carrot-shoved-up-my-jacksie smile. She's a woman, probably with PMT, on the verge of a strop. Probably because old Leonardo has made her stand still for so long, and is painting her on such a bad-hair day. I've seen it loads of times – the smile, not the picture. Seen the picture once. It's about the size of a postcard, and you can't get anywhere near it because there are always a thousand tourists standing right in front of it. That can go.'

'For a Cartier watch, the whole shebang can go. Come on.' Natalie had drained her coffee, and was hopping excitedly from foot to foot.

'Put your arm away!'

'I can't stop looking at it. It's beautiful. It is absolutely the best, best present anyone ever gave me. Totally. I love it. Thank you, Tom!'

It had cost more than Tom was expecting. He should have known they were in trouble when the snooty French assistant had offered them two comfortable leather bucket chairs, and produced a selection of watches on a velvet tray thing. Quite a lot more than he'd thought. But it had been worth it – she hadn't stopped beaming since, and had completed the rest of the whistlestop tour of Paris's major attractions with her left wrist extended in front of her. He didn't think Simon had spoilt her like this – the fool. She was like a little girl, and he felt absolutely fantastic.

'Happy birthday, Nat. Welcome to your late thirties!'

'I'm entitled to call it mid-thirties for at least another year, surely!'

'You call it what you like. Me – I'm staring down the barrel of forty.'

'You so are not. That's unusually cup-half-empty, for you.'

'I don't mind turning forty. It lends a certain gravitas.'

'It's not gravitas that worries me. It's gravity.'

Tom laughed. 'Stop fishing for compliments.'

They were sitting on the stone balustrades of some *pont* or other, with the stunning Notre-Dame cathedral behind them and its extraordinary stained-glass window, soaking up the last orange rays of a beautifully sunny day.

Natalie let out a long, contented sigh. She was tired, not the scratchy tired that made her knees ache, but a pleasant, languorous sensation.

'Do you know where we're meant to be having supper?' Tom asked.

'Not exactly, but I'm sure we can find it. It's called something like the Tavern of the Recruiting Sergeant.'

'Sounds dreadful.'

'No – it's meant to be great fun. Suze says it's very atmospheric. The sort of place where you can only eat steak and *frites*, and there's only one house white and one house red, and they come in jugs.'

'Come on, then. We've got to be back at the Gare du Nord in—'

'Two and a half hours!' Natalie had read the face of her new watch exultantly.

For atmospheric, read incredibly noisy and Gallic, but the

steak was thick and juicy, and the jugs flowed – okay, they sort of sloshed. Tom wondered if Natalie's brief to Susannah had been to find the least romantic restaurant in the capital of romance, but dismissed the thought as paranoia.

He didn't know if they'd ever be more than they were now, but if they were, he already knew that they wouldn't be your conventional romantics. He might have liked to be. He could see himself buying flowers, leaving notes under pillows and all that stuff. He just wasn't sure he could see Natalie accepting them. She was seriously out of the habit, if she'd ever been in it. He might have to see what he could do about it.

It was dark when they came out, somewhat gratefully, into the quiet street, which was practically deserted. Natalie linked arms with him and they started in vaguely the right direction for a cab. Five minutes later, they hadn't reached the place she had thought they would. 'Better have a look at the map. We're pushing it for time.'

They headed for a doorway with a soft yellow light above it, and Natalie pulled out the map. She started tracing lines with her finger to orient herself.

In another doorway across the road, a couple were kissing passionately, oblivious of their presence. It was a full-on, Robert Doisneau, filmic snog – his hands in her hair, her arms flung round his neck, their eyes closed, bodies locked from lip to knee.

Tom looked down at Natalie as she studied the map. They were very close under the lamp. He could see the gentle rise and fall of her pale chest, and the almost imperceptible throb of the pulse in her neck. Then she glanced up and saw the other couple, watched them for a second, then raised her face to him. The shadows accentuated the dip between her nose and mouth, and her lips glistened where the light caught them. Her pupils were huge and black – he could almost see himself reflected in them.

Natalie's head was asking her: Is this the man?

He wanted to kiss her so much right then that it hurt in the pit of his stomach, just under the steak and *frites*. She didn't move her face. It would have taken only the slightest movement from either of them to bring their mouths together, but they were still. It seemed like they hadn't even blinked. And everything was in that look. Everything.

Tom's heart was telling him: This *is* the girl.

A second before the headlamps on the car changed the colours of the light, and broke the moment, Tom moved away from her. And she recognised him doing it. He didn't know whether he was relieved or disappointed to see it was a taxi. The next twenty minutes were spent hailing it, garbling instructions, *très vite, s'il vous plâit*, racing through Paris to the station, running down the platform. They caught the train with what felt like seconds to spare, and fell gratefully, breathlessly, into their seats.

Natalie laughed at him. 'You look so stressed! I *always* catch trains like this.'

'*Why?*'

'Because life's an adventure, Tom.'

But twenty minutes later she was asleep, her head against her rolled-up jacket, her bare feet up on the seat next to him. Tom watched her. I wonder if she wondered why I didn't kiss her back there, he pondered. I wonder if she minded. I wonder what would have happened if the cab had been two minutes later. Would she have moved in towards me, like she did in the bedroom at the health farm? Or would she have changed the subject, made a joke? And if she had kissed me, got things started, wanted me, would she have stopped again?

Natalie went straight to her bedroom, and stripped off, letting her clothes fall to the floor unheeded. She was exhausted. But she was wondering. It would have been okay, being kissed under a streetlight in the dark in Paris on her birthday. She would have quite liked it, actually. So long as he didn't think she was only letting him kiss her because of the watch. She wasn't that kind of girl. But, then, he probably knew that. But it was okay that the kiss hadn't happened, too. She felt a bit like a teenager. Once, on Valentine's Day a thousand years ago, a boy she liked had sent her an anonymous card, but by the end of the day she had worked out it was from him, and after school they had sat together on the bus, and he had walked the long way round to his house, which meant going right past hers, and they had stood shifting from one foot to the other at the end of her drive, talking about whether or not to kiss each other for ages and ages (until Bridget and Susannah had come home, in fact, which broke the mood, such as it was). They hadn't been brave enough, that day, but they had sort of laid the foundations for the next time. And the next time they had kissed and kissed. Paris had felt a bit like that Valentine's afternoon, in the cold, on the driveway, when she was about twelve. And it was quite a nice feeling. She pulled her nightshirt over her head. She might have fallen into the unmade bed immediately if she hadn't been thirsty. She yawned and headed for the kitchen. The red light on her telephone was flashing. Four new messages.

The first was her dad, saying he hoped his money had been well spent. She thought so. She could hear his benevolent smile when he said, 'Don't bother to call your old man back, sweetheart. I'll talk to you tomorrow. I love you.'

The second was Rose, an apparently hyperventilating Rose: 'Call me, call me, call me.'

The third message was also Rose: 'Whatever time you get in. I'll still be up!'

Natalie smiled to herself, and pushed Rose's button on the speed dial. If she was looking for gory details she was going to be disappointed.

She was looking for an audience. 'Oh, Nat, I'm *so* glad you called! Pete's asked me to marry him!'

For a split second, Natalie remembered January, when Pete had whisked Rose off on Eurostar, and how she had hoped (and hated herself for it) that Pete wouldn't propose. She didn't feel that way tonight. She was instantly, bubblingly happy for her best friend and burst into tears.

Rose sounded panicky. 'Are you crying? Are you all right?'

'I'm fine. Fine. Just . . . so . . . happy . . . for . . . you . . . both.'

'Isn't it ironic? You went to Paris, and I got engaged! Makes you smile, doesn't it?'

'I'm smiling because I'm happy for you, Rosie, not because that makes me smile.'

'Well, don't come here for sympathy. You could be, if you wanted to be, if you ask me.'

'Which I won't. Now, shut up about me and tell me all about it. While simultaneously reassuring me that I get to be Sexy Bridesmaid, not Taffeta Terror . . .'

It took Rose about half an hour to impart the most salient points of Pete's proposal, and about another thirty minutes to discuss those aspects of the wedding she had decided on. Pretty impressive, Natalie thought, for someone who only got proposed to tonight.

It was almost one in the morning when she could stifle her yawns no longer, and she mumbled to Rose that she'd better get some sleep.

'So,' Rose finally remembered to ask, 'how was Paris?'

'Paris was . . . Paris was . . .'

'Yes?' Rose sounded excited all over again.

'Paris was . . . perfect.' Rose was silent at the end of the line. 'And that's all I'm going to tell you, you nosy old bag. Now, goodnight!'

She made a last mug of tea, stirred it and thought about Tom. She was plodding wearily back towards the stairs when she remembered there had been a fourth message. She almost ignored it – what couldn't wait until tomorrow? – but then, impulsively, she pushed the button.

It was Bridget. 'Nat? I don't think you're there. Was it today you were going to Paris with Tom? I know today's your actual birthday. Happy birthday, by the way. That's a bit stupid. Sorry. Not sure if it was the day you were going. Anyway, look, a message probably isn't the best way to tell you this, but I'd want to know, if I was you . . . Dad's had another stroke. A massive one, apparently. This afternoon. He's in hospital, of course, and Mum's there, too. I've been, briefly, but I don't know much, and I've had to come back home now, because of the kids . . . I'm sorry, Nat, really sorry to be telling you like this. But they think there's a chance he won't survive this one.'

Natalie sat down on the arm of the sofa. Christ. She didn't know what to do. Then the receiver was in her hand and she was calling Tom.

'Missing me already?' He sounded sleepy, but not angry.

'Dad's had a massive stroke, Tom. They think he might die.'

'I'll be there. Sit tight. Give me twenty minutes.'

He was there in fifteen. She opened the door to his insistent knock, and collapsed against him. 'I thought he was okay. He seemed okay.'

'And he still might be. Why aren't you dressed? We can go straight away.'

She wasn't dressed because from the moment she had put down the phone to when she had opened the door to him she had been sitting on the floor behind the sofa, rocking back and forth with her arms round her knees. She hadn't known what to do with herself.

Tom led her upstairs, and found her jeans and a sweater. He practically dressed her, raising her arms above her head to put on the jumper, and making her lean on him while he fed the denim over her feet. She didn't say a word.

Then he led her downstairs and out to his car.

'Thanks, Tom,' she muttered, as he opened the passenger door.

Briefly, he kissed the top of her head, then went round to the driver's side and climbed in beside her.

They made her take off her bracelet and rings, and the shiny new Cartier watch, and wash her hands in a special sink outside ITU. Tom took the jewellery from her, and squeezed her hand. 'I'm right here.'

Her mum was by her dad's bed. Natalie stretched out her hand to Anna but never took her eyes off her father as she approached him. There were machines, like on television, beeping and flashing their strange techno beat. Her father was intubated – she knew that from *ER* – where they have to stick this metal tube down your throat, 'Careful of the vocal cords' and then 'I'm in,' and 'Bag him.' They'd done that to her dad. He was asleep but it wasn't a peaceful sleep. One side of his face was all dragged down, like something powerful was sucking at it. The corner of his eye, the corner of his mouth, all the flesh of his cheek. And the arm on that side looked weird somehow, just wrong, like a broken leg is wrong-looking.

'How is he?' she asked. She wanted to touch him, but she

wasn't sure where was okay so one of her hands just hovered above him.

'They can't say.'

'Anything?'

'Tonight is critical. If he survives the night . . .' Her mother's voice broke, and Natalie turned to her. She was ashen. Her hair was messy, as if her hands had been pushed through it a hundred times, and her lips were dry and chapped.

Natalie put both her arms round her, and the two of them stayed like that for a long time.

'Bridget's been,' Natalie said eventually.

'Yes. She's telephoned Susannah. I hated making her do that, call you both, but . . .'

'Is Susannah coming?'

'I don't know. I suppose she will if she can.'

'Of course.'

They both turned to Nicholas.

It seemed inconceivable to Natalie that he wasn't about to open his eyes and say something pithy about Paris, or goad her about Tom. She almost wanted to shake him. She wanted them to put a curtain across the part of his face that was unrecognisable. She only wanted to see the familiar part.

'Can we stay?'

'They think I should go and get some sleep. They have a room . . . out there somewhere.'

'Can I stay with you?'

'You shouldn't be here.'

'He's my dad, Mum, and you're my mum. I want to stay with you.'

'You're a good girl.'

'Have you eaten anything, Mum, at all, this evening?'

'I couldn't.'

'Would you come with me, have a cup of tea at least?'

'No. I want to be here, in case . . .'

Natalie wouldn't let herself think about the 'in case'.

Tom paced the corridor outside ITU. He was desperate for Natalie, of course, but he was also shattered. They'd been up absurdly early, it was almost three in the morning and he had a meeting at nine. This is the heavy stuff, he thought. This is what you sign up for, parents, children – this is the deal. And it was the second time he'd been here for Natalie in barely four months. Poor Nat. He thought about his own mum and dad, and wondered how he would feel. It didn't seem fair: things had seemed to be getting better for Anna and Nicholas. Now this.

When Natalie eventually came out, she looked smaller somehow than when she had gone in.

'How's he doing?'

'It's too early to tell, apparently. I spoke to a nurse, and she said with a stroke this massive the first twelve hours or so are crucial. If he makes it through the night' – she took a deep breath – 'they can start to evaluate how badly he's been affected. Until then it's a waiting game. They said.'

'And your mum?'

'She won't come out. She hasn't left his side, I don't think, since they got here. I hope she'll sleep a little – they have a room here she can use.'

'Do you want me to take you home?'

'I want to stay, Tom. I want to be here. I wouldn't sleep, anyway, if I went home.'

'What can I do?'

'Call work for me in the morning and tell them what's happened?'

Tom nodded.

She stroked his face. 'You look exhausted.'

'Thanks.' He managed a weak smile.

'Still devilishly handsome, of course, but exhausted none the less.'

'I wish there was something more I could do.' He pulled his car keys out of his jacket pocket. He didn't want to leave her.

'Go, Tom. Sleep. You've done enough. You're always there for me. You came when I rang, without a moment's hesitation. You brought me to my mum and dad.'

He pulled her to him in a bear hug. 'Call me. Any time. Promise? Any time.'

She nodded and pulled her arms up into the sleeves of her jumper; she looked about ten years old. He walked into the lift and pushed the button.

May
Q for Queen Tribute Band

This was Natalie's first big night out – a planned outing – since her dad. It felt bad and good at the same time. Tom, it was always Tom, had made her come.

'Don't you think your dad would want you to? I know that's the kind of crap thing that people say at times like this when they want to justify their behaviour, but think about it honestly. He'd want you to, wouldn't he? Just like he wants Susannah to go for auditions, and he wants Bridget to go to – I don't know what Bridget goes to, toddler groups or something. This is your life, Natalie, not his. Besides, I've bought tickets.'

'Not more Wagner, I hope. I'm not in a very Wagner place, these days.'

'Definitely not Wagner. Promise. This is very, very cool.'

It definitely wasn't Wagner, but she might have quarrelled with the very, very cool bit.

'Have you ever noticed how Brian May and Anita Dobson look exactly the same? Like those poodles. Or like Charles the First. Or was it the Second. I think they both had the same hair, come to think of it. That was why Cromwell didn't like them. Can't say I blame him. It's absolutely rubbish hair.'

'Sssh. I'd be careful about slagging Brian May off in this company.'

'Am I the only sane person here, do you reckon?'

'Since when did a fondness for classic rock make you mental?'

'Classic rock! Listen to yourself, Tom. You're still a young man, for God's sake!'

'The classic-rock genre knows no age limitation, Natalie.'

The tribute band was called Queens. The merchandise in the foyer proclaimed this proudly. The tour T-shirts boasted such mega-venues as Plymouth and Basildon. Natalie hoped the name of the band was ironic, but she doubted it. She was pretty much the only person there without a visible tattoo.

'Tom? Have you got a tattoo?' She hadn't thought to ask before.

He looked at her strangely. 'Yes, actually. I have a profile of Freddie Mercury on my left testicle.'

She smacked him.

'No! I haven't got a tattoo. Or a Harley Davidson. Or a leather waistcoat with useless metal chains attached to it. I just like Queen.'

'I don't know any Queen songs.'

'Rubbish. "We Are The Champions". "We Will Rock You". "I Want to Break Free". Some of the great anthems of the twentieth century. "Bohemian Rhapsody" – possibly the greatest song of all time and, incidentally, the first ever modern rock video.'

'And, incidentally, the most insane lyrics *ever*.'

'Thought you didn't know any.'

'I know enough to know they're half-baked.'

'And my personal favourite, "Crazy Little Thing Called Love".'

'Now, *that* I remember. Mum wouldn't let me watch *Top of the Pops* when they were on singing that because there were all these girls in bikinis writhing around on motorbikes.'

'Your mum wouldn't let you watch?'

'No, and she nearly burst something over Frankie Goes To Hollywood.'

'Do you remember how hard it was to convince her to let us go to Live Aid?'

'She only let me go because you were coming. She said you were a nice, sensible, trustworthy boy and that I would be in safe hands.'

'And that is why I've always loved your mother.'

'We had a good time, that day, didn't we?'

'Yeah. We did.'

'You know what I remember best?'

'What?'

'Sitting on your shoulders for Elton John and George Michael. Do you remember?'

'Remember? I still have a neck injury that aches in wet weather. You fidgeted up there something chronic.'

'Shut up! It was brilliant.' Natalie's eyes were shining with the memory.

Tom put his arm round her shoulder. 'See? Shared experience. History. Pretty cool, isn't it?'

Natalie was about to admit that it was when she saw something.

'Natalie! What are you doing?' Without warning, she had thrown her arms round his neck and buried her face in his left ear. She smelt of onions and mustard. 'Sssh. Don't call me Natalie!'

'What would you like me to call you?'

'Sssh. Over there.'

Natalie tried to gesture with her head, but since it was spot-welded to Tom's she only succeeded in moving both of them, awkwardly.

'Where?'

'Behind me.'

'What am I looking for?'

'Who, Tom. Who are you looking for? Unless I'm very much mistaken, over there, heading this way, is Mike Sweet.'

And it was. In a shirt that surpassed even his usual, dismal styles, and a baseball cap purchased from the table in the foyer.

Too late.

'Natalie? Hiya. I didn't know you were a fan.'

Natalie swung round, a fixed smile on her face. 'Oh, yeah. Can't get enough of them. Seen them twice already.'

'Really?' He looked at her with new eyes. 'This is my lady, Erica.'

My lady? Who did he think he was? Barry White?

'Natalie works for me, down at the station.' He couldn't say 'works with me', could he?

Erica offered a limp hand, which Natalie shook.

'And I'm her man.' Tom poked her in the small of the back, and proffered his hand. 'Name's Barry.'

Great minds thought alike. Natalie stepped back, and on to Tom's big toe.

Mike was frowning at him. 'Haven't we met?'

'Terrific! You remember. Waited backstage for you after the New Year's Eve matinée of *Jack and the Beanstalk* last year. Fabulous performance. Really excellent.'

How did Natalie stop herself laughing?

Mike nodded, as though being accosted by super-fans was commonplace for him. 'Oh, yeah. I never forget a face. That was a great script.' The two men continued to nod at each other until Erica began to fidget. Natalie imagined that her skin-tight trousers might make standing still for too long a little uncomfortable. Were they PVC?

'We better go and find our seats, Mikey,' Erica purred.

Mike put his hand to his forehead in a salute. 'Better had. Don't want to miss a note. Great seeing you, Natalie. And you – Barry, was it? Have a wild time, kids.'

Natalie and Tom turned to each other, burst out laughing, and collapsed on each other's shoulders.

'*Barry!*'

'I thought the walrus of love was appropriate.'

'I didn't think it was possible for him to be worse out of the office, but, do you know, he is?'

'Thank God they went off in the opposite direction. Can you imagine sitting next to them?'

'We'd have had to watch him dance. I've seen it at Christmas parties. It's hilarious.'

'Poor misunderstood fellow.'

'My arse.'

'You have got to get a new job!'

Now there was a thought . . .

The crowd inside the auditorium erupted into applause, and the first few notes of what even Natalie recognised as 'We Will Rock You' played at an unbelievable decibel level.

Tom pulled her arm. 'Come on, Anita. Time to *rock*!'

Natalie was smiling through her wince, as he pulled open the door.

Lucy

It was horribly easy for Lucy to make time to see Alec. Lack of time and privacy was one of the things she thought would protect her from being unfaithful, but, like all the other safeguards, it failed her.

One tiny lie.

She was going shopping in London and meeting an old friend from college for lunch. She would be back lateish.

Easy.

Patrick would be busy ferrying the children to and from school. Their children. Her children.

She felt disgusted with herself, briefly, as she pulled away. It was the sight of him dressed for a day at home, Ed peering out between his legs. The knowledge that he thought she was going because she wanted a day away from him. From the depressing, dreary dullness of his unemployment and his presence. That was why he had agreed so easily.

'You deserve a bit of time to yourself, Luce.'

But half an hour later she was on a train surrounded by people, and it was simple to push him to the back of her mind.

She didn't want to go to a hotel. She couldn't have. Alec had a friend, some guy at work, who kept an apartment at Canary Wharf for when he worked late during the week. He was in New York. He'd given him the keys. 'We don't have to do anything, Lucy. I just want to see you. Whatever you want, I promise.' She told herself she wouldn't do anything, but she knew she was lying. It was time.

He was waiting for her when she arrived. He looked strangely formal when he opened the door: he hadn't taken off his suit, or even loosened his tie. As if she had come for an appointment, or a meeting.

Alec had drawn the curtains in the flat, but the strong spring sunshine streamed in through chinks and gaps and played on the anodyne modern, furniture. There were just two rooms – this one, with a small kitchen in one corner, and a bedroom beyond, with an en-suite, through wide double doors.

He had planned to offer her a drink. He'd stopped at Tesco Metro on his way there from the office, and hadn't known what to get. In his friend's fridge there was a bottle of champagne, some orange juice and milk, for tea.

He had thought they might sit and talk for a while. When he thought about Lucy, that was one of the things he most wanted to do with her. She had such a mind – you could see it beyond all the small-talk and inanities of school, domesticity and life. But when he saw her in the doorway, saw that she had agreed and surrendered and come to him, he was overwhelmed by the need to touch her without other people around, without clothes, without anything between them except how they felt.

She was wearing a cotton dress that appeared to tie at the front and when he pulled it, the fabric fell apart and he could slip his hands in and round her waist. Lucy was pushing his jacket off his shoulders, and he tugged at his tie to loosen it. Her fingers fiddled with buttons, his with the clasp on her bra, and then they stood, and breathed in and out slowly, revelling in the feeling of each other's skin.

If you had asked her, Lucy might have guessed that the sex would be furtive and fast. That the very act of unfaithfulness might mean the sacrifice of beauty and meaning. It didn't. For two, three, four hours, they were two people who, aside from the lives they led beyond, cared for each other, and at last, at long last, had the chance to show it. She couldn't believe it was anything else, and the thought occurred to her several times, through the fog of sensation and emotion, as they made love. When he trembled as she touched him, and gasped as he entered her. When he held her face very still and watched her as she came so that she knew he was with her.

They made love in the shower at the end, and afterwards he washed her hair and her body, so tenderly that she cried.

'This is safe, isn't it? You can trust this guy?'

'I promise you this is safe, Lucy. Neither of us wants to hurt anybody, do we?'

'No.' It was true. Mine is the only heart I'm risking. She repeated it in her head. Only his and mine.

On the train home she felt fabulous. Like her lips must be swollen and red with kissing, and like the smell of sex must be coming off her in waves as she moved along the carriage, searching for a seat. Her legs felt wobbly, as though she had swum a couple of miles, and her hips ached. She could still feel his hands on her breasts, on her back, moving her to wherever he wanted her, and when she remembered, she felt weak.

As the train pulled in, she glanced at the time on the station clock, and, as you do when you take a transatlantic flight and adjust your watch, changed herself back.

She'd been into Bath the day before, and bought a couple of things, for the holiday, without thinking.

She was dreading the holiday. Patrick was really looking forward to it. Thank God they'd booked and paid for it before Christmas, he'd said. Patrick always booked their holidays at least six months ahead. He would collect brochures, and spend hours on the Internet, researching destinations. He had a plan that stretched years ahead; he'd worked out which year would be the best for a trip for Disneyworld in Florida, when the children would both be old enough to scuba-dive, when they might be able to afford a long trip to Australia, to see some distant cousins he'd never met. He talked about renting a camper van and driving around New Zealand when he retired in twenty years' time. Sometimes Lucy would dawdle outside a travel agent's window, perusing the last-minute deals. Seven nights self-catering in Antigua, fourteen half-board in South Africa. Leaving tomorrow. Hotel assigned on arrival. Sometimes that seemed exciting. But this holiday had been booked last September. Patrick always got an early-bird discount.

She'd bought a dress, some sandals. Shopping. Just as she'd said. It was when she opened the boot of the car, and checked quickly that there were no tell-tale receipts in the bags that what she had done hit her.

The house was quiet when she went in. It was tea-time, and she felt a twinge of irritation that Bella and Ed weren't sitting at the table, eating and chatting. She supposed it was left to her to do. She would have smiled at her own hypocrisy, complaining at having to make the tea when she'd spent the day in bed with another man, if she hadn't felt so sick.

She was about to call out, when Patrick appeared.

He'd changed his clothes, put on a clean shirt. He looked fresh, and she felt suddenly grubby. Did she smell of him?

'Have you had a nice day?'

'Great, thanks.'

'Done a bit of shopping, I see.'

'Of the window variety, largely, I promise.' She raised the bags. 'And this is mostly sale stuff.'

'That's okay. Whatever.' He was smiling, and it jarred a little. He hadn't done it much lately.

'Where are the kids?'

'At my mum's. We went over there after school and she offered to keep them. It's half-term now, so no need to rush about in the morning, and you know she loves to have them. I thought, Why not?'

Lucy shrugged. 'Kind of her.'

'Besides, we've got celebrating to do . . .' He was coming towards her.

'Have we? Why?'

'I got a letter this morning. I got the job! The one in Bath. That I thought must have gone away. It hadn't, after all!'

'That's fantastic!' It was. Lucy exhaled – she hadn't realised she'd been holding her breath. 'That's great. Well done. I'm so, so pleased for you.' The platitudes came pouring out. She knew she should hug him, and she raised her arms to put them round his neck.

'What a fucking relief, hey?' He was too busy talking to notice that she was stiff in his arms. 'It's the same pay, more or less, as the old job, but that's okay. Good pension scheme, benefits, all that. I think it'll work out as being about the same as we had before. But it's a job, and we don't have to relocate, and the company's solid, and there's room for advancement, so – it's brilliant. Isn't it brilliant?' For the first time he really looked at her. 'You've lost all your colour. My darling girl, I know how worried you've been, but it's going to be fine now. Come and sit down. I bought a bottle of Moët on the way back from Mum's. I'll get it.'

Why did it have to be today?

She heard the cork pop in the kitchen, and the clink of glasses. He came back in, and handed her one.

'Here's to you.' She raised hers to his.

'Here's to us.' He drank half his glass in one thirsty gulp, then sat down, very close beside her, on the sofa. 'I want to say something to you, Luce.'

Oh, God.

'And I know I'm all over-excited, and I've not given you the chance to take this in, and you're probably tired and everything but, please, just listen to me and let me say it to you.'

She smiled wanly at him.

'I know these last few months have been incredibly difficult for you. I'm under no illusions that I've been anything other than utterly foul to live with. I've been moody and belligerent, and I haven't been there for you, or for the kids, probably, if the truth be known. I know I've been a complete male stereotype, and I've hated myself for it. I've been no kind of proper husband . . . even . . .' His voice faded away.

Lucy knew what he had been going to say. She could still feel Alec's weight on her, and him inside her. She couldn't bear it. She reached out and put her hand over his in his lap. 'Sssh.'

'I won't sssh. I'm sorry. That's all. I'm sorry. And I'm back now. I can be a proper husband again. Look after you. All of you.' He was close to tears again, and his eyes implored her.

She held him close to her, and told him that it was okay, that everything was going to be all right. And she closed her eyes to shut out Alec, to push back the idea of him and of today. But he wouldn't go away.

They had a takeaway curry. Lucy phoned the order through and Patrick went to get it. Lamb madras, chicken tikka masala, a naan and onion bhajis. The same curry they had had at least once a month for the last eight years.

While he was gone she scrubbed herself under a too-hot shower, but that didn't work either. She could still smell Alec. And she couldn't stop thinking about how it had felt.

She didn't know what to do now. That day, on the beach, they had told each other they didn't have answers for all the questions. Today had surely supplied them.

Literature, pop records, films – they were all in a great hurry to sing to you or tell you about love affairs. All that getting carried away by passion, swept along on some non-existent tide beyond your control. It was all bollocks, really. You were never out of control, not completely. You made the choices, you took the steps, you told the lies. You did it, and it was bullshit to let you blame something else, something 'bigger' than you. Lucy wouldn't let herself off the hook like that. You might reach the point where you came over all animal, but it was the human being in you that let it get that far in the first place.

And why didn't the books and the films tell you how it felt to sleep with your husband the same day you had let your new lover use your body for his own pleasure – to touch you in places and in ways that you had forgotten, or never known, then send it back, changed for ever, to the person who knew it best, and who had loved it longer and first?

Relief, and champagne, and a profound urge to penitence made Patrick reach for Lucy that night. Reach, for the first time in months, confident of what he was reaching for. He just didn't know that it wasn't there any more.

Lucy stopped his hand between her legs, and turned her back to him, pulling that hand over her shoulder in an embrace, so that they were lying like spoons. 'Can we start slowly?' she begged. 'Maybe tomorrow. It's just . . . well, it's been a long time, and . . . we've got the whole week, haven't we?'

Patrick lay there awake, wondering why, when it had finally felt as if everything was going to be all right, it hadn't quite been.

And Lucy lay beside him, awake, knowing that it never really would be again.

It was the first time in her life that she had hated herself.

The next morning, after Patrick had brought her tea in bed and gone to get the children ('I'll take them swimming, give you a couple of hours to yourself to do some packing or just laze around – I've got making up to do with them, too. And I can't wait to see the look on my mother's face when I tell her – I think she was more worried than we were!'), Lucy lay under the duvet, waiting to know what to do.

Alec answered his mobile phone on the fourth ring. 'Lucy?'

'Can you talk?'

'I've got Stephen. We're in the park. Nina and Marianne are in the shops.'

'Does that mean you can?'

'Wait a minute. Yes. Yep. Are you okay?'

'Yes. No. Not really.'

'You're scaring me.'

'I'm scared to death myself.'

'Has something happened?'

'Yes, Alec. Something happened.' She paused. 'We cheated.'

There was silence at the other end of the line.

'And we have to stop. Whatever it costs us.'

'Is that what you want?'

It wasn't. She had a dull ache in the pit of her stomach. 'We're going to hurt people, Alec. And please don't say that we won't hurt them if they don't find out because that makes us sound cheap and nasty.'

'We weren't that. We were never that.'

'I know. That's why we have to stop. Because I think we're both okay people, Alec, not bad ones.'

'Of course we're not bad.'

'Maybe.' She thought about Marianne and the shades of grey.

'Why now? Something's happened, hasn't it?' Why did he keep saying that?

'It has to be now.' Because I don't think I could walk away from you if we made love again. I think I would want to hold you for ever. 'Before it's too late. Please, Alec.'

'Okay. If that's what you want.'

She wanted to say that it wasn't what she wanted. That right now it was the last thing she wanted. But what was the point of that? 'I'm sorry, Alec.'

'I'm sorry too, Lucy. And, Lucy? I—'

'Don't.' She hung up on him. Was he going to say that he loved her?

R for Rock-climbing

Natalie thought about her dad every day. She hadn't done that for years. Worried like a parent does about a child. Every bit of new information she gleaned from her mother, or from the doctors when she was visiting, was fascinating to her. Each small progression in Nicholas's condition was absorbed, celebrated, reported to Tom, and Rose, discussed over and over again.

She didn't want to believe that he would never fully recover from this. Because that would mean she would have to grieve for a part of him, and she couldn't bear to do that when so much of him was still here with her. That felt like betrayal.

Life had changed completely, and yet at the same time went on as before. It wasn't the same for her mother, whose entire life had gone on hold. Natalie made time to visit him, more time than she thought she had. She spent hours in the hospital, sitting beside his bed. And when she wasn't there, she went to work, and she went out with friends, and she saw Tom, and the alphabet rolled on.

'You've done this before, haven't you?' They were parallel, about ten feet above the ground. Tom was sitting back, relaxed, in his harness.

Natalie was hanging on for dear life, knuckles white, trying to smile. Of course she bloody had. And this was the highest she had ever got. She'd had three private sessions, in the last fortnight, at the indoor climbing wall on the industrial estate, costing twenty pounds each time, with Thaddeus, the hippie instructor, who wore tie-dye Lycra and said 'cool' a lot.

Two major problems: (1.) The harness was just like the one you used for abseiling. Not flattering; (2.) And this was worse than abseiling – the person on the ground pretty much had to support your weight. The first time she fell off the wall with Thaddeus below, she was vaguely afraid that he was going to fly to the ceiling, letting her drop like a stone. He didn't. He said 'cool', and told her to get back up.

The wall was multi-coloured, the handholds sticking out at intervals, like Smarties. Small children and old ladies alike seemed to go up it like rats up drainpipes. No fear, Thaddeus said. No sense, Natalie reckoned.

It had seemed like a good idea to do something physical. She'd thought about *reiki*, but she could imagine Tom's in-credulous face . . . She'd Googled leisure activities in town, and this place had popped up. R for Rock-climbing.

It had been Bridget's idea to come for a few lessons. 'That'll spook him,' she'd said, 'if you can do something he can't.'

Good idea. Except that she was sixty pounds worse off, her arse was still like a sack of potatoes in a triangle of webbing, and she still couldn't do it. And Tom bloody well could.

He'd pronounced her choice 'epic', said he and Rob had been meaning to come ever since it had opened in the autumn and hurried off to get himself fitted for a helmet. In which he did not look like a complete idiot. Natalie's was too big and kept slipping sideways so that the tip of one ear caught on the rim. She had sworn Thaddeus to secrecy, and now she winked at him. 'I have not.'

'Okay.' He clearly did not believe her.

Natalie felt a flush of irritation. 'Did it never occur to you, Tom, that I might actually have physical aptitude for some-thing?'

'Not really.' He sniggered. 'I see you more as a cerebral girl.' She narrowed her eyes. 'But it's fantastic. Brilliant that you like it. We can come again.'

Not if she had anything to do with it. 'We certainly can.' She started climbing. Maybe if she went faster it would be easier. She looked frantically above her head for a Smartie within reach. A green one, over there. Or this blue one. Her trainer slipped, her chin smacked on to an orange one as she fell, and five seconds later she had slammed backwards into the wall, with a handhold rammed into her kidney. 'Tom?'

'You okay?' He was considerate enough to keep the snigger out of his voice.

'Can I get down now?'

Thaddeus brought her an ice pack, and she sat in the padded section reserved for children under five, watching, while Tom finished the session. Which meant getting to the top on all five of the walls, including the one with the overhang. And took an hour. Her chin throbbed, and her kidney ached. 'If I pee blood, it's your fault,' she said ruefully, when he finally appeared.

'You can have one of my kidneys.' He kissed the top of her head. 'I'll buy you dinner – your choice.'

'Fish-and-chip supper?'

'I'd have sprung for French.'

'I don't wear Lycra to French restaurants. Fish and chips will be fine.'

'You're going to have a bruise tomorrow.' Maybe a restaurant with fluorescent lighting wasn't the best idea. But the chips were good.

When Natalie got in the red light on her answering-machine was flashing. Imagining it would be Tom, and looking forward to hearing about S, she threw herself down on to the sofa and pushed the button.

It was Simon.

Simon's voice. Deep, slow, haughty.

Natalie sat up straight.

'It's me. Surprise, hey?' The briefest pause. 'I've fucked up, Nat. I miss you. I don't know what I was on before. I want you back. We can do whatever you want. We can move in. Hell, we can get married, if that's what you want. As long as I have what I want. Which is you back. Machine's probably not the best place for this kind of conversation, so have a think about it. If you're interested, I'll be at Bill's tomorrow night. Eight o'clock. Our usual table. See? I remember. Come.'

She played it once more. No 'sorry'. No 'please'. 'As long as I have what I want.' Angrily, she went to her bedroom, pulled off the day's clothes, and put on her sweats.

Back in the living room, she played the message again. Bill's. The nerve of him. Their special place. Bloody good of him to 'remember'.

They'd been there first when he'd qualified at the end of three years' clinical. She'd paid, of course. Again on his birthday, his first year as a SHO, and when he'd passed the FRCS exams. Taken his mother on Mother's Day, taken Bridget for her first outing without the baby. Been when Natalie had been promoted to producer on her show. She had piles of photographs taken in its white interior. Different hair, different clothes, different flowers in the vases on the tables. Same smiling faces.

Natalie reached for the phone, but almost as quickly put it down again. There wasn't anyone she could call. They would all tell her the same thing. Don't go. And she already knew that she would.

The next day Tom left a message for her at work. She didn't

call him back. Not telling him about Simon would feel like lying, and she didn't want to do that. The next day, she told herself, while she showered, that she was going to tell Simon to his face that it was over between them, and not to call her again. And then she shaved her legs.

She chanted the same thing to herself while she did her face, ever so carefully, and dried her hair. There was no point. He'd hurt her too badly. She wouldn't ever be able to forgive him that so there was no point. And then she chose a matching black balconette bra and dental-floss knickers.

By the time she was dressed and ready, and walking out of the house, she was thinking that everyone deserved a second chance; and by the time she pushed open the heavy glass door to Bill's she was pretty much convinced that their break could only have made them stronger.

And he looked so damn good. Smelt better. Familiar, and sexy as hell.

He was there before her, which was rare. He had ordered champagne and handed her a glass as she sat down across from him. Wordlessly she took it, and watched his mouth as he said, 'Here's to us.'

And then he talked to her. He told her stories. His private practice was going well. Coronary artery bypass grafting and aortic dissection and valve replacements. A gratifyingly steady – and steadily growing – stream of middle-aged, well-off private patients, who had eaten and smoked too much and done too little and were now paying for his Alfa Spider and his two weeks heli-skiing in Aspen.

'You'll come. We'll get you some lessons.'

During the starter she thought briefly how angry they would be with her. Rose, Bridge, Suze, Tom. But they didn't know how much she had loved him, and for how long, and how it had felt to have her dream of a future with him taken away and, now, given back. All the daydreams, all the doodlings of a life, flooding back while she listened to him talking.

And he kept filling her glass. When they had finished the first bottle, another appeared.

While she played with the main course he told her about the new house. How he'd got bits and pieces for it, but it needed her touch, he saw that now, to make it a home. In a minute, she thought, he's going to ask about me. How I've been. What I've been doing since he left me. How I feel.

But somehow, with the wine and the stories, he didn't ask and she didn't mind. This was what she'd wanted, wasn't it, for so long? He had come back. It wasn't in his nature to beg – humility wasn't his strong suit, and she loved him just the way he was, didn't she? Why not accept that he'd gone and he'd come back and be glad?

And he paid for dinner.

It seemed natural for him to come in. He'd had far too much to drink to drive the Alfa Spider home to his own place, hadn't he, and hers was so much closer? For a nanosecond the right (or was it the left) side of her brain pondered what he might have done about being stranded and a bit drunk if she hadn't let him in, but the piddled side quickly regained control and she practically rugby-tackled him as soon as they were in the living room.

Outside, Tom sat in his car. He'd been at Natalie's end of town for a late meeting this afternoon. It had turned into drinks in a local bar. He'd come to tell her about the weekend. Skiing. Dry-slope skiing. He'd booked them lessons. He knew how Simon had mocked her because she couldn't ski. Well, this time she'd be in the same boat as Tom. He couldn't do it either. She'd make a face of mock-horror, rolling her eyes at another 'in-appropriate' activity, but they'd have a grand time, laughing and fooling about, and maybe, just maybe, learning something. Z for Zermatt, if she played her cards right, he'd thought.

She hadn't answered the phone, and her mobile was switched off. He'd been about to give up when he'd seen her. She was pretty merry, he could see that. Simon was holding her up, her arm tight about his waist, and his clamped round her shoulders. Under the porchlight he'd watched Simon kiss her, feeling queasy. And then they had disappeared inside.

He sat for a few more minutes before he drove off.

Surgeon's hands. She remembered them. Delicate, careful, thorough. No rough skin or sharp nails. Soft like a woman's, insistent like a man's. Cupping her breasts with a touch that was almost reverent. Tracing down the cleft of her buttocks with the lightest strokes.

Natalie was light-headed and knew she'd drunk too much to be doing this. But it was too easy, too familiar. And too good. He knew exactly how to touch her. She arched her back and surrendered.

When she woke up the next morning, she felt terrible. She couldn't drink that much, and she was supposed to go to work, but when she sat up, the room moved with her, and didn't stop when she did. She fell back, gratefully, on to the hot pillow. It took her a couple of minutes to realise that Simon was there. He always slept on his front, with his head under the pillow. For a second she forgot whose smooth brown back it was, and by the time she remembered, she was half-way to the bathroom, her hand clamped over her mouth.

Simon came in while she was still clutching the white porcelain. At least surgeons weren't squeamish.

'Sorry,' she said.

'It's okay. Wasn't quite how I planned to herald the morning, but there'll be others . . . Do you want some water or anything?'

'A lift back to bed?'

But he'd already gone. Natalie crawled after him.

He was sitting in the middle, propped up by all the pillows, the duvet tucked under his arms like some invalid aunt. 'You shouldn't drink so much.'

People who stated the bloody obvious like that when you felt like death warmed up should be killed.

Since there was no room for her in the bed, Natalie crawled into the foetal position on the moth-eaten *chaise-longue* Susannah had bought at a flea-market. She felt the clasp of her bra – evidently thrown there last night – digging into her bum, but she couldn't be bothered to remove it.

Perfect time for a deep and meaningful.

'So, Simon, did you see other women while we were apart?'

He didn't even look uncomfortable. 'A couple.'

'Do I know them?'

'No. Of course not. I'm not completely insensitive, Natalie.'

Wasn't he?

'What are you actually calling a couple? Do you really mean two, or do you mean more?'

'Why are you doing this?'

'Because last night you waltzed back into my life – and my bed – after months and months, and I need to fill in the missing pieces.'

'Why?'

'Because I do. Don't you wonder what I've been doing since you dumped me?'

'I didn't dump you.'

'That's exactly what you did.'

'I was confused. I needed some space. I've come back, haven't I? Why can't that be enough?'

'It might be, I suppose, if I trusted you. I find that pretty hard this morning.'

'You didn't seem to have any trouble with it last night.'

'Last night you bought me too much champagne. This morning I'm seeing things a bit more clearly.'

'You're hung over. That's not clearly. Why don't you let me take you out for breakfast?'

Simon climbed out of bed grudgingly, and started to pull on his clothes.

'You haven't asked me.' Natalie's voice was very small.

'What?'

'You haven't asked me if I want to go out for breakfast.'

'What are you talking about, Natalie?' His tone was irritable.

'I'm talking about the fact that you haven't asked me anything. Not if I want breakfast, not what I did after you left me, not how my family is, how work is, how anything is. You don't even know if I'm with someone else. Because you haven't asked.'

'I assumed you'd tell me if there was anything I needed to know. And if you're seeing someone else, I feel a little sorry for him. You let me back into your knickers quickly enough – and it rather seemed to me like you were in need of a good seeing-to.'

Natalie stood up, head pounding. 'I'm not seeing anyone. And don't talk about me like I'm some sort of mare that's been put out to stud. The point is, you assumed I wasn't. Like you assumed everything else. Assumed I'd come gratefully back to you.'

'Are you going to start singing Gloria Gaynor? Because if you are, I need some strong coffee.'

'Don't you dare laugh at me, Simon!'

He was buttoning his shirt, tucking it into his trousers. 'Look, Natalie, this isn't how I wanted things to be. I'm sorry if I'm getting it wrong. I don't know what else to say to you. I've laid my soul bare here. I want you back. Nothing else really matters, does it?'

No one could have been more surprised than Natalie to find that, actually, other stuff did matter.

He shouldn't have used the word soul. It made it too, too easy to see what was missing.

She looked right at him, and waited to see what she felt.

S for Simon

It was one of those beautifully hot May days that you expect, but rarely get, in August. It had been, in fact, a gloriously hot week, and Natalie had lain out on the grass bank outside the radio station every lunchtime. She was gratified to see that her legs had lost their bluish hue of winter months, and were, in fact, almost sunkissed. She absolutely loved this time of year, when people poured out of their offices and into the pubs and bars in town, spilling on to the pavements. Men with their ties loosened, girls in pastel and primary colours, tossing their hair in the late-afternoon sunshine. Summer was sexy, and you could practically smell the pheromones as you walked past them.

Tom was waiting for her at the Lamb. He'd been there for a while – the joys of self-employment: he'd bagged a great table, and there were three empty Becks bottles in front of him. He stood up as she approached, and kissed her briefly on the cheek, his arm brushing her shoulder. 'I'll get you a drink.'

When he returned, he sat in silence opposite her, watching her drink. Natalie was a little unnerved. He seemed tense. 'So come on, then. S – I'm dying to know. Hope it's outdoorsy. The forecast says it's going to be like this all weekend.'

Tom smiled wryly. 'It was going to be.'

'What do you mean?'

'I mean it was going to be. I had something planned, but I've changed my mind.'

'How come?'

'I thought of something else.'

'Are you planning to tell me?'

Tom shrugged.

'Or are we going to sit here all evening with you being weird?'

'Simon.'

'Sorry?'

'S for Simon. Pretty bloody obvious if you think about it, isn't it? Simple.' He laughed again, but without humour. 'Simple Simon.'

'What are you talking about?'

'Stop, Nat. Please don't tell me a lie. I can't take you lying to me.'

'I wasn't.'

'You might have done.'

'Tom . . .'

'I know you slept with him, Natalie.'

Natalie coloured. Her face felt hot, and it wasn't the sunshine. 'How?'

'What has "how" got to do with it? I know.' He hadn't but he did now.

'Tom, I . . .'

'Listen, Nat, you don't owe me an explanation. Let's face it, this was only ever a game, wasn't it, this stupid alphabet thing? Served its purpose. Kept you busy for a few months while Simon sorted himself out. That's fine. But let's stop, shall we? I don't think either of us wants to play any more.'

'Do I get to speak?'

Tom pursed his lips and pushed back his chair. He couldn't look at her. He stood up. 'Just don't ask me to be happy for you. Not yet. Okay?' He raised his eyes to hers just once. 'Sorry.' And then he walked away.

Natalie wanted to go after him, but shame or fear rooted her to the spot and she had to stare hard at her hands to stop crying. When she raised her head again, he had disappeared from view.

She'd told Simon to go. She'd told him that she didn't love him any more. And he had gone. Sullenly and sulkily. That was what she would have told Tom, if he'd waited.

She was surprised to discover that Tom's walking out on her was more affecting than Simon's had been.

Lucy and Patrick

Lucy lay on the sun-lounger, her head on one side, squinting to watch Ed in the swimming-pool. He was wearing factor fifty and one of those lurid sunsuits with a legionnaire's hat so he was hard to miss. He was diving for plastic rings, which he was throwing in himself, with great enthusiasm and lousy aim. They kept landing near a snotty woman in a thong bikini, who had no business to be lying so close to the shallow end, except that it got the most sunlight each day, and she had been there for ten hours every day since they'd arrived. Ed splashed her with each throw, and splashed her more with each dive, and each time she gave an annoyed little kick and, occasionally, tutted. Lucy felt the urge to stand on the edge near her and do one of those water-bomb things – banned on the posters in municipal pools, along with spitting and petting – and see if she could drown her once and for all.

Even with the entire pharmacy's sun protection slathered over him, Ed's forearms and ears were going red. She'd take him into the shade in a minute, and pay an exorbitant amount for a plate of food, from which he would eat only the chips, then demand an ice-cream to assuage the hunger he would claim still to feel.

She loved him, though. The round baby-belly of him.

Bella and Patrick had gone to watch fishermen on the wharf.

They didn't like lying around. Bella couldn't have been more like Patrick if she had been genetically his. Was that luck? Or had Patrick made her into his own?

They had been there for four days. She'd left her mobile in the glove compartment of her car, at the airport, so Alec couldn't phone her or text, but he was in her mind all the time. They had a studio apartment – she and Patrick had a double bed in the back part, and the children slept in the front bit, on two sofas that were made up into beds every afternoon while they were on the beach. They were separated by a curtain, not a door. Each night, at around eleven, Ed had wandered in, bleary-eyed, demanding a wee, then climbed into Lucy's bed instead of making the journey back to his half of the apartment. She had welcomed him, and lifted him to sleep between them. Her human shield. She was starting to panic. She didn't know how to sleep with Patrick, after Alec, and it was getting worse, not better.

They were being very friendly. Patrick seemed relaxed, relieved. But it was still between them. They hadn't made love since before Christmas. Almost six months.

Before that, they'd always had a good time in bed. Not spectacular, maybe, but nice. Patrick was a bit too gentle for her: he would do something, then stop and ask if she was enjoying it. She'd told him, years ago, emboldened by drink, that she wasn't made of china, and that he could be a bit rougher, and he'd started that way – they'd laughed. Hadn't he even carried her through to the bedroom over his shoulder in a fireman's lift? But he'd still asked if it was okay. She'd sometimes thought, lying under him over the years, of what it might be like to be . . . just fucked, hard.

That was what Alec had done. His hands had held her hips and pulled her and placed her, and he'd lost himself in her to the point at which you knew he didn't really care, for that one

moment, how it was for her because it was bloody brilliant for
him, and she'd loved that.

So maybe she and Alec were more compatible in bed than she
and Patrick were. So what? Not for the first time she'd
wondered what it was like between him and Marianne. What
it had been like after Marianne had stopped her own affair and
come home to him. Did he do it the same way? Did she feel the
same to him? Whether he had made love to his wife since he had
made love to her. She felt itchy, way, way under her skin –
irritable and frustrated and sad. Serves you right, she spat to
herself.

Bella appeared next to her. She kissed her mum's tummy.
'Hiya, lazybones.'

'Hello, you. Had a nice walk with Dad?'

'Yes. We saw lots of fish. Smelly!' Bella held her nose, and
waved her fingers under it.

Patrick was not long behind her.

'Daddy says he's taking you out tonight. He's got a babysitter
– that nice girl, Laura, who works at the kids' club, the one Ed's
completely in love with. He says you might even eat one of the
fish we just saw getting caught. Can I swim before lunch?'

Her dress was off and she was underwater before Lucy could
respond.

Lucy squinted at Patrick. 'Is this true?'

'It was supposed to be a surprise . . .'

'But then I wouldn't have had a chance to get my gladrags
on.'

'And you'd still have looked lovely.'

'Flattery will get you everywhere, young man.'

Patrick ran a hand speculatively over her hip. 'That was what
I was hoping.'

Lucy's heart sank a little.

* * *

It wasn't fair, was it, to keep comparing? This dinner, with that lunch of chips in a paper cone. So why did she keep doing it? They weren't laughing, he hadn't made her shake easing a little drop of ketchup off her top lip with his finger, she wasn't desperate to get to the end of the meal so that she could kiss him. They were husband and wife, parents, eating dinner together for, what, the thousandth time? That should have been good too. Different, but still good. Richer, stronger, better. Maybe nothing in the universe was ever going to feel the same way again.

She drank three glasses of red wine, deliberately. They walked back slowly to their place, and Patrick paid the girl. Lucy checked Bella and Ed, one asleep so neatly, one splayed and exposed.

Patrick pulled her through to their side, and pulled the curtain, then started kissing her. She pulled away and shushed him, but he carried on, pulling her into the bathroom, closing the door behind them, and locking it. It was pitch black, and Lucy couldn't see.

He undid the zip at the back of her dress and let it fall to the floor. 'You're so lovely. My beautiful, sexy wife.' He took off his own shirt, over his head, and she heard his trousers fall too. He lifted her on to the vanity unit, where the marble was cold on her skin. A toothbrush clattered into the sink.

His hands ran up and down her body, and his kisses traced an invisible line from her neck to her breasts, then further down. Lucy tried to get into it. She put her hands into his hair, tried to pull his face up to hers, to kiss him properly and try to remember that she loved him and he loved her and that they were okay, but he wouldn't let her. She couldn't keep up – she couldn't get to where he wanted her to be. Now his mouth was working at her, his lips and tongue tracing back and forth, opening her up. But still it wasn't working. She wasn't there. It was mechanical, and forced, and she was a million miles away from really feeling him.

So she put herself back into the flat with Alec. His face, his mouth, where Patrick's was now, seeing her, tasting her for the first time. The newness and the excitement flooded back.

Two minutes later, she pulled his head in towards her, roughly, and came, hard, stifling her gasp with her fist. He laughed, triumphant and gruff, as he surfaced, then entered her. By the time it was his turn, tears were running down her cheeks, and she was glad that it was dark, and that he couldn't see them, or her lying, cheating face.

The next morning it was better. It was clear that Patrick felt as though some demon had been vanquished. They had slept naked, and when they woke, he didn't let Ed's presence stop him roaming possessively over her body. A little of his old sparkle was back. Everyone makes themselves believe what they want to believe, Lucy thought, so why can't I?

Three days later they were home, brown and tired. The children were weary of travel by the time they caught the bus out to the long-term car park, and Patrick carried Ed on his shoulders. Ed's Mr Ted kept falling across Patrick's eyes as his owner nodded and dozed above. Lucy pulled along the two wheelie suitcases, Bella beside her. They got nearer and nearer the car, and she felt herself speed up. She switched on her phone while Patrick put the cases into the boot. No flash or beep. No messages. She felt as if Alec had slapped her.

At home there was no milk, and the bread she had forgotten in the bread bin had gone green. 'I'm sorry. I didn't think about coming home.' She'd thought only about going away. And Alec.

'No problem. I'll nip out. Bella'll keep me company, won't you, honey?'

Bella nodded enthusiastically.

'Bread, milk, some eggs or something?'

'Yeah. I'll do a big shop tomorrow.' But she chased them, as the car backed down the drive. 'Better get some washing-powder too – I'll get a few loads done tonight. There's a mountain of it.'

Bella waved.

Ed lay on the sofa, reunited with his Power Rangers, thumb in, while Lucy made piles of whites, lights and darks, and tried not to think about Alec.

She'd started her period that morning, and her head and stomach ached. I'm shedding my lining, she thought. The lining that was getting ready for something that isn't going to happen now.

You stupid cow.

It was getting dark when she heard Patrick's car pull into the drive. She'd put Ed to bed, and poured herself a gin.

Different voices in the porch, then Patrick's key, and Bella tripped in, giggling with Nina. She heard Marianne: 'I know, I know, the last thing you need is visitors. We bumped into Patrick at the supermarket – he said you'd be glad to see us. I've got car-park withdrawals – I've missed you. And I'm bearing gifts – I have lasagne!'

Marianne came into the kitchen. 'You look fantastic! So brown in just a week, damn you.' She hugged Lucy, and Lucy saw Alec over her shoulder. 'Good to see you!' Marianne said.

'We're not staying,' Alec was saying.

'Nonsense.' That was Patrick. Stop talking. Stop. Lucy wanted to laugh at the absurdity of it. Her husband ushering her lover into the kitchen, grabbing a bottle of good red.

'She's had enough of me all week. Let's have a drink, the lasagne. We've lost the girls, anyway, for an hour or two. Come on.' Patrick found the corkscrew in a drawer. 'Besides, you haven't toasted my new job yet.'

'Lucy! When did all this happen? You didn't tell me! That's fantastic, Patrick. Oh, darling, congratulations!'

Marianne was hugging him now, and Alec pumped his hand. 'Great news.'

Patrick beamed. He saw her gin. 'Did you start already, Luce?'

Lucy felt as if she was wrapped in clingfilm. Around her Marianne and Patrick toasted, laughed and busied themselves turning the oven on, tipping bags of pre-mixed chlorinated salad into bowls and drinking.

She couldn't look at Alec, but she couldn't look anywhere else either. She pushed her hair back from her face, behind both ears, and studied the plate rack as though she had never seen it before. And then he was there. Reaching for the plates. Marianne and Patrick were walking away, into the living room, glasses in hand. You stupid, stupid people.

'You do look beautiful. Beautiful.'

The hairs on the back of her neck stood up.

Patrick saw them there. He'd come back for something. They weren't kissing. Alec was barely touching her. But it couldn't have been any clearer to him, suddenly, if they had been naked and rutting away on the Formica. He was standing so close to her. And the way they were looking at each other. He'd seen a painting like it once of two lovers. In a gallery. It must have been years ago – he didn't go to galleries any more. That expression people used ᴛ 'You could have cut the atmosphere with a knife.' He'd never really understood it until now. But what he saw between his wife and his friend in the kitchen, you could have sliced that. Solid, tangible and charged.

He felt as if he jumped backwards, but he didn't, of course. It was the subtlest change in direction that took him, undetected, to the cloakroom. He locked the door and leant against it, panting as though he had just run a long way.

He stayed there until he was missed and called. Then he came out and ate lasagne.

Watching Lucy while she slept had always been one of Patrick's favourite things to do. He had once told her that she slept like a child. Like an innocent. On her front, vulnerable, with all the little lines on her face smooth and untroubled. It had made him feel good, once, watching her while she slept. All sort of 'God's in his heaven, all's right with the world'. His world – the one with Lucy in it. Her and Bella and Ed.

Tonight he couldn't look at her. He felt sick. But he wondered if her face still wore the untroubled, untrammelled expression it always had.

Patrick felt stupid. A woman might have wondered, who else knew? How long had it been going on? Maybe some men would too. He didn't, although on some level he knew that that ugly, destructive curiosity would come. He wasn't angry, tonight, although that would probably come as well and, in a way, he would welcome it. Lucy probably would too. She would want him to rant and rave and call her names. There would have to be something catastrophic, apocalyptic. Otherwise there would be nothing for them to move past, get over. He didn't know if he could get over this.

Patrick and Tom

Tom had rung, asked him out for a beer. He said there was something he needed to talk to him about. They met after work at a pub they both liked, with tables leading down to a stream. It had always made Patrick feel like he was in an episode of *Inspector Morse*. It was still warm.

Tom lifted his glass. 'Well done, bro. The jungle drums have done their thing – I heard about the job. Congrats. Is it what you wanted?'

Tom was the first person to ask him that. Was it what he wanted? As if that had anything to do with it. It hadn't been about that. It was about getting a job, having one, so that no one had to talk to him or about him not having one. It was about paying the mortgage and filling the car with petrol and buying endless pairs of shoes. About holidays and new tiles for the kitchen and a pension that would keep him and Lucy in their dotage.

'It's what was needed,' he replied. 'It'll keep Mum off my back, at least.'

Tom grinned. 'No, it won't.'

Patrick smiled in acknowledgement of that truth. 'And how's the business?'

'Good. Very good, in fact. I think it's going to pay off, taking the risk. Rob pulls in the clients, that's for sure. He's good.'

They both drank again, and nodded. Like men do.

A table of young people was congregating nearer the water. People kept arriving in couples and threesomes, greeted by peals of laughter and offers of drinks.

Patrick felt old. 'What did you want to talk to me about?'

'I think Natalie's sleeping with Simon again.'

'You think she is?'

'I'm pretty sure. I saw them together at her place late at night . . .'

'You were following them?'

'No!' Tom was indignant. 'I was stopping by with something. I wouldn't do that!'

'Sorry . . . so, does she know that you know?'

'Yeah. Told her the other night.'

'And? What does she say about it?'

'I didn't give her the chance to say anything, really. I stormed off.'

'What did you expect to achieve, doing that?'

'I didn't set out intending to storm off, did I? I was afraid of what she might say. That she might tell me it was all back on again.'

'But you've no idea.'

'S'pose not.'

'I didn't know things had got going between you two.'

'They haven't, not really. I thought we were getting somewhere.'

'But nothing's happened.'

'No.'

'But . . . you want it to.'

Tom sighed. 'God, yes.'

They sat in silence for a minute or two. 'I love her, man. This is it, I think. I really love her.'

Patrick didn't have anything inside him to give to his brother.

'I mean, I've always loved her, we've been best mates for years. When I started this thing, I thought that maybe, maybe there was something else – the germ of something else that could happen between us. But I don't think I was entirely serious. It was speculative, you know. But, bloody hell, it's bitten me in the arse. And now I love her. I think about her all the time. When I'm not with her, I'm just waiting for the next time I can be, and when I am, I'm just really happy. She's funny, and smart, and . . . gorgeous. I love her. Never felt like this before. Want-to-marry-her-and-be-with-her-all-the-rest-of-my-life kind of love her.'

Patrick had never heard Tom talk like that before.

'And now this bastard's come back. He had fucking years to work out what he had, and he dumped her, and now he's come back for her. She's loved him all that time. She thought the two of them were going to end up together. That's what she wanted. How can I compete with that?'

'Have you told her?'

'How can I? I was getting round to it. I nearly told her in Paris. There was this perfect moment but I wimped out. Afraid of scaring her off. Or just afraid of being rejected. It's always been me, before, doing the blowing off.'

'You don't need me to tell you what to do, do you?'

Tom smiled. 'Not really. Just wanted to say some of it out loud.'

Patrick drained his glass. 'Another?'

'All right. That your last word on the subject, then? I'd have been better off going to Lucy.'

Patrick stood up, the two glasses in his hand. 'Lucy's been a bit busy lately, sleeping with a friend of mine.' Then he walked slowly up the grass towards the door of the pub.

When he got back, he said, 'Sorry. That was probably a bit melodramatic. There was no need to tell you like that.'

'I'm not sure you could have found a way of telling me that wasn't.' His brother raised an eyebrow. 'I'm sorry, Pat. I've brought you out and rambled on about Natalie . . .'

'Why shouldn't you?'

'Because this is a lot more serious, obviously. I presume you're sure?'

'I haven't caught them at it, if that's what you mean. But, yes, I'm sure.'

'It's so unlike Lucy.'

'It's not all her fault. I've been hell to live with these last months.'

'Jesus Christ, Patrick, she's your wife. I know things haven't been easy, but that's no excuse to run off and shag someone else.'

Patrick winced, and Tom wished he had said that differently.

'Don't make excuses for her, for God's sake,' he went on. 'How long, do you think, has it been going on?'

'I don't know. I haven't noticed. I should have known.'

'Stop it!' Tom was exasperated. 'Does she know you know?'

'No. And I'm not going to tell her.'

'Why not?'

'Because I don't know what I want to happen.'

'You're not making any sense, Patrick.'

'I know. I don't want her to leave me, Tom. I don't want to lose her, and I don't want to lose my kids. So I don't want to force her hand.'

'You can't be serious, Patrick. You can't let her carry on doing this to you, and not say boo to a goose because you're afraid of what might happen. You can't.'

'Why not?'

'Because it's not okay, Patrick. It'll eat you. It's untenable. And she can't stay with someone who's prepared to be cuckolded and walked over. So you'll lose her anyway. You have to fight, if you want her. Don't you?'

They both had to fight.

T for Tattoo

The door to Tom's office opened and he looked up expectantly. No one was due in this afternoon. A brown ankle in an absurdly high heel appeared at skirting-board level. Then a calf, then a knee. There was something written on the leg, in dark letters, big enough to read from ten feet away. 'SORRY'. The leg continued to emerge, bit by bit, through the door. 'TOM' was written in the same hand on the thigh.

Then the singing started. 'Dah dah dah, de dah dah dah . . .' The stripper's theme, just barely.

In spite of himself Tom smiled. 'What the hell are you supposed to be?'

'I'm T. T for Tattoo.'

'That's permanent, is it?'

'Well . . . no. Not on my leg. Obviously. I'd have to hope gypsy skirts were in style for the rest of time, wouldn't I? And, let's face it, my legs are one of my best features, so it seems a bit of a shame to cover them up, don't you agree?'

'I can't have a conversation with a disembodied leg.'

'Does that mean I can come in?'

'I don't know.'

Natalie started singing again, and her leg danced wildly in the door frame.

Now Tom laughed. 'Okay, come in, for God's sake, before someone sees you, you nutter.'

The rest of Natalie slid through the door. The other brown leg was wearing a bright pink Converse All Star, so her walk as she approached him was comically lopsided. She put her arms round him. 'I hated you hating me the other day.'

'I don't hate you Nat.' He held her.

'Good. Couldn't bear it.'

Tom pushed her back to arm's length. 'But we have to talk . . .'

'I know.'

'So come in, sit down and listen to me, will you?'

'Yes, Tom.' She sounded very unlike Natalie.

'Okay, Nat. I'm going to put my cards on the table.'

Natalie clasped her hands in her lap.

'I don't know what's happened with you and Simon. I'm sorry about the other day. Maybe I should have given you a chance to explain it, maybe not. Maybe it doesn't matter. You'll make up your own mind about how you feel and what you want to do. But I can't let you do that without knowing everything. Without knowing how I feel.' She smiled encouragement at him.

'When this game started, I didn't know where it was going. I genuinely wanted to make you feel better, and I knew I could. I thought that you were wrong when you said that there could never be anything between us, but I don't think, back then, that I was particularly serious either way. Maybe I saw it as a challenge. See if I could get you to fall for me . . . I don't know. It was all a bit of a joke, wasn't it?'

Natalie nodded.

'But the joke, I find, is on me. Because I've fallen for you. I've known you for more than half of my life, and in the last few months I've come to see you in a completely new way, that I don't think I ever expected. I knew you well in so many ways, but I've seen things lately I never did before.'

Natalie started to say something, but Tom was determined now. 'Let me finish. It's the most overused expression in the

English language, I know, but I'm reasonably sure that I love you, Natalie.'

'Tom.'

'And I know most people say that expecting to have it reciprocated, right then, but not me. I just needed you to know while you decided what to do.'

'Tom.'

Again, he stopped her. 'Hang on, can't you? I'm not sure I've finished. Give me a moment.'

Natalie sat still.

'I mean, I think I've finished. Don't want to over-egg it. And I don't want to sound like some sap, by the way. It's not like I'm breaking my heart. I could still get over it, Nat. It's a new love. Surface wound, not a disembowelment. I just think it could get worse, if I let it carry on. I suppose I'm saying that we'd better not carry on playing if you're going back to Simon.'

'I'm not going back to Simon.'

'You're not?'

'I'm absolutely, totally, utterly not going back to Simon.'

Tom took a deep breath, but before Natalie could say anything else, he was talking again: 'Okay. Well, that's that, then. I'm glad – I gotta tell you that if you aren't going to end up with me, he's the last other man on the planet I would choose for you to be with.' Him and everyone else. 'But I'm not stupid enough to jump to the conclusion that you not being with Simon means you'll definitely be with me. Quantum leap. I know that. So go away, and think about what I've said, and let's just see, hey?'

'Okay.' Natalie nodded. 'Thanks for clarifying things, Tom.' She was smiling, but Tom found it hard to read.

'And if you want to shoot for U, let me know in a bit, or something . . . Just let's not go for U if you're already a hundred per cent certain this can't go anywhere. Let's not do that to my heart, hey? Okay?'

Now that he'd made his grand speech, Tom was floundering. He felt a bit of an idiot. They sat there for a moment.

'So . . . go away!'

'Oh.' She sounded shocked. 'You mean go now?'

Now Tom's face broke into a smile. 'Yes, go now. Before I feel any more stupid.'

Natalie stood up.

'And I'm glad about Simon. Dickhead.'

'Me too.'

When she got to the door and opened it, she turned back. 'Tom? Let's go for U.' And then she was gone.

And, for now, it was enough for him. He pushed the insistent thought that maybe he was just like Patrick – a fool, prepared to settle for something unacceptable – firmly to the back of his mind. Natalie wasn't Lucy. And he wasn't wrong about this. The longer it went on, the more certain he became. It had been hard, the Simon business, and he hadn't liked how he had felt, but maybe, in fact, it was good.

Nicholas

'Hello, Dad. How are you?'

Nicholas grunted.

'I'll take that as a "Fine, thank you", shall I?' Natalie kissed his cheek, and they both smiled.

Nicholas felt the relief of Natalie's presence. Susannah didn't come much and he didn't mind – she was busy, and he understood. Bridget always cried. Natalie, his Natalie, always laughed at him. It would be *with* him, if he knew how to articulate it.

But Natalie knew from the twinkle that briefly hit his eyes when she arrived. She'd brought grapes, and a copy of *Heat* magazine. 'Both for me, I'm afraid. There's a limit to the gifts I can bring you, and I've passed it. Promise I'll only read the magazine when you fall asleep on me.'

He hated doing that. Sleep came often, and without warning, and he was powerless to stop it. It made Natalie laugh. 'At least with you I know when I'm being boring,' she joked. Although she never was.

She plonked herself down on the corner of his bed, and started on the grapes. 'Well, the fascinating saga of my life has an exciting new chapter today,' she said. 'I know you're agog to hear it. Tom, it appears, has fallen in love with me.' Nicholas grunted once, and gave his half-smile. 'Aha, venerable elder pleased,' Natalie said, in a mock-Oriental accent, placing her palms together and giving a little bow. 'Oh, and Simon has come back and asked me to marry him. Do you have a grunt for that?' Apparently not, but Nicholas gave her a half-eyebrow that left her in no doubt.

'Actually, I told you those things in the wrong order. I guess that proves which one I was more excited about . . .' That hadn't occurred to her before. 'So, I'll start at the very beginning . . .' Nicholas's eyelids closed. 'Now, I know you're not asleep. How could you doze through these revelations?' She squeezed his hand, and he squeezed back.

'Finally, all these months after breaking my bloody heart, Simon pops up on my answering-machine, and says it's all been a big mistake, basically. That he's had time to realise what he gave up, blah, blah, blah, usual stuff. I foolishly agreed to have dinner with him, and even more foolishly slept with him. Sorry, Dad, I know you're not really interested in the squelchy bits, me being your daughter and all. But it is relevant, I promise. Meant he slept over, didn't it, and meant I woke up next to him. Which was when I realised that, actually, some time in the last six months I'd sort of stopped feeling quite so desperate about him. And that, actually, I was kind of pissed off with him, and that, on reflection, maybe the last few years hadn't been so marvellous after all, and that he hadn't treated me quite as well as I deserve – yes, deserve – to be treated. And that maybe I didn't love him any more. Which was, frankly, *so* exciting!'

She paused for breath, and looked at Nicholas, who'd opened his eyes. 'Love these little tête-à-têtes, Dad. Although I suppose they're actually just têtes, aren't they? Haven't told anyone else this, by the way. You're a very safe receptacle for a girl's secrets, just now, do you know? So, anyway, sent Simon packing. Done and dealt with. Haven't had a flicker since, which is a huge relief. Weird, isn't it?

'And then there's Tom. Somehow – I must ask him, come to think of it – he found out about Simon, and sort of went mad. I said sorry and everything, and then he came out with all this stuff. Said he'd fallen in love with me, these last few months, when we've been spending so much time together. And that if I was trying to make a decision between him and Simon, I should be armed with all the facts.

'I know, Dad, not the most romantic declaration, but it was very touching – you had to be there.'

Nicholas tried very hard to form a word. 'And?'

'And I'm still farting around. There have been moments, no doubt, when I've looked at him and thought stuff I haven't thought before. Whether that's love or not I don't know. I know that I want to keep being with him. I love that. Being completely myself. You don't have that with many people in your life, do you?'

Nicholas shook his head.

Natalie sighed. 'I'm just confused. I'm used to falling hard and suddenly. Not slowly and gradually. So I don't know if it's what I think it is. Don't quite trust myself.'

She smiled at her father. 'And with my track record, why would I? Not sure what to do now. Want someone else to make the decision for me. Why don't you do it, Dad?'

Nicholas laughed, and looked mournfully at her.

'Go on. Raise your left eyebrow for yes, right for no. That's no use. You can only move one.'

They both laughed.

Natalie threw herself impulsively on to her father's chest. He put his good arm round her, and patted her. 'I love you, Dad. And he's a good man, isn't he?' A loud, sustained grunt.

Natalie lay there for a while, and pretended that her father was her father again, and that he could still make everything all right for her.

There was a message on the answer-phone for her when she got home. For a second, when she saw the flashing light she thought of Simon, but then she heard Tom's voice and smiled. No introduction, no preamble. No sulking. He was amazing. He really was.

'Need a favour. Call me back. I'm still at the office by the way.'

She dialled the number, and he answered. 'How's your dad?'

'About the same. We had a good talk.'

'I thought he—'

'He can't. I talk. He listens. Makes him pretty much the perfect companion for me.'

'I'll remember that. Right, that favour. I need you to swap letters with me.'

'No way. Got something in my head already for V.'

'Liar.'

'Okay.'

'Anyway, it wouldn't be as good as my V, which is why I need you to swap.'

'But we're due this weekend. Doesn't give me much time to think of one, does it?'

'You'll manage. You're a genius.'

'Okay, you win, with your empty flattery. I'll take U.'

'You'll be glad. You're gonna like V . . .'

And then Natalie phoned her mum. That was a new habit. She'd say to her dad, as she was leaving, 'I'll call Mum when I get home.' And he would smile his sideways smile of thanks. And so then she would call.

'Hi, Mum. How you doing?'

'I'm all right, sweetheart. Been to see your dad?'

Natalie supposed it was pretty obvious. The pattern. Although, honestly, she was starting to look forward to chatting again to her mother. It didn't feel like the sort of game it had been in recent years. 'Yep. He's looking good today.'

They'd stopped saying 'better', because he wasn't. There'd been that first slow, steady climb, just after the stroke, and now he was on a plateau. Didn't mean that there wasn't any more getting better to do, just that, for now, there was no change.

'I know. I saw him this morning. How are you, love?'

She didn't want to tell her mother about Simon. There was no need, now, anyway. 'I'm really good, Mum.'

'Really?'

Natalie thought for a moment. 'Yeah. Really good. I feel pretty sorted. I suppose you might even say optimistic.'

'I'm pleased, Natalie.'

It still felt like her mum was just emerging from a coma she'd been in for the last goodness knows how long, a little bit like she was a stranger. But it was improving . . .

'How's Tom?'

'He's fine. Why do you ask?'

'I saw Bridget the other day . . . and she was saying . . .'

'What was she saying?'

'Just that you two have been spending quite a bit of time together recently.'

Natalie didn't immediately respond.

'I'm sorry, love, I didn't mean to pry . . .'

'Oh, for God's sake, Mum, you're not prying. Don't go all brittle on me again.'

'I'm sorry.'

'And stop apologising. Nothing to be sorry about. Yes, we've been seeing each other a lot lately. Yes, it might even be going somewhere. I suppose I feel a bit weird, talking about it. Not just to you. The whole family. It feels like you all want it to happen so much . . .'

'I only want it to happen if it's the right thing for you, Natalie.'

'Thanks, Mum.'

'He's a lovely boy, but that doesn't count for toffee if he isn't the right boy.'

'But how do you know if someone *is*? That's the great debate, isn't it? The endless conversation I've been having with my sisters and my mates all year. Don't suppose you've got a fail-safe method?'

Anna laughed. 'Fail-safe? No such thing. I'll just say this, sweetheart. Something my mum said to me, the night before I married your dad. She said that if I couldn't imagine a life without him in it, didn't want to contemplate spending the rest of mine without him, that he was probably the right one for me. I couldn't. I still can't.'

'Oh, Mum, I'm sorry.'

'Don't be. I've had more happiness than most people. I'm still lucky, Natalie. I have you, and your sisters, and my grand-children, and my health. And I still have your father. The man I've loved, and who has loved me, for almost all of my adult life. How many people can truly say that? He's not the same on the outside, maybe, but he's still in there – you can see that too – and I'm going to love him for the rest of his life, however long that is, and whatever form it takes.'

'Have you got any of your happy pills left?' Anna couldn't have said that, even a few weeks ago, Natalie thought. 'I could do with some of what you've got.'

'I stopped taking them a while back. I was lucky there, too. Your dad got me to the doctor nice and early. I think we caught it. I know it doesn't work that way for some people. It was like . . . the pills made everything recede a bit . . . like my brain was wrapped in cotton wool for a while. They gave my mind a rest. That's the best way I can describe it to you. You know how you struggled with your maths when you were little? Long division? Something hard? You know how you'd sit there, with your books in front of you, getting more and more frustrated and confused and angry? Do you remember we'd stop for a while, and go and do something else – take the dog for a walk, or play a game of Mousetrap or something – and when you came back to it, it was suddenly much easier?'

'Vaguely.'

'Well, taking the pills was like that for me. Life unravelled itself, and when I came off them, it all seemed different again. Definable. Understandable. And nowhere near so bleak. Does that make sense?'

'Kind of.'

'And I don't want to go on about it, but I'm sorry I wasn't really around for you. I feel bad about that. About not being who you needed me to be when you were going through the mill with Simon. Or enjoying time with your dad. Or helping Bridget when Toby came. I regret all of it.'

'Mum, I might not completely understand it, but you've put us first for so much of your life. You shouldn't beat yourself up about it.'

'I'm not. In a funny way, being aware of all the things I missed out on was a part of feeling better. I have a life. I just wanted you to know.'

'I love you, Mum.'

'And I love you too. Now, back to Tom. I'm firing on all cylinders again. Close your eyes and imagine a future without him in it, and tell me how it feels.'

It was Natalie's turn to laugh. 'That's unimaginable, I'm afraid. He's always been there. Couldn't happen.'

'Of course it could, you silly girl.' Now she sounded like the old Mum – and Natalie was glad. 'What do you think a wife might make of you hanging around?'

'He doesn't have a wife.'

'He will, one day. And make no mistake. She'll make him choose.'

'Isn't that a terribly old-fashioned way of looking at it? Modern lives don't work like that. He can have a wife and a best friend who's a woman, can't he?'

'Not one he was in love with once, he can't. Not unless modern life, as you call it, has completely altered human nature. And I don't think for one minute that it has. He'll have to choose, and he won't choose you . . . You should think about that, maybe . . .'

She did – all night.

U for Urgh

'Obviously, pot-holing was my first thought, but you didn't leave me much time to plan it.'

'So, U is for . . .'

'Urgh? I couldn't find anywhere round here that did it, and I don't want to schlep half-way around the country.'

'Is that the best you can do?'

'Sorry. Had a lot on my mind lately.'

He nudged her shoulder. 'I know.'

'And I did think about it . . . honestly. I thought Under Water. Scuba-diving or something, but the budget, as usual, is limited, and it was Scapa Flow or the local baths, and, besides, you can already do it, and that would be about the tenth thing in a row that you were better at than me and my fragile ego just can't take it.'

'Aah!'

'And then I thought of Underwear. I put all my white pants in the wash with a black sweater last week, and they've gone battleship grey. But that didn't seem quite the thing . . .'

'Maybe not. Although I read a survey the other day that said most men, when the chips are down, would prefer a nice pair of white cotton panties to anything else on a woman.'

'Doesn't that depend on the arse?'

'Suppose.'

'Besides, I know that's bollocks. Do you remember when I worked in Marks and Spencer? I spent the whole time exchanging red nylon bra and suspender sets men had bought as

349

gifts for comfortable briefs – although I always thought "briefs" was a funny old word for them. Nothing brief about them. Where do you stand on the issue, out of interest?'

'I like skin, myself.' Especially yours, he thought.

'Good to know.' Time for a subject change, she reasoned. 'Then I thought I might drag you into London, and make you sit on the Circle Line for a complete journey.'

'Oh, yeah. That sounds great.'

'We could have talked. I was going to bring a tube picnic . . .'

'Can't we talk in the park? It's a beautiful day.'

'Can you think of a park-related word that starts with U?'

Tom hesitated. 'Undergrowth!'

'That'll do.'

'That's a rubbish letter.' Tom stood belligerently on the pavement, with his hands by his side.

Natalie tried to look stubborn, but with him looking exactly like he had more than twenty years ago, when she had stayed on his new skateboard longer than he had the first time he'd climbed on it, she guffawed instead. 'You should see your face! Double urgh.'

'You're going to feel so bad when you work out my V.'

'Bet you I don't.' She smacked his bum playfully, and started off down the pavement. 'Don't forget it was you who made me swap. And I'll buy you an ice-cream.'

He followed her. 'Okay. But I want your Flake as well as mine. Then we'll call it quits.'

They lay on their backs after they'd eaten their ninety-nines. The sun felt gorgeous.

'I'm going to quit my job.'

'What?'

'I've been thinking about it since J. You made me see it all in a new way. You were right. It's a crap job and I've put up with it, and that tosspot, for too bloody long. Waiting for something to happen, in work, out of work. And it didn't and I'm still there, and that's cowardly.'

'Wow. Why now?'

'Combination of things. Dad, partly. His stroke gave me a *memento mori* moment. It's not a rehearsal, is it? And I've been thinking – about you, I suppose. Not that you should get big-headed or anything. Well, maybe you should, a bit. You took a risk, didn't you? Believed in yourself. Paid off for you.'

He raised himself up on one elbow. An image, fifteen years old, sprang into his brain, of them, in the pub garden, the first time he had kissed her. They had been lying exactly like this. 'I believe in you, too, Nat.'

'I know you do.' She put her hand, briefly, to his cheek. He wasn't sure what the touch meant. 'And that helps. Don't think Simon ever did, really.'

They were both quiet. Tom lay down again.

'And Mike has just sunk to a new, exciting Sigourney-Weaver-in-*Working Girl* depth of office crapness.'

'How?'

'You know my book-club idea – the one I put to him ages ago, and the one he's been palming me off with for months with his good-things-come-to-those-who-wait bollocks?'

'Uh-huh.'

'He's presented it as his. Started his own bloody book club. He's bucking the trend, apparently, of book clubs being a female thing. He's having a lads' book club. He's going to do sports autobiographies, and novels about the twenty-first century male. Apparently. The boss thinks he's a genius.'

Tom thought it was quite a good idea. Not that he would dare say so, of course.

Natalie glanced at him. 'I know it's a good idea. But he could have said that it was mine in the first place. He could have given me a little bit of credit. But he's too small for that, the pillock.'

'You're lovely when you're angry.'

'Bugger off.'

'Seriously. I think it's fantastic. Have you done your CV yet?'

'No. But I'm going to.' Tom chuckled. 'I *am*.'

'Good. Let me see it before you send it anywhere. I'll check it for typos, gross implausible untruths, and sex it up a bit on the graphics front.'

'I thought you believed in me?'

'I believe in your utter brilliance. I believe you'd make an excellent radio – whatever, boss, presenter . . . Totally. I just think you're a bit of a ditz on the detail.'

He was right, and she knew it. 'Okay,' she said, only a little sulkily. 'You can check it.'

Tom smiled, and closed his eyes.

Five minutes later, she kicked his right leg gently. 'Are you asleep?'

'No.'

'What are you, then?'

'I'm thinking.'

'About?'

'Patrick thinks Lucy's having an affair with the husband of a friend of hers.'

Natalie sat up. 'Fuck.'

'Exactly.'

'What do you mean "thinks"?'

'I don't think he has any actual evidence. But he's pretty sure.'

'Bloody hell.'

'I know. I don't know what to tell him.'

'Has he asked you for advice?'

'Not exactly, but I don't think he's told anyone else. He's

hardly likely to tell Mum, is he? She's only just got over him losing his job. I feel like I should be able to help.'

'I'm not sure how.'

'Me neither.'

'Have you seen Lucy?'

'No. He asked me not to. Do you know what he seems to be, most of all – more than angry or sad?'

'What?'

'Humiliated. Embarrassed.'

'That's horrible.'

'I know. He blames himself. He talks about her as though the whole time they've been together he's never been quite good enough, and like he knows that, and it's almost as if he's been waiting for her to realise it and leave him.'

'Have you ever felt that way about them?'

'I don't think I've thought about it. I mean, he's my brother, but we've never lived in each other's pockets. He met her, he married her, they had Ed . . . I just assumed everything was okay. You do, don't you, unless someone sticks something like this under your nose and makes you think about it?'

'But things have been tough this year.'

'I know. That was my first thought. I mean, not that that would make it okay or anything – things get tough and she falls into bed with another bloke. But it would make a kind of sense, I suppose. And it wouldn't be . . . so huge . . . somehow, as this thing he's thinking about himself.'

'Poor Patrick.'

'And poor Lucy.'

'Why do you say that?'

'Because that's what I think. It's all a bloody mess, isn't it? It can't ever be just one person's fault.'

'I don't know much about it. Simon may have been some things, but I don't think he ever cheated on me. Mum and Dad.

Bridget and Karl. Even the luvvies. I come from a long line of relentlessly monogamous stock. I can't imagine having an affair. All that lying, deceit. How would you sleep at night? How could it be worth it, when you have what Lucy has?'

'Unless you didn't want it any more?'

Natalie and Lucy

Natalie pressed the doorbell, and waited for Lucy to answer. Tom might be able to stay away but she hadn't promised anyone anything.

She'd been here a dozen times – including the night before Lucy and Patrick's wedding, for a Chinese, a bottle of wine and a manicure. That night, when they were tipsy, Lucy had clasped her hands together and implored her to marry Tom. 'We'd be sisters-in-law. I'd love that. We could gang up on their bloody mother together!' She'd still been with Simon then, of course. Later she'd come with helium balloons to meet a newborn Ed. For lunch and dinner and drinks. Gossip and a laugh.

Lucy looked knackered beneath the remnants of her suntan. She was wearing jeans and a T-shirt and had lost a lot of weight, Natalie saw.

Lucy made tea, and they took it out on to the patio.

'Are you cheating on Patrick?' Natalie asked, her heart beating fast.

Lucy looked her in the eye. 'Yes.'

Natalie exhaled softly and waited.

'Does he know?' Lucy asked.

'He told Tom he thinks so.'

'Oh, God.'

'What are you doing, Lucy?'

'I'm buggering everything up.'

'Do you want to talk about it?'

'Desperately. Do you want to listen?'

'I'm here, aren't I?'

Lucy looked like she could really use a hug, but Natalie wasn't ready for that. 'Does anybody else know?'

Lucy shook her head. 'I don't think so. I haven't told anyone. The only person I'd have told is my best friend, and since she's his wife I can't even do that. I didn't think he'd told anyone. He's a bloke.'

'Bloody hell, Lucy.'

'I know.' Lucy picked petals from a red geranium in a terracotta pot, and let them flutter, one at a time, on to the stone.

'Does he think it's because he lost his job?'

'It isn't. It's been going on for years.' Natalie's face must have shown horror. 'Not the affair itself. That's really new. Only a couple of months, really. I mean the feeling, the stuff between the two of us. That's been there since I met him.'

'Are you expecting kudos for resisting so long?' Natalie didn't mean to sound so hard.

'I'm not expecting anything, Natalie. I'm just talking to you. You started this conversation.' Her voice was meant to sound strong, but they both heard the little shake. 'What's happened to Patrick these last few months hasn't got anything to do with it, really. I don't think. This thing between me and Alec is a story playing itself, with its own momentum. It's bad timing.'

Natalie snorted. 'Bad timing!'

'I don't mean that the way it sounds. I don't know what the hell I mean.'

'Do you know how you feel?'

'Like a girl, when I'm with him. Like a desirable, free, delighted girl. Like an absolute bitch, every other second of every day I'm not with him.'

'Do you know what you want?'

'No. Yes. I want to be with him. But it isn't that simple, is it?'

'Isn't it?'

'Of course it bloody isn't. I love Patrick. We have a life. We have children. If there was anything to be built between Alec and me, every day of the last umpteen years would have to be dismantled first. And how can I do that to Patrick? To Bella and Ed? And . . .' her voice broke '. . . I don't even know if that's what Alec wants.'

'But if he did, that's what you'd do?'

'Can you not hear me at all, Natalie? I don't know. I don't know.' Lucy was crying now. 'I'm sorry. I'm so bloody sorry that this has happened. No one will ever know how sorry.'

'What can I do?'

Lucy blew her nose and patted her eyes with the tissue. She reached out her hand across the table, and Natalie put hers into it. For a moment they sat without speaking. Then Lucy smiled. 'You can make sure you get it right, whether it's with Tom or not. Be sure that you love him – whoever he is – so much, so truly, that there are no cracks and gaps in your heart where someone else can sneak in. Work hard every day to keep it like that. Pray to God every night not to let it happen. Just get it right, Natalie.'

June

Lucy

'Alec, don't!'

His hands were under her skirt, creeping up her thighs. They were behind his car. There were people twenty feet away. She could hear them talking, planning where to rig up the canopies for shade. It was the school's annual summer barbecue. Patrick was shopping for ice to empty into big black dustbins, and Marianne was in the school kitchen, sticking marinated beef cubes on to skewers. 'I can't help it.'

She slapped away his hands. 'You have to help it. It isn't safe. There are people around.'

'Well, come with me, then. Let's go somewhere.'

'We can't just go somewhere, Alec. We're supposed to be here, working. Marianne is just inside, Patrick will be back in a minute, and the children are running riot somewhere. They'll miss us.'

'I miss you. I want you, Lucy.'

She felt dizzy with desire.

'Meet me in the wood. Five minutes. Come, Lucy. Please.'

She gave him no answer.

But she went. As always, with Alec, hearing him tell her he wanted her made her desperate for him.

It was very quiet, much cooler and dark. This was where their children did nature projects, innocently collecting leaves and insects. It smelt damp, and she heard every twig snap under her feet as she moved quickly towards where she knew they would be out of sight and sound.

Suddenly Alec appeared, so fast she gasped in something like fear, pulled her behind a wide tree and, pushed her against it, his mouth on hers, his tongue exploring hers. He pulled her cotton dress up and her knickers aside in one almost rough movement, lifted her and was inside her easily. 'Christ.'

The bark hurt her back a little. 'What are we doing here, Alec?'

But he wasn't listening, and soon she didn't care any more. He kept one hand under her bum and used the other to undo her buttons, exposing her bra, then pulled it down so that he could see and kiss her breasts. This felt so good. She felt wanton and beyond herself. He barely needed to touch her to make her come. She'd never been like that before. Sometimes just thinking about being with him took her so near to the edge that she would yelp the second his fingers or his tongue or his mouth touched her. And the more often they were together, the truer that was.

She'd come in her sleep a few weeks ago. That had never happened before either. Woken pulsing and mewling at the edge of the bed, the blanket thrown back and the sheet wrinkled and damp. She'd known Patrick was awake and, for a second, before she was fully awake, she had reached for him, wanting more. He hadn't been hard, though, and although she had stroked him, he'd pushed away her hand gently and rolled on to his side.

Alec was always hard, the minute he was near her. It was like being a teenager at the school disco again, feeling him pressing into her thigh, when he hugged her briefly and said hello. It made her feel incredibly alluring. She saw her own body differently, even. She had taken, she knew, to standing naked for a little longer after the shower, turning left and right, to look at the body he worshipped. All her nerve endings were nearer the surface, and she was thinking, all the time, about him touching her.

They were taking more and more risks, because neither of them was thinking straight. Patrick had been watching her look at herself the other evening. She'd thought he was reading to Ed, but when she turned he was in the doorway.

'You're a lovely-looking woman, Luce, lovelier now than when I first knew you.'

She couldn't read his eyes. And she had reached for her dressing-gown, tying it tightly round her waist. If she was lovelier it was because of Alec, and it didn't seem fair to either of them to show Patrick that loveliness.

Now, in the woods, they were finishing. As she came, she thought, as she often did, of Marianne's magnesium flame, and clung to Alec. They stood for a moment, with him still whispering into her ear how beautiful she was, and how sexy. Then he released her, and stood back. She felt him trickling down her thighs. They stared into each other's eyes, but in her peripheral vision she saw him tuck himself back into his trousers and fasten them, as she adjusted her bra and did up her buttons.

Alec laughed, kissed her, then swung her round briefly. 'Thank you, Lucy. Thank you.'

It seemed to her a strange thing to say.

V for Vegas

I t was bizarre. They had just taxied along the runway, and in the last minute she had seen the Sphinx, a pyramid, the Statue of Liberty and a fairytale castle.

'Are we staying in any of those?'

'I told you, it's a surprise.'

A white stretch limousine was waiting for them outside the terminal building. Tom pulled his Ray-Ban Wayfarers out of his jacket pocket and put them on. 'Oh, yes!'

'Is this for us?'

'You bet. It's the only way to travel. When in Rome . . .'

In ten minutes they arrived. 'The Bellagio – "The city's most stylish and exclusive hotel and casino. Vast and palatial, its reinterpretation of an Italian village gives it a quality not shared by many of its competitors – elegance." This is going to be amazing.' Natalie had bought the guide book at Gatwick, and pored over it for most of the eleven hours on the plane, but Tom hadn't told her until now where they were staying.

The hotel was breathtaking. The reception area was vast, with a humungous mirrored and bejewelled horse in the middle, and a ceiling of vividly coloured, elaborately blown, glass flower blooms. Ahead, they saw the vast glass atrium, with a botanical garden, and to their right the casino. People milled around, some in black tie, others in velour tracksuits. Natalie could see slot machines and, beyond, gaming tables manned by croupiers in red waistcoats and bow-ties. 'Wow.'

Tom was smiling at her. She smiled back. 'Way to trump Paris!'

They were shown to a bank of lifts, and from there to their bedroom. Natalie watched Tom peel off a couple of dollars from the wad in his jacket and give them to the bellboy. He was quite cool in Las Vegas.

She was surprised to feel a mixture of relief and disappointment when she saw that there were two double beds. No scene to be had here, then. 'Tom,' she called, 'you should see the size of the bath!'

'No, you come here – they're switching on the fountains.'

Natalie rushed to the window, and they watched the lake in front of the hotel erupt into life. The water seemed to shoot above the hotel. 'This happens every fifteen minutes, practically all day and night,' she reported. 'For no apparent reason.'

She looked like a kid, wide-eyed and excited, Tom thought. 'You're going to like this, aren't you?'

'I'm going to love it.' Her eyes sparkled. 'Thank you for bringing me here, Tom.'

Was there a moment? In the hug that followed?

'I can't believe we're doing this!' Natalie held Tom's hand tightly; with the other she gripped the headrest of the seat in front. The helicopter banked sharply and completed a second arc above the Hoover Dam.

'You okay?' Tom mouthed.

'Think so,' she mouthed back. She had no idea how they had got to the dam – she'd had her eyes screwed shut since the helicopter had started its lurching hover above the tarmac of the airport. She had grabbed Tom's thigh in panic. Forty minutes, they'd said this was going to take. She wasn't sure she could do it.

But, wow, that dam really was amazing. After a minute or so

of staring at it, marvelling at how they had built it, Natalie discovered she wasn't quite so petrified. She released Tom's hand. His fingers were white where she had gripped them. Liberated, he rubbed the blood back into them, then offered it again, but Natalie – who had retained her grasp on the headrest – waved him off. Actually, this was okay. They probably weren't going to die after all.

For the next ten minutes, they were both absorbed in the rugged terrain that the helicopter was flying over. Then the world literally fell away under them, and the helicopter was in the canyon. They followed the path of a river, flying lower and lower into this huge hole in the world, and finally landing in a clearing, with a crude wooden shelter. Natalie crouched low to exit, and Tom laughed. 'Don't laugh at me!'

'Can't I laugh with you?'

She giggled – relief at having survived mingling with the realisation of how silly she must look crawling out of a stationary helicopter. 'You can't be too careful!' she remonstrated with him.

'Oh, I think you can!'

A 'champagne picnic' was included: they were each presented with a small wicker basket containing a plastic glass, a packet of Doritos, and a dubious ham and lettuce roll. Natalie decided eating might not be the greatest idea, since the exit route from the canyon was to be the same as the entry one, but she drank the champagne quickly, facing away from everybody else.

'The pilot says that cliff there,' Tom pointed in front of them, 'is four thousand feet high. And that's just the start of it. Four thousand feet! You can't imagine it, can you? Just think, we abseiled a hundred feet, so that is . . . what? Forty times as high. Bet you'd like to go off there, wouldn't you?'

'Yep. That's really me!' Natalie shielded her eyes and gazed up – the top seemed impossibly high. A for Abseiling. They'd come a long way since then, hadn't they? Twenty-something letters. Nearly six months. She'd almost forgotten about the alphabet game. The other passengers had gone walkabout and the pilot was busily collecting up the plastic champagne glasses. Tom and Natalie wandered to the edge of the picnic site.

'Most amazing thing you've ever seen?'

'Definitely.'

'We're meaningless, aren't we? Inconsequential. Infinitely small. We're nothing.'

She punched his arm gently. 'Speak for yourself.'

'You know what I mean. All the stuff we run around worrying about and sweating over, it's bollocks, isn't it?'

'Not to us. You can't say that.'

'No, of course not to us. But I reckon if you flew everyone over here and dropped them at the bottom like this they'd come to see that it didn't matter all that much. They'd go back and live differently, I bet you.' He was thinking about Patrick and Lucy.

Natalie thought of her mother, and her poor old dad. 'Are you going to go back and live differently, then?'

'A bit.' He nodded slowly.

Natalie couldn't take her eyes off a curl by his ear. His profile was so very familiar to her. The sun was hot on her back. She pushed her sunglasses off her face and took his hand, raised it to her mouth and kissed it.

Tom turned to her. His face was very close to hers, and suddenly she kissed his mouth. A light, quick kiss.

The pilot was watching them. He'd flown into the canyon 1782 times. On the 958th time, he'd flown his girlfriend in and asked her to marry him. It was a good sort of place for that sort of a thing. He smiled to himself and gave them an extra minute or two.

'What was that about?'

'I don't know.'

Tom kissed her back, then stood up and pulled her to her feet. 'Come on.'

Back in the helicopter, Natalie took Tom's hand.

'Still frightened?'

'No,' she answered, with a half-smile.

If the Grand Canyon had been a miracle of nature, the Venetian was a man-made one. One of the vast hotels that lined the strip, Natalie had asked the courtesy driver to drop them off there after their flight landed. The guide book said it was unmissable, she claimed. Tom could cheerfully have missed it. It was hot, and the Bellagio's pool was calling him. At least there was air-conditioning.

'Who thinks this up?'

'I read about it in the guidebook. Didn't some bloke build it for his wife so they could ride around the canals of Venice without ever having to go to Italy? Isn't that genius?'

'Of a sort, I suppose. But did they really think this was what Venice was like?'

'It is, kind of. It's like Disney does Venice, isn't it?'

It was lunchtime in the real world – if you could call the Las Vegas strip, with its outdoor travelators and white tigers, real – but in here, in St Mark's Square, it was dusk. Carnival-type street performers, masked and colourful, juggled and conjured for passers-by, and 'authentic' Italian *gelato* was served off carts. Along one side was a shopping mall. 'I don't remember there being a Jimmy Choo on the real St Mark's Square.' And running through the centre was a 'canal' with improbably blue water, trafficked with battery-operated gondolas. Each one had a gondolier, of course, singing 'O Sole Mio', and 'Santa Lucia' in operatic voices too good for the dismissive audiences passing by.

'It's terrible! It's antiseptic Venice. They've taken away all its charm. It's too perfect.'

'They've taken away the smell, too, though, haven't they?' Natalie had only been to Venice in a sweltering July, on a school trip one year when she was about fifteen, and she remembered the smell rather better than the Bridge of Sighs – as fifteen-year-olds are wont to do.

'You're a Philistine.' Tom had spent a week there, the summer he went round Europe, and had loved its decaying, tatty beauty.

'Does that mean you're not taking me in a gondola?'

'Do you seriously want to go?'

'I seriously do. We weren't allowed, in the fifth form. Mr Briggs thought we'd all muck about and fall in. Besides, it cost a fortune.'

'I'm sure it'll be a complete bargain here.'

'Forget it, then. Doesn't matter.'

Tom pulled her along by the arm. 'Don't sulk. Course I'll take you. But only on the condition that you promise to come with me to the real Venice one day, and let me show you how infinitely superior it is.'

'That deal works for me.' Natalie smirked at him.

It was, of course, stupidly expensive. The couple in the queue in front of them wanted to ride alone, but hadn't paid enough for the exclusive service so they reluctantly watched Tom and Natalie climb in, assisted by their Japanese gondolier, who was no more than four-foot tall.

'Good job she can work it with a pedal,' Tom whispered.

'Sssssh!'

The 'Welcome to Venice' spiel had started. Tom shook his head incredulously and sat back.

Opposite them, the other couple started kissing. Tom tutted like a teacher. Natalie glared at him, and took a huge interest in the shops on the canal bank. But it was almost impossible not to stare – they were about two feet away and barely out of their teens. Suddenly Natalie felt old. The boy was holding his girlfriend's face in his hands, and she hung round his neck for dear life. They were lost in each other, oblivious of everyone and everything.

Half-way round, the boy broke off the kiss, and fell on to his knees on the floor of the gondola, which wobbled ominously. Tom glanced at the gondolier, expecting an admonishment, but he was smiling beatifically. When he looked back at the guy, he had assumed the age-old position, and was pulling a ring box out of his denim jacket.

'You have to be joking!' Tom muttered. Natalie slapped him surreptitiously.

'Jennifer, will you be my wife?' He had a southern drawl, and, for a moment, Natalie felt like she was on the set of *Jerry Springer*.

But Jennifer clasped her hands in delight, and tears welled in her eyes. 'I will. I will.'

Another wobble, and he was back beside her, hugging her. Then he punched the air and shouted, 'She said yes!'

Rapturous applause erupted on the canal banks, and the gondolier burst back into song. When Natalie looked at Tom her eyes were full of tears too.

'I can't believe it! You're crying!'

'It's wonderful!'

'I'm the only sane person in Las Vegas.'

'You're a killjoy. You haven't got a romantic bone in your body.'

'I bloody well have.'

'Sssh.' Now Natalie was sitting forward and kissing the young couple, congratulating then.

The guy leant forward, and pumped Tom's hand. 'Good to

meet y'all. Brad and Jen. Can you believe that? As in Pitt and Aniston. Except we're Stuckey and Jones. Soon to be Stuckey.' Jen Jones clung to Brad's arm.

Tom put his arm round Natalie. She buried her face in his neck. 'As in Pitt and Aniston! Can you believe it?'

W for Wedding

'Ha!' Natalie nudged Tom.

He nudged back. 'Ha! What?'

'W for wedding. My turn. W.' She blew on her knuckles and rubbed them on her lapels. 'Back to you, Tom.'

'Yet again you go for the straightforward, no-advance-planning-required option. I don't think you're taking this as seriously as I am.'

'Sssssh! Bit of respect for Elvis!'

At the front of the chapel Elvis, very much in his deep-fried-peanut-butter-sandwich phase, was massacring 'Love Me Tender', while Brad and Jen looked from him to each other like new recruits to the Moonies.

'Bridge and Suze would *love* this!'

'Is it going to take much longer? I thought these things were supposed to be quickies?'

'Oh, stop moaning. Don't you think it's beautiful?'

'I don't. The two of them are the end of the bloody world and this is the tackiest venue I can imagine. There is nothing remotely beautiful about it, and I can't imagine for the life of me why you agreed to do this in the first place.'

Natalie looked hurt. 'I'm sorry. I didn't realise you felt so strongly.'

Tom relented. 'I don't feel all that strongly. It's just that it's our last night – I thought we might be doing something else, just the two of us, instead of being stuck in here.'

Natalie raised an eyebrow quizzically. 'No,' he added. 'Not that.' A pause. 'Necessarily.'

'We'll go as soon as it's finished. Okay?'

'Okay.'

Brad and Jen wanted 'y'all' to go with them to a steakhouse to celebrate. 'You were with us at the start of all this, seems fitting you should see the night through with us too.' Natalie won an Oscar for convincing them that newlyweds should spend their first night of married life alone together.

'Am I cramping your style?' Tom asked, as they waved the couple off.

'No more than usual,' she joked. Then she wrapped an arm round his waist. 'Besides, I quite wanted to spend the last night with y'all too.'

They found a bar where the cabaret was going on around them all the time, and ordered drinks. It was too noisy to talk, and for a while they just sat, watching the people. There were all sorts – families with babies in strollers, silicon gold-diggers in Juicy Couture tracksuits, sipping drinks with umbrellas and looking available, blank-eyed croupiers, short-skirted waitresses and old women with a cigarette in one hand and a bucket of quarters in the other. But it was the high-rollers that fascinated Natalie. They were quiet and fast. They had entourages, and crowds gathered around them, but when they'd won, they moved away quickly. They didn't drink or smoke, just stared at the tables and gambled with thousand-dollar chips. She was both attracted and repelled by them, and she couldn't stop watching.

Tom couldn't stop watching her. Surely she could feel what he felt. It just worked. *They* worked. She was gorgeous. Her face was so animated. Those bright eyes took everything in.

'D'you reckon we've got it right this time?'

'What d'you mean?'

'Well, last time, for H, we were too drunk, weren't we, to consummate our relationship? Now we might be just drunk enough.'

'Charming. Do you have to be drunk to find me attractive?'

'That's not it. You're attractive, all right. You're very attractive. Even without my beer goggles on . . .' Natalie giggled. 'It's just so . . . weird . . . that's all.'

'Weird?'

'You know what I mean. That's the crux, isn't it? That's the switch.' She held her hands like a pair of scales. 'That's where it really shows if we've stopped thinking mates – or, dare I say, siblings? – and started thinking . . . you know, phwoar!'

Mojitos had made Tom brave. He pulled Natalie to him, not very gently. 'Let's get something straight, Nat. I'm not your brother, I never have been. And right now I don't feel very matey. And, since you bring it up, I'm thinking very much phwoar.'

She pulled back. 'Let's go dancing.'

Tom pulled her closer again. 'I'm dancing.' He started to move slowly, his hands on the small of her back.

'There's no music.' But she didn't pull away.

Tom kissed her, and it wasn't friendly.

This time, when Natalie moved back a little her eyes were wide with surprise. They stood still. Tom felt himself on the edge of something. His heart was racing. When she spoke she said only one word, and it was so faint that Tom had to bend down to hear it: 'Phwoar.'

The young guys on a cruising weekend away from their cheerleader girlfriends could see that Tom and Natalie had chemistry. They whistled, and one shouted, 'Get a room' – advice they were happy to take. The elderly couple in the lift on their way to the fifteenth floor, talking loudly about their dinner and trying not to stare (her with disapproval, him with a twinge of envy and regret) didn't doubt they had chemistry. And the tired maid, on her long journey of turning down beds and placing chocolate on pillows, could see it too. Mind you, she saw a lot of stuff.

And behind the door, fifteen floors up, one or other of them might have been waiting to get the giggles, or snap out of it, or for something to happen that reminded them of who they were and why this couldn't happen. But it didn't.

The only really funny thing that happened was that the enormous fountain that ran along the lake at the front of the Bellagio erupted into its noisy, explosive *son et lumière* show just as . . .

But that was on the third time, hours later.

And when she woke up, and raised her head to check that she was where she thought she was, and that the room was still, the red digital numbers told her that it was three thirty a.m. 'Happy birthday, Tom.'

'Mmm.' He didn't answer, unless that counted, or open his eyes, but he pulled her tighter into him, and she went back to sleep with his breath warm and comforting on the side of her neck.

Lucy

The doorbell rang as the phone did. Lucy went to the door – let whoever was ringing leave a message.

It was Marianne.

Marianne had never slapped someone's face before, and Lucy had never been slapped, so it was an awkward, unsatisfactory blow, but hard enough to leave three red welts across Lucy's face.

They both stood, shocked, on the step. Three doors down, Lucy's neighbour stared from behind her rosebush.

Marianne spoke first: 'I'm sorry. I shouldn't have hit you.'

'Yes, you should.'

They still stood there.

'Do you want to come in?'

Marianne's face crumpled, and she seemed to sink towards the floor. 'I don't know.'

Lucy pulled her into the house and shut the door behind them. 'I'm sorry.' It was woefully inadequate. Lucy felt sick.

'Sorry you did it or sorry you got caught?'

'Both. We didn't ever want . . .'

Marianne's eyes narrowed. 'Don't say "we".'

'Sorry.'

'No, I'm sorry.' Marianne's voice had taken a sarcastic turn. 'I'm sorry I interrupted you. You were going to tell me, let me guess, that you never meant anyone to get hurt. That I wasn't supposed to find out. Weren't you? I know, because that's what Alec told me.'

Lucy had nothing to say.

'What the hell were you thinking, Lucy? I mean, what the hell are you playing at?'

She couldn't speak.

'We're friends, you and me. We're friends, Lucy. And he is my husband. My husband.' Her shout grew quieter. 'And I love him.'

'I know.'

'Do you?'

'Do I what?'

'Love him, Lucy. Do you love him?'

'Yes.' She hadn't known until that moment. 'Yes, I do.'

'Well, I should bloody well hope so. It would be fucking stupid to put us all through this just for a shag.' She stared hard at Lucy. 'Does he love you?'

'I don't . . . I don't know.'

Marianne laughed bitterly. 'Well, he was never particularly good at expressing his feelings with me either.'

They both knew that wasn't true.

'Actually, I do know the answer to the sixty-four-million-dollar question. I asked him, funnily enough. It seemed an obvious kind of question to ask the husband you've just found out has been sleeping with your best friend.'

And the question hung in the air.

Marianne walked into the living room and half fell into an armchair. 'He loves both of us, poor bastard.'

It seemed right to make a cup of tea.

Marianne drank hers in silence, staring ahead. 'Aren't we civilised?' She gave Lucy an ugly smile.

'I'm honestly surprised you can stand to be in the same room as me.'

'You're my best friend.'

'Don't, Marianne.'

'Who else would I want to talk to when I find out something like this?'

Lucy looked down at the floor.

'I think that's almost the worst part of it. Has it been like that for you, I wonder – wanting to talk about what was going on, and not being able to because your lover was my husband? I don't know, incidentally, how long. I didn't ask him.'

'It started about the time of Bella's birthday party.'

'I didn't say I wanted to know.'

'Sorry.'

'Not long, then. Not that it makes a difference, I don't think. I don't know.' She shook her head. 'I can't believe I'm having this conversation with you, Lucy. How often?'

'Not that often.'

'How often? Once, a handful of times, a dozen?'

'A dozen.'

'In my bed?'

'Never.'

'In yours and Patrick's?'

'No.'

'Where, then? Apart from the woods.' Lucy's eyes snapped wide in surprise. 'I saw you. Coming out. So carefully, five minutes apart. It was fucking obvious, Lucy.'

'Marianne . . .'

'Please tell me, Lucy. I want you to tell me. Where?'

'In town, at someone's flat. Outside. In the car.'

Marianne's laugh was hollow. 'In the car. My! How abandoned of you both. Lorna and Sasha would be proud.'

'Don't.'

'Does anyone else know?'

'I don't think so. We were always careful.'

'Good of you.'

'I'm so sorry, Marianne.'

'Doesn't sound quite adequate, does it? You're sorry.'

'But I am.'

Marianne was looking at her very, very hard. 'Do you hate yourself for this?'

'I hate hurting you.'

'But you don't hate yourself.'

'I can't help what's happened, Marianne.'

Marianne stood up. 'Of course you bloody well could, you stupid cow. You're an adult. You could have walked away. You should have walked away. Don't you bloody dare to sit there and tell me you couldn't help it. That's bullshit, Lucy, and you know it.'

'I'm sorry.' What else could she say? 'Are you going to tell Patrick?'

'No. Poor sod. I'll leave that to you. You've ruined everything, Lucy. You've trashed it all. For all of us. It's over.' Her shoulders dropped, the rage seeping from her. As she walked to the door, her footfall was heavy. 'Did you tell him about me? About my affair?'

'Of course not. I wouldn't.'

'You keep my secret, but you still fuck my husband. Funny ethics, Lucy.'

She didn't have an answer. Marianne was right. She'd wanted to tell him. Months ago, as soon as she'd known. But she hadn't.

'I suppose you used it as justification. What's good for the goose, and all that. You didn't need to tell him, did you? It just gave you a licence to do whatever you wanted. I suppose I shouldn't complain. You're right, aren't you?'

'It wasn't like that, Marianne.'

'Spare me.'

'I'll stop seeing him, Marianne.'

Marianne shrugged. 'No point now, Lucy. You've started. You can't stop any of this.'

And then she walked out, back to her car, leaving the front door wide open, and drove off.

X is for X Marks the Spot

Sunday morning. A Sunday morning exactly as a Sunday morning should be. A Sunday morning after a Saturday night, spent laughing and loving, and after a long, deep sleep. And a Sunday morning where the bloke got up and made tea, and – was that the door she heard – went out and bought the Sunday papers, not just the *Observer* for the clever stuff but the *News of the World*, too, for the pictures, and came back and brought it to you in the big double bed that smelt of sex, where you lay, with the warm, soft breeze from the open window wafting over you. With chocolate croissants, even though he really hated crumbs in his bed, and hated melted chocolate on his sheets even more, but still brought it because he knew you liked it.

That was a Sunday morning.

Natalie stretched her arms above her head, then rolled back on to the cool side of the bed, pulling the duvet with her. Her body was luxuriantly tired. Later, she would go to the hospital and sit with her dad, and then, if her mother was there, she would take her home and sit with her, and open the post with her and help her go through things. Then she would come back here to Tom's, strip off all her clothes again and climb naked into this bed for him to make love to her again.

That was all she wanted to do.

But first, she might . . . just . . . go back to sleep.

She could hear him, downstairs, listening to Radio 4, and putting tea things on a tray.

*   *   *

Sunday morning. A Sunday morning exactly as a Sunday morning should be. The woman he loved was asleep upstairs in his bed, recovering from a wanton night of passion. The face he had seen in a thousand different lights, over twenty years, was now the face he could close his eyes and remember making love to. And it was all he wanted to do. For ever.

Not that they'd had that conversation. Not yet. He'd held his breath, after Las Vegas. Waited for her to freak out. Waited for her to change her mind.

She hadn't. He'd dropped her at home, her home, on the way back from the airport. She didn't have any stuff, or anything, and they were both pretty knackered. And he'd waited some more.

And two days later she'd shown up at the office, with a Sainsbury's bag of fresh pasta, pesto and raspberries, clean knickers in her handbag, and just come home with him. Just like that, like they'd always been that way. And that was Friday.

They hadn't been out of the house until he'd gone for the papers just now. And he might not have gone then, if there hadn't been suspect-looking skin on the milk. And if she hadn't said she wanted chocolate croissants for breakfast.

They'd barely been out of bed. Barely got through the bowl of ravioli. They hadn't even had any wine. When he told Rob about it – and he wouldn't be going into huge detail – he would definitely have to say that she'd jumped on him. Not unlike a woman possessed. And certainly like a woman who hadn't had a lot of sex in the last few months, and found, once he'd whetted her appetite, that she'd quite missed it. And that was a nice surprise. After all the love stuff. A bit of old-fashioned have-to-have-you-now-even-with-your-socks-on kind of thing. Very nice.

But now it was Sunday morning, and they still hadn't really talked about it. He was afraid to, he knew that. Afraid of what this might mean to her, and how that might compare with what it meant to him. He wasn't ready to hear anything other than total love. So he didn't ask any questions that might provoke a different answer. He knew he was being an ostrich but, for now, he was a happy one.

So, he put the croissants, and the newspapers, and the big mugs of tea on the tray, and went back upstairs to Natalie.

Something was tickling her. Like a fly. Natalie swatted at her skin and settled. The tickle came back, and dragged her into consciousness. Grudgingly she opened her eyes.

Tom was crouched over her, with a marker pen in his hand, and he was – bizarrely – writing on her chest.

'Is this some weird sex thing I don't know about?' she mumbled, raising her hand to ruffle his hair.

'No. We'll be trying weird sex things later.'

'Promises, promises. What, then, may I ask, are you doing to me?' She sat up.

'See for yourself.'

Natalie looked down. Tom had inscribed a perfect X, about two inches high, on her breast.

'Okay, honey. None the wiser.'

'X marks the spot.'

'Yep, indeedy.'

'X. The penultimate but one letter. Marks the spot. Where your heart lives, and mine is now lodging.'

He meant to hold her gaze, but he couldn't, so he got up and shucked off his jeans, kicking them on to the floor by the bed.

She took his hand and kissed it. 'That is the sweetest, sweetest thing you have ever said to me. Hell – that anyone has ever said to me.'

Tom felt like a kid. He climbed in beside her and held her to him.

'Of course, it's also the most nauseating.'

'Hey.' He started to tickle her, and she tried to wriggle out of his grasp.

'And, frankly, the lamest excuse for a letter thus far in your game. And your heart is on the left if I remember anything from O level biology . . .'

The tickling increased. 'You're so rude! I couldn't reach the left side . . .'

'What are you going to do about it?'

And the tickling turned into something else, and Tom didn't stop to wonder whether she had made a joke of his lame line because she didn't want to talk about it or because it was a lame line. And, pretty soon, he didn't care.

Nicholas and Anna

Natalie had bought her dad a Stratosphere snowstorm from Las Vegas. She shook it vigorously and stood it triumphantly on the tray table across his bed. 'Kitsch comes to the ward!'

Her dad smiled.

'And I have jelly beans. Your favourites.' She produced a large bag with a flourish. 'Better hide them in here.' She put them into his locker. 'I'm sure the nurses wouldn't approve. I'll get some for you every time I come. They're brilliant. You can mix together flavours and make cocktails.'

'You look happy.'

'A sentence! I should go away more often.'

He raised his good arm and made a shooing motion at her. 'Brill, Dad.' She kissed him and sat down on the bed, one leg under her, and held his hand while she talked.

'Happy? I'm flipping ecstatic!'

Behind her she heard the door and her mum's voice. Natalie stood up and hugged her. 'The old man's talking again!'

'I know. I can't get any peace to do the crossword any more.'

'Rude girls,' her dad said, but he was smiling as broadly as she had seen him smile in a long, long time.

'Did you have a fabulous time, darling?'

Natalie had rung her mother, excitedly, from the check-in queue at Virgin to tell her where she was going.

'The best. Vegas is extraordinary. I thought I might hate it but secretly like it, if you know what I mean. Actually I just out-and-out unapologetically loved it. Best city in the world. I know I should probably think Prague is, or St Petersburg, or Ho Chi Minh or somewhere worthy and beautiful, but I think I'm a bit of a Vegas girl at heart. Cultural desert – it and me. Quite literally!'

'And Tom? Dare we ask?'

Natalie felt her cheeks go pink. 'I'm crazy about him.' What was she? Fifteen?

Anna and Nicholas exchanged a glance and a smile.

'I mean, not just because of Vegas – although we did have the most wonderful, wonderful time together. I think I must have been getting crazy about him for ages. But it was so different from with Simon, and you lot were all so keen, and, frankly, that didn't help.'

'Sorry!' Nicholas said.

'It's fine now. Now I can see what you guys saw. Now I get it. He loves me, too. For what I am. For everything that I am. Or maybe despite of.'

'Rubbish. He's a lucky man.'

'Now I've just got to make it clear to him . . .'

Elizabeth Noble

Patrick and Lucy

The children were asleep. She'd been on auto-pilot all afternoon and evening. They had come home, and she had listened to Bella reading *Charlotte's Web*, tested her on her spellings, and helped Ed draw and colour in all the things that started with the letter S. She'd rinsed out their lunchboxes, and put the juice cartons for tomorrow's lunch into the fridge to cool. She'd made dippy eggs for tea, and laughed, as if for the first time, when they put their empty eggshells upside-down and pretended they hadn't eaten them.

At bathtime, Lucy sat on the mat and watched them playing together, Bella patronising her little brother in a tone that aped her parents' voices, and Ed's mood deteriorating towards bedtime, as it always did, until he slipped beneath his duvet with Mr Ted shoved down the front of his pyjamas and a thumb between his lips.

Bella wanted to watch *Coronation Street* and sat belligerently on the top stair, wet hair dripping down her back, while her mother folded the bath towels, and collected all the plastic flotsam and jetsam from the bath. Lucy spoke to her more sharply than usual, and Bella stomped sulkily along the landing to her room, muttering under her breath.

Normally Lucy would have gone after her, cajoled her into a giggle, muttering back and offering to call ChildLine for her, and they would have been friends before Bella went to bed. Tonight it was more than she could bear, and she stared at Bella's closed door helplessly, then turned and walked, heavy-footed, downstairs.

Patrick was late.

Now that she had made up her mind to tell him, she was suddenly frightened that Marianne had not kept her word. That, right now, she was pouring poison into his ear. She stared

390

at herself in the hall mirror, at the woman she no longer truly recognised. Marianne might have been right when she had said that there weren't people who would cheat and people who wouldn't – that everyone had something inside themselves that they didn't think about, understand or acknowledge. That everyone might.

But there were two different kinds of people: people who had and people who hadn't. And she had.

In the kitchen, she wondered whether she should start dinner, then heard Patrick's key in the lock.

She was gripping the sink when he came up behind her. Suddenly she had to get it out, but she couldn't, wouldn't turn round and tell his face.

'I'm sorry, Patrick. I've been having an affair. With Alec.'

She heard him pull out a chair, scraping it over the tiled floor, and sit down at the table. He put down his keys. He breathed out slowly.

Lucy turned to him.

'I know.' As he spoke, his head nodded slowly.

'Have you seen Marianne?'

'No. She knows, too, does she? Poor old Marianne.'

'How, then?' Not Alec, surely. For a moment the thought was even exciting.

Patrick waved a hand impatiently. 'Does it matter how? I saw you together.'

'Where?' It didn't matter, but she couldn't let it go. Maybe the minutiae was safer than the rest.

'In the kitchen. The night we got back from holiday.' Lucy's face was blank. 'You weren't *doing* anything, but I could just tell. It was like something fell into place. How do they say it? The scales fell from my eyes, or something . . . It was just, I don't know, obvious all of a sudden.'

His eyes sought hers. 'I'm right, aren't I?'

'I'd ended it before we left.'

Patrick laughed. An ugly sound. 'And I brought him back to you.'

'Patrick . . .'

'Is it over?'

Lucy hesitated. She didn't know. Her fists were clenched. She could feel her fingernails digging into her palms. She had to stop this now. Enough. 'I don't know. But I don't want it to be.'

'What does that mean?'

'I love him, Patrick.'

'And you don't love me?'

'Not in the same way.'

'Here we go. The I-love-you-but-I'm-not-in-love-with-you conversation. How incredibly original, Lucy.'

There was a reason for that, Lucy thought. That's how it is sometimes for people like me. That's why they all say it. Because it's true.

'Sorry,' Patrick corrected himself. 'I don't care about other people. Make me understand, Lucy. Please.'

Lucy sat down opposite him, but he was speaking again: 'But before you do, can I tell you where I'm coming from?' She didn't want to hear it, but what could she say?

'I don't want this to end. I don't want to live without you and the kids. I don't want any of the implications of what you're saying, and what it means. I'd rather live with you, here, and know that I'm second best than live without you. I think I could do that, as long as you let him go.' He was horribly afraid that he was going to cry. 'I've loved you for ever, Lucy. I fell in love with you before I even saw your face, heard your voice. I don't know how to have a life that doesn't have you in it. You and Bella and Ed.'

Tears rolled down Lucy's cheeks. 'I can't, Patrick. I'm sorry, I can't.'

'We can move away. I know it would be hard to see him every day. To keep seeing him. We could go anywhere you wanted. That job in Leeds, maybe I could get it. Or another.'

'It wouldn't work.'

'But if you didn't see him any more . . .'

'Then there'd be someone else.'

'Why?'

'Because I don't want this any more.'

Patrick threw up his arms in exasperation. 'What "this" are you talking about?'

Her voice got louder with his. 'I don't want you.'

That stopped him.

'I don't want you, Patrick. I'm sorry.'

He sat still, staring at the grain of the pine table in front of him. Why didn't she want him? Why? He had never in all of his life felt so worthless. So broken. 'I thought we were happy.'

'We were. We were little *h*, small-town, quiet-life happy. I think there's something else. I feel like . . . like I've seen it now. And it makes it impossible to settle for that kind of happy again.'

'Even if Alec doesn't feel that way?'

The very thought made her tremble, but she still knew the answer. 'Even if he doesn't.'

Patrick pushed back the chair from the table and got up. For a split second she thought he was going to hit her. Maybe she imagined it was possible because she wanted it to happen. But of course he didn't. He was Patrick. He went to the french windows, opened them and went out into the garden. She continued to sit there, staring at the wall.

Eventually, she poured them each a large whisky and took it outside. Next door someone was watering their grass with one of those sprinklers that went back and forth. One corner of the spray came over their fence, landing on the leaves of the pots she had planted.

He let her sit beside him and drank the whisky.

Lucy took a deep breath and started talking: 'We always call it you rescuing me. Everyone does. And you did. You scooped me up, after Will, and you gave me back to myself. You made me feel like it wasn't my fault that he left me, that I wasn't a disaster area that no one could stand to be near for long. I still don't know what would have happened to me if you hadn't done that.'

She knew that Patrick's eyes were on her.

'You gave me and Bella a home. And no one . . .' tears were close '. . . no one could have been a better father to her. And then you gave me our Ed.' She thought she could smell the little-boyness of him, and she inhaled. 'Our beautiful boy. And this life, this life. And I've been happy with you, Patrick. I swear I have.'

'So how can that go away?'

'I don't know.'

'But it has?'

'Yeah.'

She wanted to tell him more. 'I don't need rescuing any more, Patrick. I'm not that girl. But you still want to be that man. That's what was so hard about the redundancy business. Not losing the job – I couldn't give a shit about that – but you wouldn't share it with me. You wouldn't let me be a proper wife. You had to keep taking care of me, protecting me, rescuing me.'

'So it's my fault?'

She shook her head in frustration. 'No. They're separate things, really. That's been truer and truer, over the years. It would have been a problem in the end, on its own, anyway.' Was any of this making sense? 'Alec came along, and showed me something different.'

'Better.'

'Different.' Of course better.

'And it isn't going to pass. It isn't a phase.'

'I'm not proud of myself for any of this, Patrick, believe me. I wouldn't have done any of it if I'd thought it was a phase.'

He stared into the middle distance.

'I think, maybe, that we've been heading to this point since the day we met.'

'I can't think that — I won't think that. That we were somehow doomed from the start. That's bullshit, Lucy. I hate that you think that. It makes a lie of everything we've shared.'

'It doesn't.' Lucy risked a hand on his arm.

He shook it off and stood up. 'What are you doing?'

'I'll get some things. Go to Tom's.'

'You don't have to.'

'I can't stay here.'

From the garden, she saw the bedroom light go on. It took him about ten minutes, then the light went off and she heard him coming down the stairs. The water next door had stopped, and the night felt very quiet.

He'd been crying. Lucy had never felt so sad. At the door, he turned as if to speak to her, but no words came, and he rushed out and away.

Y for Your Place or Mine

The bar she had chosen was as equidistant between their two homes as she could make it. Actually, the place exactly in the middle, according to the milometer in her car, was a rather dubious public house with an even more suspicious clientele, so she had compromised on this place, which was just a mile closer to her house. And it was very nice – very *World of Interiors*, very London. It had an endless zinc bar down one side, with minimalist stools, and the booths were in cowhide and fuchsia pink suede. The music was the kind played by people in their late thirties, who remembered clubbing fondly but knew they were too old for it. And good lighting. There were those clever floor-to-ceiling sliding doors all along the wall opposite the bar, the ones with no handles, and this evening they were open. Outside was decked, with water features, all gentle tinkling and soft lighting. It was warm, and there was a gentle breeze. She couldn't have ordered better off a menu.

She'd rung Susannah earlier in the week, and persuaded her to post her beaded aqua Alice Temperley dress ('My première dress? Wow, you're serious!'), which had fitted easily into a padded A4 envelope, and which had been hanging on the side of her wardrobe for three days, making her shiver whenever she looked at it. Rose had provided a pair of what she called follow-me-home shoes, and Natalie had been tottering around the flat, wearing them over a pair of tennis socks, practising not falling over. She and Rose had drunk a bottle of Pinot Grigio and got giggly.

'It's going to be like that bit in *Pretty Woman*, is it? The bit where he meets her in the bar, and the crowds part and he sees her and, wham, bam, you know it's all over for Richard Gere – he's a goner.'

'Yep. If it works.'

'It'll work.'

'If it doesn't work in this dress and these shoes, I don't know what will!' Natalie was holding the dress against herself.

'So, let me get this straight.' Rose was squinting at her. 'You've made up your mind, have you?'

'Absolutely.'

'And you're sure?'

'As sure as I've ever been about anything.'

'Forgive me a minute, Nat, but I've known you as long as most people, and I've known you to be really, really sure about loads of stuff in the past.'

'Like what?'

'Well . . .' Rose thought for a moment. 'You were really, really sure that Scritti Politti were going to be bigger than the Beatles. You were convinced that you'd have your own radio show by the time you were thirty. You were convinced you'd be married to Simon . . .'

'All right, all right . . . I can't be right about everything. But I was about you and Pete, wasn't I?'

Rose nodded exaggeratedly. 'True!'

'And I will have my own radio show – you watch me.'

Again, Rose rolled her head around on her shoulders. 'I'd listen!'

'Thanks. I know. And I'm right about Tom.'

'Well, Hallelujah for that! Welcome to my world. Haven't I said that all along?'

'You might have done. But other people can't make your decisions for you, can they? You've got to get there on your own.'

'And this is a decision, is it?'

Natalie thought for a moment. 'Not a decision, no. Just a change. In me. In us. I can't explain it. I just know.'

Rose had hugged her then. 'I'm so happy for you.'

Now she just needed to tell Tom. So she was sitting in the bar on the stool, legs crossed, in the beautiful dress, with the beautiful shoes, and the knickers that matched, with the smooth legs and the makeup that had taken her an hour to put on, and the hair that had taken the hairdresser ninety minutes to make it look as though it had been put up in five. With her last thirty pounds until payday at the end of the week cooling in an ice-bucket next to her. Trying to resist the dish of oily olives in front of her (bound to drip and Susannah would kill her), and trying not to slip off the stool.

When he came in, it was the first time in her life that seeing him had made her heart do that flip thing that a thousand songs had been written about. She almost laughed. Smiles bubbled up in her. He looked sort of scruffy and a bit tired, but he looked like her Tom. And if he didn't exactly stop dead in his tracks, he did go a little bit Richard Gere. 'Blimey, Nat.'

'Hello.'

'This is nice. And you look . . . you look really beautiful.'

'Really?'

'Really.' Then he saw the champagne, and his heart did a little thing of its own.

The old, old friends who had never been short of things to say to each other were suddenly very quiet. The barman appeared and poured them both a glass, and Tom raised his to clink against hers. She couldn't see what he was thinking. He looked excited and sparkly-eyed, but she wasn't sure.

Natalie took a huge gulp and put down her glass. 'I know we're not quite at Z, Tom . . .' He raised that mobile eyebrow of his. She had a sudden urge to kiss the scar. '. . . but you've won.'

'I didn't know there'd be a winner. What's the prize?'

She took a deep breath. 'I am.' Shook her head. 'I didn't mean that. It sounded horrible. It's not that I think I'm a prize or anything like that, quite the opposite, in fact. If I'm any kind of prize it's probably the booby.' She grimaced. 'Didn't mean that either. Stop talking, Natalie. Stop talking rubbish.'

He was smiling at her now. 'Don't stop.'

'I mean . . . I mean you were right. And I was wrong.'

Tom didn't want to let himself go ahead of her. He wanted her to say it. Not to torture her, but just because if he didn't hear her say it he wouldn't believe it.

She was pink-cheeked now and, despite the pretty dress, the extraordinary cleavage and the sexy shoes, and the immaculateness of her, he liked the pink cheeks most of all. 'What are you trying to say, Natalie?'

'Don't you already know?'

'I think I do. I hope I do. But you have to say it to me.'

'I love you, Tom. I properly love you.'

'Properly?'

She smacked his leg. 'Don't make fun of me.'

He put his hand on the hand that had slapped him. 'I'm not.'

'And if you love me or, frankly, even if you're really fond of me, but actually agree that chemistry can grow . . .'

'Are you still on about chemistry?'

'I am . . . except this time . . . I have it. Big-time.'

'Properly?'

'Properly.'

He picked up her hand and kissed it, never taking his eyes off her face. He looked serious. 'Well . . .' And then the seriousness gave way, and his big Tom smile broke across his face, and that moment when they had been a different Tom and Natalie had gone, and they were back to old Tom and Natalie, except that they were new in so many ways. 'Well, in that case, I have to say that I . . . properly love you too.'

They sat, stared and smiled at each other, then Natalie kissed him hard and they smiled some more.

'So what's your Y? Unless it's W-H-Y, as in, why not give us a chance?'

'That could have worked.'

'But it isn't?'

'No.' Natalie drew herself up to her full height on the stool, and shimmied with delight. 'It's Y for Your place or mine? And,' she took the champagne glass from his hand, 'this time we're going to be sober, all the way through . . .'

July

Lucy

There was no need for this to be a secret, so why did she still feel so guilty, sitting here, waiting for him? It was a pretty incongruous venue. The coffee-shop in a crowded department store, mid-morning. Just before the end of term, it was full of mothers making the most of their last days of freedom before the six weeks of house arrest and day trips. Lucy had ordered coffee, but she didn't want it, and it had grown cold in front of her.

Alec was a little late. He apologised – parking had been difficult, he said. Then she watched him stand in the short line and order his own unwanted coffee, carry it carefully over to her and sit down.

'How are you?' she asked.

'I'm . . . I'm okay,' he said.

It was only a matter of days since they had been lying naked side by side, as intimate as two people could be, but now Patrick and Marianne were between them, and it was entirely, utterly different.

He looked tired, and she told him so.

'Not sleeping too well. You?'

Lucy answered with a small, tight shrug.

'Are you still . . . at home?'

Alec nodded. 'I think Marianne wanted me to go. At first I think she was inclined to chuck all my stuff out of the window.'

'But?'

'You know . . . neighbours, children, life . . . I wish she had. I'd rather have had her rage than this.'

'Which is?'

'I've broken her heart, she says.' Alec stared into his coffee cup. 'Patrick?'

'He won't tell me how he feels. He's at his brother's. He left the night . . . you know. He'll hardly speak to me at all.'

Alec ran his hand across his face several times. 'Christ. What a mess.'

'I'm sorry.'

'It isn't your fault.'

'But I'm still sorry.'

At the next table a toddler smashed his plate. The flustered mother dropped to her knees and picked up the pieces.

'Lucy?' Alec reached for her hand, and held it on top of the table. She waited. 'I want to stay with Marianne.'

She couldn't take her hand away. 'Is that what she wants?'

'I don't know. Not right now. She's hurt and angry, and I don't know if she'll forgive me, ever, but that's what I want to try to make her do.'

Lucy didn't say anything. She had told Patrick she wouldn't stay with him, whatever Alec decided. But she hadn't allowed herself to think this.

'I don't know how honest you want me to be with you,' he said. Jesus! How much more honest could they be than they already had been, lying in each other's arms, eyes wide open, hearts wide open. 'I love you both. I hope that doesn't make me sound like an idiot. And I don't know if it helps or makes it worse. I only know what I feel, and I've been pretty fucking confused for a while now. I love you both. I can imagine a life, a future, with both of you. But Marianne has my past as well. She's the mother of my children, she's the maker of my home, she knows me better than anyone else I've ever known, and I can't leave her.' He shook his head, dissatisfied. 'No, no that's not right. That's not fair to you or to her. I don't *want* to leave her.'

'So what was this, Alec?' It wasn't an accusation.

'This was me falling in love again. With you.'

'That can't happen.'

'I didn't think so either. But it has. Look at you. Don't you love Patrick?'

'Of course I do. He's been all of the things to me that Marianne is to you. More, maybe. But not like this – I don't love him like this. If I squeeze my eyes tight shut and try to imagine a life without him in it, I can, Alec. And it aches, but it doesn't sting. I don't know if I can say that about you.'

He didn't answer.

'You make me desperate, Alec. I want you. All the time. When I'm not with you, you're all I can think about. When I am with you, I feel completely alive. You're everything. I forget Patrick. I forget everything, basically.'

'That sounds like infatuation.' He said it in a flat, weird voice, as if maybe even he didn't believe it.

'Don't you dare tell me I don't love you because that would be more convenient for you! If I've just got a silly crush on you, you can go back to Marianne and get on with your life, and I can just be this embarrassing little blip – painful, but easy enough to get over. It'd be simpler for you, wouldn't it?' Her words were angry, but her voice wasn't. She knew she sounded pathetic.

'I'm sorry. I didn't mean that. None of this is easy for me, Lucy, believe me. It isn't easy for any of us. Please don't be angry with me.'

Lucy could feel hot tears in her eyes. 'I'm not angry. I'm frightened. I'm frightened because you're leaving me. You are leaving me, aren't you?'

'I was never with you, Lucy. Not really. What I'm doing is *not* leaving Marianne. Not if I don't have to. Not if she doesn't leave me.'

She knew he didn't mean that to sound as cruel as it did. And she knew she should stop. This was going to get undignified. But she couldn't. 'You were with me, though, weren't you? All those times. All those times we made love, and held each other and talked together, you were with me.'

'And I shouldn't have been. I hate myself for it. Not just because of Marianne. Because now I'm going to hurt you too.'

And it did hurt. It hurt like hell. More than Will's note all those years ago had come close to hurting her. How cruel only to realise in this moment – in the moment when it was taken away – how much she loved him. Her chest was tight, and she was beyond tears now. She looked at him, and knew now that she seemed tragic to him. He must be desperate to get away – he had said what he had come to say, and the rest was all pointless. But still, she knew, her eyes implored him.

He shook his head sadly. 'I don't want to abandon you, Lucy. Please know that. But I can't be the one who helps you deal with this. Any more than Marianne can be. We can't see each other. You must understand that, surely.'

Slowly, Lucy nodded. Then she stood up.

'Give Patrick a chance, Lucy. He loves you.'

She kissed his forehead, eyes closed tight, lips dry, and walked away.

Natalie

Rose, Bridget, Susannah and Serena held up their glasses.

'Here's to about bloody time,' Susannah said.

'To slow-burning chemistry,' Bridget added. Susannah rolled her eyes.

'To fairy-tale endings,' was Rose's contribution. Rose was planning her wedding to Pete, and had unfortunately taken to talking in *Brides* magazine copy. But she was so glowingly, obviously, stupidly happy that it was hard to hold it against her.

Serena just winked and drank.

Natalie wished Lucy was there. She'd tried to persuade her to come and celebrate with them, but Lucy had said she would ruin it. 'You enjoy your simple, straightforward love, Natalie,' she had said. 'You don't know how lucky you are.'

Natalie thought she did.

'Now, we want details . . . gory details . . .' Susannah rubbed her hands gleefully.

'Speak for yourself.' Serena wrinkled her nose.

'Oh, come on, a little vicarious excitement for the young mother,' Bridget begged. This was only the third time she'd been out without Karl since the baby, and Natalie was afraid she was already a little drunk.

'What I want to know,' Rose half whispered, 'is what it was like, you know, the first time you ended up in bed together. It must have been weird after all those years of not doing it.'

'Dutch courage, Rosie, to be honest, got us through the first time. Who am I kidding? It always has, I think. No change there. But later that evening, after the third time—'

She was interrupted by a chorus of oohs.

'Yes, I think it's fair to say I'd stopped worrying about it being weird.'

'Bloody right.'

They all laughed. 'And this is why men are terrified of women going out drinking together.' Serena giggled.

'I suppose the next morning, when we woke up, I was a bit nervous – the most nervous. I was sober by then, of course, and I thought, I wonder if we've made a dreadful mistake – if it's going to feel odd. And if I'd ruined everything between us, for ever.'

'Fortune favours the brave, though.'

'And it didn't feel odd?'

'No. Do you know what he said to me? The very first thing he said to me when he woke up?' They all leant forward. 'I shouldn't be telling you guys this stuff.'

'You absolutely should be.'

'He said it had been more wonderful than he ever could have imagined.'

Serena put her hand to her mouth. 'Tom said that?'

'Tom said that.'

Rose hugged herself. 'I love it.'

'I was pretty keen on it too. I mean, I still wondered a little bit – you know, we were on holiday, and holidays make you feel different – and—'

'Oh, for God's sake! I don't know how he puts up with you. I'd have had to slap you by now if I was Tom,' said Susannah.

'But now you know?'

'Now I know. We're home, back in our real lives, and I know. And he knows that I know. If you know what I mean.' How many glasses of champagne had she had? 'So it's all okay.'

'And the best bit is, you're not going to have to do all that in-law stuff.' Rose was in the middle of wedding negotiations with Pete's mother and her own that made Kofi Annan's work at the UN look like child's play.

'That's right, Rose. That's the best bit.' Serena smirked. She didn't really get Rose. She liked her, but she didn't really get her.

'Are you going to get married, then?'

'Hold on. Give us a chance. We've only been together a couple of weeks.'

'And twenty years.'

'I'm not even sure I want to get married.'

'Right!' They *all* found this hilarious.

'Rob's been trying to persuade me that we should go to Las Vegas, get it done quick in one of those wedding chapels.' Serena wrinkled her nose.

'That sounds great.' Rose was wistful. 'No mothers.'

'No way! Tacky in the extreme. At least, the one we went to was.'

'And no one there who knows you to see how gorgeous you look,' Susannah added. 'Except the groom, of course, if he counts at all,' said Bridget, sarcastically. Susannah raised an eyebrow at her sister.

Natalie nudged her friend. 'Are you up for it, Serena?'

'I might be.' She smiled. 'You never know . . .'

'There must be something in the water . . .' Natalie said, sipping champagne and beaming.

Lucy and Patrick

Patrick rang the doorbell at his own home, and waited for Bella or Ed to answer. How strange it felt to have a key that fitted into this door but be unable to use it. Because that would be going through a different door to a different world, and it wasn't his any more. It would be to trespass.

He had asked, once, since he'd moved out, if not having Alec meant that she would have him back. Asked her if he could come home, and be, if not the person she wanted now, then maybe the next best thing, the person she had wanted once. The pity, sadness and refusal in her face had killed something inside him. He wouldn't ask again.

And now all he had to do was convince himself to stop waiting for it to happen. People said was he sure it was all over. Her face had made him sure.

A second Saturday leisure-centre, McDonald's father. Was that what he was going to be? The injustice of it stung behind his eyes and ribs. He hated everything about now. Camping at Tom's. Watching Tom, so newly happy with Natalie. Lying at work, his new work, being guarded about his circumstances. And, most of all, he hated ringing his own doorbell to see his own children. But there was nothing he could do, was there? It wasn't up to him. He had asked her and she had said no.

They had agreed, at least, not to have any big, heavy, final discussions with the children. They thought his new job was taking him away a lot. At least, that was what Patrick and Lucy had let them believe. Maybe it would make it easier, eventually, when they told them that he wasn't coming home. Who knew what strange thoughts and feelings went through their minds? It was another thing he couldn't bear to think about.

Bella knew something was up, though. He was sure of it. She watched enough crappy American-import TV on Saturday mornings to have grasped that there was more to it than a long commute to work.

He had thought more about Bella not being his biological child in the last month than he had in the whole of the rest of her life. It tortured him at night to think that he might have no claim over her. No rights in her life. That he might not sit, proud and triumphant, at her graduation, dewy-eyed at her wedding, then with her child on his knee. Tom told him that Bella would always love him, that Lucy would make sure of it. That he needn't worry about it. But Tom wasn't with him in the middle of the night. He was next door, in his own bed with Natalie, at the beginning of everything. So Tom couldn't understand the fear.

It made him want to tell her. Last week, Ed had met a little schoolfriend in the café at the swimming-pool and the two of them had played happily under a neighbouring table while Patrick stirred a mug of weak tea and Bella had picked the chocolate chips out of a muffin and eaten them one by one. He had wanted so badly to slice himself open and pour all his feelings for her out on to the table in front of them so that they could both see it and know. But he hadn't. She'd put her head against his arm, tired after her swim, and he had stroked it, tucked the hair behind her ear and kissed her forehead. And said nothing.

Now he wouldn't be there when Lucy told her about Will. He wouldn't even know when she did it. It wouldn't be his decision.

Tom was angry with Lucy. And their mother had started to say something about her the other day. Something that Patrick had known could quickly turn into another life story, retold, in which Lucy had always been wrong for him, and not entirely good. He'd gone out of the room so he hadn't heard it. It wasn't what he wanted or needed, their animosity, even directed towards her. It didn't help.

He felt it sometimes, though. Rage. His anger was different. Black, unctuous and acid. It rained on him sometimes like blows. And cleared as storms do, almost as quickly as it came. He never felt rage at the door to his home. Just sadness. And longing.

Bella answered, and threw herself bodily at him. He swept her up and held her tightly. 'Sorry, Dad. We were in the garden. Ed just found the most enormous stag beetle. You've got to come and see it.'

'Well . . .'

Ed appeared and wrapped his arms round Patrick's legs. 'It's gone, thank goodness. It was disgustering.'

Patrick took one arm from Bella and reached down to ruffle Ed's hair. 'Hello, my boy.'

Lucy was the last to appear. No swing in her walk, no laugh in her eyes. She was thin. Too thin. She was wearing a low-cut T-shirt, and her collarbones jutted out sharply against skin that was pale again now, after the holiday. The last holiday. 'How are you?' she asked.

'Fine.'

Natalie had told Tom that Alec was going to stay with Marianne – try to make it work. For an hour or so he had sat on the sofa and waited to feel something unpleasant. Satisfaction? Revenge? Maybe. But he hadn't. Actually, it made the whole thing even more bloody pointless. None of them was going to be happy at the end of this horrible dance they had all done. Marianne would never be able to trust Alec again – or, at least, not for a long time. Alec would think of Lucy whenever he looked at Marianne, comparing, contrasting, missing, regretting. Lucy had lost Alec. Patrick had lost Lucy. We're all worse off, he thought. What a pointless, dry, dreadful thing. Misery in layers.

Once she would have retorted that he didn't look fine. And he would have smiled and replied that when people asked you how you were, they only really wanted to hear that you were fine. If you were worse than fine – if your cat had been run over, or your house had been repossessed, or your wife had had an affair and then left you – they glazed over with embarrassment and moved away. If you were better than fine, a little piece of them died. Wasn't that how the quotation went?

And then Lucy would probably have kissed him lightly and told him to shut up and not be such a smartass.

He didn't need to ask her how she was. He could see for himself that she was sad, diminished, guilty and lonely. It was written in her skin, and gave him no pleasure.

'Have you got your stuff, guys?' She was letting him have them overnight.

Bella and Ed scuttled off to collect their bags.

'We'll be at Tom's,' he said.

She nodded. 'Is there room for you all?'

'He's away, actually.'

'Oh.'

She didn't ask, but he needed to fill the space: 'He's taken Natalie away somewhere.'

'It's all come together for those two, has it?' Lucy folded herself further inside her cardigan.

Just as it has unravelled for us. 'Seems so.'

'I'm happy for them.'

'Me too.'

For the first time they looked directly at each other. Then Lucy smiled the kind of smile where you press your lips closer together and force the corners of your mouth to rise. Ed and Bella filled the next space with Power Rangers and Meg Cabot novels, and then they were climbing into Patrick's car, buckling themselves in and blowing theatrical kisses at their mother.

'How's the job going?'

He had been about to climb in, and her question had startled him a little. 'It's okay.'

Lucy nodded. 'I'm glad.'

That night, Lucy couldn't sleep. At about three a.m. she gave up, and made herself a cup of tea in the kitchen. The house felt unnaturally quiet and still. She sat to drink it in the dark living room. She wondered where Natalie and Tom were. A stab of pure envy ran through her. She wanted what they had more than she had ever wanted anything, yet she had never been further away from it. She remembered New Year's Eve, lying entwined with Patrick on the sofa, half listening for the chimes of Big Ben. Sitting here, opposite Alec, after the holiday. What a bloody mess.

For the next hour, she wandered from room to room, bare-foot and weepy, looking at photographs, remembering conversations, playing out scenes from their past in this home.

Grieving. It was almost five in the morning, and light outside – birdsong erupting – when she curled up in Ed's bed, under the Power Rangers duvet, and fell asleep.

Anna and Nicholas

The nurses started their ward rounds just before seven. It seemed absurd to Nicholas. What's their bloody hurry? he thought. It's not like any of us have somewhere to get to, is it? Can't a bloke get a sodding lie-in? Suppose you were dying of something. You'd be thrilled, wouldn't you, to be woken up with the dawn, lots of lovely extra time to think about shuffling off your mortal coil?

He swore a lot more inside his head, these days. He could get quite steamed up in here, when he wanted to. And being woken so early was one of the things that got him that way. He was tired, for God's sake. Why couldn't he sleep?

Anna didn't usually come until ten. By then he was glad to see her. She always brought him a copy of *The Times*. She read him the cricket and the letters page, and then they did the crossword together. Which meant, of course, that Anna did the crossword while he nodded and slurred approval or disapproval as appropriate, which allowed her the affectation that they did it together. She'd always been quicker-witted than him. And now . . .

She was so well. The other day Natalie had said, when she'd popped in on her way to meet Tom, that she thought Anna was rather enjoying having someone to look after again. Nicholas wasn't sure that wasn't a slightly simplistic view. Maybe he was flattering himself – and, God knows, with him looking like this, no one else was going to – but he thought that what she was enjoying was only in part a purpose and the fulfilment of practical needs. They were having happy times together again. Simple, happy times. He was alive. He was recovering. Slowly, sure. And, yes, maybe he'd never be as good as he was before. And maybe the next 'big one' was bigger and marching inexorably his way. He might die, he knew. At any time. But so what? So might any of us. He might have lost Anna last year, or Bridget having Toby in January. He might lose anyone at any time. So might everyone. This focused the mind, he found. Funny, because everyone else believed that it fuddled it beyond recognition. But Nicholas was still in here. And he was sitting, with his wife, for hours every day. And sometimes they might go for the longest time without talking about anything except what nine down and two across were, but that was okay.

And if she did like the caring? Then that was okay too, because he liked being cared for. He pitied some of the other poor buggers he'd seen. They looked a mess, and they didn't get enough to eat because the catering staff couldn't have cared less if they ate or not, and whipped their trays away while some of them still had the first spoonful heading mouthwards. Anna brought him things from home. Titbits from the Marks & Spencer food hall. And flowers. A new bunch twice a week.

Natalie's postcard was propped up against the vase – freesias today. It had arrived at home yesterday morning and Anna had brought it in with her. She was in Sicily with Tom. She had used a biro to draw an X on their hotel bedroom window.

Mama/Papa
Wish not that you were here – which would cramp our style
horribly – but that maybe you two were in the next town and
we could see you for sun-drenched lunch and then each
return to our Italian love nests.
Ciao!

It sounded idyllic. Things had worked out for the two of them. At long last.

For a brief moment he allowed himself to imagine walking Natalie down the aisle. He'd done it with Bridget, and loved it. That ten minutes alone with her in the car on the way to the church. Unable to take in how beautiful and grown-up and saturated with happiness and excitement she was. He'd been Susannah's witness, which had also been very special, although that proceeding had been a little unconventional. Casper's witness had been a gay makeup artist, wearing more mascara than the rest of the bridal party put together, and sporting a terrifying handlebar moustache – with pink lipgloss beneath.

And he didn't care if it sounded old-fashioned, but he'd like a full set, thank you very much. He was sure it was perfectly possible to find happiness, fulfilment and a joyous life without a husband. He just wasn't sure it was possible for Natalie. And now it looked like she might not have to try. Tom had succeeded.

So for the first time in a long time, all of his daughters were well and happy at the same time. All with good men who loved them. All fully engaged in the pursuit of happiness.

He supposed, if his life was a television drama, this would be the point at which he could lay his grey head against the pillow, smile benevolently at his progeny, all settled contentedly around him, and die.

No fear. He'd lost one year, pussy-footing around the woman he had loved his whole life, and he wasn't ready.

Z for Capo Zafferano, Palermo, Sicily

'Zhenzi, in China?'
     'Nah, you can only have one kid, and I want loads.'
'That rule only applies if you live there, Tom.'
He shrugged.
'Zagreb? That's up and coming, isn't it?'
'Nat, put the sodding atlas down. Where the hell did you get it from, anyway?'
'They had one in the office at Reception.' Natalie hadn't looked up. 'Zanzibar! Now that would have been nice.'
'Too hot, too far.'
She poked her tongue out at him. 'What are you? Sixty-five?'
'What's wrong with here?'
The sun was low in the sky, turning orange. The sand and the sea were glowing. The perfect late-afternoon summer sunlight for photographs – she'd run and get her camera in a minute and take pictures of him, lying bronzed and somnolent beside her, a Dan Brown novel long abandoned beside him.

Behind them the waiters, resplendent in their vanilla linen jackets and black ties, were starting to lay the tables on the veranda for dinner. The luxurious clink of crystal and silverware, and crisp white tablecloths fluttering in the breeze. One saw her watching him, raised his hand in a drinking gesture, quizzical. 'No, no, thanks!' He winked. Italians loved a lover.
'Here isn't too shabby.'
He smiled lazily at her. 'Would it be too nauseating altogether to say that anywhere with you wouldn't be too shabby?'

'Utterly.'

'Won't say it, then.' But his hand was on her knee.

The moment bubbled in her. She looked back down at the atlas. 'Zuckerhutl, in Austria?'

Tom sat up and snapped it shut. 'That sounds like a sexual position. We could go there—'

'Before dinner?' Her voice was shrill with mock-shock. 'Certainly not.' She picked up the atlas, and shoved it into her beach-bag. 'I'm relieved we've got to the end of this damn alphabet. I was running out of ideas.'

'Huh! Face it – all the great ideas were mine. You ran out of what little steam you had by about G.'

'I did not! What about Hotel?'

He laughed, his head back. 'Yeah, *great* idea!'

Natalie slapped him playfully. 'I'll have you know I had a Z, too, even though it wasn't my turn.'

'I didn't know that.'

'You don't know everything, smartass.'

'Well, what was it?' Natalie didn't answer. 'Come on, spill the beans.'

Sheepishly she reached into her bag and pulled out a small box. Tom's face was baffled as she handed it to him.

He opened it and took out a ring, an enormous, revolting signet ring, shiny gold, with a sort of lattice-lace thing happening round the band, and a big slab of royal blue onyx set in the top.

Tom laughed. 'What the hell is this?'

'It's a Z-sized ring. It's for you. Z. Get it?'

'But—'

'Okay, I know it's vile and horrid and deeply hideous, but it was the only size Z they had in the shop, and I was rushing, with the holiday being short notice and everything . . .'

'And you thought I might verify the size?' His dimples were

out in force now, his hilarity barely contained. He was holding the ring up to the light, spinning it round on one finger.

'I don't know, do I?'

'Tell me one thing, Nat?'

'What?' She felt almost sulky suddenly. She knew it wasn't a great ring. Okay, it was possibly the worst ring in the history of rings, but that wasn't the point, was it?

'Will I have to wear this when we get married?'

Natalie looked at him for a few seconds without speaking, but her eyes filled, first with understanding, and then with tears. She threw herself against him, and they fell back on to the sun-lounger in a tight embrace. All she could say was 'Tom.' She put her hands on both his cheeks and kissed him again and again. 'Tom. My Tom.'

He tolerated it for a few moments, then held her face still and kissed her slowly and deeply. 'My Natalie.'

Behind them the waiters stopped polishing and watched.

Later, when the sun was touching the sea, and the heat had gone from the day, they collected the ring and the atlas and started up the beach towards their room, arms round each other companionably.

'You'll do it again later, won't you? Ask me. Properly, I mean. At dinner, maybe. You know, the full-monty sort of thing.'

Tom hugged her tighter to him, and just laughed.

Alphabet Weekends

Reading Group Guide

Introduction

Natalie and Tom have been best friends forever. But Tom wants more, and he's going to prove to Natalie that they were meant to be together. He makes a wildly romantic proposition: spend 26 weekends together, indulging in a different activity from A-to-Z. In six months, he argues, they will be desperately in love. The cautious Natalie—still heartbroken over her ex-boyfriend Simon—isn't so sure.

But Tom and Natalie aren't the only ones coping with the vagaries of love. Natalie's mother is going through her own crisis, and Lucy, Tom's unhappily married sister-in-law, yearns to give in to temptation. All of them are about to learn that no matter how clever they are, love—and life—isn't always as easy as A, B, C . . .

Questions for Discussion

1. How would you characterize Natalie and Tom's childhood friendship, and to what extent does it seem like they would make good romantic partners as adults?

2. How do the friendships in *Alphabet Weekends* (between Lucy and Marianne; Natalie and Rose; and Tom and his work colleagues, Rob and Serena) reveal differing levels of trust, dependence, and affection?

3. How does Natalie's relationship with her father, Nicholas, compare to her relationship with her mother, Anna, and what are the implications of her feelings as both of her parents confront significant health problems in *Alphabet Weekends*?

4. "I'm a romantic—what's wrong with that?" In what ways does Tom challenge Natalie's idealized vision of romance?

5. Why does Natalie agree to have dinner with her ex-boyfriend, Simon? How fair to Tom is Natalie's decision to meet up with Simon again?

6. How do to the trips to the Health Farm and to Paris alter the course of Natalie and Tom's relationship and the depth of their feelings for each other?

7. Why does Nicholas's stroke enable Anna to overcome her clinical depression?

8. Why might Patrick's impotence and feelings of inadequacy after losing his job contribute to Lucy's decision to seek out an extramarital affair with Alec?

9. Of all of the romantic relationships explored in *Alphabet Weekends*, which seems the strongest and why?

10. How did the plot of *Alphabet Weekends* enable your appreciation of the unfolding relationship between Natalie and Tom?

An Interview with Elizabeth Noble

Q: How did you conceive of alphabetical activities as the organizing plot structure for your novel?

A: I got the idea, as I get a lot of great ideas, from talking with my fantastic girlfriends. They are wise and funny and smart. We were talking about how you keep a marriage— busy with work and children—fresh and exciting, and out of its rut. (And please understand, ruts are not always bad places to be—they can be comfortable and contented.) Trying new things together, having new adventures came up, and the alphabet idea followed on from that. I went A-for-abseiling with a bunch of mates and had the time of my life, and the concept grew from there. Structurally, it worked brilliantly for me—my twenty six chapters were already outlined. It gives the book its unique 'hook.'

Q: At any point in your writing were you unsure of how to accommodate the next letter of the alphabet?

A: It was important that the story came first, and the letters second. Otherwise it would have seemed contrived. When I got stuck, I would brainstorm, with my husband, with my mum, with my girlfriends, over a few glasses of wine. You'd be amazed how long the lists would get with suggestions, not all of them strictly repeatable! I had a few fixed markers—V for Vegas, for example—although I wasn't sure when I chose that one what state Tom and Natalie's relationship would be in when they got there. I was keen to start with abseiling. It showed the reader that Tom knew what he was doing, even though, for Natalie, it seemed proof that the idea was doomed. *Alphabet Weekends* was great fun to write. It took on its own momentum.

Q: Natalie and Tom's relationship is just one of many that you explore in *Alphabet Weekends*. Would you describe yourself as a romantic by nature, or are you just drawn to exploring relationships in your fiction?

A: Relationships are the whole point, aren't they? Otherwise, why are we here? Not just romantic ones, but the relationships we have with our parents, our children, our friends. They all shape us, inform who we are. I'm fascinated, too, by the way one impacts on another, so that, emotionally, nothing exists in isolation. So for *Alphabet Weekends*, I chose three romantic relationships, all in very different places. But they are happening to people close to each other, and what I particularly enjoyed exploring was the way in which what was happening in one affected the way the players reacted to others. That is how real life is, I think. I can't imagine writing a novel that didn't have relationships at its core. And as for romance, who doesn't love that?! As a woman who has been happily married for a decade, it is a wonderful job to get to write about the first flushes of love—all that breathless excitement...

Q: If you were casting *Alphabet Weekends* for a movie, who would you like to see in the roles of Natalie and Tom?

A: This is hard, because when you are writing you have your own invention of how your characters look inside your head—and, for me, that is never an actual person. But it's beyond a dream to have a novel turned into a movie (so long as they didn't want to change it too much!), and if were in charge of casting, I'd want Kate Winslet for the Natalie role. I'm a huge fan. There is something utterly real and down to earth about her. She has a great laugh and the right curves. And some big, twinkly-eyed hunk for Tom—someone like John Corbett or Vince Vaughn.

And I'd want to sit next to him at the premiere, obviously!

Q: What is your next project?

A: My next project, my fourth novel, is going to be finished around Thanksgiving 2006. The summer of 2005 was all about relocating myself and my daughters to New York City, where my husband relocated at the beginning of the year. Something of a mammoth task! It's been incredibly stressful and busy, but we are finally all reunited, in the most amazing city. Time to get back to the computer!

alphabet weekends

VEGAS GETAWAY SWEEPSTAKES!

During 26 fun-filled jaunts to new places—each including activities that begin with a different letter in the alphabet— Tom tries to convince his best friend Natalie that life together could be one big long adventure. Now you and a special friend can set off to Las Vegas for the first of what we hope will be many great adventures together. Odds are you'll fall in love, even if it's just with the casino life!

• • • • • • • • • • • • •

Enter to win a get-away weekend for 2 at a luxurious hotel in Las Vegas. Must be 21 or older to enter.

E-mail your entry to: AlphabetWeekends@harpercollins.com

Note the following in the subject line: Vegas Weekend Getaway Sweepstakes

Include the following in the body of your e-mail:

Name: _____

Address: _____

City: _____ State: _____ Zip: _____

Phone: _____ Age: _____

No purchase necessary

HARPER

Alphabet Weekends

"Vegas Weekend Getaway" Sweepstakes

OFFICIAL RULES:

1. This promotion (the "Sweepstakes") is sponsored by HarperCollinsPublishers ("HarperCollins"), 10 East 53rd Street, New York, New York, 10022.

2. How to Enter. NO PURCHASE OR PAYMENT NECESSARY TO ENTER OR WIN. To enter, please send an e-mail to AlphabetWeekends@harpercollins.com. In the subject heading please write "Vegas Weekend Getaway Sweepstakes" and include in the body of the email your name, address, age, and phone number. LIMIT ONE ENTRY PER PERSON. Multiple entries are automatically disqualified.

Each online entrant in the Sweepstakes must be the rightful owner or have authorized use of the e-mail account indicated by the entrant's e-mail address. In the event of a dispute concerning the identity of the winner submitting an entry, the winner will be deemed to be the person in whose name the e-mail account is opened. The e-mail account must be opened prior to the commencement of the Sweepstakes.

3. Eligibility. Sweepstakes open to all legal residents of the United States (excluding Colorado and Rhode Island), excluding employees and immediate family members of HarperCollins, and their respective subsidiaries and affiliates, officers, directors, shareholders, employees, agents, attorneys, advertising, promotion and fulfillment agencies and other representatives and their immediate families. All applicable federal, state and local laws and regulations apply. Offer void outside the United States and where prohibited or restricted by law.

4. Entry Period. The Sweepstakes will commence on February 1, 2007 (9:00 a.m. EST) and end on July 30, 2007 (9:00 p.m. EST). Entries must be e-mailed during the Entry Period and received by no later than July 30 (9:00 p.m. EST).

5. Odds of Winning. Odds of winning depend on the total number of entries received. Prize will be awarded. The winner will be selected by a random drawing from all the entries on or about, August 1, 2007, by HarperCollins, whose decision is final. Potential winner will be notified by mail or e-mail and will be required to sign and return an affidavit of eligibility and release of liability within 14 days of notification. Prizes won by minors will be awarded to parent or legal guardian who must sign and return all required legal documents. By acceptance of their prize, winners consent to the use of their names, photographs, likeness, and biographical information by HarperCollins for publicity purposes without further compensation except where prohibited.

6. Prizes. One winner will receive round-trip airfare from major airport nearest winner's home to Las Vegas for two adults 21 years or older as well as double occupancy accommodations for a two-night stay. Approximate retail value of prize: $3,000.

7. Prize Limitations. One prize will be awarded. Prize is non-transferable and cannot be sold or redeemed for cash. Any federal, state, or local taxes are the responsibility of the winner. Sponsor may substitute prize of equal or greater value, if necessary, due to availability.

8. Additional Terms: By participating, entrants agree a) to the official rules and decisions of the judges, which will be final in all respects; and to waive any claim to ambiguity of the official rules and b) to release, discharge, and hold harmless HarperCollins and their respective parent companies, affiliates, subsidiaries, employees and representatives and advertising, promotion and fulfillment agencies from and against any and all liability or damages associated with acceptance, use, or misuse of any prize received or participation in any Sweepstakes-related activity or participation in this Sweepstakes, including, without limitation, the following: (i) late, lost, incomplete, delayed, postage due, misdirected or unintelligible entries, (ii) any printing, typographical, administrative or technological errors in any materials associated with the Sweepstakes, and (iii) any damage to the entrant's computer, related equipment, data files, and software resulting from entrant's downloading of information regarding the Sweepstakes or participation in the Sweepstakes.

HarperCollins reserves the right, in its sole discretion, to modify, cancel or suspend this Sweepstakes should a virus, bug, computer problem or other causes beyond HarperCollins's control corrupt the administration, security or proper operation of the Sweepstakes. HarperCollins may prohibit you from participating in the Sweepstakes or winning a prize if, in its sole discretion, it determines that you are attempting to undermine the legitimate operation of the Sweepstakes by cheating, hacking or employing other unfair practices or by abusing other entrants or the representatives of HarperCollins.

ANY ATTEMPT BY AN ENTRANT TO DELIBERATELY DAMAGE THE WEBSITE OR UNDERMINE THE OPERATION OF THE SWEEPSTAKES MAY BE IN VIOLATION OF CRIMINAL AND CIVIL LAWS, AND, IN SUCH EVENT, HARPERCOLLINS RESERVES THE RIGHT TO PURSUE ITS REMEDIES AND DAMAGES (INCLUDING COSTS AND ATTORNEY'S FEES) TO THE FULLEST EXTENT OF THE LAW.

HarperCollins may only use the personally identifiable information obtained from the entrants in accordance with its privacy policy, which may be found at http://www.harpercollins.com.

9. Dispute Resolution. Any dispute arising from this Sweepstakes will be determined according to the laws of the State of New York, without reference to its conflict of law principles, and the entrants consent to the personal jurisdiction of the State and Federal courts located in New York County and agree that such courts have exclusive jurisdiction over all such disputes.

10. Winner Information. To obtain the name of the winner, please e-mail your request to: AlphabetWeekends@harpercollins.com. All requests must be received by January 1, 2008.

BOOKS BY ELIZABETH NOBLE

THE READING GROUP
Where the Books End, the Stories Begin . . .

ISBN 0-06-076044-3 (paperback)

The Reading Group follows the trials and tribulations of a group of women who meet regularly to read and discuss books. Over the course of a year, the women become immersed in the books they read together, as well as intertwined in each other's lives.

"Noble keeps engagement high as her characters connect and interconnect . . . this entertaining read is very accessible."
—*Booklist*

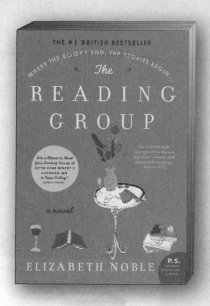

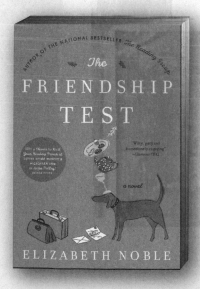

THE FRIENDSHIP TEST
A Novel

ISBN 0-06-077774-5 (paperback)

One late wine- and gossip-fueled night, four friends create a fateful test of friendship on a lark—one that challenges the very principles and boundaries of their alliance. To pass it means to never, at any cost, betray one another. Twenty years later, they must face that ultimate test. Exquisitely rendered *The Friendship Test* is a powerful testament to the depth and capacity of female relationships.